"Louis! Are you . . ."

Even as she spoke she could see that he was clearly not all right. He had been hauled by the horse across rough ground. Alarmed, Jenny put her head down to his chest. As she heard the heartbeat, her eyes focused on the cross. It had been pulled out from the shirt, and its dark surface glittered with vagrant specks of light.

Jenny found her hand reaching up to it. The metal felt chillingly cold, with a vibration deep within it.

Villette muttered a French word that she did not understand, and reached to pull her close to him. He drew her body down, until her face was next to his with the cross against her throat. For one moment she felt that chill of cold metal, quickly swept away within a bewildering rush of erotic desire.

Take him, said a voice within her. *Possess him. Devour him.*

Jenny grasped his head in her hands, pushed it back to the grassy surface, and moved her mouth down to his. Her lips were hot and swollen, aching for contact.

"No!" The Marquis was looking up, through her and beyond her. *"Not now, not to this one . . ."*

PRAISE FOR *THE SELKIE*

"A novel of subtle suspense which builds, like Mary's emerging sexuality, to a climax . . . the reader will be seduced by this finely woven fiction."
—*Fantasy Newsletter*

"A superior horror novel."
—*Washington Book Review*

to Holland Park. It was not large, but it reminded Jenny of

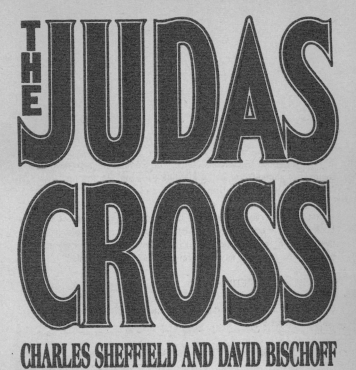

THE JUDAS CROSS

CHARLES SHEFFIELD AND DAVID BISCHOFF

ASPECT

WARNER BOOKS

A Time Warner Company

WARNER BOOKS EDITION

Copyright © 1994 by Charles Sheffield and David Bischoff
All rights reserved.

Aspect is a trademark of Warner Books, Inc.

Cover design by Don Puckey
Cover illustration by Dom Brautingam
Hand lettering by Carl Dellacroce

Warner Books, Inc.
1271 Avenue of the Americas
New York, NY 10020

 A Time Warner Company

Printed in the United States of America

First Printing: December, 1994

10 9 8 7 6 5 4 3 2 1

CHAPTER ONE

France; January 1, 1916

At the top of the hill the man halted and looked down to the river valley beyond. Dusk was settling over the landscape, with a deadly chill folded into the darkness. He shivered, tucked his right hand into his overcoat, and checked for the thousandth time that his precious burden was safe.

If his instructions were accurate, the dull gleam of silver-gray below was the frozen surface of the River Aire. All he had to do was follow it north, past Erneville and Dagonville and Baudremont, and he would arrive at the village of Saint-Amè.

And then, pray God, he would finally be at journey's end. It was almost too much to believe.

He lit a black cigar of Turkish tobacco and exhaled smoke through nostrils still red and inflamed a month after their exposure to the freezing air of the Alps. His eyes stared northeast, past the river valley. That way lay the snow-covered war front. It curved down like an invisible barrier, all the way to the border of neutral Switzerland. Those combat zones had blocked his progress again and again. Who would have dreamed, a year and a half ago when he set out on his mission, that a simple assassination in Sarajevo would have had such an effect? It was as though the whole of Europe were a glass mirror, and those two insignificant shots, fired at world's edge in far-off Bosnia, had shattered the vast, glittering surface into complicated and unpredictable fragments.

1

And would those fragments come together again, with this new year? It was hard to believe, after what he had seen.

The legate turned uneasily in the saddle, feeling the patient mare quiver beneath him. Like him, she was close to the end of endurance. He had abandoned any idea of train or motor travel as soon as he realized how tight the borders had become. It was impossible now to move even between neutral countries without running the risk of search and seizure of possessions. That risk was intolerable. He had turned to the old and slow, plodding along on horseback. An elderly, unarmed man on a tired horse attracted little attention and so was able to wander across the frontiers unseen, far from border posts. The same man in an automobile would be noticed wherever he appeared.

He straightened in the saddle and groaned. His decision not to go by car or train or coach had been the right one, but there were penalties to travel on horseback. He was suffering excruciatingly from hemorrhoids. Each day's journey was a guarantee of new agonies. His whole body cried out for a long, hot bath and a soft bed. He had not seen either for more than ten days.

Let him be there. The prayer was whispered beneath his breath. The man touched the metal inside his coat. Please, let him be there, alive, and healthy, and sane. I grow weaker, Lord, and sickness saps my very soul. I lack the strength to seek further for a Guardian. *Let him be there.*

He sighed, and clucked at the old mare to begin the walk down to the river. Self-pity was as pointless as anger. No one was to blame. The Knights of the Twelfth Apostle had made their list of Guardians in happier times. Who could have imagined that the first three choices would all prove impossible, with the legate forced to travel on, from one end of Europe to the other, in a desperate search for a fitting warden? But it had happened.

He had never reached the home of the first choice. It was on the French-Belgian border, a place he remembered as a pleasant land of green pastures and grazing cattle. The new reality mocked his memories. All that lay there now were leagues of blackened earth, strung with barbed wire, pitted with trenches, ditches, and shell craters, and dotted with the decomposing bodies of the dead. The messenger had approached close enough to see that his destination no longer existed. Then he had crossed himself, turned, and headed south and east over the frozen winter earth—to Turkey, where the second choice should be found.

Should be, but was not. The force that shattered Europe had not left Asia unscathed. Arriving in sweltering July, the emissary learned that he was two months too late. His man had died during the May fighting near Cape Helles.

And so began the long return west, with travel more and more difficult across a warring Europe that writhed and shuddered in its conflict like a man on a fever bed. The legate shuddered, too, appalled by what he saw on his travels. To cure the fever, Europe's governments were bleeding the Continent of its young men.

He had finally found the next in line for Guardian alive in Naples, and hoped his job was done. But the man was suffering from third-stage syphilis. He was locked away in an asylum overlooking the gorgeous blue of the Gulf of Gaeta and the Tyrrhenian Sea. The legate had spent three days with the man, until he was sure that the situation would not improve. Then he had again saddled the patient mare and wearily headed north, into the icy maw of winter Europe.

And now the Aire River was no more than fifty yards ahead. Chateau Cirelle and the village of Saint-Amè were only thirty kilometers off. So close, to success or a fourth failure.

It was now full dark. The man bowed his head and fingered his sacred charge.

Lord Judas, I will go on. If necessary, I will continue until I die of weariness. But hear my prayer. Let the cup pass from my hands, Lord, and give me peace.

His words were carried away on the night wind, whispering across the frozen river and vanishing into the snow-dusted hills beyond.

CHAPTER TWO

Jenny Marshall received both letters in the same morning post. She was eating breakfast in the dining room of her aunt's London town house when the parlor maid set a pewter tray between the teapot and the toast rack. Lying on it was the day's edition of the *London Times*, already unfolded to the news pages.

Until she saw the headline Jenny had been feeling half asleep. In that shadowy, familiar dining room she could close her eyes and imagine her father and Clive Dunnay still sitting across the table from her. It had been mixed pain and pleasure to see them in uniform. They had looked so handsome and confident, so determined—the two men in her life, convinced that they would come home safe within a few months, trailing clouds of victory. Then with the war over it would be the satisfying old world of family, and the exciting new one of marriage.

Captain and Mrs. Clive Dunnay. Jenny could see his thoughtful eyes and slim build, and smell the pleasant odors of pipe tobacco and sandalwood soap.

The *Times'* headline jerked her to reality. April 18, 1916: THE CHARNEL HOUSE OF VERDUN.

The battle was already in its second month, a German attempt to demoralize their French opponents by capturing the old fortified town. Verdun was for France a symbol of national honor and integrity. The seat of Charlemagne's empire, it had fallen disgracefully to the Germans in 1870; now

4

it was seen as a gateway to Paris itself. Both sides were pouring in troops and suffering horrible casualties. Neither was willing to yield.

To Jenny, the name held a more personal significance. Her father, William Marshall, was a French-British liaison officer, and he had hinted that both he and Clive might receive postings to the Verdun area.

Jenny picked up the newspaper, to reveal the small stack of mail that lay beneath it. She grabbed at once for the letters. She had received nothing from Clive or her father for over a week. That didn't mean much, since the mail from France often came in batches, with some curious delays, and letters from abroad were more often in the second post. But maybe . . .

The first envelope was a bill from Harrods. She hardly looked at it—for the second one was addressed to "Miss Jenny Marshall, c/o Dr. Ellen Blake, 92, Willesden Lane." And up in the left-hand corner, with its official crest, MINIS-TRY OF WAR.

Jenny ripped it open with the marmalade knife, smearing the envelope a sticky orange. "*We regret to inform you . . .*"

The letter that a million households dreaded.

Jenny grabbed the mail and jumped to her feet. She could not bear to read any further. She ran into the hall and up the steep stairs.

If anyone would know what to do, it was Ellen Blake.

"Aunt Ellen!"

Her niece was charging along the landing, past the bedroom. The door of Ellen Blake's study was ajar, and Jenny came crashing through it as though it weren't there.

The "study" was a wilderness of desk and files, fitted into an overflowing two-story library and collection of antiques. The morning sun was striking through narrow south-facing windows, sending spears of light through the dusty air, and the room smelled of leather, mildew, old paper, and cracked binding glue. Ellen watched as Jenny, tall and lithe, dashed along a faded Persian rug, came perilously close to knocking over a Byzantine statue, and caught a Qin Dynasty vase just before it went off its pedestal.

"Jenny! Have a care, child. That's a life's work you're

knocking to bits.'' Ellen Blake jumped to her feet with a reflection of Jenny's own energy.

Her niece had always been careless. Ellen remembered the scrapes and scratches whenever she had seen her, back home in Connecticut or here for a visit to London. It was hard to think of that gauche adolescent as an adult now, a young woman with suffragette sympathies and a life of her own. But some things hadn't changed. Jenny was an only child, a motherless princess, bright and energetic and beautiful—but a menace around anything fragile.

Ellen had been working quietly on a manuscript, magnifying glass in one hand and pencil in the other. Now, as she saw in Jenny's hand a letter with a government seal, her own heart skipped a beat. William Marshall, or Clive Dunnay? It had to be one or the other. In either case, she had to hide her alarm from her niece.

She took the letter that Jenny thrust at her. Then she reached up and carefully adjusted her glasses.

"This manuscript's a pain, you know. It's taking me four times as long as I thought it would, and I promised to have it translated by next week.'' She glanced at the letter. "Now, then, what's all this?''

Jenny stared at her, wide-eyed and unspeaking.

"From the Ministry. Well, there's no reason for panic.'' Ellen adjusted her glasses again and read aloud. "We regret to inform you . . . Hmm. it's not as bad as you're thinking, Jenny. 'Colonel Marshall has been wounded, and is now receiving treatment . . . further word on his condition as soon as possible . . .' That's it. See for yourself.'' She passed the letter back to Jenny. "William's obsession with flags and guns—he's had it as long as I've known him. I always told him that one day it would get him into trouble.''

Jenny took and pored over the short letter. "It doesn't say a word about how badly he's wounded, or how he was wounded. It could even be something completely trivial.''

But it wouldn't be. Ellen Blake did not reveal her own thoughts. She was a tall, broad-shouldered woman with fine cheekbones and a strong chin. Even relaxing at home she wore stiff, dark clothes with only a wisp of lace at the throat to relieve their stern facade. She could never look at Jenny's face, pretty and optimistic and stubborn, without seeing the late Dora Marshall mirrored there. Jenny's mother had been the same age as Ellen, second cousins who had chosen radically different lifestyles. Now Ellen wanted to say, *Just like your mother, always looking for a silver lining*. But she couldn't do that, not today.

Instead, she said, "I certainly hope it's something minor—though it must be bad enough to take him out of combat, or they wouldn't have sent a letter."

She picked up a cigarette and absently lit it. Her travels around the world had forced her to claim men's rights long ago. It was that or be unable to perform her work as an archaeologist and antiquarian.

"Out of combat." Jenny had seized on the phrase she wanted to hear. "Then he's not in a danger area anymore. Maybe he's already on his way home!"

Ellen puffed furiously, staring at her shelves of books as though for answers. She didn't want to depress Jenny, but it did no good to stir up too many false hopes. "I don't think he's on his way to England," she said after a few moments. "If that were the case, they would certainly tell us, so that we could prepare. Remember when Geoffrey Rogers at Number Twenty-three was invalided out with a piece of shrapnel through the calf of his leg—the Rogerses were told a week in advance that he was on the way."

"But first Mrs. Rogers had a letter to say he was wounded. And then in the next post they found he was coming home! Maybe there's another. . . ."

Jenny had ignored the rest of the mail while she was reading about her father. Now she riffled through the other letters, looking again for the official crest of the Ministry of War. As she reached the bottom of the stack her face became despondent. "Nothing."

"Not from the Ministry." Ellen had been watching closely. "But there is something here." She reached out, and took one of the letters from Jenny's hands. "See, this one has a French stamp. And the envelope is addressed to both of us. Pass me that letter opener, would you?"

Jenny looked on excitedly. The envelope was an expensive vellum, with a seal in red wax below an ornate crest.

"Chateau Cirelle, Saint-Amè, Meuse." Aunt Ellen frowned down, letter opener poised by the envelope. "Interesting. I thought I knew the Meuse Valley fairly well, but I've never heard of Saint-Amè. It must be a small place, or a private chateau."

"Oh, Aunt Ellen. Open it!" said Jenny impatiently.

"I will." Ellen slit the envelope and removed a single sheet of cream bond paper covered in a flowing, old-fashioned script. "It's just that I like to know as much as possible about my correspondents."

She held the page so that they could both see it, and began to read aloud.

"Dear Dr. Blake and Miss Marshall.
My name is Louis Villette. I take this liberty of writing to you without introduction, because in these terrible times the usual niceties cannot be observed. Let me say it at once, Colonel William Marshall is alive. He was injured by an explosive shell, and is staying in a portion of this chateau that serves itself as a field hospital for wounded officers. The Colonel is a gallant officer and a gentleman. My home is his home. He would write to you, but his wounds do not permit. He has requested that I take up this pen on his behalf, to send his love, to say that he misses you very much, and to tell you that he will write to you as soon as he is capable. With apologies for the poorness of my English writing.
                    Respectfully yours,
                    Louis Villette, Marquis.

Jenny had been hanging tight to Ellen's forearm as she read. Now she gave a huge sigh and released her hold. "Thank God. Oh, thank God. He's all right."

"More than all right." Ellen was staring again at the crest. "That's your father's style—recuperating at the home of a marquis. William always falls on his feet."

"Louis Villette, Marquis de Saint-Amè." Jenny repeated the words with her best French accent. "How wonderful for Daddy, and what a wonderful letter. Aunt Ellen, where is this Saint-Amè place?"

"My question exactly. Let's have a look, shall we, and find out."

Ellen went across the room to a rack of oversized books and returned carrying a big atlas. She placed it on her cluttered desk and opened it to a map of northern France. "Now, then. Where's Saint-Amè?"

It took a couple of minutes to find, a little village nestled on the Aire River. Jenny searched for nearby names that she recognized, and found only one: Verdun, where so many soldiers were dying, was twenty miles to the north.

"Saint-Amè seems to be in the middle of nowhere."

"Not really." Ellen put her finger on the map. "I've traveled the Meuse Valley, and I've been here. This is Bar-le-Duc, the administrative center of the Meuse district. It's about twelve miles southwest of Saint-Amè—not far, over easy country."

"You've been there?" Jenny sometimes had the impression that Aunt Ellen's work had taken her everywhere in the world. Name a place, and she would tell you all about it and its history. Ellen's personal knowledge of Bar-le-Duc suddenly made this part of France closer and more accessible.

Jenny was overwhelmed by the idea that struck her. "Aunt Ellen, if you know the place—why can't we go there, and look after Father ourselves!"

"Well . . ." Ellen took off her glasses and blinked at Jenny. "I know the area as it was in peacetime. But I'm not sure it's feasible to go there now, with a war raging all around it. We need to know where the front lies in this part of France. There was a new war map in the paper just a few days ago." She picked up a stack of recent newspapers. "Give me a hand to find it."

Ellen didn't say what she was thinking, which was that the letter from Saint-Amè had another significance. William Marshall was not only unable to write a letter himself, he was apparently unable to *dictate* one. He might be very seriously wounded, though naturally the Marquis was unwilling to alarm them. And if William Marshall was terribly hurt, Ellen really did not want Jenny to see him, no matter how much Jenny might wish to do so.

"Here's a map," said Jenny suddenly. "From just a week ago. It shows the front, but it doesn't show Saint-Amè."

"The village is too small to be marked. We can put that in for ourselves." Ellen was using her magnifying glass again. "I thought so. The Germans are really very close to Saint-Amè. They occupy Saint-Mihiel, here, on the River Meuse—just ten miles to the east. That puts Saint-Amè within range of the big guns."

As she spoke, Ellen evaluated the situation. She had near-term commitments for her own time, but if anyone went to France, there were good reasons why she should be the one, rather than Jenny. Jenny's spoken French was barely adequate. She was not a seasoned traveler on the Continent. She would have to make her own arrangements for travel through what would certainly be chaotic conditions. Most of all, Jenny had not seen modern war and its effects on human flesh. She was awfully young to be exposed to what she would find in a field hospital.

"Jenny, I have obligations just now. But we can go together in a few weeks. All right?"

Jenny frowned and shook her head. "We shouldn't delay. The sooner, the better. We have no idea what Father's condition might be. And I've had nursing training. I can help look after him."

"Jenny, you've had civilian training, for ordinary sickness. The wounds made by weapons—"

"Aunt Ellen, I'm not a little girl anymore. Look at me! I'm twenty-three years old!"

"You're twenty-three, but you're no Florence Nightingale." Ellen reacted to the tone in Jenny's voice. "Jenny, you have no idea what you'd have to face there. Frontline conditions are terrible, and I'm not just talking injuries. Wait until I can come with you—it won't be long. I promised Profesor McVittie a translation of this new fragment of the Gospel of Saint Peter, and I'm nearly done. I'll finish that while you brush up on your French, and we'll both go. What do you say?"

"You think I'm just a kid, don't you? No experience of the world."

"Jenny, you're an intelligent and energetic young woman—"

"You're patronizing me. You always do. I say something, and you pat me on the head and say, 'That's nice, dear.' "

"You mean what I said last night about women's rights? I didn't patronize you. All I did was point out that the most effective way to get your rights is one at a time, the way I did."

"You're changing the subject. I want to go and take care of Father. You say, 'Wait until I can come along and hold your hand.' All because of a stupid manuscript. Aunt Ellen, there's more to life than parchments and broken old pots."

"Of course there is. But my work is important."

"You think it is, but most people don't care tuppence about it. All I know is that Father matters more than a whole roomful of stuffy manuscripts." Jenny stopped suddenly. The depth of her misery was written on her face.

"Of course he does. Jenny, I care as much as you do. But we're not doctors." Ellen reached out to pat Jenny's shoulder. She knew what William Marshall would want her to do. He'd be horrified if anyone allowed Jenny to run into danger— even to see him. "What could we do, if we were there today?"

"I don't know what we could do. You're quite right, I'm not a doctor, I don't know the language well, and I don't know the country. But I feel as though I *should* be there, for his sake. A few weeks is like forever, when I know I won't be able to think of anything else."

She turned around and headed blindly out of the study.

"Jenny! Where are you going?"

"Out." Jenny tossed the words behind her. "For a walk. I feel as though my head is ready to burst."

CHAPTER THREE

Twenty miles to the north, German heavy artillery churned the French line to mud. And at the Chateau Cirelle, dinner had reached its final course.

The dining room was almost forty feet long. In brisk spring weather like this it held a winter's edge of cold, even with a fire blazing in the great hearth and the heavy screen drawn. That screen was over a century and a half old, a carved tracery of wood overlaid with heavy painted fabric. Its designs, dating back to the Royalist days of Louis XVI, depicted the floral gardens at Versailles. Resplendent courtiers wandered among the bowers. The screen had survived only because Saint-Amè was far from Paris and the centers of government. It had not seen the mad zeal of the revolutionaries.

Louis Villette, Marquis de Saint-Amè, spoke casually of that screen. In a lineage that found its roots in the eleventh century, one hundred and fifty years was no time at all.

Beyond the screen and out of earshot of the dinner guests, the maidservant set the remnants of garlic-rubbed lamb on the side table and turned nervously to the butler.

"Monsieur Monge—this dinner is so unfriendly, so cold." She had sensed the tension as she set down the first course of barley soup. She had moved more silently than usual, trying to avoid even the smallest clatter of spoons and serving dishes on the long board of polished oak. "Did I do something wrong? There is no friendliness, no jokes, no words of thanks."

12

"No, Marie, it is not your fault." Maurice Monge was a patient, nearsighted man in his late thirties. He had served as butler at Chateau Cirelle continuously since the return of the Marquis from Africa. Now he picked up and chewed a fragment of lamb, appraising its texture. "And it is certainly not the quality of the food. This is excellent!"

Marie hazarded a look past the edge of the screen at the blond man and the woman sitting next to the Marquis. "Then do you think he has found out about Mademoiselle Cecile? I think that she and Monsieur Richter . . ."

The butler shook his head. "I will not deny that something is going on between Monsieur Richter and Mademoiselle Cecile. But it is not that. Monsieur Richter has dined here many times, and the Marquis likes him very well. They talk together, of many things and many countries. Monsieur Richter is a very educated man. If his relationship with Cecile does not worry Monsieur the Marquis—and it does not seem to—then it is no business of anyone else's. Certainly it is no business of *yours*!" He wagged his finger at her jokingly. With dinner reaching a successful conclusion, he was in a relaxed mood. "If Monsieur Richter tries to climb into *your* bed, then it is something to worry about—but I do not think he plans such a thing."

Marie felt intrigued at the possibility. Monsieur Richter was a handsome man! "But then, what is it? Why is everyone so gloomy?"

Monge looked serious. "Doubtless it is the visitor. He was not at dinner tonight, because he is sick. He is taking a light dinner in the guest wing where the wounded soldiers have been housed. But his arrival is worrying the Marquis— enough to spoil an excellent dinner."

"A stranger?"

"Not a total stranger. He was at the chateau before you came here, back in January—early January, when the cold was so bitter. Since then, the whole personality of the Marquis has changed. Now he works incessantly!"

"Yes." Marie spoke respectfully. "He is like a haunted man."

"Haunted!" Monge shook his head. "And you would be, too, if you had his past. Have you not noticed that although he is an aristocrat, he has no heir to his title?"

"That must be his choice. He could be married tomorrow."

"Ah, but Louis Villette *was* married—very young, to a girl he loved dearly. They had one child, a boy, but his wife died in childbirth. And then his son, Patrice, was one of the first of our war dead. He was killed in battle, heroically, in August 1914."

"How awful!" Marie shivered. "The poor Marquis. But is Cecile not his daughter?"

"She is, but she is not legitimate. When his wife died, Louis Villette went away to Africa to escape his pain. He brought Cecile back with him. He adores her, but she cannot continue the line of Saint-Amè."

Monge paused, remembering. Then he sighed and snapped his fingers. "It is very sad. But unless you and I get back to work, the Marquis will have a genuine reason for unhappiness with *us*. And then you will have plenty more to worry about!"

Monge gave her a pat on her well-padded bottom and watched approvingly as she trotted back into the dining room. He slowly followed, eyeing the wiggle in her walk. Marie would do very well, unless someone like Monsieur Richter found her fresh youth a little too attractive. He had seen it happen too many times before. . . .

I wonder what is going on inside that man's head, wondered Charles Richter. He gave his host a curious glance. *He looks as though the weight of the world is on his shoulders*.

Louis Villette was sitting at the end of the table farthest from the fireplace. He had eaten little, ignoring the later courses of food but drinking steadily. He had continued his solitary perusal of a third bottle of Moselle and nibbled fragments of boiled crayfish and hard cracker, while the other guests proceeded through the main courses to candied and preserved fruits and liberal amounts of Chateau d'Yquem.

Richter, two seats down from the Marquis, had as always drunk very sparingly. He valued his clarity of mind. Now he sipped the syrupy golden wine and watched his host for any sign of a change of mood. At the moment the Marquis was quite unapproachable. He had joined in the discussion of centrally heating the chateau and had listened politely to the boring analysis offered by the man next to him, an official with the prefecture at Bar-le-Duc, but although the Marquis was unfailingly polite, his mind was clearly elsewhere.

It was the first time that Richter had seen Louis Villette, normally the most attentive of hosts, so indifferent to the comments of his guests. He caught Cecile Villette's eye, three places farther along on the opposite side of the table. She, too, had been watching her father closely for any sign of a thaw in his mood. Richter gave a little shake of his head. Not tonight. He wanted to postpone his conversation with the Marquis to a time when Louis Villette was in a more promising mood.

She made a little moué of disappointment, but she nodded. Richter looked at her full-lipped mouth and took in a deep breath. He had started his relationship with her for purely practical and patriotic reasons. Now the very sight of her made him physically aroused.

Cecile Villette was a woman of twenty, with striking dark eyes and a wild sweep of black curly hair. The high cheekbones, thin nose, and delicate features had all come from her father. Her mother's legacy was more difficult to detect. It lay in the darker-than-ivory skin, supple figure, glowing good health, and violence of emotional reactions. Of the friends and family of Louis Villette, only a handful knew that his only daughter Cecile was a natural child, born of an African mother during the Marquis' twelve years in the Belgian Congo. She had been educated in Paris, Brussels, and London, without anyone guessing that her mother had spoken not a word of French or English.

Charles Richter turned to answer a question from his neighbor. No, he had heard nothing new about the battle farther north. It was less a battle than a siege. Verdun had held out for more than two months, under what appeared to be the greatest German pressure of the war. The French troops and supplies continued to pour north along the Voie Sacrée, and the battered remnants would limp back a week or a month later.

The question showed that although it was only eight-thirty, the dinner party was over. By convention, with the German lines only ten miles east at Saint-Mihiel, polite dinner conversation could be on almost any subject except the progress of the war. The pain of lost or absent loved ones was concealed beneath general conversation of food, drink, clothes, crops, and hunting. The conflict was mentioned only as the guests were leaving.

The Marquis was already on his feet. Charles Richter stood up also, turning again toward Cecile. She showed the tip of her tongue between her teeth, and raised her eyebrows. He nodded imperceptibly, then made his way to the head of the table to bid good night to the Marquis.

Richter limped as he walked. A congenital deformity had left one leg nearly two inches shorter than the other, and even with an elevated shoe his resulting lameness had kept him out of the French Army. Until, he would say—not altogether in jest—they are willing to draft the blind, the deaf, and the crippled; then my turn will come.

He held out his hand to the Marquis, who gripped it warmly and smiled at him. "Always good to see you, Charles. Off again to Paris?"

"Bar-le-Duc first, then Paris." Richter returned the pressure. He genuinely liked the older man. In his own reports to his superiors, he had offered what he believed to be an accurate description of Louis Villette: an aristocrat with a strong sense of duty that sometimes seems to derive from an earlier century. Convinced of the rightness of a cause, he will pursue it to the limits of his strength and energy. A powerful friend, and a formidable enemy. The only thing that Richter did not mention in his reports was his own liking and respect for the Marquis, a feeling which seemed to be reciprocated.

"Don't wait for an invitation," Louis Villette was saying. "Come back anytime. This house is your house."

He patted Charles Richter on the shoulder and turned to say good-bye to the next guests.

This house is your house. Richter headed for the door. Louis Villette meant that. Would the Marquis say it if he knew what had been going on under his roof—and would go on again in just a few minutes?

The main doors to the Chateau Cirelle faced south. From there it was a fair walk around to the stables, on the southwest corner of the main building. As the guests left, their carriages would be brought to the front door by the hostler and be waiting for them as they came out of the building. But Charles Richter often lingered after the rest of the guests had departed, to smoke an after-dinner cigar with the Marquis. It was understood by the staff that he would go to the stables to take his own horse, without assistance from anyone.

It was a cloudy April night, with a touch of drizzle in the air. Richter pulled his cloak around his shoulders and set off clockwise around the chateau toward the stables. But once there he did not stop. He continued until he was at the northeast tower, and went back into the chateau through a narrow door there. It was a little-used entrance, leading up a winding wooden staircase to the second floor, and then along a bare and unlit corridor to another landing.

Cecile was waiting for him, standing in the darkness.

His eyes were not fully adjusted to the gloom. He saw her only as a pale shape against the dark paneling, then smelled her perfume as she moved forward into his arms. She had removed her dress and stockings and was wearing only a short undergarment that stopped at her hips. He pressed her back to the wall of the corridor, pushing against her warm body and stooping forward to bury his face in the nape of her neck. He could hear her heavy breathing in his ear, and her whisper, "*Ici, mon Charles.* Right here. Do not wait."

The perfect guest, Charles Richter thought to himself. He eats your food, he drinks your drink, and then he fucks your only daughter. But those wry thoughts did not slow his actions. He was already moving to couple with Cecile, lifting her and pushing her back against the wall, both of them too urgent in this first embrace to wait for the softness and ease of her bed. She had opened his clothes and taken him in her hands. He heard her hiss of pleasure and satisfaction at his excited state.

But there is an act worse than this, thought Richter, as Cecile guided him into her greedy warmth. I am doing something worse than this to you, Louis Villette, something you do not dream of—and something that I hope to God you will never discover.

Wartime economies extended even to the use of light and heat. At eleven-thirty the steam generator providing power for Chateau Cirelle's electrical generator was banked down until morning. Light bulbs slowly faded from yellow to orange; by midnight the light was gone completely.

In the warm darkness of Cecile's feather bed, Charles Richter steeled himself to rise, dress, and face the chilly night. Cecile slept at his side, as deeply and innocently as a child. He lay physically drained but mentally alert, listening to her even breathing.

In the middle of their lovemaking he had promised again that he would talk to her father and raise the question of marriage. It was the third time they had talked, the third time he had given his word.

Cecile was impatient but sympathetic. She knew that her father was a formidable man, and she was not surprised that Richter was reluctant to face the Marquis unless the circumstances were right. Fear of confrontation and rejection was natural.

Natural, thought Richter in the darkness; but in this case, irrelevant. Louis Villette likes me, he approves of my seeing Cecile. He knows I have money, knows I'm of good family, thinks that I have a decent amount of brains and property. He would welcome me as a son-in-law. Damn it, what I'm afraid of is *acceptance*. Cecile intoxicates me, the very sight of her makes me feel drunk. And in bed . . .

He ran his hand along her smooth flank. He had never known, never even read of, a woman with the sexual energy and inventiveness of Cecile. She did by nature things that others could not do with training.

She is warm, and tender, and loving. She would make a wonderful wife. And what I cannot bear is the thought that one day she may look at me in disgust.

He sighed, eased his way over to the side of the bed, and stepped out onto the polished floorboards. Dressing in the dark was something that had become easy after half a year's practice. He leaned forward, touched Cecile gently on the cheek, and went to the door. His knees were weak and trembly, and his neck was aching. An evening with Cecile made him at twenty-seven feel like an old man. Maybe tonight that was mostly imagining—he still had a long way to go before he would get any sleep.

The corridor outside the bedroom was pitch-black, with not even a glimmer of light from the narrow window. The sky must still be overcast. He felt his way quietly to the head of the winding staircase and went down as lightly as possible, noticing every creak of the treads. The upper floors of the chateau were a new addition to the older, fourteenth century structure that survived in the cellars and storage rooms below ground level. But "new" meant eighteenth century, and there had been plenty of time for the boards of the upper stories to shrink and warp, or floors and walls to go out of true.

At last he was at the outside door. He gripped the handle, turned it, and swore aloud. The damned thing was locked. Not bolted from the inside, as usual, but actually locked with a key—just as it was supposed to be. A stable hand had the nightly duty of locking the doors, but he rarely touched this one. He had chosen tonight of all nights to be conscientious.

Charles Richter grunted with disgust, then slowly went back up the stairs. It was not the first time it had happened. On two previous occasions when the tower door was locked Cecile had guided him through the chateau to another exit. This time he did not wake her. He knew the way well enough to the front of the chateau.

And if he were unfortunate enough to run into the Marquis as he was leaving?

Well, he had promised Cecile he would talk to her father about her hand in marriage. He grinned to himself. There would be no quicker way of guaranteeing that conversation than meeting the Marquis here and now.

Richter tiptoed along the corridor, down a couple of steps, and through a sharp right-hand turn. It was one thing to joke about an encounter with Louis Villette, quite another to contemplate it seriously. Fortunately the Marquis had his bedchambers well away from here, over in the southwest wing.

The main staircase led directly to the double doors, with a gun room off to the left and the library of the chateau on the right. The library and study had been an addition of this Marquis, when he succeeded to the line with the death of his father and returned from Africa. He had converted a high-ceilinged room with excellent light, formerly a spinning and weaving chamber, to a book-lined retreat where he spent a good part of his time.

With the front door in sight, the urge to step out more

boldly was strong. Richter was about to do so when he noticed a line of light showing at the library door. If that were the Marquis, insomniac at one o'clock in the morning, leaving the chateau would be much more difficult. The opening of the main outer door might be audible in the library.

Richter moved slowly down the stairs and crept to the library door. It was open a few inches, not enough to give a full view of the room. He could see the Marquis, tall and energetic as ever, pacing up and down in front of the big desk. Seated at that desk and not visible from the door was a second man.

"It is safe in my care," Villette was saying. "I have used the methods approved by the Brotherhood."

"Good. I am glad to hear that. I have returned at the request of the Council, to see that all is . . . well." The voice was weak and high-pitched, speaking a slightly accented French. "You did not seem so receptive when I explained your duties back in January."

"I did not expect the succession in my lifetime."

"I told you of the problems on my first visit." The other man sounded faintly exasperated. "You did not expect it would pass to you, I am sure—just as I did not expect to *deliver* this to you. We were both wrong. But if you have the Cross with you, I would like to see it one more time. Tomorrow, God willing, I will return to Trieste."

"Trieste?"

"My home." A dry laugh. "Yes, even I have a home. I have not spent my whole life as a legate, though sometimes it feels like it. My duties are finished, unless I am still on this earth when there is again a succession—which I much doubt. Ahhh."

There was a long-drawn sigh of breath, and the soft clink of metal. Charles Richter leaned forward to the crack and peered into the lamplit room. He was not particularly a snooper, but a natural human interest in overheard conversations held him where he stood. The stranger had moved forward, so now Richter could see a thin, white-haired head and a frail arm. The man was holding a dark cross on a silver chain squarely in front of him. His lips moved silently for a few seconds. Finally he cupped the crucifix in his hands.

"Thank you." His voice was stronger. "You know, when

I arrived here in January I thought that I was as weak and sickly as I could get. It was only when I surrendered the Cross to you and went on to meet with the Council in Toulouse that I realized how much the holy presence on my person had sustained and comforted me. Treasure it, Louis Villette, for yourself and for all the other Knights of the Twelfth Apostle. The Cross comes to your hands, just as it was fashioned by our lord, Judas. Treasure it. And guard it.''

The speaker had finally risen to his feet, presenting a full view to Charles Richter. Dressed in tattered black clothes, he was stooped and emaciated, with an unhealthy tinge to his skin. Louis Villette, tall and powerful, towered over him and reached out a supporting arm. ''You need sleep, brother.''

''Aye.'' The white head nodded. ''Since Bosnia I have needed sleep. There is a long enough sleep on the way for all of us, when we are laid in earth. I can wait for sleep.''

It sounded like the end of their conversation. Richter drew back into the shadows, then padded away silently toward the main door. He opened it and slipped through.

The drizzle had strengthened to a thin rain as he moved around to the stables, found his waiting horse, and mounted it.

What was the significance of the things he had just heard and seen? He puzzled over them as the horse took him quietly out of the grounds of the chateau and onto the soft dirt road that led to his stated destination of Bar-le-Duc.

But when he came to that southwest road he did not take it. Instead he turned the horse the other way and went east, along the road that led to Saint-Mihiel; the road that also led, less than ten miles away, to the French lines; and, beyond them, the war front and the waiting German forces.

CHAPTER FOUR

"What was that?"

The legate blinked and craned his neck around to stare at the library door.

"What?" Louis Villette followed the legate's gaze. The man claimed that the Cross sustained him, but he was on his last legs. Why had he tottered back here in such a physical condition? A puff of wind would blow him away.

"I heard a sound." The legate pointed. "Out in the hall."

"I heard nothing. But I'll take a look." Villette strode to the door. It had been ajar, and now he opened it all the way and peered into the darkness of the hallway. "Nothing. A bit of a draft, that's all."

When he returned, the legate was again holding the Cross cupped in both hands and frowning down at it. The old man's yellowed teeth were clenched.

"Are you all right, brother?" The Marquis touched him gently on the shoulder.

The visitor breathed in noisily through his nose and slowly nodded. "I am all right. My concern is for the Cross. It feels peculiar. Different."

"It senses massive pain and suffering. The trenches are only a few miles from here." The Marquis turned to pour himself a glass of brandy, hiding the tension that must show on his face.

"Yes. Yes, that could be it." The old man nodded slowly. "I have traveled with the Cross for so long, I am grown too sensitive. Forgive my fears. The Cross has been misused so often.''

''The record shows it.''

''Misused disastrously.'' The legate hardly seemed aware of the Marquis. He was talking to himself in a soft, dreamy voice as he crouched over the tarnished silver. ''For almost two millennia this sacred treasure, in humble, God-fearing hands, has worked toward our Lord's redemption. Is it heresy to believe, as many of the brethren believe, that the soul of Lord Judas is trapped even now within this metal, awaiting freedom? Who knows? There are few certainties.'' He looked up. ''But there is one certainty. Evil must result if the Cross is misused.'' His voice was harsher. ''Misused, Louis Villette, when a man believes that he can *control* events, rather than surrendering his own spirit to the will of God. Misused, when the power is not allowed to work in its own way.''

''I know, brother.'' Villette reached out his hand. ''I know all this. Give me the Cross, so that I can put it away and let its work continue.''

''I cannot do that.'' The legate raised his cupped hands, and a single drop of blood fell from them to the carpet. ''Behold. The test is infallible. Confess, brother, and admit that of which I am already sure: You have employed the Ritual of Abraham.''

The voice was faint, but the words carried the weight of a physical blow. Louis Villette shook his head.

''The Ritual of Abraham,'' the legate went on remorselessly, ''which may be used only by the most purified Guardian, after many years of service, and only in the direst of times. That is not you, Louis Villette, not for many years. You have betrayed your trust.''

Villette drained the brandy glass, and the stem snapped in his fingers. ''Never. That I would never do. Brother, I swear to you, before God and Lord Judas himself, matters here are under control.''

''No. You have deluded yourself, Louis Villette, as others have deluded themselves before you. The Cross is not a trinket, to be toyed with as you choose. You are playing with fire—hellfire! Tell me what you are hoping to gain by your actions.''

The Marquis sat down opposite the other man. ''Is it

not obvious, brother? I am saving my country. You must understand the situation here. Truly, the wolves are at the gate. My countrymen are dying by the thousands, by the tens and hundreds of thousands, to stop the enemy from trampling through our sacred land. You speak of dire times. Could there ever be times more dire, more need to invoke the full ritual?''

The legate hissed and craned his turtle neck forward. ''You fool! The Ritual of Abraham is powerful, enormously powerful. But using it for secular purposes is like calling down the lightning—there will be results, but no one can tell how or where they will strike. Continue this path, Louis Villette, and the consequences will be frightful. You will lose everything—your household, your estate, all that you love. And finally your sanity and your immortal soul.''

''Brother, your concern is heartening. I share your worries. I did not easily conclude that the ritual had to be employed. I am no man of blood. It was the hardest decision that I ever had to make. But the need to perform the rite will soon be over. The tide of war will turn, I know it, and my country will be safe. My people will be safe.''

''You are the *Guardian*, Louis Villette. *All* people are your people!''

''I am a Frenchman. A man of France. I have my duty to my country.''

''Do your duty—but not by using the Cross. I am taking it back to the Council. There must be a different Guardian.'' The legate stood up, straighter than before, and clutched the Cross to his chest. ''Out of the way, brother. I can find my own way to the stables. I am leaving. Tonight.''

''I cannot allow it.'' The Marquis rose also. ''Tell the Council that I know my duties, and I will honor them. I take full responsibility for all my actions. There is no worthier use of the Cross than the salvation of France.''

The legate stepped close, to stare into Villette's tormented eyes. ''Ah, brother, I know the temptation, the agony you feel when your young men are dying. But don't you see that it is patriotism and nationalism that has *caused* this death and destruction?'' He pointed north. ''Your young troops go to their deaths with glorious courage. But do you think that the Germans are any different? Do you think they love their country less? You talk of duty, but can you not see a higher duty? You must love your God and your Lord *more* than your country."

"Can you stop the sun from shining, or the rain from falling? We do not control what we love. And I love France."

"Out of the way. I am going to the stables."

"Go where you like, brother. The Cross stays with me, where it belongs. I am the Guardian." The Marquis held out his hand. "Return it."

"It leaves with me. My first responsibility is to the Cross." The legate's right hand reached beneath his cloak and came out holding a small pistol. "You are stronger than I am, brother. But you are not stronger than a bullet. I beg you, in the name of Lord Judas himself, do not make me shoot. But shoot I will, if that is necessary. Come no closer."

Villette stood still. "Brother, you are so sure of yourself. Have you asked the Cross what it thinks of this? You have carried it long and far, and you say you are sensitive to it— so ask it! Let it decide." He closed his eyes and whispered the opening litany of the ritual. As he came to the last phrase, the legate screamed in sudden agony. He opened his hand, and the Cross dropped to the floor. A wisp of smoke curled up from the carpet.

Villette scooped up the dull-glowing metal. Untouched by pain, he kissed the hot silver and looped the chain around his neck. "Where it belongs, brother," he said. "I am the true Guardian. The power of God will work through me."

The legate had his burned palm to his mouth. "There is power. But I tell you, it is not the power of God—not if you are applying the Cross and Ritual to secular uses."

"Tell the Council what you like. But go. Come back, if you will, when my homeland is safe from the German barbarians."

"I am finished with words. Surrender the Cross to me— now." The legate had lifted the gun and was again pointing it at the middle of Villette's chest.

The Marquis was surprised by the speed and power of his own reaction. He felt no anger, but his right arm clutched and swung with terrible force. The gun went flying away across the room, while the legate was hurled headfirst into the carved oak desk. He fell to the floor and did not move.

"My God." Villette stood horrified and stared down at the body. "What have I done?"

He went to the legate and gently turned him over. One eye was open, and a trickle of dark blood came from the scalp and the man's left ear. The staring eye turned to gaze at Louis Villette.

"Forgive me, brother." The Marquis mopped tenderly at the scalp wound with his kerchief. "I did not mean to hurt you. You will be all right." But even as he spoke he could see the distorted line of the legate's skull.

"Worry about yourself, Louis Villette, not me." The voice sounded half in the grave. "You are calling down the deepest curse of our Lord's passion, upon you and all that you hold dear. The powers you invoke are beyond your imagining."

"No, brother. I have studied the Gospel and the Ritual, long and hard. I have learned from the mistakes of others. I am sure that matters here are under control."

The staring eye with its dilated pupil wandered, unable to focus on Villette's face. "You deceive yourself. You will lose control, and then far more than control. You do not know your own heart, but I know. Unhappy brother! Your deepest love, the dearest soul that you will ever know, that one will be sacrificed—by your own hand—to the Cross of Judas."

"Who?" The Marquis shivered, and he bent close to the thin face. "For God's sake, who? Who are you talking about?"

"Your true love, your heart's desire. You will destroy your heart's desire."

"Who is she? Will she—"

Louis Villette did not complete the question. The Cross on its chain had been hanging to touch the legate's chest. Now it slipped free to dangle at the old man's side. As it left the body, the faint breathing stopped. The Marquis leaned forward and placed his head on the legate's thin chest. "In the name of heaven, brother, forgive me! Lord Judas, help me. What have I done?"

He lifted the Cross in his right hand. The feel of the battered metal eased his despair. From far off came a faint rumble of gunfire.

"Brother, my heart grieves for this death. You devoted your life to the service of the Cross, and your dedication earned a burial of full ceremony and honor. But I cannot provide that. Not today. Hear the guns. What I am doing is right, and the sacrifice must continue. The full ritual must be used. I have no alternative. Brother, forgive me.''

He tucked the cross once more inside his collar. Its cool touch on his chest comforted him. He crouched for a long time, head bent in prayer. Finally he lifted the wasted body of the legate and set off with it for the deepest cellars of Chateau Cirelle.

CHAPTER FIVE

Halfway between Belgrave Square and Hyde Park Corner, the reaction set in.

"We regret to inform you . . ."

Jenny could hardly breathe. She staggered to the side of the flagstoned pavement and leaned against an iron gate. Her throat felt tight and constricted; after a few moments the tears began.

Under the influence of Ellen Blake's brisk optimism, danger had been so abstract. Now death and injury were as near as the row houses lining the street, as choking as the exhaust fumes of the cars chugging past her. He could be dead at this moment, and she would not know it. Dead, or wounded and in terrible pain. That was almost worse.

William Marshall was not the man that Aunt Ellen had described, infatuated with flags and guns and military power. The memory of other seasons was in Jenny's mind, the two of them galloping through the flaming reds and yellows of fall trees. He would do anything for her. And now, when he needed help himself . . . she was useless.

Jenny wiped her tears away with her handkerchief. She must be a terrible sight, face blotchy and eyes swollen. She couldn't let Aunt Ellen see her like this, or they'd never go to France. She had to stay outside until she had control of herself and her face was back to normal.

She headed along the sidewalk, avoiding the eyes of the other pedestrians. The bus stop was four blocks away. A fast walk would help. The few men she passed in their starched white collars and black coats were a lot older than her. But certainly they were no older than her father. Why weren't *they* over in France?

Jenny recalled Clive Dunnay's wry comment on his last leave: "You see, Jenny, this is a young man's war *and* an old man's war. The old ones do the talking; the young ones do the dying."

After more than a year and a half of war, London showed little outward sign of the struggle. Jenny walked along streets filled with buses, hansom cabs, and bright new motorcars, hindered in their movement by laden horse-drawn carts and tarnished lorries. They still carried their wares to Covent Garden or Billingsgate Fish Market, just as though the war did not exist.

She boarded the 88 omnibus at Hyde Park Corner. A woman conductor took her half-pence fare. Unimaginable, two years ago . . . a woman doing a man's job. And yet it had to stay that way. If anything good came out of this war, it would be that women were finally allowed to compete with men for positions.

Jenny climbed to the open upper deck of the bus and settled into a front seat. She had her feelings in check now, more or less, but she could not stop thinking about her father. The last time she had seen him was four months ago, and then he had looked awful. He had lost a good fifteen pounds. His face was haggard and gray. He assured Jenny that everything was fine, but his hands trembled when he tried to light his pipe, and he drank more than she'd ever seen him drink. Jenny had mentioned it to Ellen Blake. Her aunt had been too wrapped up in her own world to do more than nod agreement.

But her father liked Ellen, and he trusted her judgment. So did Clive. "You say she's a funny old bird," he had said after his first meeting with her. "But she's a very competent woman. And she's fun to be with, too."

"She treats me like a *baby*," Jenny had grumped. Clive hadn't seemed to feel that was much of a criticism.

The bus groaned to a stop, and Jenny looked at the street signs. Earls Court Road. She hurried down the spiral stairs, jumped off, and headed for the trees that signaled the entrance to Holland Park. It was not large, but it reminded Jenny of the woods back home. A stiff breeze whipped at new leaves and swirled the branches into complex arabesques. She still wasn't sure of the names of the English trees and shrubs, but that was certainly a hawthorn, ready to flood the world with snowy blossom. And that was a healthy crabapple in late bud. The birds fluttered and chirped, and squirrels drunk with spring madness chased each other up and down the tree trunks.

Lucky animals. They had never heard of the war.

She sighed, and walked on among the scattered park benches. The cast-iron frames needed paint—but that would wait until the war was over.

"There you go, Papa Joffre." A voice brought Jenny out of her brooding. Right in front of her, a man was feeding pigeons. The left arm of his jacket was pinned to his sleeve, and a wooden crutch leaned against the back of the bench he was sitting on. His right trousers leg dangled empty below the knee. He held a paper bag, and attentive birds surrounded him, clucking and cooing.

"Make the most of that, Papa," he said, dropping a piece of bread crust to a fat and half-blind pigeon that stood by his foot. "And all of you, 'cause that's yer lot. You've 'ad most of my breakfast as it is."

Jenny moved to the far end of the bench. She finally felt the need to talk to someone. "They're not getting what they were used to, I suppose."

"That's the truth, miss." The crippled man returned her smile. He turned the paper bag upside down, allowing a rain of fragments and small crumbs to fall on the blue-gray mass of strutting and pecking pigeons. Eager sparrows fluttered on the perimeter, darting in to pull specks of food from beneath the bigger birds. "Back when old King Edward was alive, this lot was as fat as 'e was. Now it's iron rations all 'round. They've got to tighten their belts like the rest of us."

"Were you there—in France?" Jenny asked abruptly.

He turned to look straight at her for the first time. His face was ruddy and good-natured, with a once-broken nose and protruding ears. "I was, miss."

"My father is over there now," she said, blurting it all out. "We got word this morning. He's been injured."

"Ah." A moment of respectful silence. "Let's hope that

'e'll be all right. My old lady said that was the worst part, when she knew I'd copped one and didn't know 'ow bad it was.''

"We don't even know yet where it happened."

"That's right. That's policy. They don't want to give out too much on where the fightin' is, in case it gets to the wrong 'ands.''

"He used to be stationed at Loos." She was babbling, but she had to talk, even if this was a stranger.

"I know the place, miss. I wasn't far from there. I got mine at Wipers.''

"Ypres?"

"Ypres, Wipers—same place, and Wipers is a lot easier to say.''

"Did you ever meet a Colonel Marshall when you were at the front—William Marshall? That's my father. I'm Jenny Marshall.''

"Alf Nettleton. Nice to meet you.'' He frowned. "William Marshall. Not that I recall. Didn't meet many colonels. Which outfit?''

"Royal Scots Fusiliers.''

"Ah. I was with the Terriers—Forty-seventh London Territorials. And I was blown up early on, comparatively speaking.''

"What's it like over there?'' Jenny asked impulsively. "Excuse me asking, but I asked Father, when he was home on leave, and I couldn't get him to tell me anything.''

"Ah.'' He stared off into the distance for a moment, as though assessing the rustling spring leaves. "Duckboards.''

"Pardon?''

"I get the same question, many a time. People say to me, what's it like there? What do you remember best about the front? And I tell 'em, duckboards.''

"I've never heard of them.''

"You wouldn't.'' Alf Nettleton chuckled ruefully. "They're not something they makes speeches about in Parliament. But when I think of the front it's not guns an' gas an' field telephones I recall—it's miles and miles of duckboards.''

"What are they?''

"You know about trenches, miss?''

"Of course."

"Well, trenches are tricky things. If you don't keep 'em right, well drained and all, the bottom gets sludgy and the sides fall in. The French keep their trenches 'orrible! But even a good one gets damp, so you have to cover the bottom or all the paths turn to mud with a drop of rain and you need to be a duck to get through 'em. So you need duckboards. They're slats of wood, tied with wire or twine. And Tommy can bob on over 'em like ducks on the water." He smiled at Jenny. "There was near as much duckboards at the front as there was barbed wire—and there was plenty of that, believe you me."

He shook his head. "So if my little girl says to me, 'What did *you* do in the Great War, Daddy?' I'll have to tell her, 'Why, I put down duckboards, that's what I did.' "

The thought came into Jenny's head so strongly that it left her breathless. She had taken it for granted that she would need to go with Aunt Ellen, the seasoned world traveler. But did she? She leaned toward him. "Could a woman go there—alone? To the front? Could I go there and look after my father?"

He shifted on his seat and scratched uneasily at the stump of his right leg. "Ah. I know how you feel. But he won't be in the front line now; he'll be back in a hospital."

"So I *could* do it—I'd be allowed to go there?"

"Maybe." He paused for a moment, listening to the chimes of a far-off church steeple. "There. Eleven o'clock. I don't have all that much good to say about the French, but the Froggies' licensing hours make a lot more sense than ours. Only half an hour in the middle of the day here—hardly time to get me in the place an' out again. Believe you me, we'll change all that when we've put the boot to Uncle Willy and this lot's over."

"It's part of the war effort. Did you know the king has given up drink completely, to set an example?"

"I did. But I think if he'd spend a few weeks down in the trenches, bless him, he might start drinking again. I don't see how keeping the pubs shut helps the war effort."

Jenny realized that he had deliberately changed the subject. "Do you think I could go over there and look after my father?" she repeated.

He sighed. "You've had me thinkin' about that since you first said it. First thought I 'ad was, no, don't do it. There's sights in them hospitals I wouldn't wish on any woman. But a mate of mine was in one of the hospitals where Lady Dorothie was helping look after the soldiers, and he said there was nothing in the world to make you want to live again like the touch of a woman's hand. An' I know what it was like when I caught mine. I lay there all delirious and pumped full of laudanum, and I'd have given anything I had to see Edie's face at the bedside. So it's a difficult question, miss. Not helping you much, am I?"

"You've helped me a tremendous amount. You've made up my mind for me." She reached out, as though to touch his empty sleeve, then drew back. "I hope you won't mind me asking, but how did it happen?"

"This? You know as much about it as I do. Last thing I remember was the night before, in the dugout. I was eating bread and cheese for my supper, an' thinking I'd save a bit for breakfast. Well, they tell me we had breakfast, and the shell came in about half past ten. I was one of the lucky ones. Twenty-three of my mates, gone forever. I woke up two weeks later, wondering who I was and where I was. They told me I was short one arm and one leg—an' the rest of me bread and cheese."

"I'm going to do it." Jenny stood up, filled with resolve. "I'm going to find out where Daddy is and look after him!"

Even as she said the words, the knot of tension inside her eased. She knew it was the right decision. No matter how much Aunt Ellen objected, Jenny would go through with it.

Alf Nettleton was studying her face, flushed with color from emotion and the April breeze. "I believe you, miss. And I say, God bless you. You're just like my Edie—once she decides something, you'll not shift her. When I was being sent back home, I half didn't want to see her—because of this." He gestured at his empty sleeve and trousers leg. "She'd seen a good-looking young man leave at the railway station, an' now she was gettin' back half a bag of bones— I'd lost weight something terrible. But Edie come straight to Charing Cross, and she gave me a smacking great kiss— right in front of everybody! And she brought me home. She snuggled next to me in bed—beggin' your pardon, miss—

and she told me she'd rather have half of me than all of anybody else in the whole world.''

"She sounds like a wonderful wife."

"She is. Too good for me."

"Where is she now?"

"Why, she's at home, doing the washing. She threw me out and told me to come back at teatime. She says I make the place look untidy. So here I am, obeyin' orders again.''

Jenny held out her hand. "Mr. Nettleton, I can't tell you how much talking to you has helped me. You made up my mind for me. I know what to do now. I'm going to France.''

He reached up. "Bye, Miss. Good luck to yer. It was a real pleasure, and I'm in your debt as much as you're in mine. I like to talk, and these days I've got too much time on my hands.'' He looked down and laughed awkwardly. "Pardon me. On my *hand*. Be better when we get this lot over, an' we'll all be busy again.'' He looked down, at a soft pressure on his leg. "Well then, and what do you want?''

At their feet, the old, half-blind pigeon stood patiently waiting. "He knows his rights, miss." Alf Nettleton reached into his pocket. "Him an' me, we're not quite as spry as we was, so he always gets a bit extra when the other pigeons have all given up and gone. Come on, Papa Joffre, have a go at this.''

He bent down. Jenny watched for a moment as he fed the pigeon out of his hand with crumbs of stale bread and sausage dug from the depths of his pocket.

Alf Nettleton sang to the bird in a hoarse bass voice:

"Far, far from Wipers, I long to be
Where German snipers, can't get at me.
Damp is my dugout, cold are my feet,
Waiting for a whizz-bang to put me to sleep.''

CHAPTER SIX

Behind the German lines northwest of Verdun, Dolfi sat safe in his bunker.

The German corporal wore the corded trousers of a dispatch runner. He was sitting on a crate in front of a homemade easel, busily drawing. Occasionally he would lift his head, listen, look at an old steel-cased pocket watch, and scribble a figure on the edge of the drawing paper.

His subject was not being particularly cooperative. Finally Dolfi put down his pencil. "Fuchsl! Look this way—and stop scratching!"

The little terrier stopped as requested and lifted his head. He stood up and came to his master's side. One of the other soldiers, a man with an injured shoulder, laughed. "There you go, Dolfi, perfect obedience. One word from you and he does as he likes."

His voice was cheerful and relaxed. The German trench system near Verdun was well planned and well maintained. While French shells were banging in the distance, Dolfi's companions concentrated on making their shelter more comfortable. One man was checking the wooden supports for walls and roof, tapping the struts back into line with his rifle butt. Two others were fiddling with the homemade stove and cooking range, a heavy steel plate from a gun carrier wired across the top of an oil drum. They were adding a stovepipe, to send smoke up and out through the observation window. Two others changed a shoulder dressing. While his comrade

35

examined the wound by the light of an oil-filled ration tin with a cloth wick, the injured man was chatting with Dolfi.

Now Dolfi smiled, leaned over, and patted the dog's head. "He is obedient, but he wants something to eat. I don't have anything, until those two geniuses stop ruining the stove."

"Here." The man tapping the wall supports threw a piece of hard biscuit to the dog. "Try this, Fuchsl—I hope your teeth do better with it than mine. When are you going to teach him to roll over and die for his country, Dolfi?"

The messenger shook his head. "We're the ones who have to do that." He added a couple of pencil strokes to the paper on the easel. "Now you've started him on food, I'll never get this drawing finished."

"Show us the picture, then." The soldier with the bare shoulder craned his head. "Let's have a look at what you've done so far. Ouch!" He jerked around. "What the blazes are you doing back there?"

"Sorry." His companion was leaning close, peering at the shoulder blade. "I think I've found a bit they missed. Right here."

He pressed, and the private shrieked. "I knew it! The bastards. I said they left a bit in. Now I'll have to go back to that damned field hospital, out in the open to be aimed at by every gunner in the French Army."

"Maybe not. Let me give it a try. Hold tight, this may be tender." His friend took the flesh of the shoulder between thumb and forefinger, pushed a pair of tweezers deep in the narrow wound, probed for a moment, and tugged. "Got it!" He held up a fragment of metal triumphantly. "Did it hurt?"

The injured man let out a howl of rage. "Hurt! Course it hurt, you stupid asshole. What sort of a question is that?"

"You're always complaining. If I hadn't got that out, you'd be heading over to the hospital. How about a cigarette?"

The man with the wounded shoulder snorted, picked up a tin of tobacco, and handed it to his friend. "Roll one for me, while you're at it. I have to get my shirt and jacket back on."

"How about you, Dolfi? Want one?" The soldier was being deliberately provocative. They all knew that Dolfi disapproved of both smoking and drinking. This time he didn't draw a reaction. Dolfi was staring at his watch again, and listening.

"Let me tell you," said one of the men reassembling the stove. "It doesn't do much good to listen to 'em. All you need to hear is the shell with your name on it, and it's all over. You're up the monkey's bum." He went back to his labors, wrestling to fit the stovepipe cleanly into the metal housing.

"You don't understand." Dolfi was short, slight, and intense. "Want to know how safe you are, here in this bunker? I can tell you. It's different from what the captain tells you."

"I don't give a rat's turd what the captain says. But I'd love to know how safe we are. Are we in trouble?"

Dolfi smiled. "No. We're better off than you realize. First, we are safe from snipers and rifle fire."

"Come on, Dolfi. That's not news—your dog could have told us that much."

"Let me finish. We're safe from rifle or machine gun bullets, so that leaves only artillery and mineworks."

"What about aircraft, Dolfi?" said a man who had been up on the stepladder watching the explosions beyond the hill. Now he had returned and was lying on his stomach on a bunk. "I heard a couple flying over the lines. One of them could drop something on us."

"They're busy enough up there. More chance of you falling off that bunk and breaking your neck than being bombed. Mineworks and shells are the danger. And I talked to the sappers, last time I ran a message. There's no evidence of tunneling activity in this part of the front. So back to shells. We're beyond the range of the small mortars. The danger comes from the big field pieces, and that's what I've been timing. You can hear the French stuff go over us, and you can hear when they land. They've got their range all wrong. They're dropping the shells at least two kilometers beyond us. We couldn't be safer at a beer garden in Berlin."

The others all listened respectfully. They knew Dolfi was smart: cool in a crisis, doing more than his share of work in the dugout, uncomplaining about any hardship. His only peculiarities were his lack of interest in smoking, drink, and women.

"Maybe we are, Dolfi, but I'll still take the Berlin beer garden. There's less rats in Berlin—and a sight more beer." There was a tremendous clang as the two men holding the top of the stove allowed the metal plate to fall back into position. "There, we're done for the moment, but we can't cook on it yet. Want to draw lots for a food run up to the kitchens?"

"No need. I'll do it." Dolfi stood up. "Fuchsl needs exercise."

"Give him a good run. We don't want him crapping in the corner again. This place stinks bad enough with Jurgen."

"Bastard!" The two men began to scuffle, as Dolfi stood up and went across to the steps that led from the bunker. Before he could leave he saw a pair of polished black riding boots on the top step. "*Achtung!*" called a sharp voice from outside. Everyone in the bunker sprang to attention.

Two men slowly descended into the dugout. The first was familiar to the soldiers. He was Captain Mosteller, their own leader. But the second man was a civilian. It was Charles Richter, dressed in a dark traveling cloak and wearing insignia so senior that they all froze.

Richter recognized Dolfi from his description. He looked around the clutter of the dugout for a few seconds, then nodded. "Very good," he said. "Everyone out of here, if you please—except you." He pointed at Dolfi. "I'll tell the rest of you when you can come back."

The others filed out in an awful silence. A couple of them gave Dolfi sympathetic glances as they went.

Richter waited until they had left, then gestured at the dog, Fuchsl.

"He's mine, sir."

Richter nodded. "Then he can stay. At ease, Corporal. You may sit down. I am Charles Richter."

"Yes, sir." Dolfi nodded and sat gingerly on his usual crate. He shook his head in silence when the other man held out his cigar case toward him.

Richter took one for himself and accepted a light. "I want you to take a look at a document," he said, after a long draw at the cigar. "Read it right through, and take your time."

He handed over three pages of typewritten material and settled himself on a bunk. After ten minutes the corporal shrugged and held out the papers.

"All done?" Richter took the sheets. "Very good. Now, tell me what you have just read."

Dolfi cleared his throat. "Yes, sir. It appears to be a description of a plan for a campaign offensive, one that took place to the east of here."

"Correct. You saw the artillery list?"

"Yes, sir."

"Tell me about it. What pieces would be used, when it would be deployed, all that you can remember."

"It calls for huge amounts of artillery, sir. It was scheduled to begin with a massive bombardment on February twelfth." He paused. "But there was no such bombardment on February twelfth. It was on February twenty-first—"

"No comments, Corporal. Tell me what you remember about the ordnance."

"Five hundred and forty-two heavy guns, three hundred and six light pieces. One hundred and fifty-two giant mine throwers, thirteen 420-millimeter mortars, with one-ton projectiles, seventeen 305-millimeter Austrian mortars, seven batteries of 130-millimeter "whizzbangs"—high-velocity shells, so they—"

"I know what a whizzbang is, Corporal." Richter leaned back. "Excellent. Captain Mosteller did not exaggerate in his reports. Could you provide me with the same detail of information for any part of this document?"

"Yes, sir. I feel sure I could." Dolfi's face showed suspicion.

"I am impressed." Richter needed to address a difficult subject, but there was too much tightness in Dolfi's voice to begin at once. He nodded to the other man's feet. "I see a lot of things in these trenches, but I don't see many dogs. Mind telling me what he's doing here?"

"I found him in the trenches, sir, up on the Belgian border. He's a real trench dog, never lived anywhere else. He must have belonged to some English officer, because he understands English commands. One day last year he came running through our trenches after a rat—right across No-Man's-Land without getting shot. I fed him, and made a fuss of him. Now he's completely at home here. He loves it, and all the men love him."

"He certainly looks happy." Richter laughed. "I trust you taught him German, so he can be a loyal subject of the Fatherland?"

"Yes, sir, I did. Fuchsl, *setzen Sie!*" The terrier crouched at Dolfi's feet.

"Very good." Richter nodded. "At ease. And you, too, little dog!"

There was a long silence while Charles Richter sized up the other man. He was certainly unimpressive physically. Below average height, with a thin body, dark, badly-cut hair, and a doughy, unhealthy-looking face. Only the eyes were unusual. They were cold and thoughtful, staring back at Richter with a brooding, sinister intensity.

"I am working on a very important project," said Richter at last. "I need a man who can absorb a lot of information in a very short time, without seeing it written down, and remember it exactly. You were suggested as someone who can do that."

"I can." Dolfi stared speculatively at Richter. "But we are at war, sir. I am already doing important work. I do not like the idea of working on a civilian project."

"You will not be a civilian. You will be part of German Intelligence—and doing the most important job in the war. A task that will bring us rapid and total victory." Richter had the sudden feeling that Dolfi did not like him. The pale eyes looked right through him.

"Why me? Why not someone on the Intelligence staff?"

"You know your way around the front line—a dispatch runner could not survive without that knowledge. Your reports showed that you have an exceptional memory for detail, and you displayed that ability to me today. You notice things, and you remember them."

"That is true." Dolfi spoke absently, then burst out uncontrollably: "But you are a Frenchman!"

"I am a loyal German!" Richter barked the words and leaned forward. "If we are to work together, I will never allow my loyalty to be questioned. I was born in Alsace-Lorraine, but my parents came from Bonn. I went to the University of Heidelberg. I have been totally devoted to the German cause for the past eight years, and I have worked for Germany since the day this war started." Richter stood up and took a pace toward Dolfi. "You think that you run risk, do you, delivering messages? Look at the risk that I run. I work behind the French lines. If I get caught, I will be shot. I'll probably be tortured, though the French authorities never admit it. That's what happened to one of my liaisons three weeks ago. The same thing could happen to me tomorrow." He leaned forward and tapped Dolfi on the chest. "If you don't have that much guts, tell me now. I'll leave and look for someone who does."

Dolfi had scowled through the outburst, and flinched when Richter touched him. He sat silent for a moment, lips pouted. "I have courage," he said at last. "All the courage that you could need."

"And you don't sound German yourself, any more than I do. You sound like an Austrian!"

Dolfi gave a little nod of concession. "Viennese. But I, too, joined the German Army as soon as they allowed it." He bit his lip. "You are right. I was allowing your clothes and accent, and my hatred for all things French—their filthy trenches, their wine-sotted ways, their sluttish loose women—to bias my judgment. My apologies." He spoke gruffly. "I accept that you are as loyal to our cause as I am." He reached down to fondle the dog's head. "Very well. What do you want me to do? You will find that I am lacking in neither courage nor brains."

"Your decorations for gallantry prove that. No one with your high reputation as a dispatch runner can lack nerve or intelligence." Richter settled back in his chair. If Dolfi was willing to be conciliatory, so was he. This would be a different kind of partner. Dolfi was only a corporal, but clearly he had his own opinions on the right way to do things. He would not take instructions blindly. That was no bad thing.

"The papers I used as a test of your memory were old ones," Richter went on. "They were part of the planning documents for Operation Gericht, Marshal Falkenhayn's scheme for the conquest of Verdun."

Dolfi nodded. "The operation goes on, but the attack has already failed."

"You seem sure of that. What is your evidence?"

"It is common knowledge, all along the front. It is a military disaster. I would never permit such foolishness were

I running this war. Go into the trenches, and you will hear the same story everywhere. When half a million men are poured into one small salient, and few come out walking on their own feet, or with feet to walk on, that does not mark a victory.''

"Do you believe that German victory is possible?"

"I know it. But not at Verdun. And not through our stalemate of fixed trench warfare."

"Excellent!" Richter felt his excitement growing. He knew what he was doing, this corporal! "Hold on to that thought of victory. If you work with me, you will be preparing a completely new and crucial German advance—employing a totally different battle strategy! You know the usual technique: a great barrage of artillery, pounding for days before the attack is made and designed to beat down all resistance. It worked a couple of times last year. But now it produces an exactly opposite result. The bombardment *alerts* the enemy— they know the attack is coming, and they make plans accordingly!"

"Exactly what I have been saying here for half a year!" Dolfi slapped his knee. "Why don't the generals at headquarters see what is obvious in the trenches?"

"Perhaps they do. The new plan of attack, *der Grösste Vorrücken,* inverts that old logic. There will be no artillery fire until the very moment of advance. Total secrecy on troop movements. We want the attack to begin when the enemy is sleeping, or in church, or eating Sunday dinner. And the attack will come in a place where no one is expecting it. Surprise will be our greatest weapon."

"Wonderful!" Dolfi had moved from suspicious indifference to total involvement. "Absolutely the right way. Where, and when?"

Richter reached into his pocket and pulled out an oilskin map case. "The primary thrust will be here, through this little town, Saint-Mihiel. We already occupy it. Our forces will drive straight west, to cut through the Voie Sacrée, the French supply line to Verdun. That will assure its fall, but we will not stop there. We will advance west, and farther west—on to Paris. The fall of Paris will end the war."

"Magnificent!" Dolfi raised clenched fists to shoulder level. "When will it begin?"

"You and I will help to decide that. We must discover the details of all French troop movements and give the signal to attack at the moment of maximum vulnerability. You will move to Saint-Mihiel and be my principal interface on the German side of the lines." He saw Dolfi's hand move to pat the dog. "No, I am afraid that Fuchsl cannot go. Secrecy is vital, and he is too recognizable. Your friends here will look after him for a few months."

"But what will I tell them?"

"We will say that you got into trouble and accepted a dangerous dispatch mission on the eastern front rather than facing a court-martial. When it is over, you will come back a hero. For the time being you will be transferred secretly, and you will pretend to be a civilian. You may be required to make occasional trips into French territory. You know the risks if you are captured as well as I do. It is getting more and more difficult for me to travel, so we will need to set up a method of communication that does not call for such trips—maybe by heliograph, or carrier pigeon. We will work out all the details together before I go back. Now—are you willing?"

"I will work night and day." Dolfi looked lunatic with excitement. "I will take whatever risks the Fatherland needs. I am not afraid of danger. But when you say you will go back—back to where? Where will you be stationed?"

"Right here, at this village fifteen kilometers west of Saint-Mihiel." Richter's finger was trembling as he stabbed at the map. "Saint-Amè. A castle there, Chateau Cirelle, will be my temporary center of activities. One day you will see the chateau for yourself. It will be our military headquarters for the whole region, once *der Grösste Vorrücken*—the Grand Advance!—gets under way."

Richter looked at Dolfi's glowing face. The corporal was incredibly serious, wholly dedicated, phenomenally well informed. Just the man for the job! And with such a memory—what else might he know?

Richter hesitated. Should he ask?

He leaned forward. "Tell me, Corporal, as a matter of pure curiosity: Have you ever, in your very extensive reading, come across a reference to something called the *Judas Cross*?"

CHAPTER SEVEN

Chateau Cirelle.

Those two words had been the incantation, the magic phrase needed to carry Jenny through the past few days. She had said them to herself a thousand times, whenever her path to France seemed blocked.

Now, with the chateau itself beckoning from the bank of the Aire River, she paused and rubbed at tired eyes. She pulled on the reins of the light trap, brought the pony to a standstill at the top of the hill, and stared down at the cluster of buildings. All the energy that had brought her this far had vanished. She was exhausted, afraid to go on, afraid to find out about her father.

Chateau Cirelle!

The evening departure from London's Victoria Station had been like a dream. The platform was unlit. The great black bulk of the waiting locomotive crouched low on the track, hissing gently and blowing off white plumes of steam into the darkness. A sulfurous smell of burning coal was heavy in the air, dragon's breath that filled the glass-and-metal dome of the station.

It was not a regular troop service train. The platform was oddly deserted and silent, and the clatter of Jenny's leather boots sounded loud across cold stone and metal. She did not want company. She found an empty compartment and climbed aboard. Five minutes after she closed the heavy door, there was a clatter of couplings and a scarcely noticeable jerk.

They were on their way. The train pulled slowly away from the station, gliding south through the blacked-out streets of the city. The engine whistled once. Then they were picking up speed, faster and faster, rushing toward the chalk-sided railway cuttings of the North Downs and on to the English coast.

Chateau Cirelle, Chateau Cirelle, Chateau Cirelle . . . The steel wheels spoke the words as they ran along the polished rails. Jenny huddled into a corner of the deserted compartment, wrapped in her aunt's warm fox fur. She was tired but too tense to sleep. She had brought with her a flask of hot coffee and a great packet of cheese and bacon sandwiches. Now she took one out of its greaseproof paper wrapping and nibbled a little, but she had no appetite. She closed her eyes. *Chateau Cirelle, Chateau Cirelle, Chateau Cirelle* . . .

To Dover, to the steamer headed for Boulogne. It was a warm and silent night crossing, passengers reluctant to go belowdecks; the Channel was unnaturally calm, with a swath of moonglow on the dark water stretching out to lead them to the French coast. Jenny looked over the bows, staring ahead. Death in France, death in the English Channel. It was hard to look at that placid water and accept that beneath it cruised German submarines, seeking a chance to kill.

They made a quiet dawn docking, the men at the harbor calling to each other in hushed voices and warping the ship to her berth. Fatigue and early sunlight made everything pale and unnaturally clear.

Chateau Cirelle, Chateau Cirelle . . . Another train, this one from Boulogne to the Gare du Nord; a short taxi ride through the noisy morning streets of Paris; then on again, the train lurching through Châlons-sur-Marne and along a maze of changing tracks to Bar-le-Duc.

The first real signs of war.

This was the southern terminus for supply of troops and material to the front at Verdun. The town was filled with men and machinery. To her surprise, Jenny was ignored in the bustle of activity. A man out of uniform would be noticed. A woman could wander through the town as she chose, without being questioned as to future movements or reason for being there.

A man's war, here more than anywhere.

Jenny felt useless, irrelevant. She was supposed to be back in England, knitting scarves and sewing shirts. Her advance order for a carriage had been lost, or the equipment had been requisitioned. It took three hours of confusion and all Jenny's high school French before a pony and trap became available. Not until the middle of the afternoon could she begin the final leg of her journey.

And finally she was there, chilled and drooping with fatigue. The chateau, after her imaginings, was oddly unimpressive. Ellen Blake had checked the lineage of the Marquis de Saint-Amè, and found that it stretched back before the Norman Conquest of England. The family had lived in the Meuse Valley for at least nine hundred years, with the ancestral home always at Saint-Amè. Jenny had expected something tall, ancient, and brooding: great stone battlements, deep moat, and armored drawbridge. What she saw was big enough—it looked like a very large country house. But it was not very tall. And it did not look particularly old. Maybe a hundred years, certainly no more than a century and a half.

From her view on the hill, she could see that the main building was a great rectangle, with four cylindrical, cone-topped towers symmetrically placed at the corners. They were the highest points of the chateau, the tops of their red-brick-tiled roofs stretching up maybe sixty feet above the ground. The main building was made of mottled gray limestone, except for the flat-topped arches and windows that were surrounded by a stone of darker brown. Jenny could count seven chimneys. That was a good sign—maybe the chateau would at least be warm. She longed to sit in front of a good log fire. But heating the place must be a nightmare, with its hundred and fifty feet of windows. The chateau had a steep-sided roof of red brick tiles, and it looked out onto a square courtyard. The central section of the yard was filled with flowering shrubs, surrounded by a wide driveway of light brown gravel.

Jenny had approached from the southwest. The private road to the chateau left the main road just where she had halted. It led down the hill, through a pair of tall wooden gates, along a cypress-lined avenue, past a two-acre pond where she could see white ducks swimming, and finally on to the double doors of the chateau entrance. Jenny could see substantial outbuildings to the left of the main structure. They would surely be stables; and to the north, beyond the house, was a great expanse of level grass. On the lawn's nearer edge grew a border of dense evergreen hedge, while the other side formed a gentle slope down to the river.

Jenny had walked on similar lawns at a dozen English country homes. She could suddenly see this one in her mind's eye, bright with the awnings and pavilions of a summer fete. Did the French nobility follow the same custom? One thing was certain: They did not do so *now*, with the nation in the grip of awful war.

Jenny's thoughts returned to her father. Where would he be staying? If she knew him, he would want to be on the north side—in a room facing the main battle lines less than twenty miles away to the north.

As that thought came to her, Jenny realized that she had been drowsing at the brow of the hill for a long time. Having come this far, she was putting off her final arrival. Afraid of what she might find? She shivered and shook the reins. The light trap left the main road and began the descent to Chateau Cirelle.

As Jenny drove closer to the chateau it steadily became less appealing. From a distance the size and proportions were impressive, but near at hand she could see the crumbling mortar between the stones, the evidence of water damage on the roof, cracks in the grimy small-paned windows. Sad, but probably inevitable. The lack of able-bodied men must be even worse in France than in England, where everyone said home help had become impossible to find. That must account, too, for the deserted look of the place. An estate this size back home in Connecticut would have half a dozen groundsmen and gardeners, working every day around the property. Here Jenny could see no one.

She drove the trap on around the muddy pond, with its glum flock of ducks, on into the empty courtyard. She halted there, swung down to the ground, and stood holding the reins. Should she leave the trap here, or carry on around the side of the house to the stables? It was beginning to spit with rain, and the sky to the east was dark. In Bar-le-Duc they had talked of bad weather. She did not want to leave the trap outside if a storm was on the way. But she didn't want to leave the pony in the stables, either, without a groom present.

Before she could make up her mind she saw a tall figure walking around the west side of the chateau. He was heading away from her toward the stables, and didn't seem to have noticed Jenny or the pony and trap.

"Hey, there. Monsieur! Groom!" She shouted, and waved.

The man turned, stared, and then headed toward her. He was dressed in a dirty, dark green jacket covered with cement dust, crumpled black trousers, and long mud-splashed boots. On his head he wore a filthy beret of dark blue, and he was smoking a black cheroot. It gave off wisps of evil-smelling blue-gray smoke in the damp air. He came up to Jenny and offered her a little bow. "*Oui?*"

"*Le cheval*. My horse." said Jenny. She pointed at the pony. "I don't want to leave it out in the rain. *Je veux mettre mon cheval dans le—le*—oh, Lordie, what on earth's the French word for 'stable'?"

"The French word for 'stable,' mademoiselle, is *écurie*," the man said quietly. He had a wonderful voice—smooth, rich, and deep. "Now, if you will permit me."

Jenny was so surprised that she did not speak when he took the reins from her hands and started to lead the trap away toward the stables. She trailed along after him.

"You speak English!"

He turned and smiled at her. "I try, mademoiselle. These days I am getting a lot of practice."

She took another look at him. He was older than a first glance suggested, a big strongly built man, with a thatch of gray-streaked dark hair pushing out from under the beret. There was a pleased look on his face and a laugh in his blue eyes that made it very clear he knew she had mistaken him for a stable hand. It was a startling moment when those eyes met hers, the feeling of an almost physical impact.

"You're—oh, Lordie, are you—"

"*Vraiment*. I am Louis Villette, at your service." The Marquis turned and bowed again. "I was expecting you, but thought after your letter that you would certainly not be here until tomorrow. However, you are most welcome. I will be delighted if you will join me for dinner tonight." He gave her a broad grin. "Not in these clothes, I should add. You find me in my workman's uniform—we are making changes to parts of the chateau. Workmen are impossible to find."

Jenny looked down at her own travel-soiled coat and dress. "I'd love to have dinner with you, but I've been traveling for twenty-four hours. I'm tired out. And more than anything I would like to see my father at once, and talk with him."

Jenny saw a change in expression. The smile vanished at once. "Mademoiselle Marshall—you said to talk with him? But did you not see the reports? I have sent them from here regularly, for over three weeks now."

"We have seen nothing." Jenny felt her stomach tighten. "What has happened?"

"But they were to be passed on from our liaison, through to your own government offices . . ." Another change in his eyes. The pupils seemed to contract, to draw in to black pinpoints. Louis Villette's face turned red. "I knew it! If we lose this foul war—and we may—it will be our own stupid fault. We do not know each other's languages! We do not bother to learn, and we drown in bureaucracy! I could have given my reports, in English, to the British liaison officer. But that is not the approved diplomatic method! Instead, I must send them in French, to be officially translated and transmitted—by a fool whose knowledge of English would have disgraced a chimney sweep! And God alone knows what is sent on to you."

Jenny was alarmed at the anger in his face. He had changed from a charming aristocrat—one who was not at all ashamed to do manual work—to a man consumed by rage.

She gripped him by the arm, feeling powerful muscles beneath the coarse fabric. "Never mind your reporting system! What about my father?"

"Ah!" He looked stricken. "Of course. A thousand apologies, mademoiselle. I have been thoughtless enough to allow my own frustrations to rule me. Of course, if you have not read the reports you must be terribly worried. We can go at once, and you can see Colonel Marshall. But he will not be able to talk to you."

Jenny put a hand up to her own neck. "His throat is injured?"

"No. His throat is unharmed. But his condition is a mystery. Colonel Marshall was hurt in the explosion of a shell. He was knocked unconscious, but he had no visible injuries when he came here, except for bruises and one small sliver of shrapnel in the back of his head. He awoke, he spoke—and he made no sense at all. What he said did not even sound like English. A bad concussion, the doctors said, which would take a few days to mend. They operated to remove the shrapnel the day after his arrival here. When he awoke again, he seemed better. He said a few rational sentences, then went back to sleep. You were not told of this?''

''Not a word—all we knew was that he was here, and injured.''

''Then you must have been desperate with worry. Not surprisingly, he was unsure what had happened to him or where he was. He tried to send a message to you, but it came out of his mouth as nonsense. One week later he fell asleep and remained unconscious for almost two full days. Since then he has dipped in and out of sleep, with no one able to predict the times when he will be awake. When he speaks, it rarely makes sense. Worst of all are the times when he wakes, rises from his bed, and wanders through the chateau like a sleepwalker. When that happens he hears no one, says nothing, and must be guided back to his room. We fear he may harm himself badly—several times we have found him on the stairs. That is why I prefer the door of his room to remain closed. But there are good signs, too. He eats well when he is awake. The doctors say that he seems to be improving, he is stronger physically, but they do not want him to be moved from here. They offer no prediction as to when he will show a real change in condition.''

''Is he conscious now?''

The Marquis shook his head. ''Not unless there has been a change since noon. But come, let us go and see.''

He hitched the rein to a beam inside the stables and led the way back across the southern side of the chateau. They went in through a door at the foot of the southeast tower.

''The upper part of this tower is normally reserved for guests,'' he said in answer to Jenny's question. ''But recently we have been using the ground floor, too—the stairs are steep, and some of the wounded soldiers could not easily be carried up and down. When the first attack on Verdun took place we had nearly twenty men here. Now there is only your father. The chateau lacks facilities for treating people with bad wounds.''

They had entered a short corridor. On their right, east-facing windows showed the darkening sky. The Marquis went across to the wall and swung a short bar into position. Electric bulbs in brackets along the wall came gradually to life, strengthening from a dim flicker to a steady white glow.

''I tried arc lights,'' said Louis Villette. ''They are brighter, but high-vacuum bulbs are more reliable. When my construction work is finished there will be separate electrical controls in each room—I fear that will have to wait until the war is over. Softly, now. Your father is in here.''

He pushed open a white-painted door and walked through into the room. Following him, Jenny noticed how quietly he moved for a big man—even on bare boards, his heavy boots made almost no sound.

The room they entered was large and airy, with twelve-foot ceilings and casement windows left slightly ajar. A coal fire, banked low, removed any chill from the air. William Marshall lay flat on his back on a narrow bed with iron supporting rails at both sides to prevent the patient from falling out. Jenny tiptoed to her father's side and looked down. He was terribly thin and bony. The sheets drawn up to his chest were spotlessly clean and neatly folded back, but where they ended she could see the deep hollows of his collarbone. His clean-shaven face was pale, and his eyes were open enough to show a slit of iris.

''Daddy?'' She spoke softly. ''Dad, can you hear me?''

There was a slight movement of the head on the pillow, and a faint throat-clearing cough.

''Speak to him again!'' The Marquis was leaning over the bed. ''You are the first person in weeks to get such a direct reaction.''

''Dad!'' She lifted her father's left hand and squeezed it in both of hers. ''It's me, Jenny. You'll be all right now, Daddy. I'm here to look after you.''

William Marshall lifted his head, and his eyes slowly opened. Jenny felt the fingers she was holding close on her own. They tightened for a few moments, cold and quivering. Then he grunted again, his grip slowly relaxed, and the eyes closed all the way.

"He knows me! He recognized me. I felt him squeeze my hand." She caressed her father's cheek, her own hand trembling.

"I saw it." The Marquis reached out and gently pushed back William Marshall's right eyelid. Only the white of the eye was showing. "He knew you, I am sure of it. But now he is asleep again."

Jenny was looking around the room. It was easily big enough for a second bed to be moved in.

"I'll stay right here with him—I can have my meals here and sleep here. Then I'll be with him the moment he wakes again."

"No." The Marquis was shaking his head. "Mademoiselle Marshall—Jenny. Your father is here as my guest. It is my duty to comply with what I believe would be his wishes, were he able to voice them. He would insist that you have a room of your own, that you have some leisure time, that you not try to act as his nurse twenty-four hours a day. Please believe me when I tell you that Colonel Marshall will be well cared for."

"Oh, I do. Please don't think that I was criticizing you. You have looked after him wonderfully."

"We have done our best. Above all else he needs rest. There will be plenty of time for you to talk to your father, but you must not overtire yourself now. Can you not feel how tired you are? Do you think it would help your father if you yourself became ill?"

The Marquis had moved to stand by Jenny's side and was looking down at her. The steady blue eyes were filled with concern, and now he took both of her hands in his. She noticed that he had massive, thick-fingered hands, hard-muscled and with prominent tendons and veins. More like a blacksmith's than an idle aristocrat's! He held her tightly, hard enough to restrain her.

"You must have dinner with us, Jenny," he went on in that deep, soothing voice. "A change of clothing, a hot meal, a glass of wine, a little time for relaxation. It will make all the difference. You need it, and I will not take no for an answer. And then you should go to bed in a quiet room and have a full night's sleep. Then you will feel fit to help your father tomorrow. Come, now—he will not be neglected, any more than he was neglected before your arrival.''

Jenny leaned over, kissed her father gently on the forehead, and allowed Louis Villette to lead her out of the room. Why was the Marquis so difficult to argue with? It was not his great size, or his physical presence, or even her reluctance to offend someone who had been so kind to Father. It had to be the intensity of his manner, and that amazing voice. When he told her she was tired, she at once felt it—a physical languor that swept right through her. Louis Villette was so *persuasive*. He could have made a name for himself as an orator in any governing body on earth. After he had suggested the idea of rest, she *longed* for a hot meal and a soft bed.

Louis Villette led Jenny in silence up a flight of stairs, along another corridor, down more stairs, and finally into the curving first floor of the northeast tower. He threw open a door to reveal a curious semicircular room about twenty-five feet across.

"There. This will be your home while you are here. It was made ready for you yesterday, as soon as your trunk reached the chateau." He smiled. "At the risk of sounding rude, Jenny, let me say that I hope your stay here with us will be brief. I will go now, so that you can relax for a while. Dinner will be served in thirty minutes—informal tonight, since you will be the only guest."

"Thank you." Jenny was standing in the middle of the room, looking around her, before she realized that she had no idea of the layout of the chateau. She went back to the door and called along the corridor. "Dinner . . . where?"

The Marquis was already halfway up the first flight of stairs. "Don't worry," he said, without turning back. "Cecile will show you the way."

Cecile? Jenny was left alone to unpack her brass-bound trunk and ponder Louis Villette's words. *Someone* was taking good care of William Marshall, and she had seen signs in her father's bedroom of a feminine hand. Whoever Cecile was, Jenny owed her a big favor.

She hadn't planned on dinners at Chateau Cirelle, even informal ones. Most of the clothes she had brought were workaday blouses and skirts, easily washed and ironed. To-morrow she would locate a flat iron, but for tonight—what? After rummaging down at the bottom of the trunk she pulled out a blue woolen dress, embroidered at the neck with little bluebirds, and tight at breast and hip. It would shake out well and not show many creases. And for shoes?

She was still trying to make up her mind when there was a soft tap on the door. As she looked up, a dark-haired woman of about her own age stuck her head into the room.

"Jenny Marshall? Hello. I am Cecile. Welcome to Chateau Cirelle."

She had an unruly mass of black hair, wide eyes, an alert, laughing face, and a superb rosy brown complexion. As Jenny straightened up from trying on her shoes, Cecile came light-footed into the room and went at once across to Jenny's trunk.

"I've been *longing* to look into this since the moment it arrived," she said. "Mmm. Lovely clothes—but not English ones?"

She spoke English with a strange accent. It was certainly not French, unless perhaps it was from one of the French colonies. Martinique, maybe, or somewhere else in the West Indies?

Jenny gave her a closer look. Cecile was hard to place. Her clothes were clearly French, and of excellent quality. She was wearing a daring off-the-shoulder dress of dark brown. On most women the color would have looked drab, but with her tan skin it looked superb. Jenny noted, not altogether with pleasure, that Cecile had one of those lush, swaying figures that men seemed to rave about. She could be an octoroon from New Orleans, but somehow that didn't fit, either. What would such a woman be doing in northeast France?

Jenny gave up. "Not English clothes," she said. "Ameri-can, most of them."

"Ahh. Very nice." Wherever Cecile was from, she was not bashful. She had taken Jenny's tea-rose blouse and was holding it up against her own figure. She looked down, cock-ing her head to one side. "And it shows the breasts well. I thought English women were too dowdy to wear anything like this. I like it. It's a real man-catcher—and just my size, too."

She was as direct and open in her pleasure as a small

child. Now she pirouetted, holding the blouse against her and revealing long, slim legs as her skirt flared away from her body. "We must certainly compare clothes—you didn't bring enough with you, but I'm sure you could wear some of mine. We'll have to do it later—Father will already be waiting for us."

She stopped in midturn and caught Jenny's blank look. "He *hates* it when I'm late for dinner—and I usually am. I don't have much sense of time. We'd better go now."

She put the blouse on the bed, took Jenny possessively by the hand, and started for the door.

"Hold on, now," said Jenny as they were leaving the room. "Tell me who's who before we get there. You're Cecile, but who's your father? Are you a guest at the chateau, too?"

Cecile gave a burst of laughter. "He didn't tell you? I'm Cecile Villette—and I'm not a guest. The Marquis is my father. Come on, now—or we'll both be in trouble."

As Jenny followed her down the stairs and along a narrow corridor, she heard a powerful grumble of thunder from the open window. The whole building shook a little. She paused for a moment and looked out at the night sky. "I'm glad I got here when I did. Just listen to it! I wouldn't like to be traveling through that thunderstorm."

"You mean the noise?" Cecile gave a nonchalant shrug. "It's not thunder, Mam'selle Jenny—it's artillery. More action at the front." She laughed. "Don't worry, though, you'll soon get used to it. And then after a while you won't even think about it—until they bring in the wounded for us to look after."

CHAPTER EIGHT

"Monge!" The Marquis tapped his wineglass with a bread knife to show his irritation. "This lady should not be kept waiting. She has had a long and difficult journey, and now . . ."

Something something something. Louis Villette's French became impossible to understand as he spoke faster and faster. With weariness cramming cotton into her head, Jenny found it harder and harder to follow the language.

Monge, the butler, hopped into a speedy and red-faced reply. It was incomprehensible. Something about a servant, something about cooking. Jenny turned to Cecile for help.

"Marie." Cecile gave a shrug. "One of the servants. My father assigned her to special duties in the chateau. Monge relied on her to help here at meals, so everything is a little messed up tonight. Monge is madder than a buzz-fly because he wasn't consulted, and father is angry at the slow service."

"You don't seem too sympathetic with Monge."

"I am not sympathetic at all. Monge should have fired Marie long ago. She had too much of an eye for the guests. We all saw the way she looked at the men. And she was not too clever—just the sort who gets into trouble. Monge told me a week ago that Marie had become very impertinent. She told him she did not have to stay here, she had other options. One of the cook's helpers told me that Marie was pregnant. She is a real fly-by-night type, and I feel sure that some visitor had been making promises—a nice cheap way to get her hot and bare and between the bedsheets."

Jenny had been astonished at the way that Cecile had spoken, not bothering to drop her voice to a whisper. Even though the servants at the chateau did not know English, Jenny's own father would have skinned her alive if she had ever mentioned sex at the dinner table! And as for talking about somebody being hot and bare . . . there would have been murder on the spot.

Louis Villette took no notice at all. Once the food was safely on the table he became preoccupied, eating little but replenishing everyone's glass frequently. As soon as the soufflé had been served and eaten, he excused himself and left the two women sitting at the long table.

Jenny permitted herself a huge yawn. In spite of Louis Villette's complaints about service, the dinner at Chateau Cirelle had been a real feast. Chicken in a white cream sauce, fresh spring vegetables, a Grand Marnier soufflé—and Louis Villette, filling her glass long before it became empty.

"Come on," said Cecile. She had seen Jenny's mouth open wide. "Father won't be back—he's always up till all hours. It's nice to have someone else to talk to."

She led the way out of the great dining room and back toward the northeast tower. Jenny followed, trying to learn something of the chateau's layout with a brain that felt as though it wanted to float away out of her head. What she needed here was a *map*. Did people in the old days have such things, or did they take weeks and weeks learning their way around each other's houses?

She stared as they walked through a gallery of dark paintings, a frowning dozen of men in red and purple jerkins. The ancestors of the Marquis? Must be—but not a promising-looking bunch. Louis Villette easily won the contest for best-looking and most attractive.

Jenny stared again at the pictures. Surely she would have remembered them. Cecile was not retracing their path to the dining room, she felt sure of it.

She was about to ask a question when Cecile stopped at one door and threw it open.

"My room," she said. "The same as yours. Come on in for just a second, then you're probably ready for bed."

Jenny found herself in a room that at first sight bore no resemblance at all to the one that she was staying in. After a few seconds she realized that the furnishings made all the difference. She looked around her in amazement.

The whole central area of Cecile's bedroom was taken up by an enormous bed, at least seven feet long and seven feet wide, and covered with pillows and bolsters. It was the only thing close to conventional in the whole room. The wall opposite the window was covered with wooden masks, some of them painted with strong blacks and reds, others of unfinished wood. Most of them had handles at the bottom, so they could be held in position by the wearer. Another wall bore a crossed pair of feathered spears, with a single elephant tusk hanging above them. Next to the window was a poster-sized sepia photograph of a grave-faced black woman, full-breasted and square-shouldered, wearing a gold chain and a loose-limbed rag doll around her neck. The window itself was screened by an amateurish-looking venetian blind, constructed from light wooden poles and split palm leaves.

As Cecile flung herself flat on her bed and rolled over onto her back, Jenny went across to the low ebony dressing table. The seven-foot-long top of it was completely covered with arrays of glass and pottery jars, and the surface itself was so low that anyone wishing to use the dressing mirror would have to be sitting on the floor to do it.

Cecile sat up and gestured to Jenny to sit on the bed next to her.

Jenny picked up a jar of black cream, removed the top, and sniffed it. Ammonia, or something close to it. "What are all these?"

"Ointments. Medicines. Beauty mixtures." Cecile lay back, her hair like a black cloud on the white pillows. "If you need anything, ask me. This country thinks it is so advanced, so civilized—but in some ways it is very backward. No love potions, no safe drugs to make a woman miscarry, nothing to give added size or potency to a man. And so—everybody *worries* when they make love, instead of enjoying it. In *my* country, now . . ."

She turned her head suddenly toward Jenny and looked at her with wide, dark eyes. "How about you? Do you have a lover?"

People just didn't ask questions like that! But it was hard

to resent Cecile's simplicity. Jenny reached into the little black purse she was carrying and took out a picture.

"My fiancé. Clive Dunnay."

Cecile took the photograph and held it above her at arm's length, her head still flat on the pillow. She gave a little gasp. "But he is beautiful! Absolutely beautiful. Such expressive eyes, and such a sad mouth. When do you plan to be married?"

"We're not sure. With the war, it's hard to make any real plans. . . . Clive was sent over to France a few months ago. I have not seen him since. My father arranged for him to be moved to a station near here, as a French-English liaison officer—Clive speaks really good French—but I have no idea where he is! The War Office keeps information so secret."

"But you must find him and visit him! He will be feeling very frustrated. And you, too—if you are like me, you need much lovemaking." Cecile was still staring raptly at the picture she was holding. "Such a fine, slim body. Is he a really good lover?"

"Wonderful." Jenny had answered at once. But even as she spoke she asked herself the same question. Was he?

When she finally left Cecile's room, to collapse exhausted and not quite sober into her own bed, Jenny found the question coming back to her as she drifted toward sleep.

Was Clive a good lover? She had not wanted to tell Cecile the odd truth: Jenny did not know. Clive and Jenny had made love exactly once.

It had happened at her initiative, and she knew to the minute when the decision had been made. It was on a winter's night at the Wilkinsons' country estate, in such an unseasonably warm spell that the veranda doors were wide open to let in the breeze, and the band was playing a polka, lilting and gay. But this was not a gay time, and the dancers on the floor did not have the spring to their step and the carefree laughter that Jenny remembered from prewar parties.

Clive was holding her close, closer than convention permitted. They both knew tonight was special. He would not be leaving the country for another forty-eight hours, but tomorrow morning he would join his regiment. This would be their last night as guests at the Wilkinson estate, perhaps their last visit until the war was over. Perhaps (Jenny could not help thinking it) their last ever.

Most of the eligible men were already gone, doing their bit in France and Belgium. Margaret Peters, the Wilkinsons' married daughter and a star of the social scene before the war, had had to struggle valiantly to round up any men she could find—on leave, wounded, or on special home duties. Perhaps she was trying to remind them all of the world that they were fighting for. The Wilkinsons had given winter dances for thirty years. It was part of the solid world of traditional values, of gaiety and social manners, of music and progress. And once this business in France is over, the dance said, why, it will all go on again.

One o'clock. The band played the final bars of the polka and eased without a break into the strains of the last waltz: slow, sentimental, cheek to cheek. The talking stopped, and the lights were turned low.

Jenny had been full of a quivering nervousness for the past hour, thinking of saying it to Clive, then backing away. Finally she summoned up her courage.

"Clive." She leaned close and whispered in his ear. She could feel herself shivering. Was she really doing this? "Clive, come and see me. Afterward."

She felt the sudden tension in his arms, and waited breathlessly for his response. Was he horrified at what she had said? His face was buried in her hair.

"Jenny?" His voice was low. He was not sure he had understood her correctly.

"Yes. After the dance." Her voice was trembling.

He did not speak, but his lips touched her ear, and his arms tightened around her. She could feel her own heartbeat, racing twice as fast as usual. Did he think less of her now, for taking the lead like this? It was one thing to be a modern woman in theory, and another to practice what she preached. But Clive was as excited as she was, she could tell. The knowledge of things to come charged their body contact on the dance floor with new excitement. At the last bars of the waltz Clive held their embrace and guided her away into the warm darkness.

There had been little sexual desire on Jenny's part when she offered the invitation. Mostly she had wanted Clive to go off to France with the knowledge that she was his girl and waiting for him in England. The lovemaking had certainly been exciting, but it was too new and strange to be really enjoyable.

Even so, she was sure now that she had made the right decision.

Jenny snuggled down into her pillow in the chilly bedroom of Chateau Cirelle, dreaming of Clive and a happy future. Marriage seemed far off, infinitely unlikely. And Clive seemed a world away, even though he might be no more than twenty miles from this chateau.

She fell asleep to the distant growl of artillery. It continued right through the night, but for Jenny, sleepless for forty hours and then well fed on half a chicken, a soufflé, and three glasses of wine, the sound was no problem.

Near dawn, when songbirds added themselves to the guns, her dreams began. She knew she was in France, but the Chateau Cirelle was a different building—it had become the thousand-year-old fortress of her first imaginings, standing high on top of a rugged black mountain. The stone walls gleamed with a cold, obsidian sheen, the turrets reached almost to the lowering storm clouds, and the black water in the moat seethed and bubbled.

While Jenny watched from the courtyard below, the Marquis de Saint-Amè stood on the pinnacle of the tallest tower. Arms raised to the heavens, he called down the lightning. The thunderbolts came searing in, down to and through the body of Louis Villette. He stood there, trunk and upstretched arms outlined by a continuous violet nimbus of electricity. His hair was on fire, his black cloak smoking. The thunder was raging around him.

He turned to face Jenny and gave a great shout of triumph: "I have done it. The war is over! By my actions I have ended the war. Now there will be electricity in every room!"

As he spoke, every window in the chateau lit with a blue-white electrical glow. Then the whole building began to shine, bright as the sun, and steam came from the black moat. The light was so unbearably intense that Jenny reached up to cover her eyes.

As she slowly opened them, she realized that the intense light was the morning sun, striking in through the eastern window and shining on her bed. She heard the door of the room close, and lifted her head. Someone had been in, quietly opened the thick curtains, and just as quietly left. The only other evidence of their presence was a steaming jug of hot chocolate and a croissant on the bedside table.

Jenny poured a cup and sipped it—it was scalding, too hot to drink quickly. She looked around the room, then down at herself. She had been really tired. She had fallen into bed in her slip, hair unbrushed and face unwashed.

Who had brought the chocolate and croissant? She took a bite, a delicious but almost guilty bite, and listened to the distant thunder of the guns. She was living in luxury here, first-class service and food and drink. While Clive . . . Jenny wondered where he was now, and what he was doing.

CHAPTER NINE

Once heard, never forgotten: the scream of a 420-millimeter mortar shell. . . .

Clive had heard the sound before, but each time it was a fresh nightmare. A shrill, distant whistle, the sound of a far-off train; then a wail that grew and grew until it filled all creation.

"Get down!" he shouted to the Frenchmen at his side.

He had shouted in English, but the language was unimportant. The stretcher bearers had already dropped the prisoner and were falling to hug the muddy sides of the trench. Clive dived for the muddy, gluey floor.

The shell took an unbearably long time to hit. Clive imagined its metallic course as it sailed over the pitted ground, over Fort Vaux, over the Ravines de la Morte.

The shell struck. The ground shook under the stamp of a god. Clive, his face jammed down into the foul-smelling pool that formed the trench floor, felt clumps of soil raining down on his back.

When it finally ended he stood up, brushing himself off and looking around. The shell-shocked German prisoner with his gunpowder burns and singed hair lay facedown where he had been dropped. He had covered his head with his hands, and his whole body was quivering. But he had not been hurt. The worst that had happened to any of them was a pelting with lumps of turf and soil.

In the distance another shell exploded. Clive saw a puff of smoke veined with fire, then the ground in that direction heaved up in a great swell and spout of earth. Beneath their feet, the surface throbbed.

"We must hurry," said Clive. His words sounded asinine, and he had to fight to keep the fear out of his voice. "Another bombardment is starting."

The two stretcher bearers were standing together, their eyes frightened and rebellious. "We have to take cover," said the shorter man, a nervous private with fingernails bitten to the quick.

"There's no cover here." Clive made his voice as calm as possible. "We must go on. This is an important prisoner. Pick up the stretcher."

The two bearers remained in place, undecided. There was another screaming whistle of a shell, and another, more distant, explosion. Clive braced himself and grabbed the arm of the taller stretcher bearer. "Move, damn it—how long do you want us to stand here?"

For a moment Clive thought he had a mutiny on his hands. The Frenchmen were staring at him, eyes filled with hatred. Every scrap of common sense told them to leave their gibbering prisoner behind and run for safety. Clive tried to change his own fear into anger. He stepped closer and stared them down. "Pick up that stretcher. Do it now, or by God I'll shoot you myself."

After a moment the men nodded and bent to the stretcher. Clive could almost smell the fear coming off his companions. He felt he could see it, sense it in the air along with the waves of smoke and the far-off fires. Adrenaline and secret terror had kicked him into a state of heightened mental alertness and clarity of perception. Every blade of grass and every twig had detail and meaning.

"Hurry," he said again, and took one corner of the stretcher. The German was piled onto it anyhow, hands over head, oblivious of everything. "We'll make better speed if we all take part of the load." *And we'll all shiver less with something useful to do.*

They started out along the trench. The shells were falling more often now, sometimes three or four landing so close together that the sound of their explosions was one continuous roar.

Clive could imagine nothing worse in the whole of creation. The air was full of acrid smoke. His lungs burned, and the men coughed continuously. The muscles of his arms and legs screamed for a rest. Gobbets of mud and dirt sprayed down on them, adding to the dust and grit that filled their eyes. The landscape all around them was writhing, a chiaroscuro of fire and blood, of mud and smoke. The men were trapped in the middle of a gigantic bass drum, and the Devil himself was pounding, pounding, pounding out his diabolical rhythms. Whole stretches of raw, pocked landscape were scorched new-black.

And now came more smoke, a dense pocket of it ahead. Clive prayed that it was only smoke, not a dreaded gas attack. That would probably mean death for all of them, masks or not.

On the stretcher, the German suddenly sat up and began to scream in a terrible, high-pitched voice. He pushed at one of the bearers and tried to jump into the trench bottom. Clive dropped his corner of the stretcher and grabbed for the German's arm.

He did not even hear the whistle of the next shell. At one moment he was cursing and shouting, trying to wrestle the prisoner back onto the stretcher. The next, something had hit him squarely in the back, a titan's fist that flattened his body to the thickness of a sheet of paper. A great wind took hold of the paper body and lifted it, turning it end over end, whisking it off through a spattering rainfall of dazzling white-hot lava.

And then even the paper had gone. The lava vanished with it, and Clive was sucked into a vacuum of unconsciousness.

She was leaning over him, gazing down at his face.

Jenny. Absolutely the last person that he expected to see. What was she doing in France?

He tried to sit up, to speak. He had no idea where he was, but there was a weight across his whole body, pinning him down. He could do no more than stir feebly and say in a subhuman croak, ''Jenny?''

"Sshhh." She put her finger to her lips. She looked different. She had put on weight since he had last seen her. There was more fullness to her hips, and her breasts thrust hard against the lace of the white dress.

"I've missed you, Clive. So much." Again she put her finger to her lips, as she began to unfasten the buttons at the high neck of her white satin dress. Her eyes were locked on his, a little inviting smile creasing their corners. Bending over him, easing the dress off her shoulders to reveal creamy breasts and full nipples . . . she was gigantic, a dark shape slowly descending toward him.

"It's all right. We have to do it while we have the chance." Her voice was a whisper in his ear, mingling with the strange perpetual buzzing that started there and vibrated through his whole head. "I know you're tired, Clive. You just close your eyes and relax."

She straightened and wriggled her body. Her dress shimmied lower, over a gently rounded belly and across shapely hips. She kissed his weary eyelids to close them, and ran her tongue across the delicate line of eyelashes. The scent of her was in his nostrils—her perfume and body musk. He felt warm fingers on his chest, walking gently down his ribs and across his belly. She found him, teased him, manipulated him to a tense hardness. At last she moved onto him, drawing him in, gripping him inside her to create a pleasure so intense that it was almost pain.

As she moved more vigorously it *became* pain. Pure pain, intolerable pressure.

Clive gasped and opened his eyes. She was not Jenny. He was looking at a total stranger. Her face was inches away, her eyes staring straight down into his. While he watched, their gray warmth steadily drained *upward*, into bottomless pools of darkness. The blond tresses falling loose toward him paled, thinned, and dissolved to air. Beneath them the flesh of the face was dripping like candle wax onto his. Through the transparent skin he could see the outline of the skull itself, with its empty eye sockets and the rictus of fixed, fleshless grin. The tongueless mouth gaped open, dipping down to kiss him.

He tried to pull away, and could not do it. She was still moving on him, gripping him tighter and tighter with a bony, hard-edged sex. Her organ was engulfing him, swallowing penis and testicles into its fierce suction. Her whole body had become a dirty gray skeleton, the hands on his chest like icy claws. As she reared above him there was a shrill of laughter. He felt wrenching agony in his genitals.

Clive lifted his head to look along his body. At the juncture of his legs his groin showed a bleeding cavity. Her bone-edged maw had cropped him, clipped away all signs of manhood.

He screamed, and she screamed with him. Her voice went on and on, a wordless howl. He felt damp mud on face and hands, heard again the boom of guns . . .

. . . and sank shuddering into darkness.

Flashes of light striking on his closed eyes. Black trailing strands across them, drifting waterweed in a red-black sea. A throbbing pain from the pit of his belly, squeezing, squeezing. He could not scream. His eyes would not open.

Other sensations creeping in. Warmth on his face, wet, lumpy surface under his back. Terrible, terrible pain in his left leg and his genitals. . . .

And then, like a heart that had hesitated and was now beginning to beat again, the steady, remorseless roar of distant guns.

Clive lay face upward. Small fragments of earth fell like rain on his exposed face. The whole sky was lit like a subterranean forge where the anvil was still being pounded, far and near. In his left ear a constant steady shrill sounded, sending its tone through his whole head.

He turned to look around him. He was staring, eye to eye and only two feet away, at one of the stretcher bearers. The man's mouth was wide open in a soundless scream. The neck ended in bright white bone, cartilage, snapped veins and arteries. Clive had the sudden impossible fear that he was in the same condition, that they were just a pair of heads who would stare at each other for eternity.

He gulped in great ragged breaths of air and felt down with both hands, gently exploring his lower body. There was no gaping wound, no spilling of entrails onto muddy ground. He struggled to sit up, and agony in his left leg blotted out everything else.

He reached down and tenderly began to explore his body. Torso intact, though his khaki uniform was in tatters. Arms bruised, but no bones broken. His testicles ached terribly; he did not unbutton his clothes, but from the outside he could feel no wound nor see a sign of blood. Right leg in working order. Left leg—

He shivered. It was still there, but the flesh was ripped and blackened. Blood oozed steadily from his midcalf. He could see the white of exposed bone. He had a compound fracture of the tibia or fibula—and it made little difference which one it was; there was no way he could walk on that leg.

He inched himself upward, until he could rest his back on the trench wall.

By some miracle he had lived through both explosions. Had anyone else?

He moved at a slow, feeble crawl, dragging his left leg painfully behind him. The only intact body wore the blackened remnants of a German uniform. It was the prisoner. He lay facedown, and Clive had to use every ounce of strength to turn him over. The face's jaw was black no longer. It was white as the belly of a fish, and it dripped brown liquid. The German had been destined to die by water, not fire. He had survived the explosions, to drown in an inch of stinking ooze at the bottom of the trench.

Clive swallowed bile and looked away. He lay on the muddy floor of the trench and tears filled his eyes. It was more than pain, it was rage at his own helplessness. This was no clean and tidy battle, with intervals for the opposing sides to collect their dead and wounded. He had heard of cases where injured men caught on the barbed wire had screamed in agony for days, their comrades unable to rescue them because of the constant shelling. They hung or lay until they died of shock, loss of blood, thirst, or exposure. A rescue party in this area was too much to hope for. It could be days before anyone came by. . . .

No one else would save him. If he gave up, he was dead. He forced himself up on his straightened arms.

Damn it, you're not badly injured enough to lie down and die, he told himself. Move! Now, before you lose more blood.

He eased his way to the side of the trench. It had been almost demolished by the rain of shells. Instead of a protecting wall, it was a shallow broken-sided ditch, in places no more than knee-high.

The shells were still falling. It was uncannily like a thunderstorm, the lowering sky, the heat lightning of distant explosions, the thunder and lightning flash of near misses. The nearby open areas were riddled with shell holes, impossible for someone in his condition to negotiate. His only hope lay in following the broken line of the trench itself, hoping that it would not become impassable.

After seconds of closed eyes and steady, careful breathing, he eased off his jacket. It was terribly hot, and the air was thick and choking. He managed to tear off a piece of his jacket sleeve and wrapped it gently around his left calf. It would give no support to the limb, but at least it would slow further bleeding.

He took a final careful look in all directions.

That way. . . .

He made one brief attempt to stand up. No good—and agony. He began to crawl on his hands and his right knee. His left leg trailed along behind, seeming to hit every tiny bump in the ground. After a few minutes he stopped, exhausted. It took a mighty effort to force himself back into motion.

He crawled and crawled, resting when he could go no farther. He was wracked with pain, and then, even worse, with terrible thirst. He lay flat and lapped at stagnant water in the bottom of the trench. It tasted vile, and he forced himself to do no more than wet his mouth and lips. Back up, and crawl a bit more; then a bit more, a little bit more.

At one point he found himself lying faceup, staring at the sky. He had no idea how he had come to that position, or how long he had lain there. It would be fatal to fall into unconsciousness again. He might never wake up.

He would die in his sleep. Or a shell would find him. That was it, a shell would seek him out.

The shells are after me. They sniff all around here like bloodhounds. I know what they want; they're after my guts. They know I'm scared, they can smell me, smell my fresh blood. I have to keep moving, so they don't know quite where I am.

But why bother? Why not just lie down and rest? Is there

anything worth struggling for? Jenny. Jenny, my love, come and save me. (No, no, no! Don't be crazy. Jenny can't save you here. Move! You have to save yourself. *Move!*)

The world was growing darker. Nightfall. The guns were firing less often. He needed them, needed the lightning flash that lit the way ahead. He waited for the white light of the explosions, using it to set his next goal for crawling. If he could reach the next lightning-lit point, that was all he asked.

And finally there was something ahead. The Holy Grail of a bunker, with a lantern showing faint on the lip. When he was twenty yards away there was the rattle of a rifle sighted from the top of the bunker.

"Identify yourself!" said a nervous French voice.

Clive was so far gone, he almost replied in English. He realized at the last moment that the sound of a foreign voice was guaranteed to make the French sentry shoot.

He tried to stand up, failed, and crouched there on one knee and clenched fists. With his last strength he lifted his head. "*Je suis Capitaine Clive Dunnay.*" His swollen tongue made the words garbled and clumsy. "I am a British officer. I am wounded."

A fearful and suspicious face came into view, sighting along the barrel of a rifle.

"Hold up your hands," said the wavering voice. "At once—or I will shoot!"

Clive did not obey the order. He could not. He had pitched forward onto his face and was lying unconscious in the mud.

CHAPTER TEN

Once Jenny was fully awake, her first thought was of her father. She threw on a white blouse and light gray woolen skirt and hurried to William Marshall's room. As she went she noticed how cold it was. The sun was striking in through the windows of the east-facing wing, but it did little to take the morning chill off the long corridor.

Her first worry, that his room might be too cold, was eased as soon as she slipped back the bolt and opened the door. Someone had been there long before her. The window was closed, the ashes of yesterday's fire had been cleaned away, and a new fire was well lit in the grate. Jenny felt a new worry as she went to her father's side. If he went walking in his sleep, could he somehow burn himself in the fireplace? She detoured to look at the grate. It was all right. The metal grill around the fireplace was substantial. It would take someone aware of what he was doing to move it aside.

She went to her father's side and looked down at him. Her first reaction was one of disappointment. He was lying there peaceful but quite unconscious. Illogical as it was, Jenny had hoped that her arrival and the sound of her voice the previous evening would be the catalyst to bring him back to consciousness and full recovery.

She sat on the chair next to the bedside. She was being naive; Sleeping Beauty was for fairy stories. If he was going to get better, it would happen because he had first-rate medical care.

For nearly an hour, Jenny sat quietly watching and listening. There was no change in William Marshall's condition. At last Jenny sighed, stood up, touched her father gently on the forehead, and left the room. It was one thing in England to talk of coming over here to take care of him, and another to do it. Now she was here, she wasn't sure what she could do for him. Maybe she could feed him. He still swallowed normally, according to the Marquis, but with periods of consciousness so unpredictable it was possible that he was not getting enough food. He certainly was frighteningly thin.

At the thought of food, Jenny suddenly felt ravenous. There must be breakfast somewhere—but how would she ever find it?

Jenny returned to her room and set out to retrace Cecile's path to the dining room last night. On the way she made her first inspection of the interior of the castle. Many of the doors were wide open and she could take a look inside them.

Some old architect had been an early fan of light and fresh air. Jenny passed at least a dozen bedrooms, and every one had the same high ceilings, broad windows, and breezy feeling. In late spring or summer it must be wonderful—a perfect environment for injured men convalescing from their wounds. If the architect had set out to design a hospital, thought Jenny, he couldn't have done better than the east wing of the chateau. Of the hospitals she had seen in America and England, none had such an open, sunlit feeling. So why was her father the only patient? Maybe because the feeling was completely different in winter. Summer breezes would become winter gales. Jenny shivered at the thought, and went on along a corridor that led west, into the heart of the chateau.

The right direction—she recognized a marble table, with a great mirror above it, near the end of the corridor. But she hadn't noticed earlier that little door set in the wall on the other side, only five feet high and less than two feet across. Though it had a great bolt, the door now stood ajar. Jenny paused, pulled it open a fraction farther, and looked inside. A narrow staircase of dark stone dipped away into darkness. Fifteen steps below her it took a curve. There must be some source of lighting at the bottom. A reflection gleamed off the wall.

It looked ancient. This must be the original lower part of the chateau, the level that Cecile had said still existed as cellars and storage vaults beneath the eighteenth century superstructure.

Fascinating! Aunt Ellen would love this place. What was it like down there, in chambers eight hundred years old? Jenny hesitated, but she caught a whiff of coffee from somewhere ahead. Hunger before curiosity. She closed the little door and went on down the corridor.

One wrong turn, which took her south toward a big library and double doors that marked the main entrance of the chateau; then Jenny retraced her steps and was soon at the great dining room, deserted except for the green-coated figure of Monge. He stood at a long sideboard, peering at cutlery and silverware to make sure that they had been properly cleaned.

In answer to Jenny's carefully phrased inquiry about *petit déjeuner* he shook his head and pointed to another door at the end of the room.

"*Pas ici.* In the small lounge, madame," he said. "Since the war began, the Marquis insists that we serve only a simple breakfast."

He spoke slowly, and Jenny was delighted to find that she understood him perfectly.

"Are the others there?" She wanted to practice her French conversation.

It was a mistake. Monge shook his head and released a loud gabble of response so fast and furious that she didn't catch a word. Jenny nodded, smiled placatingly, and went on through the door he had indicated.

The "small" lounge turned out to be a room maybe twenty-five feet long. It was poorly lit by a single tall window on the south side. Although there were electric lights along two of the other walls, they had not been turned on. The Marquis sat alone at a mahogany table facing away from the window. He was drinking black coffee and poring over a big cloth-bound volume with a leather spine. At Jenny's entrance he stood up and bowed. He looked terrible: pale and exhausted, with lines of fatigue around his eyes and mouth.

"Good morning, Mam'selle Jenny." He gestured to her, indicating that she should sit down opposite him. "I thought it must be Cecile—at last. And you—did you sleep well?"

"Wonderfully." Jenny helped herself to coffee, hot bread, and cream cheese. "And you?"

"I could not sleep at all. There was bad news yesterday from Verdun. Another German attack."

"I heard artillery this morning."

"Yes—finally our artillery! I am confident that the attack has been repulsed."

A strange look of satisfaction had crossed the Marquis' tired face. He closed the cloth-bound book and pushed it to one side. Jenny stared at it curiously. She could see the Saint-Amè coat of arms embossed on the cover, and the name written beneath it, *Louis Villette, Marquis de Saint-Amè*.

"Not me," said the Marquis. He had followed her look. "My grandfather. This is one of his Commonplace Books, in which he recorded what he did and thought. He was a remarkable man. He restored the fortunes of the family and restored this building from the deplorable state created by the neglect of his own father. He was an art collector—when you have time I will show you his collection. He was a huntsman, a connoisseur of food and drink, a soldier, and an amateur scientist of some note. In addition to marrying three times and fathering nine legitimate children, he was reputed to have had numerous mistresses and countless offspring."

"The man who had everything."

"Not quite. In 1870, at the age of forty-six—my age—he lost his religious faith. His Commonplace Books record the event. It happened quite suddenly. He went to bed one night a true believer, and awoke full of doubts. Until that time he had been a central figure in his church, one who had been given custody of the church's most treasured possession. But he no longer believed in its sacred powers. One month later he took his own life."

As he spoke he was rubbing at his chest, twisting his fingers against the cloth of his dark shirt. Jenny realized that he was touching something there, some talisman that he wore around his neck (she could see the silver chain) and underneath his shirt.

This was another side of the Marquis. Yesterday Louis Villette had first been an indulgent stranger, willing to enjoy a joke of mistaken identity at his own expense. Inside the castle he had become the seigneur, the lord of the manor, a landowner proud to show off Chateau Cirelle and his family's estate. Then that night he was in turn the considerate host and the indulgent father, in whose eyes Cecile could do no wrong.

Now the lightness of spirit had gone. Louis Villette gazed back across half a century to his own grandfather's life and death, and something he saw there frightened him. Was it written in the Commonplace Book? Even if it were, the chances that Jenny could understand it were not very good—before he closed the book she had seen the writing in it, a spidery scrawl in fading black ink. She knew from experience that handwritten messages in a foreign language were hard to decipher.

Jenny hated that look of loneliness and despair. She spread butter and honey on a thick slice of warm bread and pushed it across the table. "Here. If you went to England you'd never be allowed to sit there and starve yourself. It makes you miserable. *Mangez, Monsieur le Marquis.* Eat it. You've had nothing today, have you? And you didn't have much for dinner last night."

He stared at the plate in front of him, as though wanting to refuse it. Then he looked across the table at her and laughed. "Thank you, *Maman.* Very well, I will eat like a good boy." He picked up the bread and took a bite. "Did Cecile tell you that I need to be mothered, or is it your own idea?"

Jenny felt herself blushing. Some barrier of formality between her and Louis Villette had just been removed. "My idea," she said. To hide her embarrassment she leaned across and picked up the Commonplace Book. "May I?"

The Marquis paused for a moment, with an odd look in his eye. Then he relaxed and nodded. "If you wish. Though there can be little interest for a stranger in the day-to-day account of old family matters."

She felt his eyes on her, watching closely as she turned the book around and opened it at random. As he had said, it was a diary of events—and the date at the head of each page was about the only thing that she could understand. The former Marquis of Saint-Amè had lacked the copperplate hand that Jenny associated with the past century. She could make out the odd word, but that was all. She was still staring at the first paragraph when she heard footsteps behind her.

Cecile appeared, coming to read over her shoulder. Before

she could ask any questions the Marquis had reached across to take the book.

"Not for you, sleepyhead," he said. "It's after ten. I'm glad you've finally decided to get up and start the day. But I'll take this—you really don't want to know the sad affairs of your ancestors."

"Not *those* affairs, at any rate." Cecile went to sit next to her father, across from Jenny. She gave a great yawn, not bothering to cover her mouth, and revealed a splendid set of white teeth. "That page is very boring: Grandfather gloating over the size of the grain harvest. Not the good stuff I've heard others talk about. We all know he was a famous rake— but I've never been allowed to look at those pages. Why are you reading the book *now*, Papa?"

Louis Villette shrugged. He had finished eating, and he turned to face Cecile. "Trying to learn from the mistakes of the past. Trying to learn how others have interpreted their duties. Problems of conscience, honor, and duty never change. They are the same now as a century ago."

"Well, don't try to learn too much from him." Cecile looked at her father seriously. "I know you think that my great-grandfather was a great man as well as a great rogue. But *I* can never forget that he killed himself. You have to promise you'll never do that."

Louis Villette reached out and touched Cecile lightly on the top of her tangle of hair. An expression of pride and affection filled his face. "I never will. That is the coward's way out. But now that you are finally here, Cecile, I can leave our guest to you and go off to work. Mam'selle Jenny, just tell us of anything you need or want."

"I'd like to see a little more of the chateau—last night I was too tired to take much in. And of course I'd like to spend time with Father, since that's why I came. And I'd like to know how I can send a letter to my aunt."

"All easily arranged. Give your letter to Monge, and it will go out this afternoon. I will not be here for lunch. Unless you have a preference I will instruct Monge as to the wine he should serve."

He stood up, tucked the book under his arm, and was gone.

Cecile slouched back in her chair, poured coffee, and gave another great yawn. Dressed in a long quilted saffron robe and slippers, she had clearly not yet washed or combed her hair. "Poor Papa."

"He really ought to get some rest."

"I know—he never used to work so hard. For the past few months he never has a moment to spare. No woman friends, no social life. And it gets worse! Now he doesn't even seem to sleep anymore."

"I think he is a wonderful man." Jenny was surprised to hear herself saying the words.

"Mmm." Cecile sat up straighter in her chair, studying Jenny. "Do you? Then at least we can make the evenings a little more interesting. My friend Charles should be here again in another day or two. And Papa is very taken with you. I can tell these things. We can have very nice dinner parties, even if there are no other guests. But I was thinking last night, you are not using your hair to best advantage. It should emphasize your cheekbones. If you would allow me to cut it a little here"—she leaned forward, touching Jenny's hair below her ear—"and change the way it falls at the forehead, it would make a big difference."

"I appreciate the offer." Jenny knew her next words might offend, but they had to be said. "Cecile, you're very kind to me, both you and your father. But I came here to look after *my* father, not to play at hairstyling. I would feel really guilty if I wasted my time. Honestly, I know you're being wonderful, but—"

"And a little plucking to reshape the eyebrows, here," said Cecile thoughtfully. She ran her finger along Jenny's forehead. "You have a very good line from temple to nose. A very elegant line. We should accentuate that. And I will give you a delicate spot of rouge, one that has a subtle match to your fair skin color." She leaned back. "Yes, I can already visualize the result. You will be a—what is the American expression—a knockout?"

"Cecile! Don't you know there's a terrible war going on? Not twenty miles from here! Men are being wounded, maimed, killed."

"That is true." Cecile took a big spoonful of honey from the jar and put it in her mouth. "But you will learn something, Jenny Marshall," she said, with her mouth full. "When you have been close to the front for a week or two, you will learn what I have learned. Before men go off to battle, they must drink, they must laugh, they must make love—to excess, everything to excess! Even in war, life goes on. And it must go on *more*. More laughter, more loving, more beauty—so that people can remain sane.''

She stared at Jenny, her great dark eyes completely serious. ''We will tour the chateau, so you will know your way all around it. And then before dinner I will change the style of your hair and your makeup. And I will make you so gorgeous that you will swoon in ecstasy when you look into a mirror.''

By two o'clock, Jenny was experiencing a sensation she had never expected to feel in France. She had been ready for horror at the sight of the wounded, for exhaustion, for terror and shock. What she had not prepared for was boredom.

Cecile had shown her the chateau before lunch. Once the overall structure was explained, it became much easier to find one's way around. The key to successful navigation was the fact that the three floors of the castle were connected to each other only via the central staircase that led to the main doors, and flights of stairs in the east and west wings. To reach the third floor of the northwest tower, for example, where the Marquis had his private suite of rooms, from Jenny's room it was necessary to descend to the first floor, traverse the chateau at ground level, and then go back up two flights of stairs.

Cecile had looked surprised when Jenny asked about the awkwardness of the chateau's layout. ''Always going up and down stairs, you mean? You ought to be here in winter. The winds come whistling down the upstairs corridors. The more windbreaks we have, the better. Papa talks of putting in central heating one day, with another big boiler in the old cellars; then it would be warm enough for a more open plan on the upper floors. But he can't do it yet—there are no workmen available.''

They had descended one underground flight of stone steps and peered down a dark staircase that led to the lower cellars, but Cecile refused to go any farther. They were huge, she said, three times the size of the above-ground part of the chateau. But they were also cold and dusty, she did not know her way around them, and she did not want to come back with her hair covered in cobwebs.

By midday Jenny felt that she could find her way around the main body of the chateau without assistance. She was also feeling, though she was not about to mention it, a little disappointed. The chateau was impressively big, it was pleasant, and it was full of interesting paintings and statues. And yet it did not give her the right feeling. *Chateau Cirelle* suggested something so much more grand and ancient—not just another eighteenth century country house, like a dozen she had visited for parties in England and Scotland.

"No family ghosts?" she asked Cecile. "No mysterious figures wandering the chateau at night?"

"Only poor Papa—he's terribly insomniac. I sometimes wonder when he sleeps and where he sleeps. Eugenie makes up his bed, and often in the morning the sheets have not been disturbed. He works incessantly."

For the past few weeks Cecile had been extremely busy herself, looking after wounded soldiers. Now that William Marshall was the only one left, things were quiet and she was glad of Jenny's company. But she shook her head at Jenny's suggestion that Chateau Cirelle ought to become a general hospital for the whole area.

"Why not?" asked Jenny. "Your father is fanatically dedicated to the cause of France, you have made that clear enough. And there is lots of space just right for hospital beds—the east-wing rooms are perfect. And there's acres of space in the west wing, too, for operating rooms and supply rooms. It wouldn't take much to give the place tip-top medical facilities."

"He won't do it." Cecile frowned. "And I don't know why. You're quite right; Papa thinks of nothing but the war, and ways to end it. But when I pointed out to him that most of the soldiers who had been housed here temporarily had gone, so we could take some more, he wouldn't even listen."

"Did he give you a reason?"

"He said we are within easy shelling range of the German forces at Saint-Mihiel. And that is true. But the Germans do not shell hospitals, or civilian homes, except by accident. I told him, if that was his only worry, why not use the deep cellars? A wounded man would be safe, even with a direct hit on the main building. And there is enough space down there for hundreds of men."

"What did he say?"

"Nothing. Not even an answer. He walked away—but if you want to try again, do it. I like to have the wounded men here, they are so cheerful and brave. Even the ones who had lost their sight or their limbs never let their misery show. It was always, 'Lovely morning, Cecile,' or 'Thank you, Cecile. Another few days and I'll be out of this blasted bed and back in action. Better yet, sweetheart, I'll be *in* this bed and back in action.' And they reach out and try to touch my breasts or put a hand under my skirt—men too weak to sit up by themselves! When I see the courage that our men show, it makes me weep."

They had wandered back from the lower level and drifted along to the dining room. The main course at lunch was roast hare with onions and mushrooms. Hare was a dish that Jenny had been served often in England and never particularly liked. The meat was too gamey for her taste. Here it was served Alsace-style—whole. Jenny took one look at the long body and skinned, eyeless head, and decided to settle for pea soup, bread, Camembert, and wine. Cecile made up for her lack of appetite. She ate a big helping of meat, then picked up the bones and gnawed them for remaining scraps of flesh. Jenny looked away, and drank more wine than she should have. One thing that Cecile had not shown her was the wine cellars, but they were extensive ones. Last night Louis Villette had mentioned they were down to "the last twenty cases of Clos de Vougeot '08, and the last ten cases of Le Chambertin '06."

While they were eating, the Marquis made an unexpected appearance. He was dressed in workman's clothes, his face grimy with dust and powdered stone. He picked up a piece of cheese, poured a glass of Haut-Brion, and began to eat standing. Jenny thought of asking about the use of Chateau Cirelle for wounded soldiers, but one look at the Marquis convinced her that it was not the time for it. He was miles away. Cecile stood up and went across to him.

"We have a *guest*, Papa." She steered him to a chair and sat him down. "Remember, Mam'selle Jenny here? You cannot live like an animal when we have a guest. Now, here is a plate, and here is food. Sit down and enjoy it."

He sighed, looked at Cecile, and smiled. He rubbed a hand

across his forehead and made another long smudge of gray there. "*Le Commandant*. Very well, I will obey orders."

But he had gulped down his food and wine, spoken no more than a dozen words, and was gone again in five minutes. His urgency and intensity made it impossible for them to continue with a relaxed meal. Ten minutes later Cecile also excused herself, leaving Jenny to her own devices.

Jenny wandered back to the east wing and went to sit at her father's bedside. His condition was unchanged, though he did stir restlessly in his sleep when she spoke his name. It was terrible to feel so helpless. Jenny had brought her portable writing set with her and intended to begin a letter to Aunt Ellen. But when she uncapped the little inkwell and dipped the pen into it, she found herself sitting, minute after minute, with the nib poised over blank paper.

What was there to say? That she was here, and completely useless? That Daddy was alive, but no one could give her any idea when or if he would recover? To her eyes, he seemed more restless and a trifle thinner and paler than yesterday. Cecile had told Jenny something earlier that had disturbed her greatly. When William Marshall was awake, she said, he always ate well; but in the past week he had been awake less and less. Cecile had not spelled out the implications; Jenny knew them well enough. If he were to go into a longer period of unconsciousness, they would have big problems feeding him, even with a tube. He might starve, or become so weakened that he would fall an easy victim to some other disease. Pneumonia carried off a third of the casualties of trench warfare.

After sitting with the tablet of paper on her knees for half an hour, Jenny gave up. She scribbled a bland, reassuring note, saying that she had arrived and that Daddy seemed to be recuperating. It was not exactly a lie. She signed it, slipped it into the envelope, and started off to look for Monge.

As she was closing the door of the room, the letter and writing case slipped out of her grasp. They fell to the floor and the case burst open to send loose sheets of paper everywhere. Jenny swore, made a dive, and grabbed the inkwell before it rolled over. Luckily it had landed right side up and the cap had remained closed. She knelt for a couple of minutes, putting everything carefully back in order. With the case tucked under her arm, she picked the letter off the floor and set out once more to seek Monge.

It took a while to find him. He was standing at a door on the north side of the building, at what was clearly the trade entrance. He was checking a delivery of beef and was apparently holding a simultaneous negotiation with the wizened delivery boy for the sale of vegetables from the chateau's own gardens.

He took Jenny's letter with a bob of the head, but went on with his argument and rapid conversation and then took the tradesman outside to show him something in the garden.

Jenny stood there looking after them. Now that the opportunity was gone, she realized that she had really been hoping to practice her French again with Monge. Cecile and Louis Villette spoke such good English that she was embarrassed even to try with them, but with Monge she could tell herself that she had no choice.

Jenny remained for a few more moments looking out at the garden, then began to walk slowly back toward her room. As she went she thought again that the chateau was a perfect location for a hospital. The grounds outside the north door were extensive, with plenty of flower beds and shaded walkways. If they were not well maintained at the moment, that was something where even wounded soldiers might be helpful. In England the hospital grounds were maintained these days by convalescing infantrymen. And there was no doubt that the chateau had space, plenty of it, especially if the basement levels were as spacious as Cecile suggested.

Jenny paused. She had arrived once more at the long corridor with the marble table and the mirror. The little door that she and Cecile had used to explore the first floor of the cellars still stood ajar. The snuffed oil lamp sat on the table.

Why not? Cecile was not expecting her for another hour. Plenty of time for a more thorough look around. And if she was going to convince Louis Villette that the chateau could serve an increased function as a hospital, she ought to know as much as possible about the cellar level.

She picked up the sulfur matches next to the lamp and struck one on the side of the box. The match flared into vigorous flame. Holding the lamp in front of her, Jenny crouched down so that her head did not hit the door lintel, and crept through the opening.

Cecile had not exaggerated the size of the cellars. After descending two flights of stairs Jenny found herself midway along a long, straight corridor, a stone-flagged tunnel stretching away as far as the light would show. Every ten paces or so stood a bracing arch of gray stone, supported on carved caryatid pillars.

The trick was not to go so far that you got lost. That, or follow Ariadne's example and provide a ball of string to trail out behind you. Jenny began to walk along the right-hand corridor, counting arches as she went.

After a couple of minutes she realized that the place might not be as complicated as it looked. Every third arch had a secondary corridor running off to the right. She explored a few and found that each ended in open chambers about twenty feet across. Two of the rooms were empty, but the third was filled with wooden pews, stacked from floor to ceiling. They must have come from an old chapel, part of the original chateau. The rooms were dusty and chilly, but the walls and ceilings were solid and there was no sign of damp. Put solid doors on them and any one would be a safe place for wounded men, even during a bombardment.

Jenny continued along the corridor and came to a major branch point. The branch she was in narrowed to a width of three feet and took a turn off toward the left. A broader side corridor ran off at right angles to the right.

Which one?

Jenny paused and tried to visualize the turns she had made and the distances she had covered. She thought she had been traveling back toward the rear of the house, heading for the trade entrance on the north side. But she had come a long way—she must be beyond the walls of the present chateau. The left-hand branch would take her still farther away from the house, while the right-hand one would bring her back toward it. It made sense to go right. But from sheer curiosity Jenny walked along the narrow left-hand corridor for a few more seconds.

She found herself at the bottom of a musty spiral staircase that wound tightly up and up. The top ten feet or so were dense with cobwebs, but there was a clear way through next to the railing that suggested someone else had been there not too long ago. And there was light at the top.

Jenny climbed all the way up and found herself facing a rickety door made of white-painted crossed planks. There was no latch. She pushed it open, went through, and entered an old cloister. The stone arches on each side of the walk were crumbling, tufts of grass grew on the walk, and the roof was broken here and there to show patches of blue sky.

She stepped to the nearest arch and looked out. About forty yards away stood Chateau Cirelle. Between her and the house were vegetable gardens, and beyond them the formal flower beds. Only a couple of yards away began neat rows of well-grown lettuce, onions, and peas, and beyond them little sprouting seedlings of tomatoes, beans, and squash. Close up, she could see that the kitchen garden was a good deal better looked after than the flowers and shrubs.

It made sense. The staff had a practical interest in the output of the rows of growing vegetables.

As Jenny watched, Monge appeared from the back door of the house holding a big wickerwork basket. He closed the door and headed along the path toward the kitchen garden.

She was doing nothing wrong, but for some reason Jenny did not want him to see her. Before he got close she had ducked her head back and was starting down the narrow spiral staircase. After the bright sunlight it seemed much darker than before. The lamp showed no more than a few yards ahead. By the time she reached the place where the tunnel widened, her eyes were again becoming accustomed to the light. She peered along the corridor on her left, thinking she would not bother to look at it today, then changed her mind when her ears caught an unexpected sound from that direction.

It sounded like running water. Was she already low enough to be at the level of the Aire River?

Jenny walked a dozen steps to where another upward staircase ran off to the right and a heavy wooden door barred the way ahead. The sound of water, curiously, was less here, but the walls were damp.

On the front of the door was a massive iron ring. Jenny turned it and pulled, and the door swung slowly open. It was another sizable stone chamber, this one with a ceiling that must have been twelve feet high. Halfway up the wall at the far end was a structure like an opera box—a little gallery set into the wall itself, with a waist-high railing and a long bench behind it.

The room itself was far from empty. Jenny recognized the contents from the visits she had made years before to the Tower of London.

A torture chamber.

To her immediate right, just inside the entrance, stood a long, flat bench with stout wooden bars across both ends. Manacles and ankle irons were bolted onto the bars. As a ratcheted iron wheel at one end of the rack was turned using long capstan bars, the wooden beams moved farther apart, stretching the victim on the bench. The flat surface was black and stained with centuries-old blood, sweat, and grease. Next to it was a bellows and an iron brazier, with sets of metal pincers neatly arranged across the top. The brazier and the ceiling above it were grimy and smoke-blackened with use.

Jenny lifted the lamp and looked the length of the chamber. It was all here. The parrot's beam, a bar about seven feet off the ground to suspend prisoners by the fingers or thumbs. A thumbscrew, its base black with old blood. An iron boot, with its opening at the top through which lead or boiling oil was poured. The iron maiden, the one that had frightened the youthful Jenny most of all; she had imagined being placed in that dark upright coffin, and watching the approach of long metal spikes that drove into belly, eyes and breasts as the lid was closed. There was the *mala mansio*, the "little ease," a tiny cage into which a wretched prisoner was squeezed for weeks, unable to stand, sit, or lie down. The press with its fifty-pound weights, the strappado, the hot plate of the *lamina*, the barbed hooks of the *ungulae*, the bilboes with their iron gauntlets, the blocks, tackles, cutters, and leaden balls . . . it was all here. In the center of the room, out of place in the grim setting, stood a long, rectangular table covered with a bright purple tapestry. Jenny walked to it and looked down. The cloth bore a sequence of stylized pictures, of men and women dressed in the clothing of the biblical Middle East. They showed the sacrifice of a lamb, men weeping, and women lying prostrate before a great flaming cross. A real metal crucifix, two feet high, stood on the far end of the tapestry.

At the other side of the long table, right at the end of the room, was another door. This one was painted bright red. Jenny stole over to it almost on tiptoe, her footsteps clicking softly on the flagstones. The atmosphere of the chamber was getting to her. It was oppressive, redolent of the tearing and twisting of tormented bodies a few centuries ago. She recalled the ways how, according to the Tower exhibits, torture for inquisition had been divided into three groups: *levis*, *gravis*, and *gravissima*—mild, major, and most extreme.

This room was equipped for *gravissima*, the most that could possibly be borne without destroying life. There was every sign that it had been used.

With a hand that was not quite steady, Jenny pulled open the red door. She peered through into a low room, one whose ceiling must have been at the same level as the chamber gallery above her head. The new room was in some ways more jarring than the torture chamber. Oak-paneled and cheerfully decorated, it gave pride of place to a wide, comfortable-looking bed, a brass four-poster with a crimson counterpane. But two things about it seemed out of place. There were modern electric light fittings around the walls, at variance with the general appearance of age; and the bed had a great mirror above it, with straps, loops, and hanging leather harnesses attached to the bedposts and suspended from the ceiling.

Jenny was about to step through the door for a closer look at those odd fixtures when she heard a peculiar sound, something between a sigh and a whistling groan. It came from just above her.

She stepped smartly backward and looked up. As she did so there was a flicker of movement. Something light-colored and flapping in outline had crossed the shadows at the back of the little gallery, right overhead.

She jumped back farther, holding the lamp high.

"Who's up there? Who is it?"

There was no reply. She heard a slithering sound from the back of the gallery, and a creaking of footsteps above her. They were passing right over her, heading for the staircase at the end of the chamber—the place where she had entered.

"Who's there?" Jenny cried out again. She ran back across the room as fast as she could. When she was at the door it slammed solidly shut in her face, knocking the lamp out of her hand. She heard the glass cover smash on the floor. She was thrown into total and terrifying darkness.

She groped for the door handle, her heart racing. Then she hesitated. Something was on the other side of the door—but who, or what? She was afraid to find out.

Jenny and her friends in Connecticut had prided themselves on their disdain for superstitions. For a dare, three of them had once spent an uncomfortable midsummer night in a New Haven cemetery. This was different. With shaking hands she felt her way along the dark room, back toward the other door. On the way her fingers came into contact with the cold metal spikes in the lid of the iron maiden. She came close to screaming in horror and fear.

At last she was back at the red door. From the gallery above she again heard the whistling sigh. She blundered on, closing the red door firmly behind her. She felt certain that there was another door at the far end of this room—but she had not taken much notice of it before. She was not sure how to find her way to it without a light.

Jenny slipped off her shoes and stole forward, trying to move in total silence. If only she had thought to look and see how the electric lights could be switched on! Any sight at all would be better than this solid darkness. She felt her way around the bed and across to the wall. Hands flat against it, she moved along until she felt the change from oak panel to painted door. It was secured by another heavy iron ring that turned easily in her grip.

She moved through quickly, and turned to secure the door behind her. As she turned the ring into the locked position, she was caught and held firmly from behind.

Hands lifted her, pulled her close. Her face was in contact with rough cloth. Jenny screamed, twisted her body as it was raised in the air, and felt her bare feet in contact with a wall. She kicked herself away from it with all her strength. It took her assailant off balance, and they crashed together to the floor.

Jenny kicked at the body underneath her and heard a deep

grunt of pain. She struggled to crawl away across the smooth stone. He had not released his hold as they fell. She found herself gripped tighter, lifted, and carried half a dozen paces.

One hand pinned her against the wall. She dug her nails deep into the back of it and heard a curse and another grunt of pain. Electric lights in the walls suddenly brightened. Jenny, about to sink her teeth into her attacker's right forearm, found herself staring into the startled blue eyes of Louis Villette.

"What the devil are you doing down here—"

"Why did you grab me like that—"

They stood panting, faces inches apart. Louis Villette released his hold. His face was flushed with excitement, rage, or exertion. Jenny, on shaky legs, grabbed hold of his arm to keep herself upright.

"Why did you do that?" she said. "I thought someone was going to— I thought you were—" *A boogie man. That moving white shape.*

"I am sorry." He took a deep breath, and his cheeks lost their fiery blush. "In the dark, I had no idea that it was you. I was just about to put the lights on when you came through the door. Don't you know better than to wander around these cellars without a light? When you ran into me, I was convinced you were your father. That's why I held on so tight, to restrain him."

"My *father*!"

"Exactly. We have been searching the whole chateau for him, from end to end. When Cecile went in to check on him, his room was empty. Did you go there and forget to lock the door?"

"Of course not! When you told me he had been sleep-walking, I naturally worried that he would get out—" Jenny paused. *Had she checked?* When she left his room, the contents of her writing set had fallen all over the floor. She had been distracted, picking them up. Had she been stupid enough to leave the door unlocked?

The Marquis was watching her closely. "We can talk about that later," he said. "Come on. I noticed that one of the doors to these underground floors was open, and I wondered if he might have found his way down here. But why are *you* wandering around in the cellars—and in total darkness? You could have been badly hurt."

"I lost my lamp."

Jenny explained what had happened: the white-garbed figure, the footsteps above her.

"Your father, almost certainly. It could be no one else." The Marquis swung open the heavy door that led back to the room with the crimson bed. "Come on. You have no idea how dangerous this place is for somebody wandering around in the dark."

"The steps? If he can't see where he's going—"

"That and worse." They had reached the torture chamber, and Louis Villette paused at a big square of stone set in one wall. He pushed hard on one side, and it swung smoothly open to reveal a dark opening.

"Lean over and listen," he said. "But not too close."

Jenny cautiously approached the dark cavity. Far below was a sound of rushing water. It was much too deep to be the Aire River. She looked at the Marquis questioningly.

"An oubliette," he said as they moved on. "A place where you put people you never want to see again. It dates back to the fifteenth century. I explored it a couple of months ago. Behind the stone there is a rock-walled chute, very smooth and slippery. It slides down steeply for nearly fifty meters, to an underground river. A few hundred years ago, that river was also the chateau's secret water supply. It made the place very difficult to besiege successfully. No one knows where that river comes to the surface. Put an enemy down the oubliette, and he was never seen again, dead or alive."

"Do you think Father may have fallen down it?"

"It's possible, but unlikely. He wouldn't know how to move the stone. I'm more worried about the ledges. A few of the corridors here end with a blind three-meter drop to another floor."

He strode, so that Jenny had to run to keep up.

"He went back across the level above the torture chamber," she said. "Before that he was standing in the little place high in the torture chamber wall—the one with a bench across it."

Louis Villette paused, turned, and gave Jenny a strange smile. "You mean the spectators' gallery. Nice people, you see, my ancestors. When an enemy was being tortured to death, they wanted to be sure of a good seat. I have records in the library of some of the old trials and executions—not pleasant reading. This whole area of the cellars is dangerous unless you know exactly what you are doing. There are steep steps, beams eaten through with dry rot, sheer drops. I know just where the route from the gallery would bring him out. But we are at the end of the section with electricity. We must use an oil lamp.''

Jenny waited impatiently while he took a small lantern from a wall bracket, and on the second attempt managed to light it. The wick was old and frayed, and the lamplight flickered and wavered, hardly showing the way ahead. It did not matter. The Marquis strode out confidently, apparently knowing by heart each step and turn. Jenny trailed his footsteps, peering nervously into the gloom.

Nothing. Surely Father would not have come this far, alone in the dark? He must be upstairs, maybe out in the garden. Had they looked in the gardens?

She stood still. At the end of the corridor there, at the bottom of that little flight of stone steps—what was the gleam of white?

Jenny gave a groan and ran on ahead of Louis Villette. ''Daddy!''

She crouched by the silent body. William Marshall's jawline was driven askew where the side of his face had smashed into bare flagstone. He must have tumbled headlong down the stairs. Jenny felt his hands. Ice-cold. She felt his pulse. Scarcely anything, the merest flicker.

Jenny knelt and put her cheek next to her father's. It was chill as marble. She wept aloud.

CHAPTER ELEVEN

Had she left the door open? Again and again she had gone over things in her mind and felt sure she had closed it. But then how had Father gotten out?

The rest of the afternoon had been chaotic. First they had to get William Marshall back to his room. He was a big man, and Jenny was not sure how to do it. But the Marquis simply lifted him in his arms and carried him upstairs with no effort at all.

Jenny felt sick. Her father had once been so handsome, so well-built and muscular. Now he was skin and bones. And his jaw was definitely broken. Even with her limited nursing experience, Jenny knew they were looking at a major fracture.

Cecile was nowhere to be found, and Monge was away in the village of Saint-Amè. The Marquis drove off to bring medical help. For the two hours that the doctor took to arrive, Jenny sat by her father's bed. She felt frozen and exhausted. Cecile had not reappeared, though Jenny longed desperately for someone to talk to. She had never felt so useless. She had come to help her father, and instead she might have killed him.

When the doctor finally arrived, he gave Jenny little comfort. He was short and fat, with a red face, a little spade beard, and a pompous manner. At first he gave her scarcely a glance, but as he began to unbutton William Marshall's shirt he turned and spoke rapidly to the Marquis in French. He looked at her pointedly. The Marquis offered an equally rapid and unintelligible reply. The doctor shrugged.

"I am sorry." Louis Villette sounded embarrassed as he turned to Jenny. "He says he cannot continue with the examination when you are present."

"Look, this is my *father*! Please explain to him."

"He knows. He says that propriety forbids that he perform a full body examination when a member of the opposite sex who is not a physician is present." The Marquis took her hands in his. "Jenny, I do not like Dr. Halphen, either. He is conceited and short-tempered. But he is a physician approved by the French Army, and I have no reason to question his competence. Also, I think that in this case he is quite right. It may be necessary for him to do things to your father that would distress you."

Jenny found herself quietly shepherded out of the room. At the door she turned. The doctor was bending low over William Marshall's bare chest, listening intently and shaking his head. The door closed.

It was half an hour before the two men emerged. This time Dr. Halphen did not even look at Jenny. He placed his high hat squarely on his head and walked rapidly away along the corridor.

She went to the doorway and began to push her way in past the Marquis. He held her gently, barring the way.

"Look at your father, if you wish, but I do not want you to stay for too long. There is nothing you can do. More than anything he needs rest and quiet."

"Is the doctor leaving? I want to talk to him."

"He is leaving." The Marquis smiled a little. "In a bad mood. He tried to invite himself to dinner, but I seemed curiously unable to understand his hints."

"He could have told us a lot more if he had stayed."

"I think not. He told me everything I wanted to know, and I feel sure he would have refused to talk to you. For some reason he hates Americans."

He allowed Jenny to move past him and followed her to the bedside. William Marshall's head had been strapped into a rigid wire frame supporting the jaw. A brace allowed his mouth to open no more than half an inch. The wires went inside the mouth and were anchored on the teeth, making a permanent half grin. The skin of his face had a translucent, porcelain look, with pale blue veins showing at the hollow temples. His dark hair looked thinner, grayer. Jenny had the feeling that she was looking not at her father in his vigorous middle age, but at a very old man.

"He can't possibly eat when he's wired up like this! What did Dr. Halphen say about food?"

"Food is out of the question so long as he remains unconscious." Louis Villette led her gently to the door and closed it behind them. He placed Jenny firmly against the wall, put his hands on her shoulders, and stared into her eyes. "Jenny, it would be easy enough to lie to you, but I will not do it. There is bad news. Dr. Halphen examined your father five days ago. He says that there has been a noticeable worsening of his condition since then—nothing to do with the recent fall. I asked for a prognosis. The doctor does not believe that your father is likely to recover consciousness. There is evidence of nervous tissue degeneration and loss of motor control." He paused. His voice dropped in pitch and volume. "I am very sorry."

Jenny leaned forward and rested her forehead against the heavy cloth of his jacket. Her eyes were filling with tears, and she did not want him to see it. He put his arms comfortingly around her and began to pat and rub her back. As he did so there was the sound of laughter, and a clatter of leather shoes up the staircase.

"Aha!" said a cheerful voice. "Caught in the act. I knew it!"

Jenny looked up with tear-blurred eyes. Cecile was grinning from the top of the stairs. She stepped closer and her expression changed.

"Hey, what is this? Jenny, is it your father? Is he all right?"

Louis Villette reached out and gathered his daughter in with one long arm, pulling them all together so that Jenny and Cecile were only inches apart. He held them tight. As he did so there was the sound of more footsteps on the stairs, slow and uneven. A tall, fair-haired man appeared on the landing and paused there, looking confusedly at the tight group of three people. Jenny heard a grunt of surprise from Louis Villette.

"Charles! I didn't know you'd be here today."

"Blame Cecile for that—she has a surprise dinner planned

for all of us. What's going on?'' Charles Richter was staring hard at Jenny. He had caught the tense atmosphere immediately.

The Marquis released the two women. ''Let me introduce you. Jenny, this is Charles Richter, a good friend of mine and an always-welcome visitor. Charles, this is Jenny Marshall.'' He nodded at Richter's quick look of comprehension. ''The daughter of the wounded colonel, our injured British liaison officer.''

''I am charmed to meet you.'' Richter smiled, but his eyes merely flickered to Jenny, took in her expression, then looked back to Louis Villette. *Dead?* His face asked the question.

''Colonel Marshall is seriously ill,'' said the Marquis. ''He is worse than when he arrived. Dr. Halphen has just left.'' He sighed. ''Jenny, I am sure you do not feel like eating, but you should. Cecile's idea of a dinner party may be the best thing for all of us. Come along. There is no point in standing here any longer.''

Jenny allowed herself to be led along the corridor towards the dining room. Cecile, still not knowing quite what had happened, responded at once to Jenny's misery. She took her by the hand, and did not let go. Louis Villette and Charles Richter fell into step behind them. Jenny heard a low exchange of rapid French, and Richter's grunt of concern.

''*Pauvre petite*. She looks too young for such trouble.''

''She is.'' The deep voice was bitter. ''It is the young who are suffering most in this war, Charles. Love and death have their arrows mixed. Today, old men love and children die.''

Jenny was beginning to feel faint. She found herself in the small lounge, holding a glass of rosy liquid and automatically drinking it. The taste was slightly bitter, and the drink tingled on her tongue. She raised the glass to the light and frowned at it.

''*Vermouth cassis*,'' said Cecile. ''It's quite all right, just vermouth, soda water, and blackberry liqueur. Drink it down. It will make you feel better.''

Jenny knew she was being treated like a small child. Tonight it was exactly what she needed. She obediently drained the glass, and did not protest when it was refilled by Cecile.

There was a time for drinking. She felt as though her face

had turned to stone and could no longer show any emotion. Cecile had taken her hand and was leading her through into the dining room. One end of the great table had been set with four places, clustered intimately together. Jenny found herself sitting across from Charles Richter and Cecile, with the Marquis on her left hand. They had been talking quietly; now they were looking at her expectantly.

For the first time, Jenny noticed Monge standing over by the mantelpiece, ready to serve dinner.

"I'm sorry," she said. "I wasn't listening."

"Dr. Halphen," said Cecile. "Charles does not share Papa's high opinion of him."

"He's a blockhead," said Richter. "I think we should call in another man and see what he thinks. There can be no harm in a second opinion, except maybe to Dr. Halphen's conceit. I was saying, if you agree I'll be happy to drive over and bring him here after dinner."

He looked at Jenny. She secretly thought it would be useless, but any straw was worth grasping. She did not feel able to speak, but she slowly nodded her head.

"It is settled, then," said Louis Villette. "Except that I will drive to bring him here. Come, now, Charles, no argument. You are my guest, and you and Cecile want to spend time together. Also, Jenny needs company."

Jenny had drunk four vermouth cassis, and now she was on her third glass of white wine. The pain in her temples and sinuses was gone and she felt distinctly light-headed. She stared across the table at Charles Richter. He must have been lamed in the war. She opened her mouth to ask how it had happened, then caught herself at the last moment. Suppose he *hadn't* been wounded—what then? He would feel awful. And he was such a handsome, dignified man—no wonder Cecile found him attractive. And yet he looked . . . what? Somehow, he looked—

"Monsieur Richter," she said abruptly. "You know, with your fair hair and light skin, you don't look French. You look more English—or German. That's it, you look German."

Before the words were out of her mouth Jenny knew what a social gaffe she was committing. From across the table there was a sudden widening of Richter's eyes, and a lightning flash of intense reaction shone there for a split second. Then he threw his head back and was laughing. After a moment the Marquis joined in.

"What's so funny?" said Cecile.

"The joke's on me," said Richter. He turned to Cecile. "As we were walking over from the east wing, I remarked to your father on Jenny's light skin coloring. He said she was born in America, and I bet him that she came from German stock." He lifted his wineglass. "I think we should drink to everyone who looks German and fights against them. It represents the triumph of brains over appearances."

"I will drink to anyone who fights Germans, regardless of how they look." The Marquis had lifted his glass and was inspecting the wine in it. "This war will not last forever. I cannot wait for the day when it will not be unpatriotic to drink Schloss Vollrads and Scharzhofberger again. I drink to the defeat of Germany and the end of French torment. I wish we could do more to help our brave soldiers."

"You can." Jenny swiveled to face him and almost overbalanced in her chair. She steadied herself by grabbing his arm. "I was thinking about it today—that's why I went down into the cellars. The chateau is the perfect place for a real hospital. It doesn't have enough equipment, I know that, but it has the right arrangement of rooms. All you would have to do is tell the French authorities you are willing, and they'd be delighted to arrange for the wounded to come here from the front. And Cecile and I would work as nurses, we'd be glad to. I would stay here as long as you want, do anything to help. . . ."

She paused, breathless. Louis Villette was shaking his head. "You mean well, Jenny, I realize that. But you do not know the situation. I have already made such an offer to the local authorities. But I also pointed out some of the disadvantages: no good roads out in bad weather, no medical facilities for surgery, no trained staff, and too near to the front line. You can hear the guns to the north even as we speak."

"But you were willing to have my father brought here."

"That case was exceptional. He was left at the castle because he is English and it was known that Cecile and I are fluent in English. But for others . . ." He shrugged. "Chateau Cirelle can serve as a temporary stopping point for occasional wounded, particularly for English-speaking wounded, but not as a hospital.''

"You haven't really tried. It's an *advantage* that you are so close to the front—you could bring the wounded here without dragging them along that awful road.''

Louis Villette was staring at her with a strange little smile on his lips. "Truly, Mam'selle Jenny, you possess a rare force for persuasion. I find it hard to resist.'' He turned to Richter. "Charles, make my argument for me. Explain to our guest the difficulties.''

"I will do my best. Although I may be a poor advocate for your views.'' Richter turned to Jenny. "I say this knowing it is a sensitive subject, but the interior of this castle has many dangers for a wounded man. Steep staircases, open fireplaces, dark places, when what the wounded need are safe and simple surroundings, fresh air, good food and drink—''

"Then let them have those. At the very least, use the castle grounds if you cannot use the interior. Out there''—Jenny gestured wildly around her, not at all sure which direction she was facing—"out there you have that beautiful big lawn, smooth and soft. When I first saw the chateau I imagined tents and pavilions on it. Summer is coming, the men could live there, they could be fed from the chateau's kitchens . . .''

Richter was biting his lower lip. He turned to the Marquis and raised an eyebrow. "Well? As you say, here is a rare force for persuasion.''

"I agree. Maybe an occasional wounded man here in the castle, but a bivouac of tents outside, to provide a first field hospital.'' Louis Villette reached out and took Jenny's hand in his. "Jenny, I make you this promise. Although the chateau itself is wrong for a hospital, for all the reasons we have mentioned, I will explore the idea of a field hospital on the grounds, just as you have suggested. Is that enough?''

"It is more than enough. It is wonderful.'' Jenny leaned forward and impulsively kissed the Marquis on the cheek. "And I will say what I said to Cecile: I think you are wonderful, too.''

Jenny put her hand to her mouth, amazed that those words had come out. But no one seemed to mind. Everyone was laughing. The mood of the room was suddenly lighter, as Monge served a dessert of hothouse strawberries and cream.

Finally, when the great clock in the main hall chimed seven, Louis Villette pushed back his chair and stood up.

"My apologies to all of you. If I am to bring a second medical opinion tonight I must be on my way. Cecile, our guests are in your hands."

Before he could step away from the table Jenny had leaned over and taken his right hand in both of hers. "I know I was very rude, telling you what you ought to do with your own house. But I *am* grateful for everything you have done for me and Father, I really am. No one could have done more or offered more."

He held onto her hand, long past the point of formality. Finally he bent low and kissed it. "I have done nothing, Mam'selle Jenny. Nothing. But if you stay here for a while, perhaps I can do something to change that."

They watched him leave in silence. As Jenny turned back to face the other two, she felt her chair sway beneath her. She clutched at the edge of the table. The whole room was moving up and down, and the oak paneling on the far wall rippled like sails in a strong wind. She stood up unsteadily.

"Excuse me. I feel . . ." She considered the next word carefully, and pronounced it as clearly as she possibly could, "terrible." She began to move away from the table.

"Wait for me." Cecile followed as she headed for the exit, pausing for a moment to turn back to Charles Richter. "It's my fault, this. Too much worry and wine. I thought the drink would help, but it looks as though she's not used to it. I ought to go with her and fix her up. If I'm not back in a quarter of an hour, we'll be in my room. Come along and join us."

Cecile blew him a kiss and was gone in a swirl of purple skirts. Charles Richter found himself alone at the table, while a poker-faced Monge placed a flask of Napoleon brandy and a glass on the table just as though nothing at all had happened.

"Coffee for one, Monsieur Richter?"

"Black."

Monge poured, placed the silver jug with its tiny spirit lamp beneath it on the table in front of Richter, and silently left for the kitchen.

Charles Richter tasted the coffee, lit a black cheroot, and allowed himself to relax a little for the first time since he had left Saint-Mihiel. He had made a nerve-wracking trip through the German and French lines at three o'clock in the morning. Then there had been a few hours of uneasy sleep in a wood, wrapped in his cloak and alert for any sound, followed by a slow and hungry ride to the chateau in the afternoon. He was already tired out. He was looking forward to his assignation with Cecile with a curious mixture of pleasure and dismay. Cecile expected her dues. It would be wonderful, beyond description—if only he could somehow get a few hours of sleep in first.

He had drunk no wine at dinner, but now the brandy was irresistible. He picked up the Bricard glass flagon by its dragon handle and poured a couple of ounces of spirits into a balloon glass. For a while he sat sniffing it, his mind far away.

Der grösste Vorrücken. It was progressing as well as could be expected, but there were difficulties. Dolfi was one of the problems—in some ways the main one. The man's virtues were also turning out to be his vices. He would take nothing for granted; he trusted no one. It was easy to see why he was still only a corporal, despite all his talents. He tried to run everything he was associated with, regardless of the ranks of the others involved—which must make him a pain for the captains and colonels whose orders he was supposed to be obeying. It was certainly proving hard on Richter. Dolfi had been pressing for two things: first, a visit to the Chateau Cirelle, since that was to be the German headquarters once the Grand Advance was under way.

Richter took another sniff of the brandy. A visit to this French chateau—by a man who spoke the most miserable French imaginable! Dolfi had waved away any objections. Richter was somehow expected to solve that problem for them.

And second, Dolfi had been asking, again and again, for more details about the Cross and the Ritual. A few casual words about them, and Dolfi's ears had pricked right up. He should never have mentioned the damned things to the man! Dolfi had become obsessed with the idea and had inflicted on Richter an hour's lecture on the Holy Grail, Parsifal, and German mythology.

And yet, with all his annoyances, Dolfi was still the best

contact that Richter had ever had. The man forgot nothing, left nothing to chance, tolerated no risk that could possibly be avoided. Richter was beginning to feel that his chances of surviving the war without being captured and shot by the French depended completely on that obsessive, talkative, and opinionated corporal, working eighteen hours a day behind the German lines. An added obsession with a silver cross was a small price to pay.

Richter yawned mightily, rubbed his eyes, and allowed himself a sip of brandy. He needed Dolfi, and perhaps Dolfi needed him. War made strange bonds, forced unlikely dependencies, destroyed all natural friendships. . . .

Jenny blundered along the corridor, heading for the bathroom in her own wing. And then Cecile was at her side, holding her arm and supporting her.

"Head or stomach?" she said.

"Both. I have to go to the lavatory—right now."

"Almost there. Then we'll go to my room. I have something that ought to fix you. Just lean on me. Do you feel weak or dizzy?"

"Both."

By the time they reached Cecile's room Jenny was feeling a little better. She had run cold water on her face, and the first rush of queasiness and giddiness was fading. She sat exactly where Cecile had put her, on the edge of the huge bed, and watched vacantly as the other woman went across to her long, low dressing table. Jenny felt as though her body and her brain were on different planets.

Cecile was sorting through the wilderness of jars and bottles that covered the tabletop, a frown on her smooth forehead.

"Those wretched maids—they have strict instructions not to touch anything here. But *somebody* has been in here, and they've messed up the arrangement. There *is* an order to all this, despite what you might think. Here, this is what I was looking for."

She picked up a little white jar with a tightly fitting lid, all carved from a single piece of ivory, and pried it open. With the jar in one hand and a bone spoon in the other she came across to sit next to Jenny on the bed. "This will do it. Open your mouth."

Jenny obediently swallowed the half spoonful of black jelly. Tart and bitter, it furred her tongue and the inside of her mouth. After a few seconds there was an afterburn, a feeling of heat from deep in her throat to the top of her head. The room came into sharper focus. The discomfort in her stomach was replaced by fiery warmth.

"Uhh." Jenny put her hand to her mouth to hide a series of substantial belches. "Excuse me. I'm on fire. What *is* that stuff?"

"I can't tell you what it's made from. I brought it here with me. Along the big river they use it to treat people with dysentery. I learned long ago that it's the world's best medicine for someone who's had too much to drink. No aftereffects, either."

Jenny was better, unimaginably better. She still felt the glow of intoxication, but her mind was clear and her unsteadiness had gone completely. She stood up and went over to the dressing table.

"I ought to take some of these back to England with me. Who taught you about medicines? You never told me you'd had medical training."

Cecile laughed and began to pick up and put down jars and boxes apparently at random. "I'd better not tell you what training I've had. But these drugs *work*." She lifted a jar. "See, this is a fertility medicine, a very strong one. You make up a tisane, an infusion of the herbs in hot water, and then drink it. It helps a woman to conceive, and it's an aphrodisiac, too."

"Have you used it yourself?"

Cecile gave Jenny a mock-incredulous look. "Jenny, I don't want to conceive—my interests are in the other direction. And I've never needed an aphrodisiac. I have drugs to prevent conception, too, if you are interested. I can guarantee you won't get pregnant if you don't want to. You'll just have lots of fun."

Jenny intended to protest even the idea, but the warmth in her belly would have made a liar of her. This strange conversation had her feeling hot and excited. She went to sit on the bed again, and leaned back against the pillows. "No chance of that. I mean, of me sleeping with anybody while I'm here."

"You never know—we have visitors, and some of them are worth a try. Hands off Charles, though. He's mine."

"He's extremely attractive. And he's obviously fond of you. Do you think you'll get married?"

"Well, we talk of it. But if you want me to be really honest, I don't think either one of us is all that serious. I needle him now and again, telling him that he ought to ask Papa for my hand. But he never does, and I'm not heartbroken. The main thing is, we are terrific in bed. Once he was over his old-fashioned ideas, he became the best I've ever had—and I've had my share."

Jenny had never in her life heard anyone talk so casually about sexual relationships—not even Aunt Ellen. "You must adore each other," she said diffidently. "If it's so good with him."

"Well, we certainly *like* each other." Cecile raised her eyebrows. "I wouldn't go to bed with a man I don't like, unless I was feeling absolutely desperate. But that's only one part of going to bed together."

More and more, Jenny felt like a child with Cecile. "What's the rest of it? Personalities?"

"I don't think so. Geometry is important—you have to fit together right if it's going to be really good. And smells and tastes and timing, maybe they matter most of all. Chemistry, I suppose Papa would call it, though that sounds to me like lovemaking in a test tube."

Footsteps sounded in the passage, followed by a knock on the door. As Cecile went to open it Jenny felt mildly annoyed. She was having a conversation she would never dare to have sober, and she didn't want it interrupted by anybody. Cecile made everything so logical and matter-of-fact, there were no taboo subjects at all.

As Charles Richter came into the room, Jenny could not help thinking of what Cecile had said and imagining those two in bed together. Cecile hadn't actually stated that she would be sleeping with Richter tonight, but there seemed little doubt of it.

Jenny wondered if she was an unwanted presence in the room—"playing gooseberry," they called it in England, hanging around with a courting couple when the last thing they wanted was a third person. She stood up. "I suppose I ought to be going now."

"Going? Going where?" Cecile stared at her. "Papa will be back in a while with another doctor. You can't possibly go to bed until then—and there's nothing else to do in the chateau tonight. Stay here." She saw Jenny look at Charles Richter. "Oh, don't be a goose. I'm not going to suggest we play three-in-a-bed, and I'm not going to jump on him while you're here."

"Cecile!" The protest came not from Jenny, but from Richter. He gave Jenny an embarrassed smile, and she was surprised to see that he was actually blushing. "She's not socially presentable, you know," he went on. "But please, stay here until the Marquis gets back. I want to talk to Cecile, and maybe you can help."

He hitched himself to a sitting position on a chest of drawers, favoring his lame leg. Cecile sat close to him on the floor, near his swinging feet. She crossed her own legs to reveal far more of them than was decent. Jenny looked at those calves and thighs in admiration and envy. They were so long and smooth—not like her own pale offerings, with their soft but noticeable dusting of golden hair.

She looked again at Richter, who was obviously searching for his opening words. He was so dignified and gentlemanly—he must find Cecile quite a handful. He obviously hated embarrassing scenes and wild behavior. So how had the two of them ever found their starting point? It must have been Cecile's doing, waiting in the chateau to draw interesting male visitors into her man-eating spider's web.

Cecile reached up to pat his leg possessively. "All right, worrier. Jenny and I were discussing important things, but if you want to talk instead, carry on."

Richter started to swing his legs nervously as he sat. "I feel like a thief," he said abruptly. "When I was last here, I saw and heard something that I had no right to overhear. It serves me right that it has been preying on my mind ever since."

Cecile twisted around so that she could look up at him. "But the last time you were here you were with me all the time. I didn't see anything unusual."

"After I left you. I went downstairs, as usual, to go back to Bar-le-Duc. But the door out of the northeast tower had been locked. It was late, you were sleeping, and I didn't want to wake you. So I went through the chateau, to leave by the main doors. Do you remember the visitor that your father had with him, Cecile, the last time that I was here?"

"Charles, he had lots of visitors—don't you remember, we had a full dinner party that night, and Monge was going out of his mind because Papa had assigned Marie to other duties?"

"Not one of those people; I don't mean the ordinary dinner guests. This was somebody else, somebody staying at the chateau who wasn't at dinner with us. Monge served him a private meal."

"Oh, I know who you mean. What about him? He was the dullest, most awful old stick-in-the-mud you've ever seen. He wasn't with the rest of us because he was feeling sick. I must say, he looked it. He seemed at death's door."

"Is he a good friend of your father?"

"Not exactly a friend, but he was at the chateau before in early January. Look, why don't you ask Papa about all this?" She turned to Jenny. "Charles won't admit it, but my father thinks he walks on water—he'd give him anything he asked for. Including me. But he won't ever ask. Will you?"

"I told you, Cecile, I *overheard* the two of them talking." Richter ignored the dig. "They didn't know I was there, and I'm sure they didn't want me listening. If I were to ask your father, he'd know I was eavesdropping."

"So what? You're not a spy, are you, trying to hear all his guilty secrets? You happened to be in the hall, and the door was open."

"Sure. Happened to be there, at one in the morning. How do I explain *that*?"

Richter said nothing more. Finally Cecile sighed and reached up to tug at his ankle. "Oh, all right, you stubborn man. Go on, then. Why do you care who he was?"

"Because they were talking about a cross and a gospel, something to do with Judas Iscariot. They had it with them. And they were acting as though it's a big deal, something priceless—very special and enormously old."

"Oh, now I know what you're talking about. That didn't

happen recently, it happened the *first* time the old man came. You know Papa.'' She turned to Jenny. ''My father is crazy about old books—the library is full of them. Dust and mold collectors, mostly. But anything old fascinates him. If you think I go in for mumbo-jumbo with my medicines, you ought to see the potions they describe in Papa's books. And the man had brought more old books with him. I think he was trying to sell them to Papa.''

''I have an aunt who's crazy about old books,'' said Jenny suddenly. She had not been listening for the past few minutes; now she was trying unsuccessfully to sit up all the way. Cecile's potion might work miracles and have no aftereffects, but it left you remarkably limp-limbed. ''She's my absolutely favorite aunt.''

''But Papa didn't want them,'' went on Cecile, ignoring Jenny. ''I'm sure of that, because I was sitting in the small lounge, and the two of them came wandering in. Papa said, 'This is Cecile, my only daughter—my *only child*. You see now that your fears are groundless for any improper use on my part.' And the old man began to huff and puff, and say, of course, but it was his responsibility to make sure that there would be no 'abuse,' and then he started to go on about how far he had come, and how many people he had been to see, and how bad the weather had been, and all sorts of nonsense like that. Then he talked about duty and honor for a while. Papa nodded his head, as though the old man made sense, and out they went.''

''I'm an only child,'' said Jenny. ''Like you. I wish I had your legs.''

''But he did leave the cross and the book,'' said Richter. ''I saw them.'' He gave Jenny an annoyed look as she sank down on the pillow.

''Well, he must have talked Papa into taking them—you know what a soft touch he is for a hard-luck story. But I can assure you, when I saw the two of them I didn't see any cross, just rotten old books, moldy and dusty and falling apart.'' Cecile frowned. ''But you're right, there was *talk* about a cross. The old man said, 'The cross is a sacred trust. It was in your custody in the time of your grandfather,' and Papa replied, 'Then it should not return in this generation.' ''

Jenny had been drifting in and out of the conversation.

Now she sat up again. "Did you say that it was very, very, very old? Then my aunt would like that. She likes everything old. She's old herself."

"Back to dreamland, Sleeping Beauty," said Cecile. She smiled and rose easily to her feet. "How are you feeling?"

"I'm fine. But I'm a jelly. Whatever it is you gave me, I want to take some of it with me when I go back to England. I've never felt so good inside." Jenny snuggled down into the pillows and closed her eyes.

Cecile went to the bed and bent over Jenny, looking at her eyes and mouth. She took the loose counterpane that stretched to the floor on both sides of the bed, and lifted it to cover Jenny from feet to chin.

"I feel sure that the other doctor's report is going to be bad news. I think for Jenny it can wait until morning."

She went across to Charles Richter, still perched on top of the chest of drawers. She took his hand to help him down. "Come on, she'll be all right here. I think you ought to show me your room." Her dark face was grave and serious. "Papa told me that in his absence I am responsible for the welfare of guests. He would never forgive me if I permitted you to sleep in a room unfurnished with everything a man might need."

CHAPTER TWELVE

The northwest tower of the chateau extended upward in a long and narrow needle. Near the top of it, perched ninety feet above the ground, hung an observation room. It had been built during the war of 1870, to keep an eye on advancing German forces. The spire swayed in even a light wind, and the castle servants refused to go up the wooden ladder that led to the crow's nest.

Wind was not a problem tonight. The air was perfectly calm, with too little breeze to flicker a candle flame. Louis Villette sat on a stool, alone.

The second physician's opinion was similar to Dr. Halphen's. William Marshall was a dying man. But that was not what dominated the thoughts of the Marquis. On the journey to the chateau, the doctor had told him that a new German offensive was beginning.

With that news, sleep was impossible. He shone a shuttered kerosene lantern onto the book that he held on his knees.

Here I am again, Grandpapa! What would you suggest that I do now? Throw myself from the tower, as you did?

Louis did not remember the death of his grandfather. The man had died one week before Louis's own birth. It was an undeniable suicide, and there had been a terrible fight before he could be buried in consecrated ground. Louis, in another affront to the church, had been named after him. The grandsire, the fourteenth Marquis, lived on in the memories of the castle staff, and in the rumors that Louis heard when as a growing lad he rode through the surrounding villages.

You did your best to use the Cross, Grandpapa; as I am doing my best. And you failed—as I have failed.

He opened the journal, although the entries he sought were already memorized. *Duty transcends every other aspect of civilized life.* And a few pages further on, *In a long life there must be many beginnings and many endings.*

From the little room at the top of the tower, the whole northeast prospect was revealed. Far to the north there was a flash of light, a spark on the horizon. Nearly a minute later, the sound reached the tower as the long-drawn boom of a massive mine. Louis Villette looked up. Somewhere along the war front, Death had paid another visit.

Louis brooded over the hidden landscape. The arithmetic was easy. In the battle for Verdun, four thousand Frenchmen died each day. The power to put an end to that bloodshed lay less than two hundred feet away, in the crypt where the Cross of Judas rested in its locked box. France could be saved from the Germans. But not without personal sacrifice.

The price was a handful of deaths, of innocent people. But were the troops who gave their lives at the front any *less* innocent? They were simple fathers, sons, brothers, husbands, giving their lives for the country that they loved. The true difference was only this, and it was a selfish reason: The troops who died were strangers to Louis; but the vessels of the ritual, by the time they died, must be his lovers.

Louis moved uneasily on the hard stool. He opened the book again, at random. The slit in the lantern fell on a single paragraph of a page.

> I am too mean-spirited. To achieve great goals, a man must risk the torments of Hell itself. But a France controlled by Germany would itself be a Hell. Courage, Louis Villette. We must try again, and not think of the cost.

The fourteenth Marquis was talking to himself alone, not to his unborn grandson. Soon after writing that journal entry he had given up, unable to continue his awful duty; but the words rang across the forty-six years since they were written.

Louis Villette closed the book and stood up. He leaned far over, staring down to the unseen ground beneath.

He would not give up. Suicide was no answer, much as it might tempt him. He would go on, until the war ended or his heart seized with sorrow within his breast.

And he would act *tonight*.

He looked north. The main bombardment had begun. Echoing his thoughts, the horizon there sparked and rumbled its commentary, its acceptance of greater wars and larger sacrifice.

Was there such a thing as perfect happiness in the world? Marie, lying sprawled on the bed, did not know. All she knew was that she was filled with a mixture of excitement, satisfaction, and anticipation stronger than anything she had ever thought possible.

And it had all started so accidentally!

She had been singing, singing to herself as she dusted the statues in the main corridor of the chateau's west wing. As she straightened up, duster in hand, she realized that someone in the corridor had been listening. It was the Marquis, the Marquis de Saint-Amè himself.

She curtsyed nervously, wondering if she had done something wrong. He nodded.

"Go on."

"Monsieur?"

"Go on singing, Marie. Sing some more. The same song."

At first she thought that her voice would fail her, it sounded so breathless and trembling. When she finished he walked over to her side and stood looking down at her. She had never seen him before close up and face-to-face. His eyes were astonishing, clear and blue, with startling black eyebrows above them. There was more gray in his black hair than she had realized, and his lips were fuller and redder.

"Do you know what you were singing?"

"It is a song that I learned from my aunt, sir."

"Good for your aunt. It is also a song written by Schubert—*Ungeduld*, 'Impatience,' from *Die Schöne Müllerin*. And you sing beautifully. Have you had voice lessons?"

She almost laughed—but he was not joking. She shook her head.

"Come with me."

She followed him through the castle to the topmost room of the southwest tower. There, in the high turret out of hearing of the rest of the building, a rosewood box piano stood in a corner of the music room. At his direction she had sung isolated notes, then upward runs, repeating the sequences that he played to her on the piano. She sang a trill, and finally went up the scale, note by note, as far as she could go.

At the end he stared expressionlessly at her from his seat on the piano stool. He struck one note, holding it with the sustaining pedal, and sang it himself, three octaves lower, in a smooth, rich bass. "That is B natural. You sang the one below high C, very clear and true. With training you could sing a high C sharp, maybe even a D or E flat. You should have professional training. Voice lessons."

She stood quietly, her heart pounding. He must realize that she had no money.

"Not here, of course," he went on after a few moments. "There is no one able to do a good job. You would have to go to Chaumont, or Troyes."

He stood up and came to her side. He took her face gently in his hands, turning it from side to side. "And you have good looks to go with the voice. With training, you should look for a stage career."

But then he said the words that destroyed everything. "Of course, I cannot dream of suggesting such an idea to Monge. Not at this time. He is terribly shorthanded already. If I were to tell him that you were leaving for voice training I would have a domestic mutiny on my hands."

She could not speak, but he must have seen the expression on her face.

"So we do not tell Monge," he went on. "At least, we do not tell him yet. When are you free from your duties?"

"Sunday afternoon and evening. And every day after eight, as soon as I have built up the fires for the night."

"Then I have a suggestion. For the time being, let us begin your training here. Tomorrow night, when you are finished with your work, come to this room. But not a word to anyone! For the moment this must be our secret."

He had walked back with her to the corridor, and left her dizzy with excitement. And at dinner that night he had caught her eye for a split second as she brought in a spring salad, and given the tiniest of nods.

The following evening at nine o'clock she had stolen away to the tower. That had been the beginning.

Marie did her work around the chateau in a trance, waiting for Sundays and late evenings. They were the only important parts of her life. It was more than voice lessons. They *talked* together, for hours. She told him about her childhood in Givry, about her unknown father, and the priest who insisted that Marie be given as surname the name of the parish. On her mother's death the priest had arranged for her to go into service, first in Beausite, with a family known to the Marquis, and then here.

The Marquis was so kind and sympathetic—and attractive! One part of her past that she was careful not to mention was the men: the priest who had been the first to possess her; and the head of the household at Beausite, a drunken oaf with a withered leg who had practically raped her and made her desperate to find a new position. The contrast with Louis Villette could not have been greater. He was so serious, so gentle. And so sad, brooding over the war, the loss of his son, and the millions of French deaths. After the first week she had been more than willing to give herself to him. But he did not touch her, except to place his big hand dispassionately on her lower chest and tell her to sing from *here*, from the diaphragm, and not high up in the throat.

On the second Sunday they went back to his chambers for the first time. Her throat felt constricted and tight, and she was depressed by the results.

"A glass of sherry will help," he had said. "It is possible you have a cold coming on, or some congestion in the chest. Do you feel sick?"

She did not; only miserable. And then, after three glasses of sweet sherry, sitting talking together before the fireplace in his rooms, she felt tipsy, a little dizzy, and very warm toward him. When—at last!—he put his arm around her she did not even pretend to resist. She just sighed with pleasure, put her head on his shoulder, leaned back, and closed her eyes.

At the beginning she was passive, letting him take the lead in everything. She thought it best to act the virgin, shy and unsure of what came next. But after he lifted her dress and gently explored her, he looked at her knowingly. She abandoned the pretense.

When they had been lovers for just one week he had taken her by the hand. "Come with me. I want to show you something."

He led her down one floor to his sitting room, and on to the tiny windowless study that lay beyond it. It was completely lined with books. In the corner of the study was a narrow wooden door. Louis lit an oil lamp and squeezed through. Following, Marie found herself descending a crooked stone flight of stairs. Her feet left faint marks in the dust of the steps.

They went to the bottom, then along a short landing to more stairs. All the walls were of gray stone, dusty and freezing cold.

Their footsteps were loud and echoing. Moving shadows beyond the light of the lamp seemed to crowd in on them.

"Louis! Let us go back, please. I don't like it here." She came close behind him and put her arms around his waist. "It frightens me."

"One moment more, my sweet." He turned his head. "We are almost there."

"But *where*? Where are you taking me?"

The stone walls and corridors marched off forever, in all directions. They had passed a dozen branch points, and every one appeared to lead to more identical corridors. If he left her, she would have no idea how to go back.

"This is the basement level of the old castle." Louis Villette's voice echoed in the darkness. "When the new building was constructed, a hundred and fifty years ago, it was less than half the size of the original. The old cellars and crypts extend far beyond today's Chateau Cirelle. But we are not going to look at them. I want to show you . . . this."

He had halted before a massive timber door, secured by a heavy iron ring. While Marie watched, he turned the ring, pulled hard, and let the door swing slowly open. He reached inside to a short metal bar on the wall, switched its position, and waited for Marie to move near. As she came close, the whole room slowly brightened.

"Voilà!" The Marquis waved his hand.

She gasped. The stone walls had vanished. She was standing at the threshold of a square paneled room, twenty feet on a side and seven feet high. Electric light fittings blazed from oak-paneled walls. There was no fireplace, but over on one side electrical heaters were beginning to glow cherry red. By the far wall sat a low, wide four-poster bed, covered with a crimson counterpane. In the ceiling directly over the bed was a great polished mirror, and from each bedpost hung oddly shaped loops and straps of cloth and leather.

Marie came hesitantly forward a couple of steps. "Louis, what is it? I've never seen anything like it. Where did it come from?"

He laughed and pulled the door closed. "It was designed by another Louis Villette—my grandfather. He had it built more than sixty years ago. It was his private love nest, where he entertained ladies who could never be brought into the chateau itself; gypsies, princesses, milkmaids, whores, his neighbors' wives. He was a man of broad tastes. I heard stories about this hideaway when I was just a child. I saw the plans for the place in his diaries when I came back from the Congo. Four years ago I began to explore the old castle's lower levels—and I came across this room."

"But these . . ." Marie waved her hands at the lights. "Surely . . ."

"Ah, you are quite right. I added the electricity—with my own hands." He held up a big, sinewy fist. "I put in lights and heat when I decided to renovate the area. And I put new fixtures in, where old ones were worn or rotting. But the main room here is just as he saw it for the last time, forty-five years ago. I never thought—until a few weeks ago—that I might actually use it myself."

The electric heaters were taking the damp chill out of the air. Marie came forward, her lower lip between her teeth, and tentatively pressed the surface of the bed. It was firm but springy. The counterpane, like the room, was clean and fresh-smelling. She looked up with sudden understanding.

"But Louis, how would I ever get here? I would still have to get to your rooms without being seen."

He sat on the bed and pulled her down gently next to him. "No, that would not be necessary. There are a dozen entrances to the old lower levels of the castle—one of them is even outside Chateau Cirelle, in the old cloisters to the north of the building. I can show you one that begins very close to your own room, on the south side. You could always get here easily . . . if you have any interest in the idea.''

His voice was casual, but his hand told a different story. He was beginning to caress her thigh. She looked around in high excitement. ''This is a *wonderful* place. It can be all our own, with no one to disturb us. I can cry out as much as I like—you know how I hate to hold back when I'm coming. Louis, why didn't you mention this to me *before*?''

''I did not want to embarrass you.'' He reached across and took hold of a padded strap attached to the nearest bedpost. His voice was low and intense. ''I thought of this place from the beginning, but I was not sure that you would like a room with this sort of thing''—he lifted the strap, and placed it quietly around her wrist—''as aids to lovemaking. Some of my grandfather's tastes were a little . . . extreme. These straps are designed to tie up a lady friend so that she cannot move freely. The mirror up there has obvious uses. But other devices, like those hoops and straps from the ceiling, are less innocent. Marie, I did not want to shock you. . . .''

He paused. She was wriggling single-mindedly across to the center of the broad bed, reaching out for the second hand strap and studying the way that it would be tightened on her wrist. After a moment, he stood up and went across to the wall, where the electric switch was located.

''No, Louis.'' Marie's voice was breathless, and she had turned onto her back to stare up at her own reflection in the mirror above the bed. ''Don't do that. Come back here, and leave the lights on. I want to watch us.''

That had been just weeks ago. Now Marie lay on the same bed, too excited to keep still. He had told her the wonderful news early today, in a quick conversation near the front of the chateau. The best musician and singing teacher in Chalons had agreed to take her as his student!

She laughed to herself. There was old Monge, thirty feet above her, running around half blind peering at the serving dishes—and here was she, ready to start out on her great adventure. She snuggled under the bedcovers, luxuriating at the thought. Louis was such a wonderful man. The idea of going away from him was heartbreaking. She would make their lovemaking unlike anything that Louis would ever experience—at least until he came to visit her in Chalons.

Marie pushed back the bedclothes. With the electric heaters aglow she was much too hot. Before she came down here she had drunk the tisane that Louis gave her, the one that prevented her from becoming pregnant. As usual its sweet-astringent taste made her dizzy and amorous, with no will of her own. She had worried at first when she missed her period, which usually came like clockwork every twenty-seven days. But Louis had reassured her the drug did no harm. It merely stopped a woman from ovulating.

But it made you *hot*. Marie threw the bedclothes off completely and looked at her naked reflection in the ceiling mirror. She examined it critically. Her face was pleasant enough, but her nose was too sharp and long. It was framed by blond curly hair, shoulder length. Her body was much better. Her waist was not particularly slim, but the stomach was smooth and flat and the thighs were plump and white. Her hands and feet were small, her breasts full and firm. Would she find, one day, that they had sagged and drooped? Never. Before such a day came, she would die.

She gave a little shiver. Where was Louis? She pulled bedclothes over her again. And what time was it? If only she had a watch; perhaps in Chalons she would have money to buy one. Down here in the cellars she could not even hear the striking of the big clock in the main hall of the chateau, the one whose chimes regulated events in the great house. All she could hear was the steady beating of her own heart.

Marie closed her eyes. A watch, and maybe some new clothes if Louis was generous. But Louis never noticed her clothes—he was always too keen to get her out of them. Well, she felt the same way about him. She loved to look at his body, to run her fingers along the muscular arms and over the line of puckered scar across his ribs. Best of all, she liked to see him crouched rampant over her, his eyes aglow, just before he took her. She had been learning how to excite him, more and more. Lovemaking in this room was better than it had ever been up in the chateau. There was a strangeness to it, a *bizarrerie* that the mirrors or securing straps only accentuated. Would he tie her tonight? It made her feel she belonged to him completely, with no control at all over what happened. She wriggled at the thought.

Where was he? He was so late, and she was so ready. But maybe he was talking to Monge now, telling him that she would be leaving, where she was going. That would be a conversation she'd like to hear. Monge would be furious, but there was not a thing he could do about it.

A sound of footsteps came from outside the room. Marie sat up. At last. A crash from the wooden door. A tall figure came striding into the room, black-clad, shining, and ominous.

Marie gasped and shrank back. Then she realized that it was Louis—but Louis dressed in a long, black waterproof cape, with an oilskin hat covering most of his face. He paused on the threshold, staring blindly about him.

"Louis." Her voice had a quiver in it. "Louis, you scared me. I'm here—in bed."

He came to the bedside and stared down unseeing at her naked body. "All day long," he said. "The Germans have been attacking north of here, all through the evening. It must be stopped."

So that was it! Another damnable German attack. There was nothing so guaranteed to upset him. Sitting upright, she reached out to pull him close. He must lose himself in *her* and forget the war for a while.

She took his hand and placed it on her bare breast. "I was lying here thinking about us. I can't bear the idea of leaving you, Louis. I love you so much, and we're so good together. Promise me that you'll come and see me when I go to Chalons."

He did not seem to be listening, but when his hand touched her breast he felt a tremble in his fingers. He grunted, and leaned over to look into her eyes. He pulled off his rain hat. While he was staring at her he unbuttoned the waterproof cape and slipped it off his shoulders. Beneath it he was naked to the waist.

"Marie," he said softly. "Ah, little Marie."

It was working. She could see the fever in his eyes. He took her by the shoulders and pushed her back until she was lying flat on the bed. She made no resistance as he spread her arms wide and wound broad loops of red cloth around each wrist. He bent to kiss her on the throat, then stood up and went to the end of the bed. She spread her legs wide and felt the cloth tight around her ankles.

She lay spread-eagled, filled with pleasurable anticipation. One of the wonderful things about Louis was that he did not hurry. He always made sure that she was fully ready before he began. But today preparation was unnecessary—she was ready *now*—before he was!

He went to each bedpost in turn, tightening the straps. She grunted in protest and pulled back against the tension. "Not *too* tight, Louis—you don't want to pull me apart."

He gave her a quick look, but he didn't seem to hear. Still wearing trousers and boots, he had moved again to the end of the bed. He hung a battered silver cross over one of the bedposts, then knelt down in front of it.

Marie looked on, puzzled and intrigued. This was certainly a new variation—and there was no doubt that he was wildly excited. She could hear his breath, great shuddering inhalations that came from the bottom of his lungs.

There was a mutter from the end of the bed, a rapid gabble of syllables.

Marie craned upward. "What? I can't hear you." He had tied the straps too tight. She could hardly move! "Louis, stop that and come and loosen these. You've knotted them too tight. I won't be able to grip you the way you like."

"*In nomine Patris, Filii, et Domini Judas, venite . . .* in the name of the Father, and the Son, and Lord Judas . . .''

"Louis!" She was frightened—he wasn't taking any notice of her as he babbled away at the end of the bed. He was reading from something, a big book. And the straps were hurting; this wasn't exciting anymore. "Come and let me go. Come on, Louis."

"*Ut bellum desineat, nunc potestam crucis sanctae invocamo . . .* I now call upon the power of the holy Cross . . .'' He bent lower, reaching under the bed. He was standing up, tall against the glaring lights. His face was pale, his eyes wide and gleaming. They shone round and bright as silver coins in the glow of the lamps.

He lifted his hand. And when Marie saw what he was holding, her screams began.

CHAPTER THIRTEEN

Jenny hesitated at the library entrance for quite a while. No one had actually *told* her to keep out, and the door was ajar; but she knew that this room was regarded as Louis Villette's private domain. Surely he would not mind, though, if she simply went in to sit?

The room beyond the thick door looked calm and cool. Jenny placed her fingertips on the panel of dark oak and pushed. It swung back smoothly, without a sound. She stepped inside. It was nowhere near as gloomy as she had anticipated, with afternoon sunlight washing in around the curtains.

She looked back to make sure she had not been observed and pushed the door to. It took a few seconds for her eyes to adjust to the change in light, then she was moving rapidly from one shelf to the next, struggling to translate the titles.

How were the sections organized? If only she knew the system, she could go straight to the volumes she needed.

T, S, R; alphabetical—and by subject, not author!

She hurried past *P, O, N*, on to *M*, jumping nervously at every creak of a floorboard. Magnétisme, Mahométisme, Mécanisme. *Médecine*. And now, was there a medical dictionary? This looked like one.

She felt oddly guilty as she took the book from the shelves, and was annoyed at the feeling. She had every right in the world to read medical reports on her own father, no matter how that idiot Dr. Halphen felt about it. Jenny took the slip of paper from her sleeve and settled by the fireplace, the dusty book on her knees.

In the old days, before electric lights were installed, this chair must have been the centerpiece of the room. Light from the windows struck here in the middle of the day, and firelight replaced that in the evening. The fireplace was a massive marble affair with a brick floor and a broad mantelpiece holding old framed daguerreotypes, statuettes, and a huge pipe rack. The room carried the comfortable smells of wood ash and tobacco, along with mildew, old paper, and leather.

Jenny sat with the book unopened on her lap. She was suddenly afraid to take the next step.

"Don't stop now," she whispered under her breath. But the paper she was holding terrified her. It was the second doctor's *pronostic*—the medical prognosis. The very word looked threatening.

Consultation seconde. The doctor's handwriting was curiously neat, regular loops and curls of letters in a purple ink. But the words were unfamiliar; they were a French medical vocabulary that she had never had reason to learn.

Jenny opened the book.

"Madame?"

The voice made her jump out of her skin. The book dropped to the floor. The man who had entered and was standing behind her had starched collar and cuffs, a fringe of light brown hair, and a stooped, squinting posture.

Monge.

"I'm sorry. You startled me. The door—" Jenny stopped in time. Helping herself to the doctor's note was one thing, but she had certainly done nothing wrong in coming into the library.

"I wondered, madam, if you would care for tea or coffee, and perhaps a pastry. It will be some time until dinner."

"Oh. Yes. That would be very good. Er—in here?"

"But of course. I will bring it immediately."

Jenny felt a moment of satisfaction as he turned and left. At least her French was improving. She could hold her own quite well now in day-to-day conversation. She picked up the book from the floor and was at once depressed again.

She steeled herself, and sought translation of the key phrases: *Le malade entre en consomption* ("the patient is entering a decline'') . . . *fièvre de cerveau* . . . *maladie céré-brale* (''brain fever'') . . . *fracture compliquée de la ma-choire* (''compound fracture of the jaw'') . . . *sans espoir* (''a hopeless case'').

Jenny turned the pages with ice-cold fingers. All the blood had drained from her body. She had already guessed what most of the phrases meant; the book provided unpleasant confirmation.

Father had always been there, so strong and confident and loving. If he left her life . . .

The rattle of china and silver brought her back to the world. She looked up, expecting Monge, and found Louis Villette staring solemnly down at her. His hand touched her chin and tilted her face upward. His deep voice said, ''My dear lady. You are crying.''

Jenny shook her head, denying her weeping while at the same time a tear rolled down her cheek. ''Not really. I'm sorry. It's just that I—I'm . . .''

He lifted the book and note from her lap and gave them a brief glance. ''Ah. I should have guessed. I ought to banish medical books from this household. Damn the doctors. On the basis of a pinch of knowledge and a lot of guesswork, they claim infallibility.'' He moved a low table to hold the tray. ''Cream and sugar, Jenny?''

She shook her head, still not sure of her ability to speak. He poured strong black coffee into a large cup of Limoges china and handed it to her, along with a plate containing a thick wedge of pie.

''Thank you, monsieur.''

''Not monsieur. Louis, if you please.'' He poured another cup of coffee.

''It is very good.'' Jenny nibbled at a piece of pie, with a dusting of powdered sugar and nutmeg. ''This is delicious, too. But really—you shouldn't be serving me.''

''Why not? For so beautiful a guest, it is my pleasure.'' He gave her a sad smile. ''The pleasures permitted to a Marquis are limited. This is one of them.''

Jenny returned the smile and nodded her appreciation. Louis Villette was wearing a smoking jacket and a silk cravat, an odd contrast to his usual daytime dress of rough work clothes. A meerschaum pipe was in the upper pocket, and he was absentmindedly rubbing its yellow-brown bowl with his thumb as he talked. He was as self-possessed and handsome as ever, but looking closely Jenny detected an unfamiliar glint in his eyes.

"Are you . . . angry with me?"

"Angry? Why should I be?"

"For coming here—into your library."

"A capital offence indeed." He shook his head. "Not angry, not at all. If I appear distant, it is because I have much on my mind."

"The war?"

"What else? *Is* there anything else? All the news from the north is bad—we hold on by an eyelash. And today I learned of a more personal loss. Two days ago I had an appointment to meet a young friend from Sainte-Ysette—a village a few miles from here. She did not come. I could not understand it. Yesterday, again, she did not arrive. Today I rode to the village. It has been bombed. Where her house stood there is nothing but rubble. The whole family was killed, father, mother, and daughter."

Jenny looked again at his face and saw that the expression on it was not sadness—it was desperation. She was not the only one carrying a load of misery.

"Was she—" Jenny hesitated, not sure how to suggest a sexual bond, "was she a *special* friend?"

"Very special."

"So what are you going to do?" The question was such a futile one that Jenny cringed as she said it. What *could* he do? What could anyone do?

Louis Villette reached forward and patted her shoulder. He went to the window and pulled back the drapes. The sunlight poured in, late afternoon honey. "I do all that I can do. I do *this*, I look out at the world. And I tell myself that even this war cannot last forever. Outside it is spring. The sun shines, flowers bloom, birds sing. They know nothing of war and misery. It is *our* job—yours and mine—to be like the birds. I saw your face, Jenny, when I came in. And I said to myself, she must not go into her father's room with such a face. What would happen if he waked and saw her like that? The first thing he would see is a face of mourning, full of storm clouds."

"I can't help it! I know you are right, we must be brave and cheerful, but I feel sadder than I've ever felt. . . ." Jenny paused. She felt dizzy, blurting out much more of her misery than she had intended. "I feel so . . . so *useless* here, watching the war go on and on. The flowers blossom and the birds sing, true—but the shells still fall."

Jenny could feel the tears coming again. She lowered her head and took another mouthful of hot coffee. It had a strong aftertaste, like caramel and licorice, unique but not unpleasant. The fruit tart was just as strange, and the dark brown and white dustings on its surface were not simply nutmeg and sugar. French cuisine offered an endless array of interesting flavors, but these tastes were completely new.

The Marquis was still standing by the window, his expression unreadable. Finally he rubbed his chin and walked across to her. "I am searching for an English word. Perhaps you can help me. It is what you say when you know something, but not through the paths of logical thought."

"You mean an intuition?"

"It has that meaning, but it is less formal."

"A hunch!"

"Aha. A hunch. A funny word. Yes. A *hunch* after *lunch*. I will remember it that way for the future. Now, I have a hunch about you, Jenny. I think that you love horses—and that you have ridden since you were a little girl. True?"

Jenny thought of breezy fall in New Hampshire, her tenth birthday—her own pony being led out of the stable by her father. "I *love* to ride. But how could you possibly know that?"

"I have my methods." He was smiling.

"But there's no way—" She paused. "You saw the photograph! The one Father carries of me, with my first horse."

"My secret revealed." He reached out and took the cup and plate from her hands. "But did you know that I have, in my own stables, the finest horses in the area? How would you like to come riding with me this afternoon?"

Jenny shook her head. The coffee and sugary pie were spreading warmth and comfort through her cold hands and feet, but riding had always been associated in her mind with happy times. It seemed immoral to think of it now, riding off carefree across the sunny fields of Saint-Amè, when her father was so sick.

He caught the ambivalence of her mood. "Come, Jenny." He stood in front of her and put out his hands to take both of hers. "It is not everyone who is invited to ride with the dashing, handsome Marquis de Saint-Amè."

Jenny smiled at his wry tone. He *was* handsome, but there was never a hint from his manner that he thought of himself that way. And usually he dressed like a tramp—today was a rare exception. "Louis, I would make a wretched riding companion. Leave me here. I will be better by dinner."

"You do not wish to come? That is a pity. It robs me of the only real pleasure that I expect today. But then again . . ." he was still holding her hands, frowning down at her, "perhaps it is true what they say in this country. That Americans talk a great deal and claim they were born in the saddle, but they are indifferent horsemen. Perhaps you do not ride well and you are ashamed at your lack of ability."

It was obvious to Jenny what he was doing. He was needling her. And it was working. She used his hands to lever herself to her feet. "We'll see about that, Louis Villette. Give me ten minutes and I'll meet you at the stables. I'll have to borrow clothes from Cecile. I never expected to be riding in France."

As she left the library Jenny felt another moment of warm dizziness, a blush that ran from her body all along her limbs. God. What was wrong with her? Maybe she should turn around and tell him she could not go riding after all.

Except that she did not *want* to cancel. Now that she had agreed to it, she was looking forward to riding with the Marquis more than anything since she had arrived at the Chateau Cirelle.

Cecile's old riding outfit was plum-colored, made of a soft and impractical velvet. It was a little too full in bust and hip, but it would do well enough. The only problem was that it had a skirt rather than breeches. Jenny would have to ride sidesaddle, which was not the way she preferred. But Cecile's boots were the right size, and the day was just right, too, with a touch of easterly breeze springing up to complement the afternoon sun.

Jenny arrived at the open doors of the stable and stood for a moment, allowing the familiar smells of straw and horses to carry her back. *Stables are stables, here or in England or in America.* She was feeling a steadily rising excitement—Louis Villette had been exactly right, she had *needed* to get out of the chateau, with its hushed atmosphere of sickness and gloom.

The Marquis was already inside the stable. She saw to her surprise that he was saddling a bay mare himself. Shouldn't a groom be doing that? And then she remembered again that the able-bodied young men were away at the front. What a change the war must have made to Louis Villette's lifestyle!

He had changed into narrow black riding trousers, long boots, and a green jacket, tight on his broad chest. While she watched, he threw a saddle onto the horse and cinched the girth. Then he went to a neighboring stall where a big black stallion stood, and lifted its head to look at the underside of the throat. The horse resisted for a moment, pulling away. The sinews in Louis Villette's forearms and the back of his hands stood out with the effort of holding the horse. He frowned, released it, and went on to a third stall that held a young chestnut gelding.

"He's a beauty," said Jenny, walking forward into the stable and peering at the stallion. The Marquis turned at her voice, nodded briefly, and threw a saddle across the back of the young chestnut. The stallion that Jenny was looking at was deep-chested and strongly muscled, with a night-black mane, silky coat, and alert dark eyes. Jenny at once wanted to ride him. "He's a real beauty," she repeated.

"He is," said Louis Villette. He looked at her closely. "And so, if you will permit me to say it, are you. Those clothes suit you very well. I think that American women look their best outside, in the woods and fields, rather than cramped in the drawing room. Now"—he walked across to the little mare and patted her rump, while the full tail swished up and down—"she is ready for you. Let me help you up, and we will be off to explore the fine fields of France."

Jenny patted the mare. "This one? What about the stallion?"

"Hector?" The Marquis frowned. "I think that Céline there is more suited to you."

Jenny came closer to the black stallion. He reached down and nuzzled gently at her neck. "Look, he acts as though he already knows me. I would much rather ride Hector."

Louis Villette laughed. "Jenny, when I said that Americans did not know how to ride, it was only to persuade you to come with me. You knew that; I could see it in your expression. So you do not *have* to prove anything to me. And you would find Hector a bit much to handle."

"Is he difficult? He seems very gentle. And he likes me." The stallion was still nuzzling at her neck and shoulder.

"He is not difficult. But he is enormously strong, and before he came to me he had been poorly trained. His previous owner called him Hector le Diable because the man could not get him to do one single thing that he wanted." Louis Villette had stopped saddling the gelding and stood watching Jenny fondle the stallion. "He is well trained now, but I am usually the only person who rides him. I must say he seems very taken with you."

"Le Diable. That is a much better name for him than Hector." Jenny could not take her eyes off the magnificent horse. He was so sleek and lithe, and the expression in his dark brown eyes was almost human. "Louis, I want to ride him. Even if we don't go far. Look, can't you tell? He *wants* me to ride him. He acts as though he is mine already."

"Hmm. There is ownership, one way or the other. But who conquered whom?" The Marquis stepped over to rub Hector's neck. "And who would ride whom? Jenny, look at these muscles. He is a very strong horse."

"I know. But I really am a good rider, Louis—it sounds like boasting, but I can ride a horse better than any woman I know. I've ridden every kind of mount back home, since I was a little girl." Jenny felt such an intense longing to ride the black stallion that she paused, amazed at the strength of her own emotion.

"I don't know." Louis Villette led Hector out of the stall. "Let me see you saddle him."

Jenny did it quickly and efficiently, patting the smooth flanks as she tightened the girths. The great horse stood silently, head low, until she had finished, then placed its soft muzzle quietly on her shoulder.

"Well?" Jenny looked triumphantly at the Marquis. "Satisfied that I know what I'm doing? He is in love—and so am I. We will be good friends."

"Perhaps." Louis Villette had been impressed at the way she saddled the stallion. "You may ride him, but there are conditions. You must promise that you will not run him too hard. He gets very excited at too fast a clip, and when he is running well, he does not wish to stop."

"I promise." The way she was feeling, Jenny would have promised anything to get up on Hector's broad back.

Louis Villette helped her to mount the sidesaddle, and handed her the reins. She moved on the boxlike seat, trying to adjust to a comfortable position. This type of saddle was new to her, more like an oddly modified regular saddle than a true sidesaddle.

Louis watched her fidgeting. "All right?" he said. "I know it is not a great saddle, but it is the best one here. I may as well take Céline. She was born in these stables. She knows these woods and fields better than I do—I can go out to dinner, climb on her back, and fall asleep knowing she'll bring me back to the chateau. Follow us, and do not stray from the paths."

Her excitement must be showing. "I will, Louis. And thank you." Jenny sat demurely on Hector and waited. If only she could ride him properly, straddling him instead of sitting with her legs over his right side. Half the pleasure in riding such a sturdy, beautiful creature was the feeling of surging power, moving under full control between her legs. He could probably go like the wind. She leaned over and whispered in the stallion's ear. "We will show him, Diable, won't we? We will be great friends, and we will amaze your master."

The horse's ears flickered and pricked up, acknowledging her voice.

"Come on, then, Jenny Marshall." The Marquis was already outside, turning the mare away from the chateau. "I have a proposition for you. You ask everyone, what is the war like? I thought I would show you not only the fields of France, but also a glimpse of the war scar that runs across them."

"Louis! Is that possible? Can we see the trenches?"

"We cannot go so close. But there is a ridge eight kilometers from here that permits a view of the front. A limited view, it is true, and only on clear days. But well worth seeing. And on the way you will smell the wildflowers and taste the sweetest air of France.''

As he twisted around in the saddle to make sure that she was following, sunlight reflected a gleam of metal on his chest. His shirt was open, and something nestled there amid thick hair. Before Jenny could take a close look, he had turned forward again.

She was not sure what she had seen. Curiosity lingered as she rode on after him.

The Chateau Cirelle lay in the valley of the Aire River. Climbing toward the eastern hills, Jenny realized that this was the first time she had looked closely at the countryside around Saint-Amè. On her arrival she had been too tired to notice anything, and since then she had been preoccupied with matters inside the chateau. She sat straight-backed on the stallion and looked around.

The village of Saint-Amè lay a mile to the south-west, away from the direction they were heading. It was a small place, no more than forty or fifty little brick houses crouched around the base of a stone church with its square-sided steeple. The land to the north was planted with grain, the fresh green of its spring growth carpeting the hills. They were passing through a big apple and pear orchard, young fruit already set on the trees and fallen blossoms thick on the ground.

The soft light of late afternoon perfectly matched the satisfied feeling in Jenny's head. Her heightened senses transformed the landscape into a perfect impressionist painting. A Monet, thought Jenny, or a Caillebotte, like the ones that she had seen in New York. But there were dimensions that paintings could never capture. The land here was tamed at a level of detail that Jenny had seen only in Europe—it had been *groomed* by century after century of cultivation, since Roman times. The linnets' nests in the low bushes were small, well made, tidy. Jenny could see a couple of nestlings in one of them, almost ready to leave their home, peeping out over the top of a neat cup of grass, wool, and twigs. The male linnet, red-breasted and red-crowned, perched on an apple tree branch and watched without any sign of fear as the two horses passed. Even the bees that settled on the larkspur and phlox bordering the path looked smaller and calmer than their American cousins. They drowsed on the blossoms, draining the nectar, then flew lazily away toward the setting sun.

Jenny had caught the tranquil mood, drifting quietly along behind the Marquis on her splendid horse. For the first time in days she was at peace. The air was perfumed with wildflowers and clover giving their final burst of fragrance before they closed for the night. The stillness around the two riders was almost hypnotic. And then, without warning, a menacing rumble sounded from far to the north. Jenny could feel the vibrations through the saddle.

The guns of Verdun. The spell was broken.

Beauty, cheek-by-jowl with pure horror. How could this breeze through the apple trees, the chirping of linnets, the grazing cows, and the glory of the red sunset be in the same world as blind gunfire and maimed, dying soldiers? Jenny looked up and saw that past the horizon a dark pall lay on the lip of the rise. God had taken a great brush and sullied the picture with a petulant smear.

Louis Villette turned, sensing her feelings. He slowed to allow the stallion to walk side by side with his mare, and smiled at her. "Imagine. A couple of hundred years ago my ancestors owned all this land. Thousands and thousands of hectares, from here to the Meuse River. They 'allowed' the serfs to cultivate it, in return for a meager little bit of the produce. Those were the days, eh? Back when it really meant something to be an aristocrat."

Jenny again noticed the pendant peeking from his open-necked shirt. It was definitely a cross of some kind, a cruciform shape of dull silver. "But I thought you *still* owned this land," she said.

"Not what we're riding over now. We just passed beyond the boundary of the Cirelle estate. The big change was naturally in the Revolution, in 1789. My ancestors were lucky—they lost land, but kept their heads."

"But you seem to be able to ride freely, anywhere you want." She stared across at him, finding her attention drawn to the half-hidden cross. The rhythmic movement of the medallion on his exposed chest made her very aware of his physical presence. She found herself watching *him* rather than their surroundings. He was attractive here, in the open air, even more than at the chateau.

"Oh, I'm not an unpopular figure," Louis Villette was saying. It took an effort for Jenny to turn her attention back to his words. "All the villagers know me," he went on, "and I know them. I make sure I contribute to the right local causes, I go to weddings and funerals, and I do my best to look after the welfare of the people—especially in Saint-Amè. They would have no reason to bar me from riding or shooting on their land."

"So you go shooting." Jenny did not say it, but she could not see how anyone could take pleasure killing animals, when only a few miles away similar weapons were being used to kill people.

"Now and again. It is something that I picked up from my maternal grandfather, and of course I continued it in Africa." Louis Villette drew a finger all along his right side. "If you could see my ribs, you would know that hunting in Africa goes both ways. Hunting there is like love—one is never sure who is the hunter and who is the game. Or *what* is the game."

Was his English good enough to allow him to make that sort of pun? Or was she reading more than she should from his words?

"What happened to you?" Jenny leaned over, filled with a crazy urge to see the scar of his wound beneath shirt and jacket.

"A little argument with a leopard. He had killed seven villagers. One evening I went on a social visit and was foolish enough to leave my gun behind. His claws got me, and my knife got him—eventually."

His tone was too casual. Jenny sensed that it had been a near-fatal encounter. At least Louis Villette had had a reason for his hunting—not like the bloodthirsty fools at home who slaughtered harmless stags and hares and foxes. She looked at him admiringly. According to her English friends, Frenchmen were bombastic blowhards, full of romantic clichés and always trumpeting their knowledge of love. But Louis Villette was so understated, so casual in describing himself, he was more Boston than a Bostonian.

"Must we talk of blood and hunting?" he was saying.

"There are nicer things in the world. Unless it is true that women are secretly thrilled by such things."

"We are *not* thrilled. Not at all!" Jenny could not tell if he was joking. "We are threatened by them."

"By talk of hunting?" He laughed. "So I am a threat to you, am I? When you have the fastest horse for miles around, and I a slow one. It would be easier for *you* to hunt *me*—but when I look at you, I know that you are more likely to *haunt* me."

She realized now that he was playing with words, finding pleasure in showing off his fluency in English. "I don't think you are a *threat*, Louis, not at all," she said. "In fact, to me you are a *treat*."

It took him a second to grasp, then he was laughing delightedly. "*Touché, Mademoiselle, touché!* I was warned about the superior wit of the American woman; but I never before experienced it."

He was riding close, his left thigh brushing her knees. From the corner of her eye she saw him watching to see how she held the bridle, then turning to stare at her profile. She felt her pulse quickening. He leaned over and put his hand flat on the stallion's back, just behind the saddle. She felt him swaying toward her, as though he intended to vault up behind. She waited, full of delicious anticipation. His hand was sliding forward to her waist. She turned to stare full at him, and found her hand going out involuntarily toward the battered shape of the medallion.

"Louis, what *is* this? I can't keep my eyes off it."

As her forefinger touched the metal, she gave a little cry of surprise. An invisible spark snapped across to her and vibrated along her arm.

But it was Louis Villette who recoiled, not Jenny. He pulled sharply away, widening the gap between the two horses so that Jenny lost contact with him. She felt oddly upset and would have spoken, but at that moment the air was filled with a whistling sound. It grew louder and louder, while she looked around in astonishment. There was a sudden flash of white light fifty yards in front of them.

"Look out! Keep your head down!" cried the Marquis. As he spoke, he urged his mare forward between Jenny and the burst of light. Beyond him, grass heaped up into a geyser of smoke and fire. A plume of dirt rose into the air. A moment later Jenny heard the thunder of the explosion and the air filled with smoking fragments.

She heard Louis Villette grunt in pain, while the mare he was riding gave an agonized scream and started suddenly forward. He was jerked out of the saddle and fell headfirst toward the grassy surface. Jenny saw with horror that his left foot was still in the stirrup. He was being dragged along by the pain-crazed mare.

Jenny had felt no more than a harmless spray of gravel. She dug her heels into Diable and urged him forward. The stallion leaped ahead through the still-falling rain of dirt. He quickly caught up with the mare, burdened as she was with the dragging, cursing body of the Marquis. Jenny headed Diable carefully to the side, making sure that Louis Villette was clear of the pounding hooves.

"Don't try to free yourself," she yelled. "Keep still."

A tall order, for someone being dragged across rough ground. She reached out for the loose reins, missing on the first attempt. Her second pass was successful and she brought Céline under control, slowing the mare to a halt. While they were still moving, the Marquis managed to free his foot from the stirrup. He dropped out of sight behind them. Jenny looped the reins quickly around Hector's saddle and dismounted.

"You calm her down, my friend," she said to the big stallion; then she was running back to Louis Villette, so dizzy with emotion that she could hardly follow a straight line. She dropped to her knees at his side.

"Louis! Are you—"

He groaned and tried to sit up. Then he paused and looked blankly in front of him. Jenny realized that in the mad chase her riding skirt and underskirt had split from top to bottom. Louis Villette, his face a couple of inches away from her bare thighs, was staring at them in bemused fashion. In embarrassment, she lifted his head higher, resting it against the soft velvet of her jacket and tugging her skirt back into position. He sighed, and his eyes closed.

"Louis, are you all right?" Even as she spoke she could see that he was clearly not all right. He had been hauled across rough ground, over earth and stones and bushes. His riding jacket was in shreds, and there were rips and smudges along his shirt and trousers. Most of his chest was showing, revealed through a gaping flap of shirt. She could see the scar he had mentioned, the African leopard wound. It ran all the way along the right lower ribs, a purplish ridge of scar tissue. Now that line was crossed by another half dozen scratches running at right angles all the way down to his waist.

His face was smudged with dirt. There was the blue mark of a bruise on his forehead, and his eyes had closed. Alarmed, Jenny put her head down to his chest. As she heard the heartbeat, slow and steady, her eyes focused on the cross. It was just a few inches away from her. It had been pulled out from the shirt and lay in the hollow of his throat. Instead of its earlier dullness, the dark surface glittered with vagrant specks of light.

Jenny found her hand reaching up to it. This time there was no moment of electrical contact. The metal felt chillingly cold, sticking to her fingertips. There was a vibration deep within it.

Jenny shivered and sat upright.

"Louis!"

To her relief he responded. He muttered a French word that she did not understand and reached to pull her close to him. His eyes were half open and still unfocused. He drew her body down until her face was next to his with the cross against her throat. For one moment she felt that chill of cold metal, quickly swept away within a bewildering rush of erotic desire.

Take him, said a voice within her. *Possess him. Devour him.*

Jenny grasped his head in her hands, pushed it back to the grassy surface, and moved her mouth down to his. Her lips were hot and swollen, aching for contact.

And at the last moment she was pushed away, in a pang of separation that brought her close to fainting.

"No." The Marquis was looking up, through her and beyond her. "Not now, not to this one." He groaned and grabbed at his chest.

"What's wrong?" Jenny had been staring into his eyes, and for one moment she had seen her own need mirrored there. Now he showed only pain, and she had herself under control. But her heart was still pounding so hard she was convinced he must hear it.

She looked away, wondering how much her face betrayed her. When she turned back, he had tucked the cross inside his torn clothing and was sitting up.

"Thank you, Mam'selle Jenny," he said. His voice was shaky. "Thank you most kindly. You know, of course, that you saved my life? And that surely deserved a kiss."

He managed to laugh. She realized that he had turned the whole incident on its head, dismissing it from further discussion. (Clever, and gracious. But she had wanted more than any kiss—even now she could not believe the strength of that momentary desire.)

He stood up, reaching out a hand to help her to her feet. As she gripped his left hand, he winced and turned the wrist gingerly. "Ouch. Nothing broken, but plenty of bruises. I believe we have finished our riding excursion for today. And a little brandy, I think, before we consider dinner."

"You need a lot more than brandy." Jenny was ready to bury what had just happened under civilized banter, but he was still hurting, limping along beside her. "You must have those wounds attended to. You need swabbing, and disinfectant, and bandages. Let's get back to the chateau."

"We are in agreement on that at least, though my wounds are minor." They walked, very close to each other, to the edge of the wood. The mare and stallion were quietly grazing as though nothing had happened. Louis Villette went across and checked Céline's condition. "Two tiny splinters of shell fragment, here in her neck. We have all been very lucky. That misfired shell could easily have killed everyone. Perhaps that will teach me not to bring people so close to the front."

"It was not your fault. I *wanted* to come."

"I should have discouraged it." He helped her to mount Hector, then swung with a grunt onto the mare's back. "But you proved your point, Jenny Marshall. You are indeed an excellent horsewoman. However, for the rest of today—" he winced as his left wrist took a pull on the reins, "for the rest of today, let us agree to hold ourselves to a slow walk."

CHAPTER
FOURTEEN

By the time they reached the chateau and began to unsaddle the horses, it was clear that Louis Villette's ankle was a problem. It had borne his full weight as he hung from the stirrup, and it was swelling rapidly. Even a slight pressure on it was uncomfortable. The Marquis cursed and talked of the way it would interfere with his work. Too bad, said Jenny. But she was not displeased. Louis Villette worked too hard; he needed a few days' rest.

She took over the chore of unsaddling and rubbing down Hector and Céline, while the Marquis sat on a bale of hay and examined his left wrist.

"I think this will be all right," he said. "It was just numb. I may have a bruise tomorrow."

"How about your ankle?"

That earned a grimace and a shake of his head. "Less good." Jenny went on working, aware of his eyes on her. The split in her skirt made modesty impossible. When she bent over or stretched upward to sponge the horses' backs, Cecile's ruined skirt gaped open to the hip. She tried to keep that side away from the Marquis, but it made her movements too awkward. After a while she did not bother.

So he was seeing more than he should. Well, he must have seen a lot of women in his time; and he had made it clear enough earlier that her body was of no great interest to him.

By the time both horses were groomed, Jenny was tired out. The shock of the shell's near miss and the runaway ride had left her weak and weary. She was not looking forward to a formal dinner; when the Marquis suggested an alternative, she jumped at the idea.

"Dinner in my rooms," he said. "Cecile and Charles have plans for tonight; they are going over to Pierrefitte to meet friends. Why sit at a table with this ankle, when I can lounge comfortably on a sofa in my chambers?" He was limping at her side, refusing her offer of a supporting arm. "Shall we say, half an hour? That will give you time to change, if you want to."

If you want to. That was a delicate way of putting it. She stank, of horse sweat and human sweat. She stripped to the skin in her room and swabbed herself all over with warm water. The outfit she picked out was a simple green frock, more suited to afternoon tea than a formal dinner. Another one of Cecile's loaners, but unusually demure for her tastes— did it make Louis Villette uncomfortable to see someone else wearing his daughter's clothes? If so, he showed no sign.

The shoes were high-heeled open-toed sandals of dark green. Jenny looked at her toes, peeping out from the front, and thought ruefully of Louis Villette's toes. On his injured foot they had swollen so much that he had been forced to remove his shoe as soon as he dismounted the mare.

The afternoon was already like a confusing dream poorly remembered on the morning after. The shock of the explosion was still vivid, with its plume of fire and flying debris; but she could not recall her emotional state when she had leaned over Louis. More than that, she could not *imagine* those feelings. Such an urge to possess a man sexually was beyond her experience—beyond her fantasies. Jenny stood in front of the mirror, almost ready to believe it had never happened. But if it were to happen . . .

The chiming of the clock in the main hall brought her out of her daydreaming. Five, six, seven. It had been an hour since she had left him, not the half hour he had suggested. She hurried through the main part of the building, meeting no one on the way, and headed for the stairs of the southwest tower.

He was in his chambers, sitting on the sofa with his left leg straight out along it. But he had not changed for dinner. In fact, as far as Jenny could see, he had done nothing more than remove his riding jacket. His chest still showed the bloodied scrapes and cuts, and he wore the same ripped shirt.

She went at once to his side. He pointed to the table by the window, where four dishes sat with silver covers. A bottle of wine, a square of muslin, and a decanter stood alongside them.

"Monge and the cook did their part," he said. "Duck Montmorency, and as good an example as you will find anywhere. But I am afraid that I failed in my duties. The best accompaniment for the dish is a Grands Echézeaux, my favorite of all the great burgundies. As we say, it gives the drinker a liter of new blood. I could do with that. But this bottle had thrown more deposit than usual. I was in the process of decanting it when I felt a mighty urge to sit down." He gave a wry smile. "And here you find me."

"Did you send Monge for a doctor?" Jenny walked to the table and poured two glasses of the red wine. The sight of him had brought back a faint echo of the afternoon, of her body pressing down on his.

He accepted the glass and shook his head firmly. "Of course not. A doctor, for a few scratches? Why would I do that? It is nothing to worry about. I am tired, not wounded." He took a substantial mouthful of wine.

Expecting some special treat, Jenny did the same. The burgundy had a distinctive flavor, smooth and almost perfumed, with a pronounced aftertaste that she didn't like at all. She put the glass down on the table.

Louis Villette had been watching her face and saw the grimace. "No?" he said.

"No. It's like tea that's been stewed for an hour."

"Spoken like a true lady." He took another mouthful and sighed with pleasure. "That is *le tanin*, Jenny. This bottle has more of it than usual. I have yet to meet a woman who likes a wine high in tannin. But fortunately we have other options. There is a chilled bottle of Chevalier-Montrachet open in the bucket."

Jenny poured a glass of the white wine, refusing to allow him to stand up and do it for her. She sipped it, nodded, and came back to Louis Villette's side. She frowned down at him. "All right, that's enough wine tasting. Look at you. We're going to need swabs."

"Swabs? You came here to dinner."

"Not with a man who was dragged across a field and hasn't even the energy to wash. We're going to do what you should have done when you first came in, instead of worrying about your wines. We're going to need disinfectant, too. Do you have brandy?"

He was looking up at her with startled blue eyes. "If you are suggesting that we use my best Napoleon brandy for *that*—"

Jenny felt a perverse pleasure when he shook his head in horror. "Unless you have real disinfectant, yes, I am."

He sighed. "Disinfectant is in the bedroom. There is brandy, too."

"Then come along." She helped him to his feet and supported him as he limped into the next room (clutching to his ragged chest the decanter of Grands Echézeaux and the bottle of Chevalier-Montrachet—a true Frenchman!). He didn't really need support, but she liked being in charge. He was strangely quiet—much as he had been on the way back to the chateau; preoccupied, more than injured.

Once he was comfortable on the bed, she went to the dresser and poured a couple of ounces of cognac into a balloon glass. "Drink your wine. The brandy is for swabs or emergencies. Now lie back."

He grunted as she gently lifted his left leg up onto the bed. "My dear Jenny, I am not a baby." But he did not protest as she peeled back the woolen sock.

The flesh of his ankle was puffy, with a bluish white tinge. Below that the toes had turned an angry red. Jenny shook her head, pressing gently on the instep. "Does that hurt much?"

"Not bad. Jenny, I told you, I am really in no need—"

"I don't think anything is broken. But I'm going to apply iodine and a cold-water bandage. Sit still, now."

She returned the foot gently to the floor. He went on drinking wine steadily while she wrapped the ankle firmly in layer after layer of water-soaked cheesecloth. "Right. Try standing up." He came slowly to his feet. "And put some weight on it."

He leaned to the left, gradually transferring his balance that way. "Good as new."

"Don't overdo it." Jenny looked at the neat bandage and

felt great satisfaction. She swallowed another mouthful of wine. "All right, that's the foot done. Next phase. Shirt off."

"Jenny!"

"Don't 'Jenny!' me." She sniffed at the disinfectant he had pointed out to her on the shelf of the dresser. It should be all right; it seemed to be the French equivalent of witch hazel. "You should have done something about those cuts much earlier."

"A great success as a riding lesson, eh? Not the way I had planned it."

"No changes of subject, please. We've got work to do. Take your shirt off."

"Jenny, you are a tyrant. If I take my shirt off, my insides will fall out."

"You have a horrible and childish imagination. No delays. Shirt off." She recognized the roles they were playing. She was the stern grown-up, he was the naughty little boy.

"Negotiation." He held out his empty glass. "I need my own best medicine. More treatment, in exchange for more wine."

"A bargain." Now that Jenny knew he was not seriously hurt, there was strange pleasure in giving orders to Louis Villette. "More wine, and then shirt off. How do Frenchmen manage to drink so much and not get drunk?"

"Ah." He looked at her seriously as he unbuttoned his torn shirt. "That is our special relationship with the grape. We cultivate the great vineyards, and in return we are cultivated by them. In return for our providing their well-being, they keep us happy. Are your men different? And your women, too?"

Jenny looked around the bedroom before she answered. The mention of 'her men' made banter impossible. She had looked in to see her father when she came back to the chateau, and there was no reason for lightheartedness. Somehow, in this quiet bedroom with its elegant brass-headed bed and the great globe in the corner, she had been able to forget for a few minutes. Now it came flooding back. She picked up her glass and deliberately took a big swig of wine.

"Well?" He was frowning. "Jenny, are you all right?"

Was she? Of course not. But this task came first. "I'm a little tired." She looked down at him, sitting with his shirt half off, and fought back the shiver that ran through her. "Did you know, Louis, that in America there is an effort under way to ban alcoholic drink?"

He stared at her in comical disbelief. His eyes were so bright, they seemed to spear her with their blue gaze. He reached up and took her hand in both of his.

"To ban wine?" he said. "Jenny, you are joking with me, as I was a moment ago with you. Or else your country has gone truly mad." He held up his glass to the light. "Look at that glow, more precious than rubies. Wine is a gift from God, like laughter and music and loving. Perhaps you will also prohibit singing and lovemaking? My poor Jenny, your people are so young and confused. You fled the Old World and thought you could escape human sorrows. We who have stayed here know better. We cling to the old, even when it means sacrifice. It would be easy to surrender to the Germans, to let them march to Paris and impose their terms of victory. But we cannot do that—not and remain French. Our pride is centuries deep, the source of life itself."

His voice was soft, cradling her in its quiet force and conviction. Jenny found it difficult to look away from him, or to take her hand from his. At last she reached out and began to remove his tattered shirt.

His chest was deep, strongly muscled, and furred with black hair. It was also matted by lines of dried blood, running from his pectoral muscles to the top of his trousers. There was a large abraded area above his navel, where the scratches all ran together. Wounds aplenty. But of the cross and chain that she had seen earlier, there was no sign.

Why did he remove the cross, yet not bother to treat his wounds?

Jenny puzzled over that as she picked up a swab, drenched it with iodine, and witch hazel, and drew it downward along the line of a scratch skirting his left nipple. With the dried blood out of the way, she saw to her relief that Louis was right, the scratches were shallow. As she applied more iodine, another chest wound caught her attention. Right on the breastbone, partly obscured by new growth of hair, his flesh showed a cruciform scar. It was quite symmetrical, two inches long and two across. The scar tissue of the cicatrix was sharp-edged, quite different from the ridged and purple scar over his ribs. She paused, holding the cloth motionless against his chest.

"What have you been doing with yourself? This looks like a burn."

"Exactly what it is." The deep chest heaved as the Marquis drew in a long breath. He was lying flat on his back, eyes staring up at the ceiling. "Something that hurt a good deal more than anything I have suffered today."

"But how did you do it? Surely you must have known it was hot before it touched you."

"I ought to have known. But oddly enough, Jenny, I didn't expect anything of the kind." He touched his hand lightly to the top of her head while she bent low over his chest. "You see, I am often a fool, not only when it comes to taking innocent people into dangerous war zones."

She was frowning over the long cut, swabbing it clean so that no source of infecting material could remain. The touch of his hand on her head created an unexpected tension between them. His other hand appeared suddenly in front of her face, holding her wineglass.

"Here. Since you are so busy, the least that I can do is offer you this." He tilted the glass, and Jenny was forced to swallow.

"No more," she said. "A nurse ought to remain sober." She took a quick glance at the bottle of white wine by the bedside and saw that over half of it was gone—and Louis himself had been drinking only the red Grands Echézeaux. No wonder she was perspiring as she worked! She began to clean a fourth scratch as he continued:

"But it is certainly good that I am the injured one and you are the skilled nurse. I dread to think what would happen if you had fallen off Hector, and I with my clumsiness was trying to swab your chest."

The image shot at once into Jenny's mind: Louis Villette, bending over her on the wide bed, delicately sponging her bare breasts. The vision was so intense and tactile that Jenny had to pause in her work. Her heart was beating rapidly, and the cross-shaped scar in front of her eyes swam closer and filled the whole field of view.

She stayed with her head bent, glad that his hand was still touching her hair. It shielded her expression from him. The memory of the afternoon became bright and immediate. But it was not the memory that was so disturbing—it was the fact that her mind clung to it avidly, rather than recoiling in horror or disgust.

Jenny forced herself to concentrate on her work. She had only two more wounds to clean. She took a fresh swab and poured iodine. She was perspiring, and so was he. There was a sheen of sweat on his bare midriff, and she could smell the scent of his body. Not unpleasant at all. Lavender, strong tobacco, and some other indefinable aroma from the body itself.

One of the remaining wounds was longer than the rest. It extended past his navel, down past the point where she could see. The lower part of the gash was hidden by his belt and trousers, the upper part ran up into the scar on his breastbone. Some branch on the ground must have been trapped under his body, scoring his unprotected flesh until it was broken off by the force of his movement. It would be the most dangerous injury of all, especially if a fragment of bark or twig had lodged beneath the skin. That wound had to be thoroughly cleaned.

Jenny eased his trousers downward a little over his body to reveal the lower end of the scratch. The lines of musculature of his midriff were as perfect as any sculpture. She cleaned the wound carefully, working her way upward and concentrating all her attention on those few square inches of flesh.

While she was working, Louis Villette moved his hand slightly, from her head down to the nape of her neck and her shoulders. He was rubbing them soothingly, palpating the muscles beneath the skin.

"So tense, Jenny," he said, his voice resonating down to his fingertips. "Such tight muscles, when you should be so relaxed. And your touch on me is so gentle, so tender."

"Louis." Jenny's own voice came from far away. "Louis, where is the cross?"

"Cross?" He was suddenly tense.

"The one you wore on your chest this afternoon. What did you do with it?"

There was a sigh, of complaint or pain, and the whispered words, "Lord, Lord, Lord." Louis Villette took his hand slowly from her shoulders and reached into his trousers pocket.

Jenny looked down along his body. As the dark cross appeared, her hand reached out to take it from his hand. This time it was warm to her touch, warm and soothing. She placed it over the scar on his chest and closed her eyes. The afternoon's urgency became a softer ache.

"Louis?" Her voice was a whisper.

He said nothing.

"Louis? Do you . . . . care for me?"

His laugh had no humor. "Too much. Too much. *Lord, Lord, Lord.*" There was a groan of resignation. "Thy will be done."

She heard the change in his voice on those last words. But who was he talking to? Jenny opened her eyes. His hand was clasping the cross, and he was staring straight at her. But this was a different Louis, a younger, carefree man, his eyes alight with longing.

"Jenny," he said. "My Jenny."

He did not speak again, but he pulled her head once more to his chest and began to stroke her throat. Jenny, crouched over his body, was unable to move or breathe. The dizziness she had felt earlier in the day overwhelmed her. Her sensations had been drawn to one place, tightly focused into the single locus of Louis Villette's hands. She could hear blood beating in her inner ear, sense the tension in the muscles along her back and haunches, and feel the dizziness that came from holding the same bent position for too long. She had finished cleaning his injuries. Now she was waiting. The sponge dropped to the floor. She had no control over her body's movements. She was waiting, waiting, waiting.

Why doesn't he move? said the disembodied Jenny. *What is he doing? Why doesn't he do something?*

When he brought his hand around to her chin and turned her head so that she was staring into those brilliant blue eyes, Jenny knew that the wait was over. There was no question in her mind what came next. His hands were caressing her shoulders, peeling back the green frock, moving it away from her breasts and down her body. He kissed her gently on the mouth, murmured words of love, and lifted her easily along his body so that his lips could reach her nipples.

Jenny clutched at his head, stroking his hair, carried away on a rising tide of excitement.

"Be careful, Louis," she said, seeing the urgency that tightened the muscles of his body. "Dear Louis. Be careful. Don't hurt your ankle."

He laughed, deep in his throat, and put his hands to her breast. "My ankle! Jenny, my love, you are a wonderful, kind woman. You touch me. You touch my heart." He lifted her above him so that she was staring into the blue of his eyes. She saw tremendous tenderness there, tremendous urgency. His gaze went into her soul.

He held her close and rolled over on the bed so that he was on top. She felt him removing the rest of her clothes, and then his own, and she automatically said, "Louis, Louis, what are we doing?" at the same time as her body pushed responsively against his.

He paused for a moment and pulled away from her, while she longed for him and hated the stupidity of her words. Then his mouth came down on hers, warm and thrilling, still with the taste of burgundy on his lips. "I cannot hear 'no,' my love," he said softly. "Now I must give back to you the joy that you give me."

Jenny lay with eyes closed while his hands and lips roamed everywhere on her body. "Oh, Louis," she said. "Louis, Louis, Louis." She was being carried away on a warm and gentle stream, a broad tide of feeling too strong to resist. His tongue moved over her like an artist's brush, painting passion and intense pleasure. She nuzzled his chest, feeling the hair against her cheek and tasting the iodine that she had applied.

She was past any thought of resistance, but Louis did not hurry. He was exploring her whole body, touching her neck, her earlobes, her cheeks, her breasts; he moved on steadily to her belly and inner thighs. "Open to me, Jenny, open all to me," said the soft voice, and then he was caressing the furred mount and the sensitive lower lips. While his fingers slid easily inside her, his mouth again found her nipples. The combination was too much to bear. Jenny gasped, while the soft lower touch smoothly and knowingly explored her and his mouth wandered across her neck and breasts.

His touch found a new pleasure point on her lower body, and Jenny cried out. "No, Louis, no!"

"Do not say that, Jenny." His voice was a whisper. "Listen to your own body."

The gentle stream that had been carrying her along was suddenly rushing into a ravine, water whitening and roaring around her. She could hear a steady pounding in her ears—her own heartbeat. It was time. She reached up to grasp his shoulders and pull his body closer.

"Not yet, Jenny, not yet." He moved lower, his tongue seeking what his fingers had found before. Jenny's back arched upward, lifting her from the bed. She groaned, a long moan of pleasure and pleading.

Not yet, Jenny, not quite yet.

Did he say that, or did she imagine it? She clutched at his shoulders, on the very brink of some unguessable precipice, while his body adjusted its position above her.

His organ was touching the entrance. She was waiting for him . . . breathless, suspended in limbo while he teased her. He was hovering on the edge of her . . . hovering . . .

When it finally came, the long, steady entry seemed for a moment like a release of tension. But then he was moving deep inside her and she was lifting to a whole new plane of pleasure. He thrust rhythmically into her, responding to or controlling the pattern of her pelvic movements. Jenny did not know which. She had no control, of her body's movements or of anything else in the world.

After a few minutes the orgasm, her first ever, came bursting inside her, uncontrollable, filling her whole body with heat. She cried out wordlessly and dug her fingers into his back. He was pushing strongly inside her, hard and swollen, and she was drowning in pleasure—dying of pleasure. It was another eternity before she felt the quiver and jerk of his own release, throbbing within her.

He sighed then, as though with unendurable grief, and said, "Ah, Jenny, Jenny, Jenny." His body relaxed, to lie flat against her.

She held him tight, rocking him back and forth, feeling the sweat between them. For the first time since they had begun, it occurred to her that he might be in pain. There had been no sign of it in his actions, but the salt of their sweat must be stinging the scratches on his chest.

She could feel him dwindling within her, slowly withdrawing. She held him tighter, then turned her head to look across the bed. The swab she had been holding was still there, where it had fallen from her nerveless hands. Jenny reached across and picked it up.

"Louis."

He opened his eyes and smiled at her.

"Louis. Roll over. I have to do your chest."

"My chest feels wonderful."

"But I might have got—got spit in your wounds."

"Your spit would never harm me." But after he had kissed her gently on the lips, he rolled onto his back.

"Lie still." She took the iodine and swab and gently cleansed all the wounds on his chest a second time. She did it slowly and lovingly, aware that his eyes had opened again and he was staring at her naked body. He reached out and touched the curve of her buttocks. "Jenny, my love, you have a perfect body. Perfect."

She went on swabbing the long scratch that went all the way down to his abdomen. His penis lay slack against his belly, shrunken and vulnerable like a closed flower bud. She touched it timidly, and dabbed the swab along it. Louis sighed, and his organ stirred under her hand. Jenny watched in wonder as it grew at her touch, pushing its broad blind head upward along his stomach.

She moved her fingers along the underside of it, with its smooth and silky skin. "Does it—" She hesitated. "Can it grow big and hard again?"

Louis did not reply. He did not need to. While Jenny held his penis, it had been growing steadily in length and thickness.

Louis's hand moved to her neck, pushing her mouth gently downward. It was clear what he wanted. After a moment's hesitation, she took the bulbous head between her lips. The soft, tender skin was warm, and as she moved her mouth on the shaft, it gradually swelled to full hardness. Louis murmured with pleasure.

He ran his other hand from the curve of her buttocks to touch her between her legs. After a few minutes his grip moved to her waist, turning her body. He positioned her above him, then slid her slowly down onto his erect organ. The penetration this time was quite different, a long, steady flow of quiet pleasure.

"The way of the lazy Frenchman." He was smiling up at her. "This time, you do all the work."

Jenny moved up and down on him, learning the muscle movements and the rhythm. It was good to give him pleasure. Better like this in some ways, because she could control his movement within her. She would not reach a climax herself, she was already sated, but there was indescribable pleasure in their closeness and in the compression of her sex organ on his.

It was a real surprise to feel herself reawakening, tightening on him as he reached up to take her nipples in his mouth. His hands moved again to her buttocks, pressing them hard and pulling her all the way onto him. Jenny looked down, seeing the high color in his cheeks and the swollen veins in his forehead.

"Louis. Your wounds."

It was a token protest. Again he began to stroke and kiss, to whisper words of love. She felt new heat in the pit of her stomach. The river was here again, and once more Jenny was moving off downstream. He was pushing harder beneath her, more urgent and insistent. She closed her eyes and gave herself up to pure sensation.

Faster and faster, harder and harder. But this time the climax was more difficult to achieve. Instead of carrying her away on its great tide, it became an exquisite agony, an orgasm that Jenny was squeezing out of her own soul. She rode him hard, forcing him deeper into her, gasping with the effort.

It took forever to arrive, but finally it came. She gave a great cry, while wave after wave of compression tightened her onto him. Louis shuddered beneath her, lunging upward to his own moment of dying.

This time he stayed hard within her for a long time. She crouched astride his body and felt herself dissolved into a warm pool of lassitude. There was no energy left in her. She stared mindlessly down into his face. He looked content, for the first time in days. His blue eyes were half closed, and there was a dreamy little smile on his face.

He was drifting off to sleep. Jenny eased to his side, careful not to disturb him. If she woke him, she was afraid that he might get up and leave. She did not want that. She wanted time with him—time to lie close, time to drift and dream.

She stretched as much as she could without disturbing their position, and felt the flex and play of unsuspected muscles in her thighs and lower belly. She would be sore tomorrow. Louis had been gentle, but he had been very insistent.

She was too overwhelmed to feel sleepy. Too surprised— too *shocked*. That was the feeling. Underneath everything else, under the glow of pleasure, the lazy, stretched-out mindless languor of physical satisfaction, under all that warmth and sweetness, Jenny was shocked that her secret mental image of Louis Villette as lover had become reality. She was shocked at the strength and beauty of his body; shocked that lovemaking could be so intense; shocked that she felt no trace of remorse or guilt at what had happened; most of all, shocked at the things he had done to her or asked her to do to him— and at the response of her own body and mind.

She yawned, and closed her eyes.

You touch me, you fill my heart. . . .

He had said it of her, but she could say it equally well of him. When he first kissed her, his lips still carrying the soft perfumed taste of his favorite wine, she had given up thought of resistance. When, a minute later, his mouth found her breasts, she had given up thought of modesty.

You are more beautiful naked than I would have dreamed. . . .

He had said that, when he eased off her dress and flimsy undergarment, to leave her naked except for the open-toed sandals; but she could have equally said it of him. His whole body was strong and trim, with well-defined muscles and white skin. She looked him over from head to foot. Louis Villette was beautiful. Jenny was drowsily aware of his thigh next to hers, and of the swell of his chest.

He was more than beautiful. He was perfect.

CHAPTER FIFTEEN

The Sacred Way's appearance did little to justify its high-flown name. It was a rutted two-lane road, repaired and resurfaced every few feet of its length. In places it was little more than a broad line of gravel.

But it was certainly busy. The truck that Clive Dunnay was traveling in encountered a continuous convoy of vehicles moving in the opposite direction, ferrying supplies and soldiers from Bar-le-Duc and Souilly to Verdun. Parties of workmen all the way along it were filling in holes in the road and shoring up its broken shoulders.

After two minutes lying on the pallet in the back, Clive had moved up to sit with the driver. The springs in the truck were terrible. The front seat, uncomfortable as it was, at least had some padding. It was better to be shaken and jarred out in the fresh air than to take a worse pounding on the dark canvas-covered truck bed.

The driver accepted Clive's change of seat with a nod. "That proves you're getting better, sir—a ride in the back of this crapheap will kill or cure you. I wish I'd my own truck, but it's having transmission problems."

Private Holloway was a broken-toothed Cockney who drove with a cigarette perpetually between his lips. He rolled them one-handed, somehow manipulating tobacco and paper without running off the road. For the first few miles he had driven with eyes half closed, exhausted or more likely hung over. Now he was waking up.

Maybe it was the change in surroundings, thought Clive. Although they were only five miles from the field hospital where he had spent three interminable weeks, the pall of battlefield smoke had been replaced by bright sun and high, scattered cloud. Occasional craters marred the rolling ground, but they only served to contrast with this region of pasture and farmland, carpeted with dandelions and dotted with grazing cows. Clive breathed in lungfuls of fragrant air. This was paradise.

The truck suddenly stopped by the side of the road. Clive looked at the driver in alarm. If they broke down here, he would have trouble walking more than a few yards, with his crutch and injured leg.

"Problems?"

Holloway shook his head and pointed to the sky. His face had come alight. "Look at them!"

Far off to the right Clive could make out three dots moving steadily north. "Airplanes? Will they attack?"

"Not us. French planes, sir—Nieuports. On their way to bomb the German lines." Holloway watched with rapt attention until they disappeared from sight in the morning haze. Then he shook his fist. "That's the way to fight a war! Right above the Germans—instead of splashing along like a toad in the muck. Those fellows up there are lucky." In his enthusiasm he had allowed his cigarette to go out without rolling its replacement.

They damn well *have* to be lucky, thought Clive. Did Holloway know that the life expectancy of a flier at the front was less than a month?

They were finally leaving the Voie Sacrée, making a sharp turn to the left onto an agricultural road, mere parallel cow paths wandering off into hillier country. The ride became bumpier. Clive's leg was beginning to throb again, though on the positive side he realized that for the first time in weeks he was not continuously aware of his testicles. But that might change if the road became any worse.

His thoughts were interrupted by another cry from Holloway and the sudden buzz of low-flying aircraft. Staccato bursts of machine gun fire echoed across the valley ahead.

"Dogfight!" shouted the private, and the truck halted again. He climbed down from the driver's seat. "Come on. Let's get a good look."

Good look! The aircraft were roaring right overhead. Clive opened the door and carefully climbed down. The jar when his injured leg met the ground made him grit his teeth, but that concern vanished when he heard the stutter of a machine gun. He leaned back on the side of the truck, squinting up into the brightness of a breezy May sky.

Holloway was shading his eyes with one hand and pointing up with the other. "I told you, sir—a Nieuport 17. And the German's a Fokker, an E-1. Get him!" He was screaming up into the air. "Get the bastard!"

The two aircraft banked steeply and flew directly into the sun. Clive could see nothing but glare for a few seconds. When he picked them up again, the smaller plane was hard on the tail of the other and both were heading straight for the truck in a power dive. Clive crouched against the fender, but the two airmen had no eyes for anything below them. They pulled out no more than a hundred feet up, close enough to make out the painted cross on the German monoplane and a marking like a bird's head on the stubby biplane that pursued it. Spurts of fire coughed from the machine gun mounted on the French plane. Bullets pumped into the Fokker's fuselage and engine.

"Got him," cried Holloway. "The German's a goner! Oh, no. Don't follow him, man—he wants you to do it!"

As he was shouting and waving, the Fokker used its downward speed to sweep up into a tight vertical loop. At the top, when the plane was flying along upside down, the pilot made a half-roll. He was suddenly in level flight, right side up and moving in the opposite direction.

"I knew it. An Immelmann! Our fellow must be a beginner." Holloway was practically crying, his arms reaching up to the planes. "Don't try to follow him, man! You'll never make it."

His scream was unnecessary. The pilot of the Nieuport already knew he was in trouble. Trying to follow the German into the loop but with slightly less airspeed, he found his plane close to a stall while its propeller was still pointing vertically upward. To save himself he was forced to give full left rudder, turning in that direction and converting his ascent back into a dive. By the time he had regained full control the

Fokker was on his tail. Spandau machine-gun bullets stitched a pattern along the side of the plane, and no new acrobatics could shake his pursuer.

But as the two planes again hurtled toward the ground, a stream of smoke appeared from the German's engine. The earlier French bullets were finally doing their work. The German pilot ignored the widening plume of black and held the Fokker glued to its target. His bullets ripped and shredded the right-hand wings of the biplane. It began to yaw in its flight, and at the same moment the engine of the pursuing Fokker burst into flames. The pilot was lost behind a dense cloud of black. Unable to see, he turned away and put the plane into a climb. Within a few seconds, flames were spreading along the fuselage. The Fokker turned, slipped sideways, and fell. Its engine went silent. The propeller jammed to a fixed position. There were five long seconds of quiet, flaming fall, then the *crump* of explosive impact less than a mile away.

"Got him!" Holloway was shaking his clenched fist. "Got the swine."

But the Nieuport was in bad shape. It was wobbling back toward them, engine coughing and sputtering. It moved in a strange crabwise fashion, yawing badly and losing height. While they watched, it banked and executed a slow circle.

"Looking for somewhere to land," said Holloway. "Can't make it back to base. Come on." He climbed into the truck, and Clive laboriously followed. They could see the vibrations in the Nieuport as its erratic motor shook the whole structure. Strips of fabric fluttered from the lower right wing. The pilot was struggling to maintain a straight line, heading for a small field no more than half a mile away. When he was almost there, he must have realized that he was going to overshoot. He pulled the nose up and stalled out twenty feet above the ground.

There were a couple of seconds of silent fall, then the crash. The plane collapsed on impact into a tangle of broken struts and stringers.

"Hold tight," cried Holloway. "We have to get him out before it catches fire."

He had begun the day a sleepy but careful driver. Now all

caution had disappeared. When a hedge sat between them and the crashed Nieuport, Holloway did not look for a gate. He set a course straight for the thin pillar of black smoke and accelerated.

Jesus Christ. Clive grabbed at the windshield with both hands. *If there's a ditch on the other side . . .*

Before the thought was complete, they were through in a shower of twigs, leaves, and hawthorn blossom. They could see the wreckage now, the broken tail of the Nieuport sticking up like a twisted cross. The plane had narrowly cleared two trees and piled into a haystack. The private drove the truck right up to the wreck.

"He's still in there!" he cried. "Must be unconscious. Come on."

Clive found intention easier than action. He dropped out of the truck and found himself flat on his face in the mud. His good leg had buckled under him. He struggled to his feet and began to hobble after the energetic private. Holloway was quite right. The pilot, complete with goggles, flight cap, and leather jacket, lay at an unnatural angle against the control panel. Tongues of flame were licking up the fuselage from the shattered engine, and smoke streamered out in black and white ropes.

Holloway wasted no time. He pushed a broken piece of lower wing out of the way and reached up toward the pilot.

"He's alive! Help me get him out."

Easier said than done. Clive was balanced on his right leg, bracing himself against the fuselage. He leaned into the cockpit and grabbed one of the pilot's arms. The man groaned, and the limb twisted at an unnatural angle in Clive's grasp.

"It's broken."

"Pull anyway." The private had undone the pilot's webbing belt that held him in the cockpit, and was lifting his legs. "A broken arm won't kill him."

Clive grabbed a double handful of leather flying jacket. His eyes filled with tears from the smoke. He pulled as hard as he could, while Holloway gave a great heave at the other end. Suddenly they were all tumbling toward the ground together. Apparently the man had been conscious enough to help with a sturdy shove of his feet. Clive shouted in pain as

Holloway's head banged his left knee. There was an ominous sizzling sound from the Nieuport's engine.

"Away!" shouted Clive, and the three men scrambled and crawled to hide behind the truck. The Nieuport became a solid tree of flames. In a few more seconds it convulsed with the explosion of the gas tank. A shower of burning struts and fabric flew over them and dropped smoldering fragments onto the truck itself.

While Holloway was jumping around to make sure that the fabric top did not catch fire, Clive bent over the fallen pilot. One arm was obviously broken, and there was some sort of head wound. It was difficult to tell how serious that was, because the face and forehead were blackened with smoke.

Clive carefully removed the goggles, and the man looked up with glassy, semiconscious eyes.

"Thanks, pal," he whispered.

Clive sat up straight. "You speak English!"

"Yeah. You, too." The pilot coughed. "So what?"

"What are you doing, flying a French airplane?"

The man did not reply at once. He was staring dreamily up at the sky. "Hey," he said. "Did you see that Hun go down? My second. Guess we got each other good, eh?"

"You're American!"

"No kidding?" The pilot was coughing again, forcing smoke and fumes out of his lungs. "You sort of have to be when you're from Iowa." He struggled to sit up. He was long and lanky, and the thin face was friendly. But now that adrenaline was no longer pumping, he was clearly in pain.

"Just lie still," said Clive. "Don't try to stand up, and I'll check you over for wounds. You've got a broken arm, you know."

"Yeah. That ain't all. Take a look at my ribs on the right side. I think one or two of them aren't quite the way they ought to be."

Clive gently explored the rib cage. The other man lay back with his teeth clenched and did no more than hiss when Clive touched the injured arm. Streaks of sweat were showing on the blackened face.

"Mostly bruises," said Clive at last. "Except for that arm. You're lucky—the way you and that German were going at each other, you ought to look like a piece of Swiss cheese.

Your head's burned and bleeding a bit. I think you got a ricochet from a wood splinter.'' He turned to Holloway. ''Any medical supplies with you?''

''Dunno.'' Holloway went to the truck and reached under the driver's seat.

''We need burn ointment for the head,'' said Clive. ''But the arm's a bigger problem. How about a splint?''

''No. We'll have to make one.''

''Painkillers?''

Holloway shook his head.

''Don't worry about me, fellows,'' said the pilot. ''Get me back to base. I'll be fine.''

His words did not match his appearance. He had started to shiver, and his face had a gray pallor. Clive turned again to Holloway. ''He can't go to Bar-le-Duc in his condition. We have to splint that arm. The doctors will set it properly when he gets to base, but it needs support when we move him. We can't have him bumping along with that fracture in the bottom of the truck. How do we get a splint?''

Holloway nodded up the hill. ''There's the cart track. The man who works these fields must live on the other side of the rise. There should be plenty to make a splint there. As for getting him back to Bar-le-Duc and his squadron, forget it. He's going to be grounded for a while with that arm, no matter what he thinks.''

''Can we drive to the farm—without plowing through another hedge, I mean? We've had enough of that for one day.''

''Down the hill, through the gate, and back up.''

''Let's do it. Spread any blankets you've got in the truck bed, and we'll lift him in.''

The American was staring at Clive and frowning when they came to lift him up. He had noticed the cast on Clive's leg. ''You want me up in the truck?'' he said. ''Well, for God's sake, ask me, then. I don't need help from a crippled Limey— I can climb in there better than you can.''

''Which is saying very little,'' said Clive. He sighed and struggled to his feet. ''What's your name?''

''Walter Johnson.''

''I'm Clive Dunnay. All right, Walter Johnson, I'll race you into the truck. First one there gets the farmer's daughter. The way I feel, I hope I lose.''

* * *

"Hold tight. This isn't going to be pleasant." Clive took hold of Walter Johnson's arm and turned to Holloway, who stood ready with splint and bandages. "This is going to hurt like hell. Why for God's sake were there no painkillers in the truck?"

"I don't know. It's not my truck. Either they weren't issued or they were all used up."

"Hold on to him, then."

Clive dug his fingers into the muscles of Johnson's upper arm, probing, feeling for the break. There was already swelling there, enough to make it difficult to gauge how the broken bones lay. He pulled down on the elbow, and there was a shuddering gasp from the American. As Clive tried to line up the ends of the fracture, Walter Johnson groaned and writhed on the farm's kitchen table. Holloway held him tightly, while the white-haired farmer looked on.

"One minute more." Clive could feel the bone ends grating together, but the limb was coming straight. Sweat was running down his forehead and into his eyes. "Now, Private, the splint. Hold on, Yankee, we're almost done."

"Sooner the better." Walter Johnson spoke through clenched teeth. "Get some of that firewater ready. I need it."

"One minute more. Hang on."

It was more like five minutes before Clive had the arm splinted and wrapped. By that time the American's shirt was soaked with sweat. When Private Holloway helped him off the table, he swayed on his feet.

The farmer spoke approvingly to Walter Johnson.

"He says no French pilot could have behaved with more courage," translated Clive. "From him, that's the highest praise. Here, wrap these blankets around you. How are you feeling?"

"Just marvelous." Walter Johnson gave a shiver and a huge yawn. "Christ, I'm tired."

"That's natural. You're going to feel more and more sleepy." Clive passed him a clay cup. "Drink this, then let's get you out to the truck."

Walter Johnson took a swig of the straw-colored liquid and pulled a wry face. "Jesus. You could fly a Nieuport on this stuff. What is it, fermented bat piss?"

"Nothing you ever heard of. The farmer distills it himself, out of cheap wine. In principle it's brandy—but you were right when you said firewater. All right to move now?"

"I can walk."

They made their way slowly out of the farmhouse, Clive hobbling, Walter Johnson leaning on Holloway's shoulder. The old farmer hovered around them, smiling and chattering.

"He says he's always glad to help soldiers," said Clive. "Especially a brave pilot who dares to ride in the air. His son and his son's sons are away fighting. There were two of his grandsons already killed in the war, and he wishes that he could help by fighting himself."

Walter Johnson gave another huge yawn and paused at the farmhouse door. "Boy. How long was I unconscious out there? It's almost dark now."

"Only for a couple of minutes." Clive stared at the sky, then turned again to the farmer. "This looks bad."

The man nodded. "I have known it since morning. We have a rainstorm on the way. Where are you heading?"

"The two of us are going to Saint-Amè," said Clive. "And I suppose we will be taking the American there, too."

"That road will become impossible." The farmer removed his beret and scratched his head. "I have room for only one person in the house—but the barn is warm and dry, and I have plenty of blankets."

Clive hesitated. The sky was black, it was already late afternoon, and a real torrent seemed to be on the way. It took no skill to read the lowering sky. He turned to Private Holloway.

"Any problem for you if we stay here overnight? I don't think our American friend should get soaked to the skin on top of everything else. He's in bad enough shape already."

Holloway shook his head. "Can't do it, sir. I must get back with this truck, and pick up my own from the repair shop. But I agree with you, the American shouldn't travel tonight. If you stay here, I'll pick you up tomorrow in my own van—and you'll find travel in that a lot easier than the rattlebox we were in today."

Supporting Walter Johnson between them, they followed the farmer into a dark and crowded storage room with a wooden cot crammed in among bins of potatoes and parsnips. Long strings of onions hung on the walls.

"No problem if you feel hungry in the night," said Clive as they lowered the pilot gently onto the cot. "Enough food here for a year."

Walter Johnson did not reply. As soon as his back encountered the hard mattress of the cot, he was asleep. Clive tucked two blankets around the airman's legs. While he was doing so, Holloway was loosening Johnson's jacket and shirt. He straightened up holding a thick leather pouch.

"On his belt," he said. "He'll sleep easier without this digging into him."

He held the pouch out, weighing it on the palm of his left hand. The two men stared at each other speculatively. The farmer had gone back to the kitchen. Walter Johnson was unconscious.

"We have to do it," said Clive at last. "I feel sure he's just what he says he is—no one could fake that dogfight. But there have been German infiltrators. We'd be failing our duty if we did not check his credentials. Be my witness that everything goes back in the pouch exactly as it came out."

He untied the leather lace of the wallet and picked out a thick packet of papers.

"Need more light." He led the way back to the kitchen, where the farmer had already put onto the table hard cheese, raw onions, and a jug of red wine.

The first item was an American passport. Walter Johnson, twenty-five years old, from Dubuque, Iowa; aviator's papers; a card indicating that the bearer, Walter Johnson, had been inducted into the French Army and was protected by the covenants of war as a French soldier; a fat wad of francs.

And then something more intriguing. "Look at this. He's not just an aviator. These are press credentials. Apparently he writes articles about the war for a syndicate. He's got a couple of old articles in here." Clive showed Holloway the grimy newsprint. CRISIS IN VERDUN; DEATH OF FRENCH HERO DRIANT; and THE AIR WAR: FLYING WITH KIFFIN ROCKWELL. "He's genuine. You get out of here before it rains, and we'll see you tomorrow."

As Holloway left, Clive stepped to the window and took a

last look at the sky. He felt uneasy about the delay, but surely one more day did not matter. Colonel Marshall wouldn't be waiting for him. He probably didn't even know that Clive was injured, still less that his aide and future son-in-law would be convalescing at the same chateau.

CHAPTER SIXTEEN

Warm and dry the barn had certainly been, and that was all the farmer promised. He had said nothing about clean, or vermin-free.

Clive sat in the front seat of the truck and imagined he could still feel insects crawling up and down inside his shirt. The straw that he had slept on had rustled all night long as a variety of small animals went about their nocturnal business. It had been hard to sleep, with rain beating down on the wooden roof above and the busy straw beneath. He wriggled his shoulders. If there was any sort of bath at the chateau, total immersion was the first order of business.

He turned to Holloway. "Will there be hot water at the castle?"

"Yes, sir. At least, that's what I hear." The man grinned his broken-toothed smile. He seemed to be in great spirits. "All modern conveniences, they say. But I haven't been there yet, sir."

"But you said you reported to Colonel Marshall. And you were his batman."

"For a while, sir, but not since he was injured. I was supposed to go to him, but they kept me over in Sector Three. I haven't seen Colonel Marshall for over a month." Holloway craned his head around. "How's he doin' in the back?"

Clive turned and peered into the interior of the truck. "Still out cold. I'm wondering if he's all right."

"I'm sure he is. We've had men get banged up like that and sleep for three days solid. He's comfortable enough."

No doubt about that, thought Clive. No wonder Private Holloway had been keen to get his own truck back. It was a luxury vehicle compared with the French loaner he had been driving. Somewhere on the way he had found a great pile of feather mattresses and was taking them with him to the chateau. Walter Johnson was lying on top of a stack of a dozen, like the princess in the fairy story.

There was scarcely room for the American pilot and the mattresses. The whole interior of Holloway's truck was stuffed with supplies. Clive had looked at the heaps in amazement when they loaded Walter Johnson aboard—tins of bully beef, blocks of hard pipe tobacco, blankets, strings of onions, soap, copper kettles, woolen cardigans, boots, pots and pans, postcards, cartons of foot powder, tins of cigarettes, a small barrel of brandy and another of rum, a portable stove, chests of loose tea and bags of coffee beans, folding chairs, yellow oilskins, briarwood pipes, whole cheeses, a wrapped block of rock salt, buttons, needles and thread, decks of playing cards, and an enormous khaki tent complete with a ridge pole that stuck ten feet out of the back of the truck and made every tight corner in the road a driver's challenge.

"I didn't say anything when we started out." Clive jerked his thumb toward the crowded back of the vehicle. "About that lot. I assumed you were taking it all on somewhere. But if you're *staying* at the castle . . ." He let the question float in the air.

Holloway laughed. "Doing it on the come, sir. I heard word there's a new temp'ry 'ospital in the castle grounds. That means a market for all sorts of comforts, so I brung a pile with me. My own tent, too; I got no taste for French army bivouacs. Anyhow, we'll see soon enough if I'm right, because there it is." He shifted down to third gear and nodded ahead to the chateau at the bottom of the hill. "Take a look, sir. Goin' to be 'ome sweet 'ome for a while."

The two men studied the prospect in silence.

"Looks decent," volunteered Holloway. "Bit quiet, though."

An understatement. Clive saw half a dozen drab gray tents, but no people. There was no smoke coming from any of the castle's seven chimneys as the van drove at a stately pace along the approach road and around the pond.

Holloway gave the weedy surface a close look. "Carp in there, I'll bet. Good eating, but you have to soak 'em live in clean water to get the taste of mud out."

He drove the truck in past the main gate and along to the first and biggest of the tents. "Here we are, sir. I think we'd better leave the American gent where he is for the moment. No point in wakin' him up till we know where he'll be goin'."

Clive climbed stiff-legged down and ducked his head into the flap of the biggest tent. He recoiled at the smell of grease, vomit, and gangrenous flesh. The man sitting half dressed at a little table just inside seemed oblivious to his surroundings. He was cutting into a piece of cooked liver on a tin plate.

"Eh?" He glanced up questioningly.

"I am seeking my superior officer, Colonel Marshall." Clive had recognized the uniform and spoke in French. "I am Captain Clive Dunnay."

"Corporal Trouffeau, at your service." The man made no attempt to stand or salute. "A colonel, you say? We have no one of such a rank here. But there is talk of a colonel who has been housed for some time at the chateau itself. You should try there." The corporal pointed toward the main building.

"Thank you."

"I'd show you the way, only—" Corporal Trouffeau swiveled his body a little away from the table and waved casually downward. His left leg ended just below the knee in a bulky white bandage.

"I'm sorry. I had no idea . . ."

"Don't worry about it." Trouffeau jerked his thumb back toward the darker interior of the tent. "We're all lucky ones in here. Still got our eyes, guts, and peckers. If you want to see some bad cases, go take a look in the last tent." The corporal nodded to Clive's crutch. "I see you got one, too."

"It's nothing." Clive spoke with true feeling. The bones of his leg were slow to knit, but at least they were all there. "Stay right where you are. I can find my own way."

He limped across to the main body of the castle and knocked hard on the great double doors. No one came. After a minute or so he turned the iron ring and pushed one of the doors open. He found himself in a tiled hallway that led to a broad staircase. Descending those stairs was a middle-aged and stoop-shouldered civilian dressed in a bottle-green jacket.

He paused on the bottom step. "Yes. May I help you?"

"I hope so." Clive reached into the breast pocket of his uniform. "I am Captain Dunnay. I am seeking my superior officer, and I am supposed to remain here for convalescent leave until my leg is healed. Here are my papers."

The man ignored the proffered packet. "There is a mistake. We have no more soldiers reporting here. You have come to the wrong place."

"This is the Chateau Cirelle?"

"That it certainly is. I am Maurice Monge, majordomo of the chateau."

"Do you have a Colonel William Marshall staying here with you?"

"We do. But he is supposed to be the only one. You should be outside, at the bivouacs."

"They directed me here. Colonel Marshall is my superior officer." Clive tapped the packet of papers. "These were signed by General Balfourier himself. They order me to report here. I also have with me an American pilot who crashed and was injured near here yesterday."

Monge took the papers at last and peered at them. "I do not know. Something is wrong here. Your papers seem to be correct—"

"They are certainly all in order."

"Perhaps. But I feel sure that the Marquis did not agree to this. He has already gone far beyond what was expected in permitting the placement of a field hospital right outside the chateau. That places impossible demands on our staff and kitchen equipment." He waved the packet. "I must discuss this with the Marquis. And he is not here at the moment; he is over in one of the neighboring villages."

"I can wait. And meanwhile, can you tell me how to reach the quarters of Colonel Marshall? He may have been receiving official communiques, but I feel sure that he will want my personal progress report on the battle around Verdun."

Monge gave him a strange look. "I can tell you how to get there, certainly. Colonel Marshall is in the east wing. But beyond that . . ." He shrugged and gave Clive directions.

Odd duck, thought Clive. Not too friendly. Blind as a bat, too, from the way he looked at those papers. Maybe that's why he's not in uniform—he's certainly young enough to fight.

The instructions Monge had given were clear enough at first, but then Clive came to a place where he did not know whether to proceed along a corridor or head up a narrow staircase. It shouldn't make much difference; he was certainly heading in the right general direction. After some hesitation he climbed the wooden stairs, made the next left as directed, and found himself at a partly open door. If he had understood Monge correctly, this was it.

He knocked, at the same time pushing the door open.

The first thing that met his eyes was a bare-breasted black woman. She was staring fiercely at him from a huge picture that hung on the wall opposite the door. The glare she projected out of the frame was so arresting that it was a second or two before Clive was able to take in the other contents of the room. Half of it was occupied by a great bed, with a pink and black silk coverlet. And in the middle of that, sitting cross-legged and barefooted, was a striking young woman. She was wearing a long orange dress, a gown more suited for an evening ball than the middle of the morning. With a length of black thread in one hand and a tiny needle in the other, she was peering at them one-eyed and trying to thread one through the other.

Clive took in the rest of her appearance while he stood tongue-tied in the doorway. She was young, maybe twenty-one years old, with a fully mature figure. A great mass of unruly black hair stood out from her delicate-featured face, and her complexion was of a type that Clive had never seen before. The skin was smooth and unblemished, with a curious tan, like a blushing English skin shining through a tissue-thin sheet of ivory.

"I'm sorry," he said stupidly. The intense look on her face was unnerving. "I must be in the wrong room."

The woman jumped lightly off the bed, revealing a flash of long, brown legs. "Aha!" She smiled. "And what a surprise you are going to be! Wonderful. We had no idea you were coming. This way."

She walked past Clive, stopping to peer into his face with

her head cocked on one side. "You are even better-looking than the picture," she said mysteriously. "But so thin. And your poor leg!" She walked off, still barefoot, along the corridor. Clive followed, feeling half-witted. Of all the reactions you could imagine if you burst into a strange young woman's bedroom, this was not on the list.

A little farther along, the woman stopped at a second door. She gave a tap on it, then flung it open. "Surprise!" she cried, and went in.

Clive cringed. What was this place, a combined hospital and madhouse? To be announced to his superior officer as though he were an unexpected gift delivered to Colonel Marshall at a Christmas party . . . He straightened up nervously, did his best to march forward on his crutch and injured leg, and hobbled into the room. There was a tremendous scream from within, and a delighted laugh from his escort.

"Clive!"

He looked to his right. There, standing against the open window, was Jenny Marshall.

Jenny had been staring out across the front gardens of the chateau and thinking about the future. Neither she nor Louis Villette had mentioned it, but since they had become lovers, two facts loomed larger and larger. Jenny had found something in her life completely new and unexpected, a sexual and emotional relationship she had never imagined; she could not envision a future without it. At the same time, William Marshall's condition had deteriorated.

He was dying. If that happened, could she stay here, never returning to England or America? She would like that. The thought of life without Louis was so painful.

Clive had been little in her thoughts. He was somewhere out there, reliable and brave and conscientious as always— but he had nothing to do with today's problems. He was *another* problem, one that would eventually have to be addressed. Sometime. Not now. Now she felt the touch of Louis Villette's fingers, the warmth of his breath and lips, the ardor of his lovemaking . . .

And suddenly Clive was here, standing in the doorway. A different Clive, pale as a sheet, so gaunt that the bones of his face jutted out of the white skin. Crippled, bandaged, helping himself along on a crutch. Hollow-eyed. And the look in those eyes . . .

"Clive!" Jenny's cry was a mixture of many emotions, shock and horror and guilt and grief. "What happened to you?"

She went across to embrace him. His appearance at that moment was just as though he had walked in while Jenny and Louis Villette were making love. She put her arms around his shoulders (such thin shoulders; blades of bone) and avoided his eye.

"Jenny." Clive's voice was as unsteady as she felt, and his hold on her oddly uncertain. "Jenny, darling. What are you doing here?"

But his mind answered before she could. Jenny was here to look after William Marshall. That accounted for her failure to answer his letters, while he had been suspecting her of finding some other man in London during his absence. . . .

"I think you both need something to eat and drink." Cecile broke the strange silence. She came forward and took Clive's hand firmly in hers. "And it's time we introduced ourselves. I'm Cecile Villette." She turned to Jenny. "And he is even more handsome in person than he is in a photograph. You are a very lucky woman."

She turned and headed for the door.

"No! Don't go!" Jenny's voice was panic-stricken; but Cecile did not stop.

"I'll be back in a couple of minutes," she said over her shoulder. "And you don't need me for your reunion."

Clive stared after her. "Jenny, who *is* that?"

"That's Cecile. The daughter of Lou—of the Marquis of Saint-Amè." Jenny finally looked at Clive's eyes. "Did you—did you meet the Marquis?"

"Not yet. But I suppose I will." Clive removed his arm from Jenny's waist and hobbled across to sit on a chair by the bed. "After all, I'm a guest here, though I gather I'm not welcome. What's he like?"

He was bending over to place his crutch on the floor and could not see Jenny's face.

"He's . . . very nice," she said after a moment. "Very civilized." *Civilized enough that he won't give any hint to Clive of what the two of us have been doing whenever we've had the chance*. "The Marquis has been very good to Father and me. We've had everything we needed."

"That's great." Clive eased his injured leg to a different position. "I wanted to see Colonel Marshall as soon as I got here, but I mistook the directions and couldn't find his room. How's he doing?"

"Oh, Clive. Not well at all." Jenny moved to him, put her arms around him with real feeling, and rested her cheek against his jacket. She wanted to give an unemotional account of William Marshall's condition, but it was impossible. She began to speak, and before she was done tears were in her eyes. "And you're injured, too," she finished. He looked ten years older than when she had last seen him. "Clive, what happened to you? How did you get hurt?"

Clive took a deep breath. "Well, I'm not sure how to describe it—"

He looked up with relief as Cecile came hurrying into the room with a tray of pastries and coffee. He did not think he would ever be able to talk about the noise and the confusion and the smells. Most of all, he could not talk about the fear that had gnawed at him in the trenches. If Jenny ever learned of that, she would recoil from him in disgust.

"I'm not staying," said Cecile as she went to the dresser and put down the tray. "I just want to drink one cup of coffee with you, as a toast to your reunion, then I'll leave you to yourselves. I told Monge that you will not be down to dinner; he is to make up cold dishes and put them under covers on the sideboard in the small lounge. You can help yourselves when you feel hungry."

"Cecile, you're just too good to us," said Jenny. "I didn't realize you were going to bring this yourself, just as though you were one of the castle servants." She turned to Clive. "Monge thinks that he runs the chateau, but the real boss is Cecile. She has Monge wrapped 'round her little finger. If you want to stay here, you have to do what Cecile tells you."

"That is exactly right." Cecile turned to Clive, holding out a tray containing three large cream-filled pastries and an oversized cup of coffee. She smiled. "I am the 'real boss,' as Jenny puts it. In your case, Captain Dunnay, your orders are simple. You must eat well, and drink well, and put on weight." She paused in front of him, looking him over from head to foot. "You are very handsome, even so thin, but if you were mine, I would insist that you add a few more kilos here and there. You need good food three times a day, and good brandy every night."

Clive blushed and Jenny laughed, more relaxed than she had been since he first entered the room. "You heard, Clive. You must do as Cecile says and put on weight."

"And you must keep an eye on him at skin level, to make sure he does." Cecile handed a filled cup to Jenny and went to the door. "I think it is time you had some privacy. He can meet Papa later, when he arrives back from his trip."

"Oh, don't go." Jenny was dreading a conversation with Clive about Louis Villette. "You haven't said a word to Clive in French. And he's completely fluent in it—far more than I'll ever be."

"Really?" Cecile looked at Clive with new interest. He shrugged. Cecile smiled and threw a question at Clive that was far too fast and informal for Jenny to grasp. Clive blushed and shook his head, while Cecile tossed her head back, laughed, and pirouetted out of the room with a swirl of skirts. She closed the door firmly behind her.

"What was all that about?" asked Jenny.

"Oh, she was just asking me how I learned to speak French."

"And that made you *blush*?"

"Well, it was the way she put it. She asked me, did I have the services of a long-haired dictionary? Which she guarantees is the fastest way to learn. Is she always like that?"

"Like that, and worse. She's half African. Sometimes the wild side of her gets out of control. She has a boyfriend, Charles Richter, who's the model of a proper French gentleman. But the things that Cecile says to him, and about him, in public! What she just did to you was nothing. But she's still wonderful."

Clive nodded. "I thought so, too."

But I haven't told Jenny that I think she's wonderful yet, or how much I missed her. And she hasn't said anything to me. She must see a change in me—and it's not just that I've lost weight.

Clive drank coffee and looked surreptitiously at Jenny. She

was staring out of the window. There was certainly *something* different in her manner. At first it could be explained by the shock of his unexpected arrival, when she had thought him far away. But she was still avoiding his eyes. Jenny had always been forward and direct; now she was avoiding face-to-face conversation. Was it the strain and worry about her father? The two of them had always enjoyed a special bond, closer than any typical father-daughter relationship. She had made the reckless trip here, to within a few miles of the front, to be with him. This whole area wasn't safe—a German attack could come tomorrow, or a long-range shell demolish the building. But William Marshall would have done that sort of thing himself, in a similar situation. He was a great model for any soldier: casually courageous, as though courage was never a thing to be sought or proved.

Clive thought of Jenny and her father and felt envious. The horrors of the front line came unbidden to his mind.

He stood up. "I ought to go and look for my own room, Jenny. I'm going to need a new dressing for my leg. Harry Holloway promised to get one for me, and it's probably waiting there."

That touched Jenny as nothing else had. He saw her expression change from distant to concerned. She came to his side and reached out tentatively to pat his arm. "I'm sorry, Clive. I've been so selfish. I never even asked how you are feeling. Does it hurt badly?"

"Not now. Itches." It was wonderful to have Jenny looking at him again with affection. He smiled at her. "If you still fancy your chances as a nurse, maybe you'd give me a hand to change the dressing later. I make a mess of it when I do it."

"Of course I will." She took his arm and gave it a squeeze, aware as she did so of how thin it had become. Just muscle and bone now, with no trace of fat.

They began to walk slowly around the perimeter of the room, Clive casually picking up or touching everything he saw. He always did it, inspecting any room that Jenny stayed in. She thought of Cecile's words when she had mentioned that habit: "Of course he does. He's claiming your territory as his—putting his *scent* on things, like a lion or a leopard."

She had laughed at Jenny's expression. "Just because we're civilized on top doesn't mean we're not animals underneath. Thank goodness."

Clive was doing it now. He reached up and touched the crystal chandelier, then went across to the wall, where a landscape that was either a Turner or a good imitation of one caught the crystal's refracted light. He put his hand on the frame and rubbed his thumb along the varnish.

"The Marquis certainly provided you with a pleasant room." He picked up an antique paperweight, a diamond-shaped piece of amber with an old French gold piece, a louis d'or, embedded within it, and touched the rounded edge. "It's a marvelous place to be sent for recuperation." He put the paperweight down suddenly. "God, Jenny, but I'm really sorry to hear about your father. I feel as bad as if it were my own father."

There was no doubting his sincerity. Clive Dunnay did many things well, but Jenny knew that lying had never been one of them.

"It's a good place," she said. *And you're a good man. My poor, sweet Clive, I know you couldn't tell me, when I asked what it was like at the front. What have they done to you?*

Clive saw the change in her eyes. There was a loving look, a look of tenderness. He pulled her to him and awkwardly kissed her on the lips. She kissed back willingly enough, but there was a flatness to it. Clive could remember very well how he had felt back in England. Ready to burst with love and sexuality. The slightest touch of her flesh had been exciting. Now something was missing in their embrace. Missing, he was sure of it, in *him*.

"Jenny, I ought to take a bath and rest for a little while before I put a fresh dressing on. My leg doesn't look good at all, I'll warn you. If you'd rather I did it all by myself, I'll understand. You've got enough worries without my adding to them."

Jenny heard the sad question behind his words. Do you want to avoid me, he was saying. Then all you have to do is stay away from my room.

She stood for a moment with her forehead resting on his cheek, then tilted her face up and kissed him lightly on the lips. "Go and have your bath, and try to rest. But don't put your fresh dressing on alone. Wait for me, Clive. I'll be knocking on your door in an hour and a half."

A nap, a hot bath, and a glass of Bordeaux made quite a difference. One thing it couldn't do, though, was make him fatter. Clive tightened the new bandage around his splint and skinny calf, stood up, and stared at his reflection in the mirror. He picked up a comb, ran it through his wet hair, and wondered who the stranger was glaring back at him. He had never realized before how much fat the average man carried on his body. No wonder Jenny didn't find him attractive. Quite apart from the failings of the inner man, the outer man was too thin to be handsome—despite what Cecile had said.

There was a light knock on the door, and Jenny came in. She walked up behind Clive and he caught a hint of a flowery French perfume, subtle and intriguing. She had changed her outfit, too, to a pale mauve dress tight at the waist and cupping her bosom. Another change in Jenny. She had never worn anything so exotic in England.

"That's more like the Clive I remember," she said. "Let's get your leg fixed and done with."

"It is done." Clive turned and put his arms around her. "I decided to have a go on my own. It's less of a job than I thought."

She was warm, she was soft, and she smelled delicious. And yet as he kissed her, a part of his mind raced with alarm.

What the devil was wrong with him? For months and months he had yearned for Jenny. And yet now, with her in his arms, flesh pressing against his, he was not aroused. There were tentative stirrings of desire, but they seemed automatic and abstract. The sensual part of him floated free, a balloon drifting above his body and connected to it by the merest shred of nerve.

He held Jenny tighter. He wanted to lose himself in her, to forget the months in France. He needed to regain a feeling of solidity and self-confidence. Jenny had closed her eyes. Perhaps she needed to lose herself, too, to cut herself off from the recent past.

He kissed her. She pulled away from him and ran her hands

over his back and shoulders. "Have I ever told you how good you look in uniform?"

"Good, maybe, if you like skeletons. I'm just rags and bones."

"I thought you were a bit fat before. You look good thin. How was the bath?"

She was being as nice as she could. He held her close, wondering why he felt so little response. "It was heavenly. Hot water. You can't imagine how wonderful it is, Jenny, to lie in a warm bath when you've grown completely used to filth and muck."

"I can try to imagine it." She looked at him earnestly. "Clive, you've been through so much, I know that, even if you don't want to talk about it. I feel so guilty when I think how easy everyone at home has things. What you need is rest, and quiet, and a chance to forget the horrors."

He ran his fingers along her cheek and touched her chin. "I've thought about you constantly, Jenny. When I was traveling or lying in my bunk, I wondered how you were doing all the time."

He lay full-length on the bed and drew her down by his side. "You're here now. That's what matters."

He kissed her again, and began to ease off her clothes. She lay with eyes closed, breathing deeply. He felt clumsy, she did not move, and it took a long time. When he was finished, he rested his head against her breast and relaxed for a few moments. This was what he really wanted to do, to lie in peace and forget all the pain and misery. He had dreamed of this for four months: Jenny, holding him close and loving him.

But there should be more. He kissed the hollow of her throat, feeling her soft pulse there, and moved to lie on top of her. Jenny gasped. He hovered above her, in the right position to enter.

The right position; but something was wrong.

Clive heard the roar of artillery and saw beneath him the skeletal, empty-eyed Jenny of the trenches. Instead of hardening, his penis became softer. His mind moved far away, uninvolved. He rubbed against her, hoping that the contact would stimulate him.

It was not working at all.

Clive could not move.

Jenny opened her eyes. "Clive? Are you all right?"

"I'm all right." *What's wrong with me?*

"Is it your leg? Is it hurting?"

"No, my leg feels fine. It's just—I don't know, I suppose it's just that, well, that it's been a long time."

He knew how false and feeble that sounded. His whole midsection felt numb and lifeless, waterlogged and heavy. There was no energy, no spirit in his insides or lower body. He rolled off to lie beside her. There was another flash of memory, of bursting shells and broken bodies.

It's fear. I can't make love anymore. He was sweating, and his breathing was ragged.

"Clive." She was whispering in his ear. "You don't understand. It's not you, and it's not your fault. It's me. It's . . . I can't say it, but it's not you, it's my fault."

"No. No, Jenny."

"You don't understand." She turned away from him, and her voice was sad. "You just don't. It's not you."

Not him? Clive didn't feel numb anymore. He felt an eruption of emotion, an outburst of anguish so powerful that it destroyed thought. Jenny wasn't asking too much when she expected him to make love to her—she was asking only what she ought to be able to expect.

Jenny's hand was on his shoulder and neck. She was stroking him gently. "Clive, don't look like that. The world hasn't ended—I'm as fond of you as ever."

He looked at her face, and the caring there was obvious. He sighed and took her in his arms again. "Oh, Jenny, I don't know what to say."

"Don't say anything. You don't *need* to say anything. I understand. I know what happened."

"No. You can't possibly."

"But I do. I didn't understand before. I thought it would be for *you*—that you needed me that way. But I didn't realize that I've been—that you would sense that I—"

"Jenny, you're not making any sense. And you're trying to make excuses for me. It won't work."

"Shush." She put her fingers on his lips and held him close. "This is what you need, Clive. This. You are a brave, good man, with feelings. Not a machine."

"Jenny, I do love you. I really do."

"I know. Hold me close. Dear Clive. Think how many men would give anything to be here, lying in a quiet warm bed. Be happy that you're alive, as I'm happy to have you here."

Alive, but half dead, thought Clive. He lay silent, holding Jenny. Long after she fell asleep he was still locked in thought. He stared into the darkness, unable to sleep, and blessed the dark.

He wondered, bitterly, if he would be able to look Jenny in the eye in the knowing light of day.

CHAPTER
SEVENTEEN

From victory to defeat, from triumph to disaster—in the space of two seconds.

A sideslip and a vicious turn saved him from the Fokker's first diving attack. Now to pull the Nieuport out to level flight! It almost ripped the wings off—Walter heard every strut and wire screech. Then he was behind the other plane, closing on it, machine gun pumping bullets into its body and engine.

He had the German cold, guaranteed, his second kill of the day; and then the Fokker went into a short, steep climb. Walter knew he must not follow, knew that the German maneuver was the one he'd been warned about. He had to veer away, out of danger. But his hands would not obey the message from his brain. He followed the other aircraft in full pursuit. It went up and up, rolled out in a way that seemed impossible, and was suddenly closing on Walter's own tail.

Sideslip. Violent turn. He was behind the other plane again, machine gun stuttering. It did a steep climb and roll. He tried to follow. It was suddenly on his tail, bullets chewing into his Nieuport. . . .

Sideslip and turn, get behind the other plane . . . sideslip and turn . . .

Walter shuddered into wakefulness. He lay staring at the brown roof of a tent. He was alive; and he would never, no matter how long he lived, forget what an Immelmann roll looked like.

He took a deep breath and slowly sat up. Where the devil was he?

Fragments of memory wandered in. The crash. The need to get away from the plane before it caught fire. Two men helping, a scramble across rough ground to a gray-painted truck. And that was all.

Or almost all. There was a memory of dreadful pain from his left arm—pain worse than anything he had ever imagined.

Walter looked down. The limb was neatly splinted and bandaged, hanging in a canvas sling. No doubt about it, the arm was broken. He had known that as the plane hit the ground. There had been a tremendous impact against the side of the cockpit. Even in the general uproar and confusion he had heard the bone snap. Now it didn't so much hurt as generate a persistent and ill-defined itch all along his upper arm.

A broken arm. What else?

Walter tenderly explored his body with his right hand. Plenty of aches. Neck, right-side ribs, right hip, right knee. He stood up slowly, testing the leg. All sore, but nothing terrible. He had fallen on his right side when he heaved himself out of the Nieuport, and in a day or two he would have some spectacular bruises.

The tent was a big one, ridge-poled and large enough to hold a dozen people. He was on an army cot near the entrance, one of four scattered around the tent. As he limped toward the open entry flap, he heard a rapid rattling sound outside, a high-pitched and well-defined burst of noise. No wonder he had been dreaming of aerial combat—whatever the damned thing was, it sounded just like a Spandau machine gun!

The sun was high in a cloud-free sky, but the ground outside had been recently doused with water. Walter swore. Soaking ground, and naturally he was shoeless. Whoever had carried him into the tent had left his jacket intact but removed his flying boots.

The rattle came again from outside. This time it was followed by another sound, dull and regular: *whomp, whomp, whomp, whomp*.

He *had* to find out what that was—and where he was.

Walter prowled the inside of the tent and found his own boots, polished as they had not been polished since he had bought them, leaning against the far wall. Pulling them on one-handed was a lot harder than it sounded. The only way he could do it was to wedge the boot against a storage box and push down with all his weight while he pulled the back of the boot upward. He forced his foot into the second boot, wondering how he was going to get them off. That would be a two-man job.

He went to the tent flap and stepped outside. The tent stood on a large open patch of grassy ground, level and well kept, with half a dozen smaller tents and a low wooden building about twenty yards away from it. Beyond them was an impressive structure of gray stone with a red-tiled roof and tall, cylindrical towers at each corner of the building. The strange *whomp*ing sound was coming from somewhere closer to the building.

Walter headed in that direction. As he approached the tents, a short file of men appeared from behind one of them. The leader was a corporal who limped along on two crutches. Every man behind him wore a gray bandage across his eyes and walked with one hand on the shoulder of the man in front of him.

"Hey!" Walter stepped closer and launched into his desperate French. *"Mon ami, bonjour. Comment allez-vous?"*

The line halted in confusion, while the leader stared curiously at Walter.

"Aviateur? Ici?"

"Sure. *Pilote de* American squadron. *Escadrille* American." Walter raised his hand and dived it toward the ground. "Shot down. *Tombé*. But where am I? *Où suis-je?"*

Instead of answering, the corporal gestured behind him. *"Anglais. Comprenez-vous?"*

"Oui." But Walter really didn't. He went off obediently in the direction that the other man had pointed, while the file of blinded soldiers started moving again behind him.

Gas attack? Probably. Which meant that chances were fifty-fifty that the men would regain their sight.

Walter came to the point where he could see what lay beyond the lower wooden building. Between it and the towers of the house someone had strung two long parallel lengths of clothesline. Hanging from those, swaying a little in the breeze, were three carpets, each at least twenty feet long and fifteen feet wide. And by the left-hand carpet, the one with a floral pattern on it, stood a man, hitting rhythmically— *whomp, whomp, whomp, whomp*—with a heavy carpet beater. Clouds of dust rose into the fresh morning air and descended on everything within five yards. While Walter Johnson watched, the man stopped, coughed furiously, and walked to the end of the line. He pulled on a rope, there was the sharp clicking rattle of a turning ratchet, and the whole set of carpets advanced a few feet along the line.

Walter walked across to the sweating, dust-covered man. He was bare-headed and wearing a long, gray smock that covered him from neck to knees.

"Where am I? What is this place?" Walter spoke carefully, in his best attempt at French. Almost no one else in the squadron had bothered to learn more than a few phrases about food, drink, and women, but Walter was glad he had made the extra effort.

The man stared at him with bulging eyes and went into another spasm of coughing. "Chateau Cirelle," he said at last. Then he went on, in a broad Cockney accent, "No good to talk French to me, sir—I only know about ten words of it. *Vooly-voo coochay avec moi*, an' that's my lot. How you feeling?"

"Rotten. But what am I doing here? I'm supposed to be back with my squadron, not in some country palace. I have to get out of here."

"Captain Dunnay sent word to your lot, and they said you was to stay here for a few days until you're fit to fight." The broad-shouldered man put down the carpet beater and stripped off the smock, to reveal a khaki uniform beneath it. He stood to attention. "'Scuse me, sir, I should have done this before, but I was too busy chokin'. Holloway, sir, Private First Class, Forty-third Worcestershires. I brought you here."

Walter reached out his hand. "Walter Johnson, with the independent American Air Squadron."

The private looked surprised at the gesture, but took the outstretched hand and shook it. "At your service. I'm the one did your boots, too, sir." He nodded his head to Johnson's feet. "They came up really nice."

"This is very strange. I was flying the French lines, and I must have come down not far from them. And now I'm in the middle of the British sector."

"No, sir. My chief was British liaison to the French, so we was stationed in Souilly. Then he got injured and he was sent here. And yesterday I came to 'elp look after 'im. You must have been real out of it after that crash. Don't you remember me?"

"Not a thing."

"Me and Captain Dunnay, we dragged you out of your plane an' put the first splint on your arm. Did a good job, too—no need to reset it. The captain's inside now." Holloway jerked his head toward the chateau. "They've been gettin' a room ready; you were just dropped off outside here temporary. The tent's for me and a couple of noncoms. We stay separate from the French troops 'cause we're not wounded."

Walter felt his belly rumble. "Any chance of breakfast?"

"I don't know about meals in the chateau, sir, 'cause it's gettin' on for twelve already. You can give it a try, but maybe they won't want to feed you until lunch. If they come on awkward, come back out here. I can get you something. I've got a little Etna stove around the back. I can do hot chocolate, bully beef, and biscuits."

Private Holloway began to pull the smock back over his tousled hair, while Walter Johnson took a closer look at the dusty carpets. "Surely they don't have you doing house-work?"

"Not exactly, sir." Holloway patted the nearest carpet. "Good quality, these. The Kachli Afghan, here, an' those two Persians from Hamadan. They were sittin' in a dust heap in an old storage room at the back of the chateau. Once they're cleaned up, they'll be worth a packet."

"Where did you learn about carpets?"

"Poplar, an' round the East End." Holloway gave Walter a wink. "There's a lot of things to be 'ad 'ere, sir, if you just know where to look. Anytime you want anything—food, drink, clothes, supplies, a little company, you name it—drop by the tent. Maybe I can help you."

"Harry Holloway Enterprises, eh? A little *company*? Female company? How would you manage that, in the middle of nowhere?''

"I've got a business partner, sir, takes care of it. Are you interested?''

"Interested? God, I'm fascinated. But not right this minute. I ought to step inside and pay my respects.''

"Very good, sir. But watch what you say when you go inside. I don't think your arrival was too popular with the feller who owns the place. I heard him and a French major goin' at it hammer and tongs. Somebody decided to send us here without telling the Marquis, and then a couple of other shell-shocked Frenchmen are supposed to arrive here tomorrow. You was like the last straw, see—*nobody* expected you —not even the French major. He seemed about as mad at your arrival as the old Marquis.''

"It's great to be popular. Thanks, and let me go and say thanks to Captain Dunnay. I don't think I'd have got out of that plane without help.''

Walter went to a door of the castle set at the base of one of the round towers and stood by it for a moment. Should he knock? That seemed ridiculous—the place was so big that the chances were no one would hear him. After a few seconds he opened the door and went inside, self-consciously straightening his uniform and buttoning his shirt.

He found himself at the foot of an uncarpeted wooden staircase. There was evidence of neglect, with cobwebs on the curving ceiling and dusty, unwashed windows that looked out onto extensive gardens. Walter climbed slowly, his wounds waking after the long sleep. At the top he held the railing and listened.

It was perfectly still; no sign of anyone, no sounds of voices or of people working.

Walter walked along a corridor that ran all the way across the front of the chateau. Nobody. He was finally in a main hallway, with a huge window overlooking the castle gardens on his right and a ten-foot-wide staircase curving off to his left. He went down it and was at the main doors of the castle. He peeked into a big deserted library, with its old, wrinkled-back books running in walnut cases from floor to ceiling, then went on toward the rear of the house. There was a marvelous smell of cooking coming from somewhere in that direction.

Before he had gone a dozen steps, one of his questions was answered. There *were* other people in the chateau. In a small study, seated at a carved escritoire, was a blond-haired man. He was bending over a square black box about five inches long and two inches deep.

"Hi, there," Walter said softly. "*Bonjour.*"

At the sound of his voice the man jerked upright and dropped the box onto the desktop.

"*Mon Dieu.*" Charles Richter stared at Walter in obvious surprise. "Who are you? And where did you spring from?"

Richter was running out of energy. He had been loading the camera with new film in the little study, but he was more than half asleep. His official French work during the day, Cecile in the evenings and half the night, and then his new nighttime scouting—it was too much. He was going to make some terrible blunder if he kept this up much longer.

When he had first realized that the Marquis went off on regular midnight roamings, it seemed like the perfect chance to explore the chateau. Every other night, Louis Villette could be relied upon to disappear at about eleven and not be back to his quarters until close to dawn. When Richter had mentioned the nocturnal wanderings to Cecile, she had run her hands lasciviously along his bare chest. "What did you expect, my Charles? Papa is in good health, he is not an old man, and there is no one here in the chateau—unless he takes Jenny's eye. I hope that the woman is beautiful and worth the effort."

As soon as Richter was sure that the schedule of the Marquis could be relied upon, he began his own explorations. He looked at Louis Villette's private quarters first. That had turned up nothing, just travel-stained clothing and a number of musty books of no apparent interest. Since one of them was open on a window seat, Richter took a look at it: a diary of some kind, handwritten (or hand-scrawled—it was nearly illegible) in a big blue-paged ledger with ruled lines. Richter was carrying the camera, but there was nothing interesting enough to photograph. He had already taken general shots of the exterior and interior of the chateau.

He revised his opinion of the possible importance of the books when he investigated the cellars and subterranean levels of the chateau. He might not have gone there at all but for the accident to William Marshall—Cecile had suggested that the lower levels were nothing more than damp, grimy storage areas.

The torture chamber was fascinating, but for the bloody history of the castle rather than for anything useful in today's war. The equipment was all old and rusted. He tried to work one or two pieces and decided they would probably not function even if someone made a serious attempt to operate them. The spectator's gallery could be reached from the level above the torture chamber, or through a steep wooden ladder in the corner of the bedroom next door. Richter had ascended a couple of rungs, felt the old wood creaking beneath his weight, and retreated.

The subterranean bedroom was more intriguing. The basic paneling and furniture were thirty or more years old, but the draperies and bedclothes were new and freshly laundered. The long mirror above the crimson-counterpaned bed was unspotted and brightly polished. Leather harnesses and padded manacles hung from the ceiling and were attached to the bedposts. They looked new and strong. There were two padlocked teak cabinets along one wall, and a tall teak wardrobe against another. The wardrobe was filled with costumes, old and fading, the attire of everyone from milkmaids to cardinals.

The locks were strongly built but simple. Richter took out his key set and in less than ten minutes both doors were open. The larger cabinet added to the impression created by the bed and mirror. It was filled with the trappings of perverted erotica: whips, masks, spiked collars, bindings, leather funnels, ticklers, dildos, clysters, and single strands of half-inch spherical ivory beads. Like the costumes, they showed signs of both use and age.

Sitting within the smaller cabinet, oddly out of place there, was another of the musty old journals. Richter sat down and took a closer look at it. He had plenty of time. The Marquis would not be back for hours.

The name engraved on the cover was Louis Villette, Fourteenth Marquis of Sainte-Amè; grandfather of the present

Marquis, and long since dead. The dates covered a period in the fall and early winter of 1870, from August 2 to January 3 of the next year. If the book had not already been open there, Richter would probably have skipped over the entry of September 2. Most of the journal was an endless catalog of facts about the French defeats and German victories in the Franco-Prussian War. In 1870 the Germans had broken the French Army, forced the surrender of Paris, and gained in settlement the provinces of Alsace and Lorraine.

The crabbed handwriting was unsteady and uneven, filled with slashes and smudges that spoke of strong emotion.

September 2nd. Again, a total failure. The fighting will continue, but the war is over. Our forces have surrendered at Sedan, and there is nothing more between the German Army and the gates of Paris. I have made five attempts, and had five failures. Five; nothing compared with tens of thousands, and with success I could accept them. But crowned with failure, five deaths remain to haunt me.

What am I doing wrong? The circumstances were right. She was certainly pregnant. She swore that the child was mine. The Cross burned bright, the Gospel was to hand, the Ritual was followed exactly. Yet this morning I learned that Sedan has fallen and we have surrendered.

It must be the Ritual! There are subtleties that I have not yet fathomed, elements that are misunderstood. I see these possibilities:

1. The woman must be a virgin—not merely puella, *as I have assumed and the commentaries suggest, but* virgo intacta.

2. An incantation in Latin may be insufficient; it must be in Aramaic or Greek.

3. The Cross must not only be present, it must be worn on the body of the Vessel or the Guardian.

4. The book of the Gospel must be physically present also, and used in the ceremony in some precise and unspecified way.

> 5. *The ceremony must not be preceded by*
> *sexual intercourse; there must be no coupling of*
> *the profane and the sacred.*

Charles Richter skimmed through the rest of the entry, then set the camera for its closest focus and tried for a two-second exposure. The light in the room should be adequate.

He leafed through the other pages. A quick scan showed nothing else about Cross or Gospel. There were numerous references to the not-so-private life of the Marquis scattered through the book:

> . . . *flower-picking in Sainte-Isème: Lucille again;*
> *a noble savage.*
> . . . *Jacqueline; the bordellos lost an asset when*
> *she was born a Marchioness.*
> . . . *Sophie, in Baudrémont—five times, for the*
> *glory of God.*
> . . . *in Verdun, with Juliette. Haunches like a*
> *brood mare and cunny-grip like a vise. She*
> *wore me to an ecstatic shade.*
> . . . *sweet Marguerite, on her sixteenth birthday.*
> *So fair, so white, so red.*

The second cabinet was almost empty. It contained only one brass box, locked with a bronze padlock and crusted with a patina of age. Richter lifted it, assessing the weight. He turned it upside down, listening to the contents clatter from bottom to top. Not metal, whatever was inside. It sounded like leather or paper.

It was frustrating. The most interesting thing was almost certainly right here in the chest. And chances were it was the Gospel, the Ritual, or both of them. Should he take it with him? Dolfi would be desperate for a look.

Richter hesitated, then at last put the box back in the cabinet just as he had found it and closed the doors. His explorations so far had been invisible. With the Grand Advance still in preparation, they must remain that way.

He headed up to the main floor of the chateau. He had no foolproof way of sending to Dolfi the film he had just taken, but at least they now had a much better method of getting messages across the lines. A safe and quick method, too, unless Private Koontz from the Signal Corps balked at the unpleasant duty. That was a possibility; Richter had seen the expression on Koontz's face when the technique was described to him, and the private learned what his role would be.

Richter checked that no one was still walking the house, then came quietly out to the corridor. He closed the door to the cellar and went up to the little study.

It was there that Walter Johnson had found him, many hours later, fiddling again with the camera and longing for a few more hours of sleep. Richter knew that the new method for sending messages would be very useful; but most important of all, he now knew how Dolfi could visit Chateau Cirelle and see it for himself with minimal risk. He had thought of it earlier in the day. Tomorrow night he would tell Dolfi about it.

On the other hand, maybe that was not a clever idea. With new people arriving at the chateau every day—and this Walter Johnson was the latest example—Richter doubted that Dolfi should be coming here at all.

CHAPTER
EIGHTEEN

"On an infantryman's wages? How much does a private make in the British Army?"

"I think it's thirty-five pence a week. Don't ask *me* how he does it."

Clive Dunnay was standing with Walter Johnson at the entrance to the big tent and peering inside. Provisions and supplies were stacked everywhere, leaving little space for the camp bed in the middle. From over in one dark corner came the subdued crooning of half a dozen chickens in a wire cage, and two pigs were asleep near the door flap. A green parrot peered suspiciously at them from a perch beneath the tent's main ridge pole. It cawed a greeting. Of the tent's official occupant there was no sign.

"And all this lot." Walter swept his good arm around in a gesture that included everything in the tent. "Where does he get it from?"

"Harry trades—anything and everything. He's probably at it now; but he said he'd be here. Let's wait outside for him."

Clive dragged two empty tea chests out of the tent and pushed one across to Walter Johnson. Both men pulled out pipes, but with one arm in a sling Walter could neither fill nor light his. He waited while Clive cut tobacco from a twist of dark shag, rubbed it to shreds between his palms, and stuffed them into the briar. Walter put the pipe stem in his mouth, then had to wait again while Clive lit a match and held it for him. He nodded his thanks as he got the pipe going.

"One more thing you can't do one-handed," he said. "I never dreamed there were so many. Did you ever try to button your fly with one arm in a sling?"

Clive gestured downward at the cast on his left leg. "Did *you* ever try to empty your bowels when you can't bend your knee?"

"No—but you're better off than me. You only have to take a crap once a day."

The two men had spent the whole day together. Jenny seemed to be avoiding Clive after last night's debacle, and Walter was lost without his typewriter and his flying companions. He was itching to tell the tale of his aerial battle to the American newspapers; but with his broken arm he couldn't even write longhand.

The pair had wandered through the interior of the castle, their pace limited by Clive's crutch-assisted hobble, until Monge politely suggested that they might prefer to enjoy the sunshine and the fresh air.

In other words, get out of here, said Walter when Monge had left. They moved outside and took up seats by the side of the chateau, away from the wind. A bottle of wine, and then a second one, made talking easy.

"He *did* say he'd find me a typist?" asked Walter for the tenth time.

"He promised it." Clive puffed on his pipe and watched the cloud of blue smoke drift up into the afternoon sun. "Don't worry. He'll deliver."

"An English-speaking one."

"If you need it, he says he'll find one who speaks Swahili." Clive paused. There was a terrible sound of clashing gears from down the hill. "That must be the truck now. He'll tear the transmission apart if he uses the clutch like that."

The truck with its fabric top had come growling up the hill toward the chateau, its red-, white-, and blue-painted emblem bright in the sunlight. While Clive and Walter watched, it mysteriously veered off to the right and disappeared behind the stables. The sound of the motor ceased.

"What the devil is he doing?" Clive struggled to his feet and grabbed his crutch. "There's nothing around the back."

"There must be. You stay where you are—you can't walk worth a damn." Walter Johnson knocked his pipe out against the heel of his boot. "Let me see what he's up to."

He hurried down the hill and around the grassy plot by the back of the building. At first it seemed that the truck had vanished completely. Then Walter spotted its front end jutting out from behind a storage shed. As he came closer, he could see that the driver's door was open and the rear step of the truck was lowered.

When he moved around the truck, the scenery changed dramatically. Instead of dull paint and fabric he was looking at a pair of women's legs, and a tight, well-shaped behind in a white cotton dress. Their owner was bending far over the truck's tailgate, struggling to pull something from inside. She bent further, and the back of her skirt lifted another couple of inches.

Walter watched without speaking for a few seconds. It was a sight too good to waste. Then he coughed gently and said: "Hello. Anybody home?"

The woman jerked upright and turned to face him. Walter was looking at a well-groomed blonde in her late twenties, fair hair swept high off a smooth forehead. Lipstick-red lips, elegant nose, and well-defined cheekbones. About five-five, he guessed, without those heels. Her blue eyes were humorous and lively, and she didn't seem put out by his sudden appearance.

"Well, hello to you. How long have you been here?" Her voice was throaty, with an accent that Walter vaguely recognized as Cockney.

"A minute or two." His second look confirmed his first. She was a knockout. "I'm Walter Johnson."

"Oh, Harry told me you'd be here." She gestured him forward. "Give me a hand, will you?" She bent forward to tug at a wooden crate, and Walter had another good view of a terrific pair of legs. "I'm Penelope Wilson," she said over her shoulder. "Penny for short."

Walter came to her side and took hold of one corner of the crate. "I'm glad you put it that way—'Give me a hand'— because I've only got one working. How long are you staying here?"

As Walter was speaking, the door of the storage shed opened and Harry Holloway appeared, accompanied by Monge. The Frenchman squinted at Walter, shook his head, and set off at once for the chateau.

"There," said Harry. "You've buggered it." It was not clear who he was talking to.

"Buggered what?" said Walter.

"We had a deal going. Hothouse fruits for navy rum. Now you've scared him and I'll have to start again." Harry nodded to Penny. "I see you two already met. Did you bring it, love?"

"Right here." She nodded at the wooden crate. "It weighs a ton. And I had a terrible time driving this thing."

"I heard you stripping the gears when you were still back in Souilly." Harry was heaving at one of the wooden strips on the crate, levering it upward. "Dark rum, twelve bottles of it. A hundred and sixty proof, for the injured boys here. They'll knock it back like mother's milk. I was afraid from the sound of the engine Penny would have smashed the lot on the way here. Come on, you two—lend a hand."

Walter and Penny were standing motionless, staring at each other and taking no notice of him.

"If you don't have to leave in a hurry, would you have dinner with me?" said Walter.

"Well! You don't waste much time, do you? You've only known me about ten seconds."

"I told you he was a fast-talking Yankee," said Harry. "Look, I've got to go down to the chateau and sort out my deal with Monge. Why don't you two go to the tent and have a glass of my booze, get to know each other."

"The tent!" said Walter. "I forgot about Clive Dunnay. He must be wondering what's happened to me. Penny"—he turned to her—"I can't really offer you dinner, because I'm only a guest myself. But I'd love to drink Harry's gin with you."

"Not gin." Penny linked her arm through Walter's and led him around the stables. "Anything but. Give me a holler when you need me, Harry," she said over her shoulder.

Clive was still sitting on the tea chest when they arrived at the tent. He certainly didn't seem to be waiting impatiently for Walter's return. He had rolled the left leg of his trousers up to the knee and was bending over to look at his splinted calf.

"Itches like fury," he said when he realized that Walter was there. "Makes me want to tear the bandages off and have a good scratch. Hello, Penny Wilson, I didn't realize you were here."

"Just drove in. Wait a minute." She disappeared inside the tent, and the two men heard a clattering of wooden boxes. There was a loud squawk from the green parrot, and a quite recognizable "Pretty Penny."

"Took me months to teach him that," said Penny when she emerged. She was carrying a bottle in each hand. "Where did those blinking pigs come from?"

"The spoils of war," said Clive. He had his doubts about Penny, but she was certainly a cheering influence. "How do you find your way around there in the dark?"

"Experience." She held out one of the bottles. "Walter, this is gin if that's what you want. And this is peppermint schnapps—Harry keeps it for me, but you're both welcome to share it."

She sat down by one of the tea chests, pulling her skirt demurely downward and tucking it around her legs. Walter took the bottle of gin (good quality Hollands—how did Harry get his hands on it?) and sat down next to her.

Penny knew Clive from Souilly, but she had heard nothing of Walter's adventures. The men spent the next quarter of an hour telling her the whole story. She was fascinated by the air battle, sitting openmouthed when Clive described the bullets pumping into the fuselage of the Nieuport close to Walter, then the burning engine of the Fokker and the fall of both planes.

"What do you do if the aeroplane catches fire and you can't bring it in to a landing?"

Walter gave her a quizzical look. "You have a choice. You stay in and cook, or you jump out and squash."

Penny patted his leg and shivered. "I wish I hadn't asked."

The level in both bottles was steadily going down. Clive could feel his head beginning to swim. He and Walter had been drinking since early afternoon, and he'd lost so much weight since he came to France that the liquor was having a big effect. He thought of the drinking that went on continuously, on both sides of the line, to add courage and drown sorrows. The whole war was being propelled by alcohol. Dutch courage, produced by genuine Hollands gin. In Clive's case it had failed to produce the required bravery. And Jenny must have sensed it.

His train of thought was interrupted by a whistle from the stables. Penny sighed and stood up. "That's it. No more peace for the weary. Harry needs me—I wonder what he's talked that poor old bloke from the castle into now."

Walter took the half-empty bottle of schnapps from her hands and walked with her a little way in the deepening twilight toward the truck. When he came back he was grinning and shaking his head.

"Quite a little lady, that one."

Clive raised his eyebrows. It was none of his business. On the other hand . . . "This the first time you've met Penny Wilson?"

"First, but not, I hope, the last. Why?" Walter flopped down on the tea chest and upended the bottle he was holding.

"Well . . ." Clive shrugged. "Penny's very nice. But maybe she's not exactly what you think she is. Not what you hope she is."

"She's not?" Walter frowned. "Tell me more."

"I've seen her around quite a bit in Souilly. She's very pleasant, but she's . . ." Clive hesitated. "Well, I don't know what you'd call it in the United States, but back home she's what we'd call a lady of easy virtue."

"I sure as hell hope so." Walter laughed, very loudly. "Clive, old buddy, that's *exactly* what I think and hope she is. You had me worried there for a minute. I thought you were going to tell me she was Harry's private property."

"No, not that. But there have been others. Maybe a lot of them. Don't you . . . er, don't you *mind*?"

"She's got the pox?"

"No! I'm sure she doesn't."

"Well, then." Walter was peering at him in the twilight "Clive, my young savior of the Empire, how old are you?"

His voice was a little slurred on the consonants. He had drunk more than Clive.

"Twenty-seven."

"All right. And I'm twenty-five. But let me tell you, that's *old* for an aviator in this war. You know the figures for the air squadrons as well as I do. Once they go into flying service, the pilots last about six weeks. I'm twenty-five, and I may not see twenty-six. I *think* I will, and I expect to live through this war and last to a ripe old age. But that's the way we all feel until we cop one. I'm not looking for a wife. I don't want to *marry* little Penny. I just want to have fun, the way I guess you have fun—pardon my mentioning it—with your Jenny. Hell, even if Penny *did* have a social disease, I'd take the risk. I might not live long enough to feel the symptoms."

He sat back, staring up into the evening sky, where the first stars were appearing in a growing overcast. "Anyway," he concluded, "the bottom line is that Penny will be coming to my room at ten o'clock. We made the arrangement as she was leaving, and that gives me a few hours to get the effects of the booze out of my system. I hope all this doesn't shock your British socks off."

It didn't, but Clive felt hollow inside. Walter's sexual self-confidence was obvious. The American pilot wasn't filled with self-doubt, about war or women. He had a certainty about him that Clive had never known, even before the war.

"Who's that?" said Walter, breaking into Clive's thoughts. "Coming out of the castle."

Clive looked from the tent to the bulk of the chateau, dark now against the evening sky. A cloaked figure was emerging from a door at the foot of the northwest tower. It was a man, looking carefully around him before he closed the tower door. Sitting by the curved canvas of the tent, without lights, Clive and Walter were invisible.

"I think it's the Marquis," said Clive after a moment. "It's his size and build."

"What's he doing, creeping out of the side door like that?"

"Why shouldn't he? It's his chateau."

"Yeah—but that's the whole point. He doesn't *need* to

creep about like a spook. He *owns* the place." Walter stood up, not quite steady.

"Where are you going?" Clive kept his voice as low as Walter's.

"Nowhere special—just being a little bit nosy." Walter set off down the hill, trailing the Marquis with exaggerated caution.

Clive watched him go. If he keeps that up, he thought, he'll fall over something in the first fifty yards. And then his own attention was drawn to a second figure emerging from the chateau, this time from the southwest tower.

What *was* going on here? The second figure was a stranger, but he walked with a definite limp. It had to be Cecile's boyfriend, Richter, whom Clive had heard about but not yet met. The man was carrying a cylindrical object under his arm, and like the Marquis he looked carefully around him before he closed the door and set off across the grass toward the river.

What was he carrying so carefully? And what was he up to? Clive's duties in military intelligence had lain dormant since the shells near Fort Vaux had knocked him unconscious. Now that interest came to life. Even if nothing significant was happening, it wasn't up to Walter Johnson to show Clive his job. He stood up slowly, reaching for his crutch, and began to hobble after Charles Richter.

In less than a minute he knew he was going to lose him. The other man was lame, but unlike Clive he was accustomed to his lameness. He could move over the rough ground by the Aire River far faster than Clive, and he knew just where he was going. Clive had to pause frequently to find his bearings or make sure he was not about to fall into a ditch or over a fence. It was almost dark now, with a low bank of cloud moving in to hide moon and stars.

Finally Clive gave up the attempt. He stood still, looking down to the riverbank. Richter was there somewhere, in among the rushes and sedges. But where he was, or what he was doing, was beyond Clive's powers to determine.

Clive turned and groped his way back toward the chateau. It took a long time until he was once more at the entrance to the tent. There was no sign of Walter Johnson, but the bottle of gin was there, with a note in clumsy block capitals underneath it: LOST HIM! SON OF A BITCH CHEATED AND GOT ON A HORSE.

Walter, writing with the wrong hand. Another wasted effort. Clive rubbed at his itching leg and went on into the chateau. Maybe he would see Jenny there. He was not sure whether that thought gave pleasure or pain.

CHAPTER NINETEEN

At its closest point to the Chateau Cirelle, the Aire River widened into a muddy meadow. The ground there was flooded every year for a couple of weeks, and it always remained soft and slimy underfoot.

Charles Richter picked his way forward across a set of harder banks of earth. He had scouted out his route well by day and could move dry-footed over the swampy ground. Around him were shoulder-high reeds and osiers, and across the river stood a thick bank of taller willows which made approach from that direction impossible. He worked his way to a point close to the riverbank itself, where a dry spot about eight feet across was entirely shielded by tall reeds. He put his package on the ground and unwrapped the oilskin protective cover.

The instrument he pulled out was simple enough. It consisted of a powerful flashlight, with a long collimating tube shaped to direct all the light in one tightly focused direction. Unless an observer sat right in the narrow field of illumination, nothing would be seen. A much smaller electric light, throwing a tiny spot of light only half an inch across, enabled Richter to make adjustments to the setting and to check the time on his pocket watch.

He looked up. It was overcast, but the chance of rain was negligible. Visibility was good. At ten o'clock precisely, when it was fully and finally dark, he turned on the flashlight and began to signal.

He neither expected nor received an answering blink of light to acknowledge that his message was being observed.

The cloud layer above Saint-Amè and the Chateau Cirelle was a thin one. It began at three thousand feet and ended before four thousand. Just above the upper edge of that layer, hovering motionless and silent as an anchored ship on a white, billowing ocean, hung the zeppelin. The night was so calm that the slightest effort by the propellers kept the great ship poised in a fixed position.

From the forward gondola beneath the ship three thick ropes hung straight down like a triple anchor cable. They were inch-thick plaited strands of best Manila fiber, all connected to a single powerful winch in the lower part of the gondola. They passed down through the cloud layer, a thousand feet of line that terminated at a small cylindrical basket with a stout metal frame and floor. The wicker wall of the basket came to waist height and was no more than three feet in diameter. Inside it, peering over the side and looking uneasily down at the dark and silent landscape surrounding Saint-Amè, stood a German soldier. From time to time he looked up, trying to draw comfort from the shifting and featureless bottom of the clouds. The three ropes, connected at equal distances around the edge of the basket, felt like his only contact with reality. Whenever he leaned out to look at the ground, he took one rope in each hand and clutched so hard that his knuckles showed white.

The German group had practiced the maneuver several times down on the ground. However, it had taken all Dolfi's sharp tongue and forceful personality to urge Private Koontz into the basket once they were high above the clouds. The private had complained of a toothache and a bad chill. Dolfi had given him his own greatcoat and told him to get on with the job.

"Don't you value your self-respect as a soldier? Don't you want to do your duty to the Fatherland? Into the basket, Koontz, and to work!"

Koontz had finally climbed in. He wanted to be a good soldier. But his silence as he was lowered through the clouds owed more to frozen fear than ready acceptance of his role. The descent through the cloud itself had been quite tolerable. There was no sense of height or motion when the basket was actually within the cloud layer. Nothing was visible. Koontz was surrounded by a thin, impalpable mist, closing in on him and in some indefinable way buoying him up. That had changed when the basket finally plunged out into clear air. He became precariously poised high above the ground, totally dependent for his life on three threads of rope. The ground was infinitely far away, and his head swam with vertigo.

"Private Koontz." Dolfi's voice, clear over the field telephone that hung down to the edge of the basket, interrupted his uneasy thoughts. The phone had its own line, a thin shielded wire that ran parallel to one of the three supporting ropes. By design, Dolfi was out of sight and earshot of the other two men crewing the Zeppelin. They remained aft in the separate engine compartment. He had easily convinced his superiors that in this mission secrecy ruled all other considerations. "Private Koontz," he said again. "Attention. Can you hear me?"

"Yes, sir." Koontz came out of his glaze of fear. A familiar voice—even of a disliked and arrogant superior—was comforting in these circumstances. "I hear you very well."

"You are in position?"

"I think so, sir." Koontz gulped and looked again over the side. "But I can see no details on the ground—only the general line of the river. And no signal."

"It is twenty seconds before ten o'clock. Watch for the identifying signal; it should go on for at least one minute."

"Yes, sir." Private Koontz clutched two ropes, bent carefully over the side, and stared down. Even Dolfi must be feeling the tension—his voice did not have its usual calm confidence. Damn the man. If he was worried about how the job would be done, why didn't he come down here and do it himself? Because the idiot didn't know Morse code, that's why! If Private Koontz had ever suspected that a position in the Signal Corps might lead him to a terrible job like this, he would have asked for a transfer to the infantry on the eastern front.

Far below, near a distinct bend in the river, there was a sudden point of light. It flashed on and off in a regular sequence. A short blip was followed by a longer one, then by another short one. The whole pattern was repeated over and over.

Koontz risked freeing one hand to grab the field telephone. "I see it, sir. He is sending Morse code for the letter *R*. It is our man."

"Excellent. Stand by for the message."

After the introductory sequence, it finally came. Letter by letter, the flashlight on the ground dribbled out its message. Word by word, Koontz interpreted it and passed it on to the waiting and impatient Dolfi.

The information on French troop movements was sent first. It continued for nearly twenty minutes. At the end came a different signal. There would be a two-minute break before additional information was sent on other subjects.

Koontz relayed that fact and added, "I think we are drifting south-southwest. There has been movement of the signal with respect to my position."

"Noted." Dolfi's voice was cold. "I will initiate appropriate action."

There was a vibration in the ropes supporting the basket as the propellers took the airship to a corrected position relative to the ground signal. Koontz hated that—it made the basket sway and roll and feel even more insubstantial.

"Continuing message," he said when the unpleasant movement was finally over. "New subject: access to chateau. Possible by posing as shell-shocked and mute French soldier. Two such specimens already passed through, thus credibility no problem. Uniforms and I.D.s available from prisoners. Suggest access to French territory across line at Saint-Mihiel. End of subject."

Again there was a wait, while Koontz, his duties over for the moment, looked nervously down and then up. The bottom of the clouds was a shifting, wispy succession of strange shapes and fancies. Sometimes he felt as though he could reach up and grasp the moving vapor. He looked over the side again and shuddered. The situation was more tolerable when he was interpreting signals and had no time to think. The slim ropes holding him three thousand feet above the land of hostile France looked frailer than ever.

"Admirable!" Dolfi's voice sounded over the telephone. He seemed pleased for the first time in the evening. "Is that the end of the messages?"

Koontz was staring down again. Two long signals, two short, two long. "No, sir. He is sending a comma. There is more."

"Damnation." In the gondola, far above, Dolfi was itching to get back to German territory. Richter's suggestion would work; it felt exactly right. Dolfi had learned to trust his instincts. In twenty-four hours he could be in French uniform, a bandage around his head and on his way to Chateau Cirelle. "What else does he have to say? Surely he is almost done."

"Signal begins, sir." Private Koontz cut off his superior's flow of words and pulled the greatcoat tighter around him. His tooth was hurting and it felt a lot colder in the basket. "New subject: Cross and Ritual."

Those words aroused within Dolfi the oddest mixture of excitement and rage. The Cross! He had told Richter that anything about the Cross was to be treated as a matter of the highest secrecy, never to be mentioned to anyone—and here was the whole thing, passing up through the field telephone.

"Have reason to believe Cross itself at chateau," translated Koontz through the field telephone. "Gospel and other document probably in possession Marquis de Saint-Amè. Will try to confirm. End of message." Koontz paused. "Sir, I said that's end of message. Anything else?"

There was no reply. A thousand feet above him, Dolfi was pacing furiously in the little gondola. The Cross! And the Gospel! Treasures more sacred and powerful than the Grail itself. He had known they were real, from the first moment he had heard them mentioned. They were his for the taking, in the castle at Saint-Amè. All he had to do was make his way over to the Chateau Cirelle—Richter, fool though he might be, had pointed the way—and help himself.

Dolfi ignored the yammering from Koontz far below. It was hard enough to think this through without idiotic interruptions. Apparently he had overestimated Richter's instinct for security, for what could be said and what should be kept secret. Well, there was a lesson in that. Dolfi was struck by another thought. Richter was an inevitable complication; he had to know about the Cross. But why should there be others? Secrecy was important above all things. There was no reason why anyone else should have the knowledge, and there were excellent reasons why they should not.

He weighed the factors in his mind. There would have to be explanations, but he could provide them.

He pulled out the sawtoothed bayonet that he carried at his right hip, and tested its edge on his thumb. Like a razor. As it should be; he kept his equipment in absolutely first-rate working order. He must be careful when he impersonated a French soldier—the lack of care of their equipment was typical of that slipshod race. Dolfi's mind was already working on the problem of the journey to Chateau Cirelle as he walked across the gondola to the drum and ratchet of the great winch.

It was a pity about his greatcoat.

Far below, Koontz was becoming impatient. He had called into the field telephone half a dozen times without receiving any reply. Was it possible that the thing wasn't working and all the last part of his message had been lost?

He shouted into the telephone mouthpiece again. "Do you hear me? I am ready to be hoisted up. The message is finished. Do you hear me? Hurry up—I am cold down here."

Instead of a spoken reply, there was a strange trembling in the rope that he was holding with his left hand. He stared at it, perplexed that just one rope would vibrate like that. Suddenly the tension in the rope vanished. The whole thousand-foot length of plaited fiber came dropping silently out of the cloud layer, past Koontz's startled face. The basket, supported now only on two points of its perimeter, tilted far off the vertical and swayed dangerously.

Koontz screamed and grabbed the two remaining cables. "Help!" He was shouting into the swinging field telephone, too frightened to take hold of it. "Get me up. One of the cables has broken."

There were a few moments when the basket seemed to be rising into the cloud layer, close enough to touch the white, swirling surface. Then the rope in his right hand shivered and lost its tension. While the basket swayed and lurched, the cable came dropping out of the sky, falling past Koontz. He was looking straight down for one moment and saw the rope turning and coiling as it fell, still attached to the side of the basket.

He clung to the one remaining rope and fixed his feet firm on the floor. He did not scream, but frantic gobbling noises came from his wide-open mouth.

When he felt the third rope going, he was still unable to cry out. His lungs lacked air. He gave a strange groan, faint, high-pitched, and whimpering, and he waited. There was one awful split second of free fall as the basket began its drop, then his clawing hand fastened onto the dangling field telephone.

The basket spun away out of sight, loose ropes coiling and writhing about it as it fell. Koontz clung to the telephone receiver with a madman's strength. One-handed, he pulled himself up until his other hand could grab for the thin wire.

The telephone had been made for cold and damp and tough field conditions. It had not been designed for simple strength. At the moment when his fingers were closing on the wire, the connections ripped out of the receiver. His wild grab missed the end of the wire by inches. The wire whipped out of reach. He saw it vanishing far above him.

And now, at last, Private Koontz could scream.

CHAPTER TWENTY

Louis Villette rode north from the chateau for one mile, then turned east. He crossed the Aire River at the only other ford within six miles of Saint-Amè, lifting his soft leather boots so that the waist-high water would not wet them. He had too long a night ahead to tolerate damp clothing.

Hector was calm and surefooted in the water, and whinnied softly when they were halfway across. The big black stallion had made the trip enough times to know what came next. The low overcast of cloud made the night almost totally dark, but Hector padded steadily and confidently across a river meadow and was soon on a dirt road that lay shrouded in a knee-high blanket of spring mist. Black-cloaked and black-hooded, the Marquis became an invisible figure on an invisible horse.

Nine miles from the chateau, the road passed a pair of deserted farmhouses, each with its own stable and outbuildings. Louis Villette dismounted and walked Hector to one of the barns. He took the saddle off the stallion, pumped fresh water into the trough, and made sure that there was plenty of dry hay available. He patted the horse on the neck and was rewarded with a friendly push from the coal-black muzzle.

"Patience, Hector. I will be back before daybreak." He closed the door of the barn and headed east.

All the farmhouses that he passed had been abandoned. Of the farmers who had left during the German advance, few had had the nerve to return for more time than it took to collect their most precious possessions. Then they had fled west, seeking safety closer to Paris.

The area was scattered with French sentries and observation posts, but there was little buildup of forces. Even the trenches existed only in a broken pattern. The Marquis, picking his way across the fields, sought the shadow of hedgerows and shrubs. He made steady progress. Before midnight he had crossed the quiet and deserted No-Man's-Land between French and German lines and was on the outskirts of Saint-Mihiel itself.

The town sat squarely across the Meuse River. At Saint-Mihiel, the Germans had successfully taken the town and occupied both riverbanks. Substantial German forces were living within the town itself, and others bivouacked just across the river, on its eastern side. The town was under a strict curfew from nine at night to five-thirty in the morning, but the sentries had been monitoring that curfew for more than one and a half years with never a sign of a problem. By midnight they had found their niches and sheltered spots and were sound asleep. The worst trouble they expected was to be caught by their own officers, and few of those would be out late unless there had been an interesting party. Then the principal job of the sentries was to escort their fuddled superiors safely back to their own beds.

Even so, Louis Villette took no risks. He walked softly, pausing at every corner and surveying the street ahead before he ventured into it. The town was old, tranquil, resting on its foundation of twelve hundred years of history. Enemy occupations came and went; this one, too, would pass away. The church clocks were chiming one when the Marquis came to a small low-built stone house on a quiet side street. He stepped up to the shutter on the front window and looked in through a narrow crack in its left-hand side. A single candle had been placed on the bedroom dresser. Satisfied, Louis Villette went to the unlocked door, walked up the two stone steps, and went in. He was in the kitchen of the house.

The interior was totally dark.

"Late tonight," said a quiet woman's voice. "Problems?"

"Not with the sentries. I had to go slower than usua**l** because I hurt my foot a little."

"Let's go into the bedroom."

Louis's eyes had been adjusting to the dark, and now he could see a faint white shape in front of him. He followed it across the crowded and tiny kitchen into the next room.

"Does it need attention?" The woman had turned to him as he moved close behind her.

He shook his head. "It hurt when I did it, but now it's all right."

The woman gestured to a wooden chair and went to seat herself on the narrow bed. She was in her early forties, dressed in a long, grubby robe. She looked much older because she was gray-haired and stooped and had lost all her front teeth. Years younger than Louis Villette, she could have passed as his mother. Her complexion was dark and wrinkled, and she spoke French with a strong Italian accent.

She looked at the Marquis expectantly, and he reached inside his cloak and produced a small leather pouch and a calico bag filled with coffee beans. She took them without a word and went back into the kitchen. He wondered again where she kept her money. Obviously, it had to be somewhere where a German search party would never find it. Behind the stove? In with the flour or sugar? Up in the cobwebbed rafters? They were all too obvious. She would have found somewhere subtle.

She was gone nearly five minutes. He waited impatiently, eyes closed. When she came back from the kitchen she was carrying a huge mug of black coffee and a glass of absinthe. She handed both to the Marquis and went to sit down again on the bed.

He put the absinthe on the windowsill but sipped the coffee. "Thank you, Gabriella. Anything for me?"

She gave him a gaping smile. "Of course. I earn my pay. First suggestion. Jeanne Hermite lives on this side of the river. She is fourteen years old, and becoming pretty. Her parents know that the German soldiers have their eyes on the girl. Monsieur Hermite would welcome a chance to get Jeanne safely away, out of the occupied region and into French territory. Thanks to me, your name is known to them. They would put the girl into your safekeeping if you assure them you can get her safely across from German to French territory and to their relatives in Montargis. If you agree, I can tell you how to get to their house."

"Very good. But it must be done immediately. She must come with me tonight."

"Tonight! Then it is impossible. They will need at least two or three days to prepare her for the journey."

"Tonight."

"Then Jeanne Hermite is out of the question."

"Are there others?"

"Monsieur, it is impossible. Without notice—"

"Gabriella, you know me well. I do not exaggerate. I tell you, I have no choice. It must be tonight."

The woman shook her head. She was silent for a few moments, eyes dark and calculating. "Perhaps there is one way. It is more risky, but it is your only chance."

"I accept risk."

"On the other side of the Meuse River, close to the eastern edge of town, lives the Raymond family. They have four daughters. The oldest two have already been taken as mistresses by German officers. The fourth daughter, Lisette, is only eight years old. She is safe. But the third daughter, Agnes, is fifteen. She is pretty. Two days ago a German officer stopped by the house on some pretext, but he did not fool them. Every hour they wait and worry, expecting another knock on the door. Monsieur Raymond is desperate. He would entrust his daughter to you in a moment, I am sure of it—if you can reach her and carry her to safety."

"She is across the Meuse River." Louis Villette was frowning.

"Exactly. Eighty meters across, no ford, and only one bridge usable. You would have to cross it, with Agnes." Gabriella coughed and pushed her hair back from her eyes. "But that can be arranged. There are plenty of small boats if you know where to ask."

Louis Villette looked at her and reached into his cloak. A second small leather pouch changed hands, and again Gabriella disappeared into the kitchen for a few minutes.

"Now listen closely," she said when she returned. "I do not want to write this down." She looked at the Marquis with thoughtful dark eyes. "You will have to do a little climbing."

"I can do whatever is necessary."

Louis Villette listened carefully, then stood up. As he left the house, he wondered just what Gabriella believed he was doing with the girls who left occupied Saint-Mihiel for French territory and "safety." The brothels of Paris or Marseilles, or the camp followers of the French Army? White slave trading to North Africa? Chances were she did not care. Sometimes he thought that Gabriella hated Germans and French equally. But she was intelligent, and even reliable—for money she would do anything, and there was no chance that the Germans would pay her as much as he did.

He walked upstream, staying away from the river until he had reached a place where the houses stood right on the bank. Many had stone steps that led down from their gardens to a mooring at water level. He counted houses carefully, then stepped through an open gate and along a stone path bordered with flowering roses and peonies. At the end of it, six stone steps led down to a small landing where a wooden rowing boat was moored to an iron ring.

He rowed slowly and quietly across the river, to a similar small landing on the other side. He saw nothing but the V-shaped ripples of water rats, but he knew that this whole area of the river was much busier than it was officially supposed to be. The Germans looked the other way at the trading of produce from one side to the other—much of their tea and coffee came across the river, in exchange for gasoline and farm produce.

Before he tied up the boat, Louis Villette took out his watch, opened the face, and carefully felt the position of the hands. It was already almost two-thirty. He had to be back at the chateau by morning. He walked quietly to the gate that led into the street, then paused. There were lights ahead—too many of them. Even at this hour he could hear talking and see moving lanterns. It might be impossible to do anything tonight about Agnes Raymond.

He stole along the street, keeping always in the deepest darkness. At the corner that led to the main eastern road, he halted.

He was looking at rows of German tents and lines of parked vehicles and gun carriers. There were thousands of them, standing in the shade of the avenue of oaks and cypresses that bordered the road.

This was no small-scale maneuver. He was seeing the buildup for a massive German advance, more substantial than anything since the beginning of the Verdun offensive.

Could such a great array of men and machinery be assembled here unknown to French intelligence, with the area around Saint-Mihiel so little protected by French forces? Louis Villette remembered very well the months before the battle for Verdun. The French generals had ignored all evidence of German buildup and had actually pulled the best troops and artillery away to other war efforts. It seemed to be happening all over again, here at Saint-Mihiel. But there was one crucial difference: The Germans already occupied the west bank of the Meuse River. From here, they could march unhindered by fortifications or geography toward Bar-le-Duc and on to Paris.

Louis Villette had to return to Chateau Cirelle. If anything called for the immediate invocation of the powers of the Cross, this was it. Here was a greater threat to the safety of France than anything since the first German offensive.

But he hesitated. He needed all the information that he could get, and he would never have a better opportunity. The German troops were too busy to keep a close eye on the dark river. He had another hour to find out all he could about the size and disposition of the German forces.

He also saw that he had no choice now. The Cross itself must have led him here to observe this new German force, and to tell him that he needed Agnes Raymond as he had never needed any Vessel before. He had to find the girl and return to the chateau with her. Somehow he must snake his way through the German forces, locate the Raymond house, and bring her with him. Risk had become irrelevant.

He inched forward toward the first line of gun carriers, assessing the size and weight of the artillery. It was so dark that for the moment he felt in no danger.

He was still forty yards from the vehicles when a low growl came from the darkness. Suddenly two low shapes appeared on the ground just ahead of him.

Louis Villette froze. Guard dogs. The first he had seen in this area of the front, and the last thing he had expected to encounter. They would be trained to immobilize and kill anyone who ran. He felt for his pistol, then paused. Even if he could kill both dogs—which was doubtful—the sound of the shots would be fatal for him. He would have a thousand Germans after him. The way back across the river would close at once.

He reached to his belt and pulled out a sheath knife. If he could kill them both, quickly and quietly, the sound of the scuffle might be taken for a nocturnal chase after rats or cats.

The dogs were still crouched low to the ground, but they were inching steadily closer. Louis Villette decided to tackle the left-hand one. It was slightly bigger. If he could achieve a quick thrust to its throat . . .

As he was lifting the knife, there was a laugh and a whistle from the darkness. "Siegmund! Siegfried!" said a nearby German voice. "Here."

"Damn it." A second voice sounded even closer. "If those dogs are off after that Frenchman's bitch again—"

The voice stopped. A flashlight had been switched on. Louis Villette was standing full in its beam.

CHAPTER
TWENTY-ONE

Where was he?

Jenny walked outside the chateau, listening to the dull muffled thump of guns to the northeast, like the pounding of a wounded heart.

Where was Louis?

When he had not come to her last night, she had assumed that she would at least have breakfast with him. But he had not come home. That was not totally unexpected if he had more war business than usual to attend to, but it *was* unprecedented. During the six weeks of their *belle affaire* he had often set out for his *assignations de la guerre*, but he had always returned. Even if it was very late and he did not see her that evening, he would be sure to share a *premier déjeuner* with her the next morning. It was as though he had to, that somehow in seeing her he received the energy and life that was drained from him in his war efforts.

This morning, though, he was nowhere to be found. Nowhere.

She had wandered through the chateau, then sat for a couple of miserable hours by her father's bedside. At the insistence of Monge she had taken coffee and a hard roll there, plus a wedge of cheese. The poker-faced servant was not worried at all by the Marquis' absence. He assured Jenny that sometimes these things happened. But he must have realized on some level that she and Louis had become close, because he seemed to take pains to make sure she was well attended to. Today he seemed concerned about her mental and emotional health in the absence of his master. The Monge prescription for a lonely heart: cheese.

Now as she walked she took the uneaten wedge that she had hidden from Monge at breakfast, and thought to nibble the sharp, tangy stuff. She found, though, that she had no appetite. She had felt ill when she awakened and it had been all she could do to get her coffee and bread down, sitting in that gloomy bedroom. Sheer misery? Or something more than that? She had her suspicions.

She pushed those thoughts away. Think of something different, something to make you happy.

Closeness.

That hardly seemed the correct term. Yet there didn't seem to *be* a correct term for what she and Louis shared. Just an incredible, resonant, sweeping set of emotions that tore through her like some breathless symphony.

Intimacy. And *happiness*.

That seemed like a sin, here and now. She walked past the hospital tents and saw half a dozen wounded soldiers hobbling about on aimless exercise walks. Even from a distance she could smell the harsh medicines and salves and the foul odor of gangrenous flesh. Suddenly she knew she had to get away for a while, away from her ailing father, away from the sick and the dying, away from this dark and lonely war. Away. Normally the arms of Louis would be enough to calm her and give her what she needed. Now, without him, she felt that she needed to get into the fields of France, his own beloved countryside. Maybe she could feel closer to him there, and it was closeness that she needed now above all.

Even though she was walking west, it seemed as though she could not escape the war. She heard trucks rumbling along a far-off road. The shelling continued its distant grumble. The very air now seemed tainted with the death and misery of battle. Even though she'd never been to the trenches, their misery seemed to reach out and cover the chateau and all its environs with a palpable atmosphere of doom. Sometimes she wished that the field hospital—in a sense her own creation—were not there. Sometimes she wished she hadn't decided to be Florence Nightingale. Sometimes, like now, she wished that the only people in the world were she and

Louis, shrouded by their love and listening to the song of the linnet.

But today there would be no linnet rhapsody. Although the day was fine and the bird was singing, it could not reach her. The scene was beautiful as ever, but now its beauty was like a landscape painting in a museum. She got no taste or smell or feel out of it. She felt dead inside, dead except for her feelings for Louis, valiantly pushing away the dread that she felt, the fear for her father, the uneasiness about the war—and, yes, the guilt that filled her mind whenever she thought about Clive.

Jenny glanced back toward the castle. Poor staunch, brave, uncomplaining Clive, who asked so little. He was somewhere in there now. At some level she loved him still, and she would trust him with the world. But she had been deliberately avoiding him. He must know it. What he did not know—could never know—was the delirious excitement that filled her heart whenever she thought of Louis.

That was what she must recapture now. Jenny sat down at the crest of a hill, looked away toward Paris and peace, and allowed her mind to stray back toward a happier time . . .

. . . one week into their physical relationship. They had said practically nothing to each other after a light dinner. They had simply made love, ecstatically and repeatedly.

Afterward they lay in Louis's rooms, covered in furs by an excellent fire. He was sipping brandy, but all that she would accept was more of the sparkling Burgundy wine that she had drunk with their meal. She loved it, although Louis spoke of it disparagingly as "not a real wine."

He stared into the fire, his eyes troubled.

"It is a sad thing to think, my love, that something so beautiful as our union was caused by something so horrible as this war."

He seemed racked by some kind of deep spiritual pain, and Jenny thought it best only to rub his strong naked back soothingly, rather than embrace him. It was as though he needed to suffer through the pain of this paradox: From war, love.

She thought about that herself for a while, and then she

said, "I don't think we should look at it this way, Louis. Maybe sometimes fortunate people find others to comfort them in times of need. You well know how I feel about Clive, and the commitment I once made to him. I would never have made that commitment if I had known I was going to meet you—and yet, I met you at a time when I needed you, when Clive could not give me the comfort I needed." She shook her head. "Though *comfort*, Louis, is far too mild a term."

He shook his head vigorously, tossed down the rest of his brandy, and flung the glass into the chimney-place.

The shards sparkled in the firelight, and the smell was violent and immediate, an interplay of fiery warmth with grim cold that hovered on its edges.

"You do not understand."

"Louis. Louis, are you all right?"

He shrugged and sighed. Looked back at her with something in his eye that she'd never seen before they'd become intimate. Something admiring, almost worshipful—the look of a man who was listening to the most beautiful melody he had ever heard and could hardly bear the ecstasy.

"Yes. I am all right. I am sorry. I am sometimes too much the victim of my moods." He slid over to her and embraced her with great power and great fervor, silently gripping her as though he could not believe what was in his arms—and then in a moment he became soft and gentle again, almost like some great, purring cat.

"Louis." Just the feel of his name on her lips said it all. He was like some god who had come to her, some answer to prayers she'd never known she'd uttered. "I understand."

"*Chérie*. How could you understand? How could you possibly? You are not me. You cannot delve into my mind, my past—"

He shuddered, and suddenly he was like a helpless child against her breast.

"Louis. Shush. Just be still. We are together now. This is what matters."

"No. I must speak my mind." He turned and looked at her. "When I was a little boy, my mother—she was very cold, distant. I was alone much, forced to entertain myself. Nonetheless, my father trained me well in the ways of the world, and so when I became of age I could wend my way well amongst males and females.'' A smile, a little gleam in his eye. "However, I certainly preferred females."

"You Frenchmen! You think you are so very different."

"For good, for bad?"

"That is not for me to judge. Not now, not after the time I have spent with you. Not after what I have learned about the ways and depths of passion."

"Ah—well—let me confess to you. I was quite the ladies' man. I made it a study. Suddenly I had much attention. I relished it, I studied the methods and techniques . . . I looked forward greatly to the act of love. And yet, with every conquest, with every frisson of love spent within a woman, there was only ashes afterward. Always. But with you, it is different. You are excitement, beyond belief. And you are also languorous calm, a bouquet of flowers and wine, you are soft, loving warmth and ease. Somehow I love you even more when I am spent."

"Louis, I know. I feel the same way."

"Shush. Allow me to finish. You see, I had long since given up the hope of real love. I was intended for it—made for it in a way that men of modern times are not, I think—and yet for all these years my heart has been empty."

"But your wife . . . and Cecile's mother?"

"They loved me, I think. And maybe I loved their love. But love *them*, the poor women themselves? Perhaps a little. Not the way it is with you, though—'' He whispered something in French.

"What?"

"*Pardon.* I said, *la demande du coeur* . . . the heart's prayer, its request. No, not quite that. Its *desire*. I feel a heart's desire I never knew I had. That, Jenny, is what I feel for you."

His words reverberated in her like the last chords of some majestic organ prelude, echoing and lingering on in a cathedral streaming with holy light, wandering on as though it would never fade.

A strange feeling possessed her.

Ancient.

Mystical.

There were depths of love, physical and spiritual, that she

had no idea existed before, and yet she found herself tumbling into them now.

Every inch of her body was aware of Louis's presence, attuned to him, transported by him.

She had thought herself exhausted physically, and yet she felt a glow coming over her. She had to share with him something deep within her—and yet the immediacy of new physical need for him squashed that.

She reached out, stroked his strong back, ran kisses down his shoulder in a soft and gentle way that was pure instinct. Their body scents mingled, merged with the smell of the fire, created a sudden heat of renewed desire.

In a few moments, helplessly, he was on her again, passionately creating the physical dance that mirrored their emotions. She felt the truth of his love, felt it to her very core. When, long-drawn minutes later, she again gasped out in shuddering release, it was his name she spoke over and over, with a new and fervent understanding of the incredible bond they had created. . . .

A butterfly had settled gently down on a flower near where she sat.

The scent of fresh grass, the taste of the reds and oranges of wildflowers. Cool breeze, warm sun.

Abruptly she emerged from her reverie. Memory had drawn her fully back to that time with Louis, and she shuddered with remembered passion. She felt the need for him grow in her, an ache in the pit of her stomach.

Now, on the crest of a hill facing the fields of France which her lover loved so, she remembered something she had wanted to tell him that night, would have told him if she had not succumbed to that amazing rekindling of passion.

When she was a little girl and her father had read her fairy tales, William Marshall always called her 'my little princess.' And when she roamed the Connecticut countryside around her home, she had told herself her own stories, her own fairy tales. In these stories she was the main character, and she would dream about that special prince who would come to make her happy ever after.

Her conceptions had been bright with imagined details, filled with sprawling castles and intricate kingdoms . . . and yet, she'd never had the prince quite in focus. She could never figure out what exactly he would look like, or be like, or do, or precisely how he would make her happy.

Now she knew. Knew who that prince was, what that prince would do.

The prince was a Marquis.

He was her heart's desire, as she was his. But she had not told him that, or that he was her prince.

Where was he?

The thought hit her again, with irresistible force. Jenny rose, brushed herself off, and started her lonely trek back to the chateau.

When she still had a hundred yards to go, she saw Monge walking directly toward her. Since he seldom left the chateau, it could be no accident. He had clearly come looking for her.

Bad news? About Louis? She ran to meet him, nervousness and lack of breath corrupting her French when she reached him into a rough stammer. "Louis—the Marquis—is he—is he all right?"

"I assume that the Marquis is quite all right." Monge gave her a little formal bow. "Although, Mam'selle, he has not yet returned."

"But you were coming to meet me."

"Indeed I was. To give you a message."

"From Louis?"

"No." Monge held out an envelope between finger and thumb. For him, that was the height of informality. Back at the castle it would have been presented to Jenny on a silver salver.

"Not from the Marquis," Monge went on. "It is from a lady who describes herself as a relative of yours, a Dr. Ellen Blake."

"Aunt Ellen!"

"Indeed? In any event, she wishes you to know that she has arrived in Rembercourt. This letter is for you to read. And she adds that at your earliest convenience, she would like to meet with you."

CHAPTER
TWENTY-TWO

Might as well face her and get it over with.

Clive made the decision as he walked back into the chateau. He went at once to Jenny's room. To his secret relief, she was not there. He went on to the next corridor, checking William Marshall's room. His superior officer lay silent and unconscious, with the face of a dead man. There was no sign of Jenny. Clive sat down at Marshall's bedside.

A man gave up an easy life, money and comfort and respect, for this. For a lonely, almost invisible death surrounded by people who wouldn't even understand his last words. That was one terrible thing about war: Deaths were so frequent and numerous that the loss of a single individual became insignificant—except to those who loved him.

Clive had been writing home randomly and infrequently, always putting a casual and cheerful face on everything. As he stood up from William Marshall's bedside, he resolved to write more often; and to tell, if he could, the truth about the war. There were too many glowing reports of 'splendid morale,' written by visitors who spent less than an hour near the front. This war needed a shot of reality—like the man in front of Clive, a life slowly fading with no one able to help.

Clive was in a thoroughly black mood when he wandered back along the corridor, knocked on Walter Johnson's door, and went in. The American pilot had been moved into the chateau at Jenny's suggestion. He was whistling tunelessly and doing his best to shave one-handed. He had the mirror propped on the windowsill and was making lethal sweeps across his cheek with an open razor.

"Ever try doing things with the wrong hand?" he said as Clive came in. "It makes you as clumsy as a baby. Where did you disappear to?"

Clive sat down on the bed. "Went after Richter. I didn't find what he's doing, though. He headed off for the river, too fast for me."

"Up to no good?"

"Chances are he's following Harry Holloway's footsteps and doing a bit of illegal trading. But it might be something worse—and part of my job is security leaks."

"How could he leak anything down at the river? There's nothing there but frogs and fish."

Clive shrugged. "There could have been somebody waiting for him."

"You've got too much imagination," said Walter. "If anyone was waiting, it was a girl in the bushes. You saw my note?" He drew the razor slowly and carefully up the underside of his chin. "The Marquis was easy until he got to the edge of the grass. Then he climbed on a big black horse that had been tied to a tree, and *whoom*, that was it."

Clive did not answer. He was staring moodily at the floral pattern on the bedspread.

Walter rinsed the shaving soap from his face, looked critically at the result of his efforts, and picked up a towel. "Look, I don't know how long you're proposing to sit there imitating Hamlet, but I want to remind you that I've got a date arriving here in ten minutes. I'm sure Penny could handle both of us, but that's not my idea of fun. Get my meaning?"

Clive nodded and stood up.

"And cheer up, buddy," went on Walter. "Army life may be nasty, brutish, and short—that's why you've got to have fun while you can. Go find Jenny, and show her what a fine upstanding specimen of British manhood can do."

She already knows that. Clive went back along the corridor to Jenny's room, knocked, and went in. She was still not there. He sat down on the bed and rubbed at his calf. No pain—but what an itch!

He lay back and closed his eyes for a second. He was still there ten minutes later when Cecile entered the room. She was dressed in a white silk blouse and a pleated skirt of bright cerise, and was carrying an armload of clothes.

"For Jenny," she said as he sat up. If she was surprised at his presence, her manner showed no signs of it. "Isn't she back yet?"

"Back. Back from where? I didn't know she'd left."

"From Rembercourt—ten kilometers west of here." Cecile stared at him. "Where have *you* been all day? You weren't at dinner."

"What on earth is she doing in Rembercourt? There's nothing there."

"There is now. Her Aunt Ellen has arrived. Do you know her?"

"Very well. Jenny lives with her. But I didn't know she was in France."

"Word came to the chateau early this afternoon that her aunt had arrived in Rembercourt, and Jenny set off at once. She didn't tell you?" Cecile was frowning at Clive, deep lines furrowing her dark forehead. "Excuse me, but I do not understand you two at all. You are attractive people, you are in love, and you have been separated for months. Then, when you meet again, you act as coldly as strangers. You should be overjoyed, touching all the time, unwilling to be parted for a moment. Instead you ignore each other. You go off, you stay outside the chateau, you do not come back even for meals—" She broke off. "And why do you keep doing *that* all the time, to your leg?" Her expression changed from accusing to sympathetic. "Are you in pain?"

Until she spoke, Clive had not been aware that he was rubbing his left shin. "It doesn't hurt." He rubbed again, this time deliberately, and smiled up at Cecile. "It *itches*— worse than you can believe. As though somebody put a lot of fine hairs under the bandages and was moving them up and down. I'm being tickled to death."

"Do not joke about this." Cecile came forward and knelt at the bedside, taking Clive's calf in her hand. "There should be some irritation as the break in the bone knits together, but what you describe suggests an infection under the bandage. Can you walk?"

"Well enough."

"Then walk. We are going to my bedroom." Her manner

had changed completely. Instead of criticizing him, she had taken charge. Clive allowed her to support him on her arm as they walked to Cecile's room. He was placed on the edge of the wide bed and told to lean back and roll up his trousers leg. He did so, and Cecile burst out laughing.

"English underwear." They had been speaking French, but now she switched to English. "Designed to boil the wearer—you should boil puddings in them. Roll it up."

Clive meekly obeyed. It was pleasant to be fussed over and told what to do by an attractive woman.

"Right." Cecile had gone over to the wall and taken down a fearsome knife, with an eighteen-inch blade and a leather handle. "Now, this should not hurt, but it may. Let me know, and I will act accordingly."

While Clive looked on uneasily, she began to cut away the bandages, dressings, and splint. It certainly hurt, but not enough to complain about. Finally she was down to the bare skin, stitched and bruised, and was leaning over it closely. "As I thought. There is some mortification—not too bad, and we can take care of it. Lie back."

She went to the dresser and Clive heard the clatter of bottles and jars. Cecile was muttering to herself in a language that was neither English nor French nor, as far as Clive could tell, anything that owed its roots to Europe. After a minute or two she returned holding a pot of grainy dark green paste. "Medicine is strange," she said. "This is a strong poison. Take it by mouth and you would be dead in a day. But applied externally, it will work a miracle on your leg."

She had taken a dollop onto the ends of her fingers and was placing small amounts at carefully chosen points on the mottled blue-black surface of Clive's leg. She was also probing now and then at the dark wound with a small knife. That did hurt, quite a bit, but Clive gritted his teeth and hung on. While she worked, she hummed softly, almost inaudibly. Her attention was focused completely on her work. "I understand now," she said finally. "You should have told Jenny that you were in pain and it was affecting your feelings."

"That isn't the problem!" Clive blurted it out, then wished he hadn't. He had told the truth instinctively about what was *not* the difficulty, but he couldn't possibly talk about what was.

Cecile was sitting cross-legged on the bed. She leaned back and moved her attention from Clive's leg to his face. The high-voltage look from those big dark eyes went right through him.

"So tell me what is the problem. I have to work this ointment thoroughly into your leg. While I am doing it, I will turn off the light and leave only a single candle. You must lean back, relax, and talk. Begin at the beginning, when you came to France, and tell me everything that worries you. But tell me in *French*, not English."

Clive leaned back and closed his eyes. Everything? There was too much to tell.

He began with the trenches. As he spoke, the sights and sounds and even the smells came flooding back. The gunfire, the maggots, the stench of decayed flesh, the weary frightened men. He told her of the dead, powder-blackened face of the drowned German soldier lying in the stagnant mud of the trench. He saw it still, waking from sleep. He confessed his own terrors, his fear of castration after the shell hit, his nightmare of the spectral Jenny. Somehow Cecile had realized what Clive never would have guessed, that speaking of these things *in French* allowed him to describe them in full detail, with an impartial point of view that made honest speech possible.

Cecile said nothing. She was invisible, gently massaging ointment into his leg. Finally Clive came to his arrival at the castle. He was able to talk of his meeting with Jenny, and of the shock of his own impotence.

He stopped, and opéned his eyes. Cecile had finished with the ointment on his leg. Now she was sitting with her chin cupped in her hands, staring at him. In the candlelight her face was all soft angles and shadows, pensive and beautiful. He could not see her eyes at all.

"Poor Clive," she said. "You honestly believe all this nonsense? That any man who is intelligent enough to be afraid of being killed will become impotent?"

Clive had not quite said that, but she had summarized his feelings.

"So the problems with Jenny are all your fault," she went on. "Do you believe that?"

"I think that women sense fear," said Clive. "And they despise it. And then the man can't—the man—"

"*The man*," said Cecile. "This man." She reached forward and touched his lips. "This very attractive man who believes he is a coward. He would not appeal to any woman, right?"

Clive gave her a look full of misery and doubt.

"He would prove impotent," went on Cecile, "even with a woman who found him handsome and stimulating. He would not be able to make love, right?"

She had moved a little, so that although she still sat cross-legged, her bare ankles and calves were visible. Clive looked at them, then glanced away. Cecile had a body that made Jenny look boyish. She leaned toward him, and he was staring right at her full breasts.

Quite deliberately and casually, Cecile began to unbutton his jacket and shirt. When his bare chest was revealed, she laughed softly and ran her hand across from nipple to nipple. "I have wanted to do that since first I saw you. Now, I must not do all the work. My blouse, and then my skirt. And then the rest. *Do your duty, Captain Dunnay*." She gave the last command in English.

Clive fumbled with buttons and hook-and-eyes, and caught his breath as a glowing body came into view. Cecile wore her nakedness with no embarrassment. She moved behind Clive, placed her breasts close to him, and reached around him.

"Sauce for the goose, sauce for the gander." She unfastened his trousers buttons. And when he was finally naked, she sighed and took him gently in her hands. "So beautiful, so shapely. When I was eight years old, my mother told me of the most dangerous snake in Africa. Beware the black mamba, she said. It can run faster than a speeding horse, and its bite is death. But more than that, beware the white mamba. Once bitten, you will seek its bite again and go to the ends of the earth to get it. And she was right. Come, my white mamba."

Clive was rising irresistibly in her grasp. Everything that had gone wrong with Jenny was going right tonight. He had never felt so excited. He reached out to stroke Cecile's breasts, and she moved her body against his hand like a stroked cat. He began to climb on her, but she pushed him back.

"No. Your leg is hurt." She moved above him, and murmured her delight. "But here you certainly do not need a splint."

She lowered herself slowly onto him. He penetrated smoothly and easily, while she sighed with satisfaction. After a moment she began to raise and lower her hips, teasing him so that he was almost dislodged at the beginning of each stroke, then reentered her completely and deeply as she pushed down.

The feeling of pleasure that her movements gave him was almost too intense to stand. He was not sure how much of it he could take. But after a few seconds, before Clive was even close to a climax, Cecile groaned, quivered, and sank down on him as far as she could go. Her eyelashes fluttered, and her eyes rolled up so that only the whites showed. She clutched his shoulders and brought her breasts hard against his chest. He heard her shuddering breath in his ear.

After a few moments she lifted her head and sighed. "Sorry. That was quite a surprise. I was more excited than I knew." She kissed him hard on the lips, then sat up and began to move again, very slowly and carefully. "Gently," she murmured. "Oh, God, I'm so sensitive there now. That was delicious, absolutely delicious. Easy. Easy. Gently."

Clive found it hard to obey those instructions. He could feel her internal muscles gripping and squeezing him, like a slowly pumping heart. Her body was against him, and the odor of her filled his nostrils. She was beginning to move more vigorously again, her eyes wide open and staring down into his.

There was no way that he could restrain himself for more than another second. He was swelling uncontrollably inside her. He grabbed her buttocks and pulled her hard toward him, at the same time pushing up violently into her. She responded to the spasm of his orgasm with a thin, high-pitched moan, and moved frantically up and down on him. He squeezed, so hard he could feel their bones creak, and thrust up again.

Then she was lying flat on top of him, her hair over his face and her mouth at his ear. "Sweet," she whispered. "So sweet, so sweet."

Clive kissed her neck and leaned forward to run his tongue along her shoulder. Her soft skin was salty with perspiration. She stirred against him, and put her fingers to his cheek.

"Mmm." She wriggled a little. "I like that. You have a gorgeous and exciting body, Clive. I love you when you are impotent. Be impotent with me anytime."

Clive smiled. He was feeling wonderful. For the first time in months he was relaxed and enjoying life. He knew there was a terrible load of guilt waiting for him when he thought about Jenny and what had just happened; but for the moment he could not think of it.

He put his hand to Cecile's head and turned it so that he could look into her eyes. "How did you know? How could you possibly be so sure that I was not impotent?"

"Ah." She snuggled against him. "I could say I have an infallible instinct in this. But the truth is simpler." She laughed softly. "If I could not excite you by my own efforts—it turned out to be very easy—I could call up reinforcements. On the dresser there, I have a salve that comes from my hometown. It is called *rashstithril*, and it is made from the sap of a lily flower. It would give an erection to a dead man. It is supposed to be infallible."

She sighed and rolled off Clive to lie by his side. He reached out and put his hand contentedly on the curve of her belly. It was warm and slightly damp. He felt Cecile's hand touch his thigh, then her fingers trailed gently upward.

"Let us rest here for a while, nice and close," she said. "Then we will see what happens." She rubbed him gently. "I think I know the answer. But if we have to, we can always call on *rashstithril* for a little assistance."

CHAPTER TWENTY-THREE

The news of Aunt Ellen's arrival in Rembercourt, only a few miles away from Chateau Cirelle, had filled Jenny with a mixture of pleasure and nervousness. It would be nice to see her aunt again, but the last thing that Jenny wanted was Ellen's dabbling into her relationship with Louis or—worst of all—suggesting that she ought to head back to London.

No matter what Aunt Ellen said, she was staying. That was *final*.

Jenny tied the mare outside the inn in the middle of Rembercourt, straightened her shoulders, and walked inside.

The main room of the hostelry was low-ceilinged, dirty, and hot. Dozens of flies and fat bluebottles buzzed around the grimy windows or struggled helplessly on sticky flypapers suspended from the rafters. They did not seem to worry Ellen Blake. She was sitting contentedly in a window seat, drinking black coffee and reading a little blue-bound book with thick yellow pages. As Jenny entered, she pushed her glasses up onto her forehead and gave Jenny a long, evaluating stare. Then she smiled.

"That's one question answered. You're not wasting away here. I've never seen you look so well. The Meuse Valley agrees with you, even with a war going on." She patted the window seat. Sit down."

Jenny sank to the cushions with a feeling of relief. Aunt Ellen was the same as always. "I had trouble getting across the supply route. That's why I wasn't here last night."

"I wondered about you." Ellen placed the book she was reading on the seat between them. She tapped it. "François Villon. If you ever want to know how it feels when a woman loses her looks, read his poem *Regrets de la Belle Heaulmière*. Good thing looks aren't everything. How is William doing?"

"Oh, Aunt Ellen, he's doing terribly. He's so sick." Jenny's other worries vanished. She grabbed her aunt's arm. "He's getting weaker and weaker. The doctors don't believe he will get better and if you saw him, you just wouldn't know him."

"I'd like to see him." Ellen put her arm around Jenny and patted her shoulders consolingly. "It's a good thing you came here, Jenny. The War Office is a disgrace. All they give out are half-truths and untruths. If it weren't for your letters, I would think that William was recuperating from some minor flesh wound. But after your last note I decided I'd better see for myself. How was he wounded?"

Jenny started to talk, and found herself blurting out more than she had expected. She told of meeting the Marquis, of how she had seen the chateau as a possible field hospital for other wounded soldiers, of how Louis Villette had disagreed. How she had persuaded him to permit a bivouac for the wounded on castle grounds. And then—the hardest part to tell—how it was her own carelessness in going to the castle cellars that had led to William Marshall's disastrous fall.

Ellen listened in silence. When Jenny mentioned the ancient castle levels beneath the present superstructure, an expression of interest came to her face, but she kept her attention firmly on what Jenny was saying. At the end of it she shook her head. "An Englishman's home is his castle—you're used to that. But don't forget that in this case a Frenchman's castle happens to be his home. It's a bit much to tell the Marquis that he ought to fill his house with wounded men if he doesn't want to. Is he patriotic himself?"

"Terrifically! He's absolutely dedicated to the French war effort, and I've never met anyone who cares more and thinks more about ways of ending the war. He'd do *anything* to produce a French victory."

Anything? But not use the inside of the chateau as a hospital or convalescence center? Ellen Blake was finding it difficult to build a consistent mental image of the Marquis de Saint-Amè. Jenny's enthusiastic voice didn't match her words.

"And he's not in the least pompous or stuck up," Jenny went on. "When you come to the chateau, you'll see for yourself. He does most of the construction work around the castle personally. He wears the raggiest old workmen's clothes—you'd never know he's a Marquis."

Starry-eyed! Ellen wondered how much accurate information she was likely to get from Jenny about the Marquis. "Why is he doing construction work? Is he going to agree to use the castle as a hospital after all?"

"Well, no. Not exactly. He's been modernizing the chateau. Putting in electricity and cleaning up the cellars. But he's not destroying any of the old part." Jenny hurried on, well aware of Ellen Blake's views of people who regarded anything old as mere junk. "When he adds modern features, he's careful to preserve the original work just as it was. There's a terrific amount of space down there, under the newer buildings. Enough for dozens of people."

"But he won't agree to letting that be used for the wounded, either?"

"Not yet. Actually, there are a few wounded people at the castle right now—Clive is there. He was blown up at Verdun. He got a broken leg."

"But he's all right?" Ellen had noticed a curiously awkward tone in Jenny's voice, and a flush on her cheeks.

Jenny hesitated. "Well . . . he's not—not really better yet. He says he wants to get back into battle, but I'm not sure he does."

"And how about the Marquis? If he's so strong and patriotic, I'm surprised he's not in the army."

"I suppose you're right." Jenny frowned. As usual, Aunt Ellen had asked a question at once that Jenny had never thought to ask for herself. Louis was young enough to be in the army, and he was certainly fit enough. There was an unspoken accusation behind Ellen Blake's words.

"I never asked him," said Jenny at last. "But he is very brave."

"Maybe he was in the fighting earlier and was injured? Has he been wounded?"

"He didn't *mention* being wounded. But he wouldn't talk

about it, even if he were hurt quite badly. He has been injured, though, because he has bad scars on his body.'' Jenny hesitated. Would Ellen ask her how she had come to see Louis Villette's bare chest? It was unlikely—Ellen wasn't one for conventional behavior.

"From bullet wounds?"

"No. One was from a leopard—nothing to do with the war—and the other is a deep burn scar, a cross, right in the middle of his chest. It looks as if somebody branded him. I don't know how he got it, but it must have hurt terribly.''

Now Aunt Ellen was frowning at her in a way that left Jenny uneasy. "That doesn't sound like a war wound. In fact . . . hmm. I was hoping to come and see William two days from now, but maybe I ought to come sooner. Would there be a room for me tonight?''

"Tonight!" Jenny bit her lip. "That's a little soon—the staff are very overworked. How about tomorrow, and I'll ask Monge to have something ready?''

She was relieved when Ellen Blake nodded and turned the conversation back to Clive and William Marshall's wounds. The one thing she did not want to talk about was her feelings for Louis Villette.

They spent three hours together, and as always Aunt Ellen was an understanding audience. But Jenny felt guilty as she finally rode away. She had lied to her aunt. There was plenty of space at the castle to provide an extra room. Jenny was sure that the Marquis would not mind, and Cecile would love to meet Ellen Blake. The inn in Rembercourt was mean and dirty and the food was poor, nothing like the fare at Chateau Cirelle. There was no doubt which one her aunt would prefer.

Jenny was tempted to turn the mare around and go back to invite Ellen to leave at once and come with her to the chateau. Only the thought of Louis prevented her. She had to be in his room when he returned, and she absolutely had to talk to him.

She did not know what she was going to say, but it would not be an easy piece of social conversation. How do you go about telling a man that you think you are pregnant with his child?

When Jenny had gone, Ellen Blake spent a long time sitting alone in the inn's dining room. She was a woman who had spent her adult life piecing together small fragments of information to make a larger whole. Early in her career, she had worked for two months reconstructing an Etruscan vase from hundreds of tiny shards. Her professional specialty often seemed like a repeat of the same problem, though now she worked with information rather than pottery fragments.

She would take many small, disconnected facts, mentally spreading them out on the sheet before her. Then she had to pick them up, by twos and threes, and turn them and illuminate them from different directions, to see if any pair or trio could somehow fit together to make a single larger fragment. And while she did that, she had to be aware that there was a single, whole story as the end objective. It was the simultaneous focus of attention on detail and grand design that was the hardest part of the job.

Now she had a handful of odd facts to work with. The shape of a cross, burned deep into the chest; that rang a bell in Ellen's memory. It was part of an old ritual, the initiation for a group known as the Knights of the Twelfth Apostle. They were a near-legendary order, who supposedly ceased to exist in the fifteenth century. They had believed in the holy powers of a lost Gospel, and they became full members of their sect through a ceremony that involved a branding or "trial by fire," in which the shape of a cross was burned onto their naked chest. Did the sect still survive? Was Louis Villette a possible member?

They had supposedly been widely scattered, influential people, all men, who shared little beyond their allegiance to the Gospel. And there was—but here the picture on Ellen's mental vase grew very shadowy and dim—there was an ancient legend of the cross itself, reputedly made by Judas Iscariot, imbued with strange powers and constituting the sect's most sacred relic.

Ellen had a quarter or a third of the mental vase in position. She had just been provided with a possible chip from the rest. If the telephones were still in working order between France and Scotland, she had two calls to make to Edinburgh. And then her visit to Chateau Cirelle might prove far more interesting than she had realized.

CHAPTER TWENTY-FOUR

"So what have you been up to?" The man behind the flashlight was invisible to Louis Villette, but his voice was more amused than concerned. "Don't you know it's the middle of the night? All you people think about is money—we could have put a bullet through you, as well as slapping you with a big fine, and never a question asked. What do you have there?"

Smuggling. The Germans assumed he was a smuggler between the French and German sides.

"Wait a minute, Dieter." The second voice cut in, less relaxed. "Siegfried, Siegmund, hold him! Get your hands up and identify yourself. I don't recognize you—and I know most people in Saint-Mihiel. Who are you?"

Louis Villette slowly raised his hands. He still had a small bag of coffee beans, enough to justify a claim that he was a smuggler. But how could he give a plausible address?

"I live behind the French lines," he said, speaking German. "I was told there is a good market here for coffee."

"A wonderful market." A man in uniform and holding a pistol stepped forward into the light. He held out his hand. "I'll take that as a gift. We'll see what comes next."

Louis Villette reached inside his cloak and handed over the coffee. His pistol was there, but the odds were just too great to try anything.

"No, Dieter, wait a minute." The invisible companion moved the light to sweep the Marquis from head to foot.

"He's about as much a coffee smuggler as I'm the crown prince. Look at his clothes and his cloak. Look at his boots, for God's sake! I'd give a month's pay for a pair like that." The light steadied on Louis Villette's face. "I don't think we've got a smuggler here. We've found ourselves a much rarer bird. The special orders were to keep an eye out for spies and French observers. I think we've found one."

"Now, don't be ridiculous." Louis Villette made his voice as exasperated and impatient as he dared. The exasperation was real, and most of it was at himself. He had wanted to impress Gabriella with his wealth, because she cared a lot about such things. But it was a mistake. He should have worn old clothes. "If I were a spy, don't you think I'd be dressed differently—in German uniform, or as a river man, so no one would know I'm French? All I wanted to do was sell a little coffee. Hell, I'll give it to you, gladly, if you'll just let me go home to Pierrefitte."

"No. I don't buy that. Dieter, give him back the coffee. We're taking him in."

"Aw, come on." Dieter was still clutching the bag. "Why'd you want to be a hero? It's late. Let's take this and send him back across the river. This town's full of Frenchmen every night bringing stuff in. How's he any different from the rest?"

"Give it back." The voice was determined now. "And you, come quietly. Or I'll set the dogs on you."

They marched northeast. Louis Villette led the way, closely followed by the two hounds. His captors stayed three paces behind, guns unholstered. They walked for over a mile, past hundreds of armored cars, troop bivouacs, and gun carriers. Finally they came to a good-sized farmhouse, a sector head-quarters for army operations. He was handed over to four officers, who had to be rousted out of bed before it could be done. Louis Villette was methodically searched at gunpoint. The battered cross and chain aroused no interest. Both sides claimed God as an ally in the war. The only reaction offered by the German soldiers was a whistle of surprise when the gold coins he was carrying were discovered.

"Thinking of financing the war effort for us?" said the senior officer, a gray-haired captain with an immense curling mustache. "Or is this your idea of beer money?"

"I was hoping to buy gasoline. It is in short supply in Pierrefitte."

"For that much money, you could buy a whole car." The officer threw the heavy pouch onto the table and went on with his inspection of the Marquis' belongings. "Ah. This is really you, is it?" He was holding up Louis Villette's engraved visiting card. "The Marquis de Saint-Amè?"

"I am the Marquis de Saint-Amè, that is correct."

"A real live Marquis. Never caught one of them before." The captain was gradually improving in his mood. He had handed the coffee beans over to a private, and interesting smells were coming from the farmhouse kitchen. "I thought they'd chopped the heads off your sort back in the Revolution."

"They missed a few of us."

"Well, that's a pity. It means we'll have to waste a good bullet." The captain accepted a tin mug of coffee and pushed another one across to Louis Villette. "Spying. You'll be heard by a military tribunal, of course—lasts five minutes, if they're feeling patient. Then you'll be shot. Tough luck, but that's war. Drink your coffee. Sorry there's no brandy to go with it."

"Thank you." Louis Villette forced down a sip of hot, strong liquid and pulled a face. The high-quality coffee had been loaded with molasses. "Are you the tribunal?"

"Us? Good God, no." The captain was genuinely amazed. "You're a Marquis; you ought to rate at least a colonel— maybe a general. And we've got a war to fight. We'll ship you north of here first thing in the morning. For tonight, you can stretch out on a cot. I'll make sure you get a good breakfast, as good as we get ourselves. Just one thing more." His voice was casual, but his face was serious. "Don't try anything. I'll post guard dogs outside your door and window. If they get their teeth in you, you'll beg to be shot."

Jenny.

If he had ever needed her, he needed her now. At this hour, when everything in the world said that the situation was hopeless. The thought of her gave him the strength to go on, to withstand even this ignominy.

"Why waste good food and drink on the swine," the driver

was saying, "and then waste petrol? It's him and bastards like him that keep this war going. Without their spies, they'd have buckled a year ago. If I were running the war, you'd see some differences. It'd be a quick bullet, and all over."

As far as the speaker was concerned, Louis Villette was not even present. The Marquis had not indicated to the men in the car that he spoke German, and the other man assumed he did not. The open car bounced along under weeping skies. Villette was bareheaded, and his cloak had been taken away from him. The greatcoated driver was doing most of the talking, while his three companions smoked rank cigarettes and grunted their agreement. One armed man sat on each side of their prisoner in the rear seats of the car, and a guard dog lay behind them on the floor, silent but awake.

The area through which they traveled showed the marks of devastating shelling and bombing. The land was pocked with craters and crossed by rolling thickets of barbed wire. Louis Villette sat with eyes closed. There was nothing to be done, nothing to say.

If only it were possible to sleep and recoup his energies. But he was too cold and wet. He had managed maybe one hour before the farmhouse was bustling with dawn activity. The breakfast food was unappetizing, thick slices of fatty ham and bloody-yolked duck eggs, hard-fried in pig's lard. He had forced himself to eat until he could not stuff in another bite, and he had drunk milk, water, and coffee until even the Germans looked surprised. He was determined to keep up his strength.

The tribunal was going to be a formality. No one had worried that he was seeing the military buildup; they knew he would never be in a position to tell about it.

He felt sick, and it was not the greasy food that he had forced down. It was knowledge of failure. He should be at Chateau Cirelle. With the German Army poised for a killing stroke across the Meuse River at Saint-Mihiel, it was clear how vulnerable the French were. A rapid German march west to the Voie Sacrée would cut that lifeline, and after that the road to Paris was open, with the French and British forces far away to the northwest. If the Cross were ever to exercise its force, now was the time. But without the ritual, the powers of the Cross were limited.

The driver was pulling the car to a halt. They were in another small village, outside a substantial wooden building.

"All right, shitbag." The driver turned and pointed his finger at the Marquis. His voice was filled with venom. "Inside. Better bend down now and kiss your ass good-bye. I've seen 'em go in, but I've never seen one come out alive."

Louis Villette stepped down from the car. Ignoring the threatening gesture from a guard, he walked across to stand in front of the driver. "I would suggest, *mein Herr*," he said in cold and correct German, "that you pray I do not come out alive." He leaned over to put his face inches from the other man. "For if I do survive, I will find you and cut your heart out. My family was noble when yours was swinging in the trees."

While the driver cowered back, the guards led the Marquis into a hall furnished with one long wooden table and five chairs. Three of the chairs were occupied, and a noncommissioned officer stood at attention by the side of the table.

"You are Louis Villette, Marquis de Saint-Amè and a French subject?" The man in the middle spoke in a bored voice, without raising his head.

"I am."

"You were captured early this morning behind our lines. You are a civilian, not a French soldier. Do you have anything to say on your own behalf?"

"The town of Saint-Mihiel is part of the sovereign state of France. As a French subject I have every right to be there."

There was a creak as the man on the right leaned far back on his chair. "Come, sir, that argument is not worthy of you. Saint-Mihiel is now German territory, as you well know. Let us not waste each other's time."

The speaker was a much-decorated colonel of a Bavarian regiment. He was in his fifties, with grizzled hair and a tan, lined face. He stared at Louis Villette with half-closed blue eyes. "Are you willing to tell us the nature of your activities in Saint-Mihiel? Please do not insult my intelligence by suggesting that you were there to trade coffee for gasoline."

He pulled a cigar case from his breast pocket, opened it, and held it forward. Louis Villette took one. The colonel reached out with a petrol lighter and took a cigar for himself. "Well?"

"I have nothing to say."

The man in the center nodded. "Your brevity does you honor." He looked at his two companions. They nodded. "You are found guilty of spying behind the German lines. You will be executed by firing squad. Writing materials will be available for any messages that you wish to send. I am sure you understand that these will not be sent at once, in case they contain information harmful to our cause. Do you, Herr Villette, have questions or comments that you wish to have recorded?"

"Since I am to be executed, it would be nice of you to tell me *when*."

"As soon as approval comes from general headquarters." The colonel on the right gave a grim smile. "Being a Marquis has, I am sure, had advantages already in life. Now it extends your time on earth until we have a sign-off for you. Any other questions?" Louis Villette shook his head. "Then this tribunal is complete. Corporal, take the prisoner away, and give him food and drink if he requests it. He is a brave man. He is not to be mistreated."

Louis Villette was marched out of the main hall and into a side room containing a single chair and a hard cot. The door closed.

CHAPTER
TWENTY-FIVE

He was early. Charles Richter shielded his eyes from the wind and looked at the fast-moving clouds on the western skyline. In fifteen minutes it would be dark.

He tied the two horses to a young ash tree and crouched behind the stone wall across from an old barn. Cupping his hands, he struggled to light a thin black cheroot. Cold, blustering gusts blew out the first three matches. When at last he succeeded, he pulled his coat around him, found the most protected spot along the wall, and sat smoking until the last red touch of sun was gone. He was nervous and edgy, but he forced himself to sit quietly.

Dolfi arrived an hour late, shivering and frowning. A stained white bandage circled his head and left temple, and he was wearing the uniform of a French infantryman.

Richter jumped to his feet as Dolfi appeared. "Trouble?"

"Nothing that a little warmth won't cure."

Richter offered a brandy flask. "Damnable weather."

"No. The best we could hope for except fog." Dolfi refused the liquor and rubbed his chilled hands together. "No one wants to be outside on such a raw night. I came through the lines without seeing anyone."

"You are late."

"A last-minute call from general headquarters. You will be glad to hear the news. The Grand Advance is set for two days from now. The buildup is complete. The only thing that could cause its postponement would be exceptional weather.

You and I are to proceed as agreed. When the advance begins and we hear the artillery, we will secure the chateau." He stood up. "Let us be on our way. We should take advantage of this cold weather."

"In a moment." Richter moved to stand in front of Dolfi and walked slowly around him. "A good fit. And the uniform is plausible."

"It is filthy! Not fit for a pig."

"That makes it just right." Richter paused. "Those boots—are they French Army issue?"

"Of course!" The corporal bristled. "Every detail is correct. I checked it myself."

"Let me look at your papers."

Dolfi reached into his breast pocket and pulled out a packet of material wrapped in a thin pigskin wallet. Richter inspected every item closely, pausing for a long time over one of them.

"This paper assigning you to the Chateau Cirelle—where did it come from?"

"It's a forgery, but it is based on a real document found on another soldier, one who had been wounded and sent to convalesce near Compiègne."

"The signature on this sheet, Colonel Lemonnier, is that of a dead man. He was killed two weeks ago."

"And his signature on the paper is dated fifteen days ago." Dolfi gave one of his rare smiles. "It was a subtle question: Should I use an old date and a dead man, or a recent date and a live one? I decided that dead men have one great advantage: They are not around to be questioned." Dolfi looked at Richter shrewdly in the flickering light of the little lantern. "Herr Richter, you are nervous. You begin to make me nervous, too. What is the problem?"

"Your visit to the chateau. I am not sure it is a good idea for you to go there at this time. The Marquis has disappeared without telling anyone where he was going. The staff are uneasy, and more alert than usual. And I continue to be worried about the British liaison officer."

"Colonel Marshall? I thought he was too injured to be dangerous."

"He is. It is his assistant, Captain Dunnay, that I worry about. He is curious and intelligent. And he has time on his hands to be inquisitive."

"Never mind Dunnay. I am much more worried about the colonel. Are you *sure* about him? It would be quite in keeping with the British to *pretend* he is injured, so that he can roam as he chooses."

"No. He is gravely hurt. When we get there, you can see for yourself." Richter handed back Dolfi's papers. "One more thing to keep in mind. If you have anything to tell me or ask me, do it now. Once we reach the chateau, you will be Private Bâchet, shell-shocked and mute. Remain silent, no matter what the circumstances. It was hard enough for me to get you into the castle at all. And it will be impossible for me to talk to you. There is no reason why I should speak German to a wounded French soldier. Any last questions?"

"News of Cross or Gospel?"

"Nothing."

"Then I have no more to say or ask." Dolfi's voice took on an edge. "Except to remind you, Herr Richter, that I need no warnings to remain quiet. I am as aware as you are of that requirement."

Dolfi spoke as though he were the superior officer. Richter bit back his irritation, snuffed the lamp, and led the way to the horses.

As he had expected, Dolfi proved to be a deplorably bad horseman. Richter got him onto the mare easily enough, but the German corporal was in danger of falling off whenever they came to broken ground. They crawled toward Saint-Amè. It was two in the morning when the two men arrived at the chateau stables, and Richter led Dolfi in silence around the main building.

He had no intention of going in through the front entrance. At Richter's special request, Dolfi would be housed within the chateau itself. He would be placed in the servants' quarters, in a small ground-floor room that Richter had furnished with a cot, stove, and lamp. An ordinary soldier must not have too much luxury. And a location well away from the main visitor's wing of the house minimized the danger of interference from Dr. Halphen, whose interest in patients seemed inversely proportional to their distance from the chateau kitchens.

They rounded the rear of the building, and Richter opened the creaking wooden door.

"Good evening, Monsieur Richter," said a quiet voice.

Richter jumped and swung around to face the shadows. "Who is that?" He looked quickly behind him. Dolfi was there and, thank heaven, he had made not a sound.

"Walter Johnson."

Richter could see the vague outline of the American against the stone wall of the chateau. "What are you doing here, out in this cold?"

"Just said good night to a young lady." Johnson gestured at the staircase behind him. "Miss Wilson went back to her room. I'm heading for mine." He took a step forward and peered at Dolfi. "More wounded?"

Richter nodded. "A bad case. Blown up in battle near Fort Vaux—can't speak, doesn't seem to know who he is." He gestured at Dolfi, who looked the part, pale-faced and slack-jawed. "Got to get him to bed now; he just arrived. We'll try a few days rest, see what it will do."

He felt that his voice was betraying him, hoarse and out of control. There was no logical reason why he would be making arrangements for a newly arrived and injured private. But Walter Johnson didn't seem to care. He was yawning and nodding, and standing with the slumped shoulders of an exhausted man. He moved past Richter and Dolfi into the chilly night.

"Can't beat a little rest. That's what we all need. G'night."

Dolfi watched him lurching along the wall of the chateau. "Drunken swine," he said softly.

"No talking!" Richter spat the words out, louder than Dolfi had spoken.

The corporal looked at him calmly. "Herr Richter, I do not plan to endanger your life or mine. But we must set times and places where it is safe to speak. How else can I obtain answers to my questions or tell you what I have discovered?"

"I thought it was agreed we will talk only when we are outside and no one is near us."

"As a standard procedure, yes. But we must use judgment. There may be urgent need for conversation." Dolfi looked quietly at the taller man. "And in the event of a disagreement over when and where we should talk, let me remind you that security is my responsibility more than yours."

He turned. Richter looked at his back. At the moment, he wished that the man in front of him was as shell-shocked and unable to speak as he pretended to be.

CHAPTER
TWENTY-SIX

Jenny was miles away, but Louis felt her presence with him in his dour prison cell.

He could sense that she was thinking of him, back at Chateau Cirelle. He was supposed to be having breakfast with her this very morning. She would be wondering about him, asking where he was, worrying, missing him.

He tried to use thoughts of her to channel his own efforts. He had to concentrate on the present situation. Most of all, on attempting the impossible: escape.

Once they realized that Louis spoke German, the guards were quite willing to talk to him. They confirmed what he already suspected, that he was held prisoner in the small town of Hattonchâtel, about twelve kilometers northeast of Saint-Mihiel. The Meuse River lay twelve kilometers west, but there were no roads in that direction. The only highways led to Verdun, to Metz (deeper in German territory), or back to Saint-Mihiel.

They had taken his weapons, his money, and his silver cuff links. After protests they allowed him to keep his boots and the tarnished cross and chain. He could not complain about his treatment. The food was peasant fare, but it was more than adequate, as much as he could eat and plenty of beer. Louis spent much of the day lying on his cot, resting and thinking. Three times he was taken out of the cell to use the toilet. The guards and dogs were always there, watching his moves.

Early the following morning he heard marching feet in the yard beyond the building. He looked out of the barred window, with the waiting dog on its leash outside. It stared up at him. When he pushed his arm through the bars, it growled and came to its feet. The animal looked starved, ready to attack anything.

By standing at the window and craning far to the right, Louis could see across the yard to an area of flattened dirt beyond. A line of riflemen appeared and stood side by side near the end of the area. Louis heard the command, saw the rifles raised, and heard the volley of shots. He could not see the target, but he did not need to. The firing squad formed a file and marched out of sight.

The despair was so strong, it was a physical force on him.

It covered him like a cold sheet of ice. But unlike ice, it did not numb as it advanced. Instead it consumed with a terrible razorlike intensity, draining everything of color and light and sensory impression.

Louis had been pacing to keep his mind under control, to focus on something other than the grimness of his surroundings, as though in movement he could hold back a force that loomed over him like a brewing storm. Inescapable and omnipresent.

But the storm could be held off no longer.

He sat down on the rickety cot. It smelled of mold and urine and squeaked under his weight, but it held well enough.

He took out the Cross of Judas and stared down at it.

It was cold as ice in his hands, and its ancient metal—the metal that had been in so many other hands, including the hands of its creator—was rough with power and promise.

As he held it he could feel its puissance, feel the purpose and promise and resolve that began to banish his despair. He had not held it so until this point, because he suspected what might happen. Even now, he was tempted to dash it into the corner. He clasped it hard, concealing it within his palms, feeling the chill bite of it against his skin.

Jenny. The word seemed to come from the cross itself.

No. Never. He recalled his own words to her. *You are my heart's desire.*

It was quite true. He thought of her constantly. The way

she touched him, the smell that enveloped her clothing, the sweet muskiness of her hair, the gentle vibrato of her voice. The urgency of her love, the gentleness of her spirit. Such wit, such gleaming goodness and love and tenderness. The blend was something he had never encountered before, never expected. It was something he needed in his life, had always desired in his soul of souls, his heart of hearts, never before aware of, never acknowledged.

So good, so pure . . .

Passion had become transcendent, beyond the mere flesh of their beings.

Jenny. The cross suddenly burned warm in his hand.

"No," he moaned softly, his head descending toward his folded hands as though in prayer.

To you alone, Louis Villette, she is the spirit of love. How many young beauties of France were just as sweet to their lovers. . . . Beauties languishing now, as their men rot in the fields of battle. . . . Beauties who will soon endure the horror of domination by barbarians whose ways will wipe out the cherished traditions of France, its culture, and its language. Rape? Pillage? These are gentle words for what will be perpetrated upon a brave and beautiful land. And the glory, honor, and nobility in all that is French will be trampled into the dust.

He could hear music now, somewhere from the corridors of his soul. The beautiful music of his beloved country. It swelled him with pride. Only a Frenchman could understand that pride, that rare and Gallic perfection of being, that happy confluence of terrain and climate and peoples that was the soul of France.

You hear it, Louis. This pinnacle of civilization must be preserved. This pure rare vintage. . . . Your home cannot be desecrated.

Louis knew that the voice was right. For when he had no one, he would still have his country, with all its wealth of sights and sounds and swelling love. Its music, art, wine, its beloved people. . . .

He could not see it crushed under the marching boots of an ancient enemy. Rather than that he would gladly sacrifice himself. All of him, his body, his heart, his soul.

Your heart's desire?

Something wrenched within his chest. He felt a sureness, a rightness. Doubt faded away. . . .

The cross spoke again, but not this time in words. It sent vibrations of certitude and pure bliss. Louis felt it reinforce his own conviction. The signs that he had seen in Jenny were no illusion. She was with child.

She is with child. The cross burned its confirmation.

The death of his heart's desire. As the legate had predicted, his own heart purified in the Ritual of Abraham.

The cross could ask no greater sacrifice. There could be no greater call on its powers. France would be saved.

His body went rigid with purity of purpose, with righteousness of cause.

His mind was suddenly clear and cold as ice.

I know what I must do.

And I know how I must do it. But it can be done only at the chateau.

I must get back to the chateau.

That afternoon the Marquis had an unexpected visitor. A second chair was brought into the room, followed by a choleric, bald-headed man who wore a general's uniform.

"Helmut von Steiner." The man nodded his greeting, but did not offer his hand. He sat on the chair and gestured to the Marquis to sit down also. "You are Louis Villette, Marquis de Saint-Amè?"

"I am."

Von Steiner stood up and lifted his hands to his shirt. He opened the top three buttons to reveal a cruciform burn scar on the chest beneath. "In the name of the Lord Judas."

"And of the Lord Christ," responded Villette. "Which house?"

"Bavarian Grand Order." Von Steiner looked at the door of the room, then checked the window. "I saw your name in the dispatch. You are the Guardian." It was a statement, not a question.

"So long as I live."

General von Steiner raised an eyebrow. "Which will not, I fear, be very long. I brought with me the confirming order for your execution. It will take place tomorrow morning."

"You can do nothing to change that?"

Von Steiner shook his bald head. "I cannot, nor would I. We follow the same High Lord, but our nations are at war. Is the Cross on your person?"

The Marquis nodded.

"May I see it? Only to look upon it."

Louis Villette reached into his shirt and lifted the Cross and chain from their position next to his bare chest. Helmut von Steiner stared at it for a long time.

"Thank you," he said at last. "Like most Knights of the Twelfth Apostle, I did not expect to see the Holy Cross before I died. That is a rare privilege. And now, the prime purpose of my visit. I have arranged to stay overnight at Hattonchâtel. Tomorrow, when the execution takes place, I will be watching. I will take the Cross from your body and make sure that it reaches the hands of the appropriate envoy. You have my word on this, even if it takes my life. The succession of the Cross will continue."

"Thank you." Louis Villette bowed. "Herr General, you have taken a great weight off my mind. It is one of life's ironies, but I was captured in Saint-Mihiel while working with the Cross. The war is the source of all our woes, not the Holy Cross."

"A war that has gone mad." Von Steiner nodded slowly and stood up. "You are right. Karl von Clausewitz taught that war is a political instrument, a continuation of state policy by other means. But he was not thinking of a war like this— a war that is killing half the youth of Europe, man by man. This war is international madness. I have lost three sons. And yet my honor commits me to a German victory."

"And mine to a French one."

The two men shook hands, slowly and formally.

"Tell me one thing more, if you are willing," said von Steiner. "Is there blood on your hands in the name of the Cross?"

"Much blood. I have sought to use its powers to end this war."

"Ah." General von Steiner sighed. "Then I and all our Knights are deeply in your debt. I will do my best to repay it. You are a brave man, Herr Villette. In happier times, I would have been honored to welcome you to dinner at my mess. As it is, you have my sacred word: I will arrange for the return of your body to your home; and I will assure that the succession of the Cross continues.''

He frowned. ''To end the war, you say? *Solely* to end the war, whatever the outcome—or to seek a French victory?''

''I believe that a German victory would destroy Europe.'' Louis Villette did not hesitate with his reply.

The German's expression grew murderous. ''Then damn you. You are abusing your trust! The Cross should not be defiled by fighting the cause of a single nation. It serves a higher cause.''

''It should be used for the *highest* causes, whatever they may be. My actions are appropriate.''

''They are not!'' Von Steiner gripped his sword handle. ''Be glad that you are the Guardian and have special privileges. If you were not, I would tear the Cross from your dead body today.'' He stepped backward toward the door. ''I warn you: If you apply the power of the Holy Cross to favor the French or for any secular reason, you will damn your soul.'' He took a deep breath, fighting for self-control before he left the room and had to encounter the waiting guards. ''*Auf wiedersehen*, Herr Villette. To our next meeting—in the future life.''

The door closed. Louis was still holding the Cross in his left hand. He stared at it for many minutes, his chin resting on his chest. All his earlier certainty and strength of purpose had faded.

Was that my last hope for salvation?

Did it just walk out that door?

Should I call him back? Should I pass on the Cross to him, fall on my knees, and beg the Lord God for salvation for that which I have done? And think to do.

Thus would I save Jenny.

But also thus would I abandon France to damnation.

He could feel the power swelling in the Cross. It was a huge power, but directionless. Inchoate, unpredictable. Only by force of will and ritual could it be bent to the mind of man; yet like electricity, it flowed as a cosmic current along the path of least resistance. It was the power of God in mankind, a single Trinity, the power of dreams and hopes and tears, the blood in the sand of many nations, the shrieking outrage of noble people under the yoke of tyrants.

*Lord Judas. You betrayed Jesus himself to save your peo-
ple—and yet it was no betrayal, because it was the God in
you that became this power.*

It was God in masks, working His will.

Now the mask was worn by a being named Louis Villette.

And the will of the mask could not be diverted from its
purpose. For if the Kingdom of Heaven was upon the earth,
then surely it held sway in the fair land of France, above all
other nations!

Jenny, forgive me.

*Lord Judas, help me. It is an awful thing for a man to know
his destiny.*

By evening a change in the weather was well on its way.
It had begun during a fine May afternoon, when a northeast
wind began to rise. At four o'clock the board roof across the
yard began to lift and rattle. By six the wind was close to
gale force. The guard dog was almost out of sight, tucked at
the limit of its leash in a corner away from the chilly gusts.

The Marquis was standing at the window at seven o'clock
when the guard brought his dinner: cold roast pork, boiled
potatoes, and sauerkraut. Louis Villette took a gigantic portion from the tray.

As always, a second guard with rifle at the ready stood
outside the room at a safe distance. The backup guard was in
his late thirties, with a great pudding belly and several chins.
He shook his head admiringly when he saw how much meat
and potatoes the Marquis was taking. "The world will lose a
great trencherman tomorrow, *mein Herr*. It is a rare man who
can eat as you do, knowing what is in store for him. But
what's wrong with our sauerkraut? You should take some—
it is excellent."

He pointed at the dish. The first guard nodded at Louis
Villette. "He's right, you know. It's first-rate; I had it myself
for dinner."

The knowledge that they were feeding a prisoner his last
meal made them more friendly. In addition to the food, they
had provided a bottle of Moselle.

Louis Villette smiled and shook his head at the offer of
sauerkraut. The guards retreated and the door closed. Later
that night, when the Marquis made his last trip of the day to

the washroom, he handed back the empty plate. "Fine show!" said the fat guard approvingly. "I hope I'll do as well when my time comes."

The wind had continued to rise in force; it was howling and whistling past the building's wooden walls. The temperature had dropped fifteen degrees in an hour. The fat guard slipped an extra blanket to the Marquis as he was led back to his cell.

Lights-out was at nine. The guards checked a last time to make sure that Louis Villette was lying quietly on his cot. They added another dog to guard the door. By ten o'clock the building was quiet except for the noise of the wind.

At ten-thirty the Marquis rose to his feet and went across to the window. The guard dog was lying at the limit of its chain, out of the wind. Louis Villette whistled softly and saw its ears prick up. He went to the cot, bent down by it, and reached underneath. Hidden next to the wall was the food that the Marquis had been storing there for the past day. He had eaten the vegetables, but he had kept all the cooked meat. There were two or three pounds of beef, pork, and ham.

He went to the window and tossed a piece of beef to the dog. It sniffed at the meat, gulped it down in a second, and looked expectantly up at the window. The hound was ravenous. Louis Villette waited a couple of minutes, then threw a second lump.

Over the next two hours he fed the dog every scrap, fat and gristle as well as lean meat. He kept the pace slow, so that the animal could not bolt all its food and vomit it up again. When there was no more, the hound walked heavily across to the wall, out of the wind, and flopped to the ground.

Louis Villette waited half an hour, then took hold of one of the window bars in his big hands. He closed his eyes and concentrated his attention on the Cross on his breast.

Lord Judas. Give me strength, if I am ever to have strength.

He pulled with all his might. The Cross burned on his bare flesh. The bar buckled slightly toward him, rising a fraction in its setting. He heaved again, the muscles in his arms and back knotting with the strain. His hands began to bleed across the palms. He ripped off a piece of his shirt, wrapped it around his open hands, and took hold again.

Now, Lord Judas. He felt a vibration through his chest:

Tingling currents of power flowed from the Cross to his aching hands.

Now!

The bar came free in one great heave.

Another ten minutes, and all the bars were out. He pushed through the blankets from his cot, then forced his head and shoulders into the opening. It was a tight fit. He wriggled until he was hanging head-down, and gave a final push outward to drop onto the hard ground.

He lay still for a moment, listening. The guard dog was sound asleep over by the wall.

Louis Villette stood up, collected the two blankets, and crept away along the sheltering wall of the building. It was an unpleasant, blustery night, with a biting wind. Even though it chilled his cloakless body, he was thankful for its swirling cold. Few guards would be keeping watch tonight if they could find a warm berth inside.

Half an hour later he was a mile away from Hattonchâtel. He headed west cross-country and made slow progress. The moon came and went behind banks of broken cloud, filling the night with moving shadows and false alarms. When the first glimmer of dawn showed in the sky behind him, he went to earth. He walked for a quarter of a mile in a shallow water-filled ditch, to confuse tracking dogs, then crawled into the middle of a dense thicket of elder and blackberry. As the sun came up, he pulled the blankets around him and closed his eyes.

Coatless, hatless, chilled, bleeding, and exhausted, Louis Villette was five miles deep in German territory. The desperate need to return at once to Chateau Cirelle was like a coiled spring inside his chest, but he had no food, no money, and no way of moving safely around the countryside. The German Army would be on the watch for him constantly, perhaps with a reward for his capture.

But he was alive; and he was free. Louis Villette pulled the blankets around his ears and slept his deepest sleep in many months.

CHAPTER
TWENTY-SEVEN

Dolfi awoke before dawn.

He came awake instantly, convinced that something was wrong. After a few moments lying tense in the darkness, he realized what it was. The familiar noises of distant guns, clattering weapons, and snoring companions had disappeared. Chateau Cirelle was *quiet*—so quiet that it had disturbed his sleep.

Dolfi hopped out of bed. The tiny pressure stove sputtered and flared for a few moments when he pumped and lit it, then settled to a steady blue flame. He put a pan of water on to heat while he went outside and relieved himself. The first hint of light was touching the line of the horizon and showing the dim outlines of the castle gardens. It was freezing cold, and when he came back he was shivering.

He made strong, sweet coffee and sat on the edge of his bed, thinking. How far did he trust Charles Richter? Not in terms of loyalty to the German cause; that seemed well established. But was he a good information source about the Chateau Cirelle?

Dolfi was a methodical man. He had to know the exact layout of the chateau, its ins and outs, its exits and its entrances, before he could feel comfortable. At the same time, he wished to *savor* the place. Already he felt like its secret master. In less than two days, the Grand Advance would be under way and he would be in charge, holding this old structure for the glory of the Fatherland. He must know the chateau more intimately than Richter's maps and descriptions permitted. Richter had told him to stay hidden, and he had not argued; but it made little sense. Why risk being behind the French lines, if all he did was skulk in his room? He had to reconnoiter, and there would never be a better time than this predawn tranquillity.

He tucked matches and candles into his pocket, buttoned his coat, and slipped out again into the castle gardens. If he were stopped by any of the staff, his role as a confused, shell-shocked soldier would explain his wanderings. That was the brilliance of Richter's plan. Dolfi could be found anywhere in the castle, and encounter sympathy rather than suspicion. He adopted a hesitant shuffle and wandered along to the central part of the chateau. As he went, he compared what he saw with Richter's description. The man had done a good job. The configuration of doors, towers, and windows was just as Dolfi had reconstructed it in his mind. He suspected that he would be able to find his way through the interior with ease. But he needed to *see* it, to experience it personally. Richter didn't seem to understand that a house was more than a collection of rooms.

The first door he came to was unlocked. It led into one of the kitchens. He stepped quietly inside, enjoying the warmth. There was enough light for him to manage without his candles, even though the fires under the big ovens were just gray ashes. They had not yet been fueled for the day's cooking. He took a fragment of old bread from the top of one of the ovens and bit into it as he went. The kitchens of the chateau were big enough to cook for fifty people. It would make a splendid base for German operations as soon as the advance had rolled through.

He heard sounds from the scullery. There was a clanking of pots and pans, and the clatter of wooden clogs on the flagstone floor. Without hurrying, he moved through another doorway and came to a well-carpeted corridor. He could visualize exactly where he was and where he was heading. This corridor led to two others. The right-hand path went to the front of the house, including the library and the dining room. The left branch was guest quarters. Four rooms along on that side, according to Richter, he would find the British colonel.

A dying man, or a major threat?

Dolfi would find out. He had heard Richter's opinion, that Marshall was at death's door, and he had dismissed it. Richter had his talents, but he lacked caution. Any British colonel, in a place that was a main objective of the German High Command, was a danger. And when you added in the fact that the man in question served in British Intelligence . . .

The door was closed. Dolfi paused and listened for a few moments. No sounds within. The corridor was deserted in both directions. He turned the handle and opened the door a few inches.

Even before he went inside, he realized that Richter was right. There was a smell in the air, the unmistakable, cloying smell of desperate sickness and slow dying. The heavy curtains were drawn, and Dolfi had to wait for his eyes to adjust to the deeper darkness. When he stepped to the bedside and looked down, he saw the slight movement of the chest, rising and falling in the shallowest of breaths. And that was all. He could not see the expression on the face.

He lit the bedside candle and held it close to the unconscious man.

He was looking at the wild hair, sunken cheeks, and pale gray skin of a corpse. The jaw had been wired into position, as though the whole head were held together by dull strands of metal. Only the breathing said that there was life in the body.

Dolfi reached out one hand, spanning the scrawny throat. He had killed Englishmen and Frenchmen already in this war, but only from a distance, through the impersonal action of bullet and shell. If he chose, he could now kill this enemy directly. One minute's pressure on the windpipe, and William Marshall would be snuffed out of existence as easily as a candle.

He pulled back his hand. Suppose a doctor could tell that the colonel had not died from natural causes? The chateau would swarm with soldiers and police. Dolfi stepped away from the bedside. William Marshall was already dying. Killing him would be pointless. War called for self-sacrifice, not self-indulgence.

He left the room as quietly as he had entered it. William Marshall had been one object of interest in the chateau, but by no means the main one. Now that he was satisfied that the British colonel could be no threat, Dolfi felt free for other exploration. According to Richter, farther along this corridor he would find an entrance to the castle cellars.

He walked on until he came to the door, and stared at it curiously. One thing that Richter had not mentioned was its small size. It could be no more than five feet high, and narrow to match. The wood was cracked and scored with age. When he eased the door open, a smell of damp and decay wafted up to him out of the darkness.

Richter had told him that the cellars were lit by electricity, but he had to keep to his role as a sick, shell-shocked man wandering mindlessly through the castle. That man would not know how to use the electricity. It would have to be a candle, and he would make do with the limited light that it could provide. He pulled the door closed, to be out of sight of anyone in the corridor, and found himself in total and overwhelming darkness, on the edge of the long flight of stone steps. He pulled a candle from his jacket, fumbled with the matches, and finally got one lit. When the candle wick caught, its flickering yellow light allowed him to see all the way down the stairs.

It took a few moments to get his bearings. The chamber he wanted, if Richter's description was accurate, lay *that* way, off to the left. The other direction would lead to the part of the cellars beneath the chateau's vegetable garden, and finally bring him out at the old cloisters. It had been too dark to see those cloisters last night, but maybe he could explore them later today.

For the moment, he had higher priorities. He went along the corridor, taking little notice of the barred rooms or stacks of old church pews. He could not allow himself to be distracted; Richter would come to his room looking for him a couple of hours after dawn. When he came to the paneled bedroom he ignored the bed with its overhead mirror and padded restraining straps and went at once to the cabinets.

Locked, as Richter had said; but secured by old-fashioned and simple padlocks. He had come prepared for that.

He spent little time with the wardrobe, or with the larger cabinet. What he was looking for would be in the locked box within the smaller cabinet.

Dolfi held his breath as he worked the padlock and finally felt it click open. The teak door swung outward. He had his first sight of the book and the brass-bound box, and grunted with satisfaction. Then he cursed.

That idiot Richter! He had said that the box was made of brass and had a brass padlock. True enough—but what he had not mentioned was the type of lock. This was not the simple, clumsy device that secured the wooden cabinets. It was a doublet lock, requiring two keys to open it. The second, smaller one had to fit into the larger one's hollow shaft. None of the picklocks that Dolfi had with him would be any use. He tried for a few minutes, until it was clear that he was getting nowhere.

He felt his anger at Richter rising. The man seemed to have no concept of the possible importance of the Cross of Judas, and no interest in its powers.

Dolfi picked up the box and turned it over. There was a dull sound as the contents moved within it. He turned it again and listened more closely. Richter had suggested that the Cross was not inside, that the sound was wrong. But Dolfi did not accept that. The sound would be different if the Cross were wrapped in something—maybe in leather or gut. And that is what it sounded like inside the box.

It was time for direct measures. The box had to be regarded as expendable. Dolfi reached into his pocket for his clasp knife. He opened the short, thicker blade and turned the brass box upside down. The lower part had been made from a single sheet of brass that had been cut, the sides bent upward, and secured to each other with brass L-plates and rivets. The body of the box was sturdy and firm, but the rivets that attached the hinges of the lid were badly corroded. When he pushed the knife blade under one and levered upward, there was a squeaking sound of strained metal and the rivet head broke off.

Now he was committed. There was no way that such damage could go unnoticed. He pushed the blade into the narrow space that showed between the body and lid of the box, and turned as hard as he could. Another rivet gave way. One corner of the box was suddenly gaping open. He could use that to get better leverage with the long blade of his clasp knife. After one more effort, the hinge side of the lid could be pivoted upward; at last he was looking into the silk-lined interior.

He moved the candle to throw more light on the inside. Lying on the bottom of the box were three scrolls and a thin, gray-backed book.

No Cross—unless it was hidden under one of the scrolls. He delved beneath them with his fingers. There was nothing else in the box.

He swore.

Of course there was no Cross! What a fool he had been!

A great fury possessed him, and he smashed his right fist onto the top of the solid wooden cabinet. *The Marquis had the Cross with him*—he would never allow it out of his presence. And Louis Villette was not here.

All this was so obvious. Why had he and Richter not realized it at once? Because they had allowed themselves to be blinded by the existence of a mysterious brass box!

A *locked* box, said Dolfi's subconscious. Perhaps everything was not lost. Why would anyone lock up the contents of this box unless they were important? The books and papers could do nothing without the Cross, but they could be part of the Gospel or the Ritual. And according to the diary that Richter had found—the other book, the one lying in the cabinet—both Ritual and Gospel were essential for the full use of the Cross. If he had these, he might at least have some bargaining power.

He lifted the scrolls and examined them. They looked old, and they were in Latin and Greek, languages that he did not understand. The little gray-bound book was more accessible. It was written in French. Although the writing was old and faded, even Dolfi could make out some of the sentences. But it was senseless for him to waste time with it. Richter would be able to read off every word with ease.

Dolfi replaced the scrolls and the gray book and fitted the lid back on the box as best he could. He locked the cabinets. Anyone who walked through the room would see no change. With box and book under one arm, he headed for the stone staircase, wondering how late it was. In his interest in the box he had lost track of time. Perhaps Richter was already in his room, wondering what had happened.

That thought added urgency to his steps. He was walking

fast when he came to William Marshall's room near the end of the corridor. He turned his head as he went past, looking to make sure that he had not left the door open. As he did so, he heard voices and the sound of footsteps from the turn in the corridor just ahead.

He froze.

If he ran away down the corridor, he would never reach the door to the cellars before he was seen. But he was within a few feet of William Marshall's room. He eased the door open and slipped inside. The colonel was sleeping as he had left him, breathing with a shallow, rapid movement of his chest.

There was a rattle from the other side of the door. It was opening! Dolfi ran to the bedside. He allowed his shoulders to slump, and stared dreamily at the sleeping colonel.

His peripheral vision followed the strangers as they came into the room. Two men wore the plain smocks of medical orderlies. The man walking between them and doing all the talking was short and bespectacled, with a square spade beard. Dolfi recognized him from Richter's description. It was the physician, Halphen—the last man in the world that Dolfi wanted to encounter!

Dr. Halphen continued to rattle along in rapid French as he came through the door; from his companions' bored expressions and the doctor's tone, he was delivering some kind of lecture. Suddenly Halphen stopped talking and gave an exclamation of surprise. He walked over to Dolfi and asked him a question he could not follow, then spoke to the orderlies. They shook their heads.

The doctor took Dolfi by the arm and reached up to his bandaged head. Dolfi shied back, putting a frightened expression on his face, and touched his fingers to his ears. One of the orderlies stepped forward to take Dolfi by the other arm, smiled at him, and said loudly and slowly: "Do not be afraid. You are hurt. We will help you."

Dolfi understood, as much from the man's actions as his words. But the one thing that would be absolutely fatal would be an examination of his "injuries." And escape was impossible—both orderlies were big, powerful men in excellent condition.

The other orderly said something too rapid for Dolfi to

grasp. The doctor shrugged and pointed to the door. As he did so, the man holding Dolfi reached out and whisked the book and brass box from under his arm. Dolfi made a grab at them, but the man shook his head. "Not yours," he said, loudly and clearly. "Not your books."

Dolfi was seething, but the books had to wait. More than anything he was worried about a possible medical examination. As soon as the orderly released him, he turned and made a dash for the door.

They were too quick for him. One of them grabbed his arms, and the other pushed his face close and said loudly, "Wait here. We will come back." He pointed toward William Marshall, where Dr. Halphen was making a brief examination. "Stay with your friend. We will come back soon. You understand? Soon!"

And then all three were gone, slamming the door in his face and locking it firmly behind them. He banged on it a few times until he realized that his knocking might increase their resolve to keep him locked up. Then he turned and leaned on the door, while his mind threw off a hundred wild thoughts.

How long would they be gone?

Not long, he was sure. They would worry about a wounded soldier of unknown condition, left alone.

What could he do?

Once they examined him, they would see that he was in perfect health. They would realize that he was a spy.

What to do? He ran to the window and looked out. It was locked, but he could open it easily enough. More important was the fact that it offered a ten-meter drop onto hard cement. He would break his legs, even if he hung from his hands.

He turned around and scanned the room, looking for some alternative. His eye fell on William Marshall, and he heard the colonel's shallow breathing.

That was it. That *had* to be it. At the very worst, it would throw attention away from him. At best, he would be able to slink off into the shadows. But it had to be done *promptly* before Halphen and his assistants returned.

He ran to the side of the bed. There had been no change in Marshall's condition. Dolfi jerked a pillow from under the colonel's head and clamped it over his face. In a few seconds the supine body's legs began to kick and the arms to flail uselessly in the air. Dolfi, detached and observant, kept up the pressure. Not too much—not enough to cause visible marks. Just cut off the supply of air for the right length of time. He continued until the movement of Marshall's arms and legs grew feeble and spastic; then he lifted the pillow and returned it to lie under the colonel's head.

And now he wanted the others back, as quickly as he could get them. The Englishman was struggling for air, with the gasping and wheezing easily audible from the doorway. The thin hands were clawing upward.

Dolfi hammered on the door with both fists, moaning and yelling. In a few seconds the key outside was turning and the two medics burst into the room, followed more slowly by Dr. Halphen. Dolfi pointed to the bed, where William Marshall was gasping and writhing in a most satisfactory fashion. The three men took one look and moved to the bedside. They lifted Marshall to an upright position, while Halphen opened his black bag and looked for stimulants.

Dolfi faded quietly into the corridor. He paused by the door, to see if the box and book were there. They had vanished, and he dared not search for them.

He ran away around the bend in the corridor. At the moment he had only one goal: sanctuary. He had to find a hiding place, and it could not be his own room, where people might go to find the injured and bandaged French soldier. But in Charles Richter's room, no one would think to look.

CHAPTER
TWENTY-EIGHT

At dawn, the guest quarters of the chateau had been deserted. Now, when it was important for the place to be empty, people seemed to boil out of every door and corridor. Where in God's name were they coming from?

Dolfi crouched in a curtained alcove, waiting for the latest group to pass. First it had been one of the orderlies, haring down the corridor too fast to notice anybody. Then, just as Dolfi was ready to venture out again, a stooping, green-jacketed servant had come hurrying the other way, soon followed by two others. Dolfi ducked back into hiding. At this rate he would never reach Richter's room and safety.

What time was it? Had William Marshall died? Was that the reason for the excitement?

He could bear it no longer. He had to leave and take the risk. As he pulled back the curtain, he again heard voices in the hallway. He crouched back, pulling the curtain across. They were women's voices, speaking English—and they had halted right outside the alcove! Thank God it was dark in here. He could see them easily enough through the gap between curtain and wall. They were both wearing coats, as though they had just come in from outside, and they were talking animatedly. He could understand nothing of what they said. One was young and attractive—Jenny Marshall, from Richter's description. But who in blazes was the other? She was tall and intimidating, and she didn't look like anyone who was supposed to be at the chateau. Dolfi didn't like the way she stared around her, taking in everything she saw with shrewd observant eyes. He recognized in her evaluative glance something of his own habit of observation and assessment. In other circumstances she could be a formidable opponent. But not here, and not now. Dolfi had learned something in this war that he would never forget: Human intelligence was important, but power defeats even the highest intelligence. And in one more day, Dolfi would wield supreme power in Chateau Cirelle.

The stooped man in the green jacket was coming back along the corridor. He also paused outside the alcove and spoke to the women. Dolfi cursed, and shrank back farther into the darkness. Was everyone in the whole castle going to assemble here and jabber away at each other? Dolfi saw the troubled frown on the man's face. He must be Monge, who according to Richter was so nearsighted that he was a negligible threat. Monge was speaking to Jenny in slow and careful French, his voice grave. Dolfi caught the words "Monsieur Marshall" and "very serious." Jenny Marshall clutched for support at the arm of the other woman.

She asked a question, and Monge nodded. He beckoned to them to follow him. As they went along the corridor, Dolfi had a new moment of fear. Suppose Marshall was recovering and conscious and could describe what had happened?

Dolfi waited until the footsteps had faded around the bend in the corridor, then went scurrying along in the opposite direction. He needed twenty seconds of good luck, in which no one wandered across the path he was taking. . . .

Turn left, left again—this should be it. If not, he was in bigger trouble. He threw open the door and went inside.

Richter was sitting on the bed in his shirtsleeves. His eyes widened at the sight of Dolfi, and he went immediately to the door and closed it. "What the devil are you doing here?" he burst out in a low and furious voice. "I told you to stay in your room this morning until I came to you."

"I had to go out."

"Why? It was strictly against orders."

"I had to look for the Cross. During the night, I realized something that should have been obvious to us a long time ago. When the Grand Advance begins, the Cross will not stay here. The Marquis will take steps to protect it and move it away.''

"To hell with the cross. You are endangering the whole advance by your recklessness. Do you want to have the whole chateau searching for the Cross, in every room? What did you do with it?''

"I did not find it. It was not in the cabinets, and not in the box. The Marquis must carry it on his person."

"The box? You looked in the box? How did you manage—''

"I broke it open. The Cross was not there." Dolfi stared at Richter, ignoring the other man's anger. "Are you sure you once saw it—you did not simply hear them talk about it?''

"Yes, damn it, I saw it—with my own eyes, as clearly as I can see you." Richter stared at Dolfi in disbelief. "You say you *smashed* the box? And left it for the Marquis to find?''

"No. I brought it with me, the box and the book, away from the cellars.''

"Then where are they? I don't see them.''

"They were taken from me. You see, I ran into Dr. Halphen and his assistants—I had to smother the British colonel.''

"You did *what*? Then it's all over. You arrogant madman, don't you see your cover is blown completely?''

"No, it's not. They took me for a shell-shocked French soldier—I did not say a word to any of them. I got away while they were looking after the colonel.''

"Oh, my God." Richter stamped across to the dresser. "You mad fool. I bring you to the chateau at great risk, I settle you safely in your room, I tell you to wait for me there—and what do you do? You blunder through the castle like a dumb ox, letting the doctor see you and killing wounded officers, hunting for a crazy Cross that has nothing to do with our mission. Is that your idea of discretion?''

"I did not kill him. I used him only to distract the doctor's attention so that I could escape. Herr Richter, control yourself. Don't you see that I had to get out of there? An examination would have been a total disaster. And before you decide that all is lost, remember this: The Grand Advance is ready to begin! Tomorrow morning the tide of the German Army will sweep through here, and we will need to hide no longer. But we cannot afford to let the Cross get away! Even if the Marquis escapes, the Cross must be ours.''

Richter stared at his accomplice. ''And the book and box? Where are they now?''

''They were taken from me by the medical attendants. They are probably near William Marshall's rooms, or perhaps they have been returned to the chateau library. You must find them.''

''Me! Are you mad?''

''Do you want me to do it myself—to wander around the chateau, not able to ask a sensible question, and in constant danger of meeting Halphen or his assistants? I think *that* would be madly foolish—but if you will not go, then I will. I say again, we must obtain the Cross before the advance begins, or it will be snatched out of our hands.''

Richter was pacing up and down by the bed. The more he saw of Dolfi, the less he trusted him. The corporal had become a madman, obsessed with an irrelevant cross, and unheeding of risks. He was a loose cannon in the chateau, equally likely to fire at friend or foe. And yet there was no way to get rid of him. Richter stopped and pointed his finger at Dolfi. ''If I do it, then you will stay here. Do you hear me? You will not move from this room until I return; not for exploration, not for curiosity, not for food, not even if the damned castle catches fire. Do not go wandering about like the madman that you seem to be. You do not seem to realize it, but we are both in grave danger. Stay here.''

Dolfi nodded. ''I will stay.''

''*Whatever* happens.'' Richter slipped on his jacket and went to the door. ''And remember, there is plenty of time to shoot German spies here before the Grand Advance begins.''

''Well, what's she like, then?'' Penny Wilson gave Walter Johnson a friendly little nudge with her knee under the table as she asked Harry Holloway the question.

''Not what you'd expect—not what I expected.'' Harry was still in uniform, but his shirt was open at the neck and he had a glass of schnapps in front of him. ''You're expecting me to say she's an old gargoyle. She's not. She isn't young, but she's not bad-looking. A few years back she must have been a real bobby-dazzler. She'd give you a run for your money, Pen, in a dim light.''

"That's what Clive says.'' Walter Johnson had been badly hungover early in the day, and he was sticking to weak scotch and water, as sedative more than stimulant. "He knew her in England. I've got to meet this woman, Harry. You or Clive will have to introduce me.''

"You don't need introducing.'' Penny was the only one without a glass in front of her. On principle, she would not take a drink before breakfast. It was three o'clock in the afternoon, but she had only been up for half an hour. When it came to parties, Walter Johnson made Penny's old boyfriends look like amateurs. "Ellen Blake's American, same as you,'' she went on. "You can just go up to her and slap her on the back.''

"You've not met her,'' said Harry.

The three of them had found a quiet corner of the chateau in what Walter called "No-Man's-Land de Cirelle.'' It was over toward the east, with servants' quarters on the north side and guest rooms on the south. In between was the little room that Harry had discovered, not much more than an alcove with a wooden table in it. It was the perfect place for a quiet talk. The rest of the castle was not a comfortable place at the moment. With the Marquis absent and no one knowing where he had gone or when he was likely to be back, the normal schedule of the chateau had been suspended. Monge, expected to give orders instead of taking them, had gone to pieces and seemed unable to make even the simplest decisions. More like a morgue than a castle, complained Walter. It had been his idea to hide away and recuperate from last night's excesses.

"Wait till you do meet Ellen Blake, Penny,'' went on Harry. "She'll put you in your place sharpish. She did it to me before we even left Rembercourt. I'd got a couple of the carpets I'd found here, all cleaned and draped over a joist in the back of the van. She looked at them for a second or two, then she says to me, 'I hope you didn't pay much for this one. It's a fake.' And she was right! She showed me the pattern of knots on the back, and what it would be like for a genuine Ardabil carpet. To me! And you've heard me, Penny,

I've boasted to anyone who'll listen about how well I know rugs.''

"Did she say why she's here?" asked Penny. "It can't be for carpets."

"I know why she's here," said Walter. "Jenny Marshall's mother is dead. Ellen Blake keeps an eye on her. Maybe she'll take her back to England."

"Not a bad idea," said Harry. "See if you can get Ellen Blake to take me as well." He stood up. He had been making lists of figures on a white card with a thick pencil. "Right. I have to go see Monge. And if you two really want to meet Ellen Blake, now's the time."

"Are you going to see her?"

"I don't have to, but I might as well. I promised to take her for a look round the chateau. She already seems to know a lot about it—before we even got here she made me stop the car at the top of the hill, where you can see the whole building, and just from a look at the outside she told me how old it was and who had done the stonework. But the bit she's most interested in is the old stuff, down in the cellars. I said I'd like to see 'em, too."

"What the devil for?" Walter drank the rest of his scotch and water. "I was told there's nothing down there but masses of old junk."

Harry laughed. "Old junk when you buy, antiques when you sell. She's a woman you can learn a lot from. She can tell the value of things better than I can. Want to go with me, or would you rather go somewhere else?"

Penny looked inquiringly at Walter and gave his knee another nudge under the table. He shook his head. "Not today, Josephine. I'm not God's gift to women at the moment. My brain feels two sizes too big for my skull. Let's tag along with Harry and meet old Aunt Ellen. Are you still game for tonight, though?"

"If it's still on." Penny stood up, tightening the ribbons around her waist. "How formal is it? I mean, can I go like this?"

"I'll ask Clive. It's Cecile's outing; she must know. Come on, let's tag along with Harry."

Like the alcove they were leaving, Monge's private rooms were in a no-man's-land between family and servant quarters.

Harry Holloway led the way confidently through the interior of the chateau, stopping once to inspect a small bronze statue.

"Now, then, Harry," said Penny. "That's not for sale, even if Monge tells you it is."

He grinned at her. "Just looking."

Monge's living quarters matched the man. They were crowded away beneath the curve of a staircase, and the brown-painted hallway seemed to squint at visitors from under the overhang. The majordomo opened the door slowly at Harry's knock and peered out suspiciously. He seemed horrified to find three people instead of one.

Harry sighed. "You two wait out here, or he'll never agree to anything. I won't be long."

He disappeared inside. Penny sat down on one of the stair treads and leaned her back against the wall. She patted the tread below her. "Tell it to me again, Walter. How you're going to become America's top air ace, and survive this war, and carry me off to Iowa, and get married and raise six kids and live happily ever after."

Walter rested his head comfortably against her breast, closed his eyes, and did not speak. She sighed. "Oh, all right, then." She began to stroke his hair, rubbing her fingers across his temples and the line of his forehead. "Forget the rest of it. Just make sure you survive the war. And tonight, do what I tell you and lay off the gin. I think Harry must have made that lot himself."

They had not moved when Harry Holloway emerged twenty minutes later. He looked puzzled, and he was carrying a long box under his arm.

"More antiques?" said Penny as he came up to them. "Or more junk?" She moved Walter's head away from her.

"I don't know." Harry put the box down on the stairs. "If this war lasts long enough, I'm going to learn sufficient French to find out what's going on. Monge gave me this because, he says—I think—that it belongs to Colonel Marshall. But I'm sure it doesn't."

"So why didn't you tell him?" Walter was feeling a lot better.

"I tried to. He says that the doctor's orderlies gave it to him this morning and told him it came from Colonel Marshall. According to Monge, he has never seen it before in the chateau and he knows what's in every room. So Colonel Marshall or one of the new visitors must have brought it. He's asking me to take charge of it.''

''What's inside it?''

''A couple of books and a few rolls of paper. All written in French and Latin and Gawd knows what else.'' Harry opened the broken lid of the brass box, and the three of them peered inside.

''Maybe they're valuable,'' said Penny.

''They don't look it.'' Harry closed the lid. ''I don't think you'd get two bob for the lot down Charing Cross Road.''

''Do you want to drop them off at the tent before we go any farther?'' said Walter.

''Don't need to.'' Harry tucked the box under his arm. ''It's not heavy; I can cart it along with us easy enough. Come on, let's find Ellen Blake.''

It was her worst nightmare. Jenny hurried along after Aunt Ellen. She was not crying . . . but her throat felt raw and her eyes were stinging.

''That's my girl,'' said Ellen as Jenny came alongside her. ''Chin up—that's the only way to handle it.''

''Monge says that Halphen thinks that Daddy is—''

''Wait and see, Jenny.'' Ellen gripped her by the arm. ''Don't believe the doctors; they're all idiots. We'll do everything we can.''

She led the way down the hall. Behind her, Jenny could not stop the dreadful logic of her thoughts. It had happened again. Even though she had been right here in Saint-Amè, again she had been unable to help her father when he needed her most. This time there was a special guilt. Father had been taken worse while she lay in Louis Villette's bed, longing for the return of the Marquis. She had put worries about her pregnancy and Louis Villette's unexplained absence over her concern for her father. He could have died right then, for all the good that Jenny had been. Monge said that he had been this way for at least two hours, but no one knew where to find Jenny. She would never forgive herself for that.

''I tried to pretend he was not so terribly sick,'' she said. ''But I knew he was. Aunt Ellen, I've made such a botch of everything.''

Ellen waited for her at the door of the room and squeezed her arm. "You haven't. And for all we know, this is a false alarm—you've already told me what an ass Dr. Halphen is."

She opened the door without knocking. The doctor was by the bedside. He stared at them disapprovingly as the two women came in. Ellen Blake ignored him. She walked to the bedside and stared down at William Marshall. He was pale and frail as a ghost, breathing raggedly, eyes staring open. She waved a hand across his face and the eyes did not follow it.

Dr. Halphen frowned at Ellen and said something sharply to her in French. She straightened up and responded with a few sentences in a cutting tone. He started back, reddened, spun on his heel, and walked across to look out of the window.

"Aunt Ellen, what did he say?" Jenny could not take her eyes off her father. She was afraid that every breath might be his last.

"He told me we had no right to be here and we ought to leave at once. I'm afraid I was a little impatient with him. I told him that we were close relatives, and if we chose we could come here at any time. I also said that if the condition of this patient reflected his best French medical skills, he ought to stick to treating the venereal diseases for which he was clearly well qualified."

Ellen Blake's tone was light, but her expression was grim as she leaned over William Marshall's body. It did not need a doctor to make this diagnosis. Death was close, hovering dark above the rumpled bed.

Jenny sat at her father's side and took his hand. So cold and thin—not the hand that had held hers for so many years. Deep valleys ran along the back of it, exposing translucent veins and emphasizing the line of each finger as it ran toward the wrist. The sunken valleys of flesh had a gray-blue cast, turning the long-nailed hand into an alien claw.

Jenny hardly noticed Clive and Cecile tiptoe into the room and stand whispering next to Ellen Blake. She was listening to her father's breathing, excruciatingly ragged and shallow. The wires holding his jaw in position had become skewed. The smell coming from him was making her gag, it was so stale and sickly. Clive came to Jenny's side and patted her on the shoulder.

"Daddy, I'm here," said Jenny.

Had his eyes flickered for a moment? The icy film on the staring pupils seemed to thaw and the eyes quivered in their sockets.

"Dad, it's Jenny." She rubbed his cold hand in both of hers, willing some of her warmth and energy to transfer itself into his body. "Can you hear me? It's Jenny. I love you, Daddy."

She was sure she was getting through to him. The wired mouth was moving feebly, the lips working against the metal braces.

Clive squeezed her shoulder. "Again, Jenny. I'm sure he heard that. He recognized your voice!"

"I'm here, Daddy. I love you. Aunt Ellen is here, too."

"I'm here, William," said Ellen gruffly. "We're here to look after you."

"Ellen." The words were a faint, grating whisper. The bulging eyes rolled sideways. "Ellen Blake."

"That's right, William." Ellen put her arm around Jenny. "You always said you'd know my croaking voice anywhere. Say hello to Jenny."

"Jen-ny." The word came out as two syllables, but it was unmistakable. The eyes focused on Jenny.

"I'm here, Daddy. Just lie quiet." She held his hand tightly, and tears welled silently from her eyes and trickled unwiped down both cheeks. Through watery eyes she saw another man entering the room. It was Charles Richter. He paused at the bedside and said a few words to Cecile and Clive, then went prowling restlessly around the bedroom, looking behind curtains and peering under dresser and wardrobe. He halted by Dr. Halphen, who was still glowering by the window, and held a low-voiced conversation with him. The doctor shrugged and turned his back deliberately on the group at the bedside. Richter moved to the other side of the bed and nodded a greeting.

"*Jenny*." William Marshall's voice was louder and clearer. "Jenny. Pillow. Can't breathe . . . ." His eyes were fully knowing, fully alert. He was trying to sit upright on the bed.

Charles Richter leaned forward, staring at the sick man

with a terrible intensity. The box and books were not in this room, but he dared not leave when Marshall was conscious and apparently rational. If the man was about to tell of being smothered by a French soldier . . . "Halphen!" Richter turned and spoke loudly to the doctor. "Colonel Marshall says he is having trouble breathing. Quickly, bring a stimulant for him. At once!"

He waved to the doctor, drawing the attention of everyone in the room. It was unnecessary. As suddenly as it had begun, William Marshall's burst of energy ended. His body stiffened, and his thin fingers tightened on Jenny's arm. While she watched, he took one long, shuddering intake of breath. The following exhalation was calm and slow, rasping softly in the depths of his throat.

Jenny waited in agony for the next breath.

She would wait forever. His grip relaxed, he sank back on the bed, and the light in his eyes went out like snuffed candles.

She knew in that moment that he was dead.

Halphen pushed Charles Richter out of the way and bent over the body. He felt the pulse, rolled back an eyelid, and shook his head. His look at Ellen Blake was more triumphant than sympathetic: *I told you so!*

Ellen took Jenny in her arms and drew her away from the bedside. "Come along, my dear." Her voice was firm. "There's nothing we can do. I'm going to take you along to the lounge, if someone will show me where that is, and you're going to have a strong cup of tea. I'll take care of everything else later on."

Jenny shook her head, but she allowed her aunt to move her away from William Marshall's silent body. As they stepped toward the door, she saw Walter Johnson and Penny Wilson standing horrified on the threshold. They had arrived just in time to see the final crisis. Now Penny stepped forward and took Jenny's hand in hers.

"You poor love." Her voice was warm. "Come on, now, go with your aunt." And to Ellen Blake, "Don't worry about a thing here. Jenny shouldn't spend any more time in this room. Walter and I will stay and take care of everything."

The others were drifting toward the door, Charles Richter leading. He didn't want to get involved in anything here—

he had too much to do elsewhere. The brass box was still missing, though William Marshall had died without implicating Dolfi.

Richter frowned. Maybe that was a fact that he ought not to share. Dolfi would be more controllable if he thought they were hunting him all over Chateau Cirelle.

Richter moved off along the corridor, not seeing Harry Holloway hurrying toward the room from the other direction. Holloway had both arms full. He had been delayed a few minutes, picking up the latest batch of mail addressed to Colonel Marshall. As soon as he reached the room and saw the expressions on Jenny's and Penny's faces, he knew what had happened. He halted aimlessly in the doorway.

Clive came across to him, shaking his head. "That the colonel's mail?" he said quietly. "I suppose I'll be handling it from now on. I'll write a dispatch about his death for you to take over to general headquarters." He looked back at Jenny, but she was still surrounded by Ellen, Cecile, and Penny, and she was taking no notice of what was happening at the door. "We'll have to arrange for bagging the body and making shipment back for burial in Yorkshire," he said softly. "That's what the colonel told me he wanted, if anything happened to him. Can you take care of that?"

"This afternoon." Harry Holloway took a deep breath and handed over the packet of mail in his left hand. The brass box was still tucked under his right arm. "We've just lost a damned good man, sir, if you don't mind me saying so."

"One of the best." Clive shook his head. "Have a drink for Colonel Marshall tonight. I'm certainly going to."

"Yes, sir." Harry forced a smile. "I'm going to take that as an order. Excuse me, sir, but while I'm here I've got another question. Monge gave me this stuff"—he tapped the box under his arm—"and said it came from here, from Colonel Marshall. I feel sure it didn't, because it's just a lot of foreign writing. But I couldn't get Monge to understand, and he gave it to me anyway. Books and papers, they are. I don't know what to do with them. It doesn't seem right to throw them out until somebody takes a look at them. And I can't read them."

"Let me take a peek. I can probably tell you what they

say." Clive handed the packet of mail back to Harry, took the box, and looked inside it. He unrolled the first few inches of one of the parchments. "No, I can't, though. At least, not easily. This is all in Old Latin. It would take me a week with a dictionary to work out what it says. Dump it in the library and let's forget it." He rolled up the parchment, put it back in the box, and was about to hand it to Harry. Then he paused and shook his head. "No, I'm not thinking straight. I've got a better idea. Ellen Blake does this sort of thing for a living. Let's give it to her and ask her to take a look at it when she has some free time. Then we can decide if it should go in the library or in with the rubbish."

One more day! Then this nonsense could end.

Why had he ever agreed to bring Dolfi into the chateau? So far it had meant nothing but trouble. But how could he have predicted that the man would change so completely? One word about that damned Cross and Gospel, and the cautious, responsible corporal of the first few weeks was replaced by a rash lunatic with no sense of danger.

He opened the door. Dolfi was waiting, skulking in the corner. As soon as he was sure it was Richter, he jumped out at him.

"What about the books? And the box? Did you find them?"

"Not yet. I had something more important to deal with."

"Nothing is more important than that!"

"The Grand Advance and a German victory are vastly more important! And you may have jeopardized those in your attack on the British colonel."

"What has happened?"

"He is dead. An unnecessary death. Who knows what knowledge of British troop movements that man held in his head? And now it is all gone."

"And good riddance." Dolfi waved away any suggestion of William Marshall's importance. "I had to do it or be caught by that pig of a French doctor. He died without speaking, did he?"

"I don't think so. I believe that they suspect you, and they will be searching for you. Now do you see what a mess you have made of things? You cannot go back to your room."

"So I will stay here."

"No. That's too dangerous. Cecile Villette often visits my rooms, and anyway there are the servants. They wander in here half a dozen times a day, to make up the bed, to sweep, to fill the water jug—there is no predicting when they will appear. Already we have run considerable risk by your being here."

"War always involves risk."

"Which is why *unnecessary* risk must always be avoided. For the rest of today and tonight—until the Grand Advance begins—you must go outside the chateau. I know the perfect place. It is sheltered, it is close by, and it is never visited. Do you know the cloisters?"

"You have talked of them, but I have not seen them. I proposed to look at them later today, if things had not gone badly this morning."

Gone badly! Richter cursed under his breath. Hear how Dolfi put it! He never agreed that anything was his fault! If only he had had the sense to stay in his room, as ordered . . .

"The cloisters are at the end of the garden. They lead down into the old cellars, but no one goes that way. You will be quite safe there for one day. I will make sure that you are amply provided with food and drink. I will take you there now. And this time, you will *stay where you are told*!"

Dolfi's pale eyes frowned in thought. He nodded. "Very well. But you must not lose sight of our need to obtain the Cross. If the Marquis returns, I want you to inform me of that."

"You have my word. If that happens, I will inform you as soon as I can. And I will continue to look for the box and the papers. I searched Colonel Marshall's room when I was there, and they are not there. But remember, the Grand Advance comes *first*—more important than any papers, or any cross. And a bloodless conquest of this chateau is central to the advance. Do you understand me?"

Dolfi nodded. But his eyes had a glint that Charles Richter did not like at all.

CHAPTER
TWENTY-NINE

For hours after the sun rose, consciousness for Louis Villette, Marquis de Saint-Amè, remained a fickle thing, a random flame that illuminated dark mist.

Jenny.

It was not just a name, but a physical presence, insinuating itself through his thoughts. His muscles hurt, yet the hurt in his heart was far greater. His mind cried out for the perfumed comfort of love and trust, the assurance that only she had ever been able to give him.

His brain pulsed with fever, bubbling into dreams. . . .

"Louis. Louis, come to me."

She stood before him, naked but for a gauzy chemise that caught the moonbeams slanting through the window. All about the room, on tables and shelves and mantelpiece, burned a lovely chorale of candles.

"Louis. Come to me. Take me, use me, do what you must do. I am yours, always and forever. I give myself to you, to your need."

The breeze, the sweet breeze, filled with the intoxicating smell of his homeland, wafted in to make a ghostly dance of her gown. It carried the smell of her to him, a supplication and confirmation amid ceremonial candles.

He realized that he was naked as well. Naked but not cold, burning with inner warmth.

He stepped toward her, and she embraced him. The energy between them coursed and blazed with passion. Somehow they were as close as lovers could be, although he was not erect and she was only holding him.

Her touch was pure surrender, beyond all passion. She looked at him in that special way of hers, a glowing presence in the candlelight.

"I know, Louis. You are a great man, and I love you. But your cause is greater. I understand. I offer myself, and I do it gladly."

Louis realized that he was holding the Cross in his hand. But the Cross had grown, and somehow it had become a knife as well—a blazing knife, filled with celestial light. The blade sang a ringing song of glory and truth.

She stepped back, rending the flimsy undergarment, exposing her naked breasts. She stood before him, head held high.

"You must, Louis. Time is short. *You must*. For the sake of France."

"For France!" He raised the gleaming cross-knife, drove it into her waiting chest. Blood spurted . . .

. . . and he cried out; for the pain was wholly his.

By noon the fever had faded. The thicket became unpleasantly warm. Louis lay flat, bramble thorns biting into his side. His mouth felt like cotton, his tongue a piece of dried meat. The last drink that he had taken was a bottle of wine, fifteen hours ago. He thought longingly of the ditch that he had waded through to confuse the guard dogs. Dirty or not, he would drink from it now, gladly. He made an inefficient fugitive. Even when he did his best to anticipate difficulties, he overlooked the most obvious problems.

He dared not stand up or look around, but he crawled a few meters in each direction in turn, stripping ripe and half-ripe berries, sucking nectar from sweet pink clover, and chewing grass stems for their moisture. As the sun crept past its zenith and the shadows began to lengthen, he pondered his next move.

He *had* to get back to the chateau and use the Cross against the German advance. That was the overpowering need, the force that drove all his actions. Yet the task seemed impossible. Between him and Chateau Cirelle lay the French and German lines, filled with men who were nervous, watchful, and trigger-happy. The German front had undoubtedly been alerted for his possible attempt at a breakthrough into No-Man's-Land. The French troops had no such directive, but they did not need one. They would fire at anything approaching from the east.

The Meuse River added to the problem. For most of its length in this region, the river's banks marked the battle line. The Germans were on the east bank, the French on the west. The single exception was Saint-Mihiel, where the German advance had allowed them to occupy both sides. But the Marquis had closed that path himself by crossing the lines there in the first place. The watching force at Saint-Mihiel would certainly be more numerous and vigilant than anywhere else.

All afternoon and early evening he lay quiet and thoughtful. By seven o'clock the sun was setting, and the silent land was shrouded with shadows. He risked standing up and looking around. There was no sign of human activity. The farmers had vanished from their fields, frightened off by warnings or threat of battle.

Louis Villette picked up one of his blankets and headed west. Three fields farther on stood an old farmhouse. He walked to it cautiously, and found it deserted. He made a quick survey of the interior. It might be safe for an hour or two, but it was one of the places that any search party would explore. A human habitation would attract German attention.

There was also little to be had here. He found a handful of stale wheat flour in a deep pancheon, together with a small basket half filled with sprouting potatoes and parsnips. On a higher shelf of the pantry stood a moldy slab of cheese, maybe a kilo in weight. He dropped that into the potato basket and added a couple of huge onions from a string on the wall. He started for the door, changed his mind, and came back to the kitchen range. In one of the drawers next to it he found a bone-handled kitchen knife with a good point and a long, sharp blade. He dropped that in with the cheese and vegetables and moved to the outer door. At the pump in the yard he halted and drank until he could swallow no more. Then he was off, still heading west. Well clear of the farm, he sat on a stone wall and began to eat. Beneath its thick layer of molds the cheese was quite edible. Less could be said for the potatoes and parsnips. He took one bite of each, then confined himself to cheese and onions. He ate quickly, cutting off chunks with the kitchen knife and gulping them down almost without chewing.

When he was done, he looked up again. The sky was clouding over with a low, flat stratus cover that threatened a chilly evening and a slow, persistent drizzle.

Even before he found food in the farmhouse, he had made up his mind what he must do. That piece of good fortune was not enough to change his decision. As long as he remained behind the German lines, the risk of discovery and recapture would not diminish. He would have to show himself somewhere to obtain food and drink, and every occasion would be a new and unknown danger. And as long as the Cross was missing, von Steiner would make sure that the intensity of the search was maintained. The problem of crossing from German- to French-held territory would become no easier with time. So the attempt should be made *tonight*, as soon as possible; and the fact that he had no idea *how* to make the attempt did not alter the correctness of his logic.

He walked steadily west. The land was beginning to roll into long, forested folds. The river could be no more than a mile or so ahead. He dropped the blanket in a ditch—reluctantly, because he had been using it to protect his head from the slow drizzle—and walked on, crouching low and moving slower. At every field boundary he paused and surveyed the ground ahead for signs of troops.

He rubbed his sleeve across his damp forehead and reflected that there was one other thing in his favor. After days in the same clothes and sleeping in the rough, no one would pick him out by the quality of his attire. His shirt was filthy, rumpled, and torn; his trousers stained with mud and blackberry juice. Even his soft leather boots would pass muster now; they were scuffed and battered beyond recognition. He could be an itinerant tinker or laborer or vagabond Gypsy, though in a place where no sane laborer or Gypsy would venture.

The river was still invisible ahead. He could tell from the change in the treeline against the sky that it was no more than half a mile away; and he was right at the brink of the line of German defenses and guard posts. He could head around them, but that would mean forcing his way through the patches of woods that separated the guard units. He was sure he could not move silently enough; crashing through the brush was a guaranteed way to get shot.

Louis Villette squatted down and stared toward the river. He fingered the Cross on his breast. The silver was cool between his fingertips. *Lord Judas, give me inspiration, or all my work will be in vain. Help me now, and I will serve a billion years in hell itself.*

There was a mutter of German voices from way off to the left, and the clink of a metal can. Louis Villette smelled cigarette smoke and a wonderful aroma of roast meat. He crouched in the darkness, salivating. Suddenly the Cross seemed warmer in his hand, turning him *toward* the path, drawing him closer to the enemy.

Think: Only one kind of person could get near enough to the river to stand a chance of crossing it; that person must be a German soldier—or someone wearing the uniform of one.

He had been carefully avoiding the paths that led to and from the guard posts. Now he crawled silently through the darkness until he was behind an elder bush only two yards from one. He waited. After about ten minutes, a group of three soldiers went from the guard unit toward the rear lines. Louis Villette could see fires back there, the sign that a field kitchen was in operation. Five minutes later a party of four came wandering along the same path, chattering cheerfully and guiding their way with a shuttered spirit lamp.

It was another half hour before Louis Villette heard what he wanted: a solitary soldier moving along the path that led to the guard post. The man was grunting and puffing to himself, and even with a lantern he seemed unsure of the way. The Marquis crouched in the shadow of the bush, the kitchen knife in his hand.

No sound. It was imperative that there be no sound at all.

He stepped forward and brought the knife upward, reaching under the front ribs to let the long blade strike to the heart. There was a single, louder grunt, almost of surprise more than pain, then a jerking body was leaning on Louis Villette while warm blood pumped out onto his shirt.

He had caught the lantern before it could fail. He pulled the man off the path into the thick shrubbery, placed the lantern on the ground, and turned the flame to its lowest level. There was still enough light to work with. As he examined the soldier's body, he realized why the man had been grunting and complaining. He was carrying a flamethrower, complete with fuel tanks, and the whole thing weighed over seventy pounds. Louis Villette knew that the weapon had been used to terrible effect in Verdun, to smoke soldiers out of the corridors and tunnels of the forts, but it was a surprise to see the weapon here—unless it was going to be part of the German advance through Saint-Mihiel.

He stripped the dead German of his bloody jacket and put it on over his own shirt. It was a miserably bad fit, and the trousers were worse. He measured them against himself, and abandoned the idea at once. They would be just ridiculous— a foot short in the legs. They would make him more conspicuous, not less. He began to move the flamethrower away to concealment in the bushes, then paused. The bulky canisters and the long, ungainly nozzle provided such an unusual and characteristic appearance to their bearer that they would mask any other oddity of appearance. And it was no secret that other soldiers avoided anyone carrying a flamethrower, for simple reasons of survival. Originally a super-weapon, it had changed to become a suicide device. Opposing troops concentrated all their fire on anyone carrying the canisters and nozzles of the flamethrowers, killing them off before they could bring the weapon to bear. Anyone who was close by— friend or foe—was likely to be sprayed with blazing oil by an injured operator.

Louis Villette lifted the harness and eased himself into the straps. He flexed his shoulders. No wonder the German soldier had grunted. It was a massive weight to carry forward at a run into battle.

Fortunately he would not need to attempt that. With his head down, the Marquis plodded on toward the river. He grunted a gruff "*Guten Abend*" to the forward camp as he passed and attracted only a wary greeting in return from the three men standing there drinking hot cocoa from metal mugs. But he was aware of their eyes on him as he trudged by, and when the river was still fifty yards away he heard louder tones of conversation from behind him. There was an exclamation, and the cry, "That's not Jurgen!" and "Why is he going to the river?" Then a shout, "You! Halt, or I fire!"

At once he was running through the muddy flatland at the edge of the river, uncertain how far ahead the water stood. He heard running feet behind, crashing through reeds and bushes, moving much faster than he could. He took a few irreplaceable seconds to slip out of the harness and drop the flamethrower onto the wet ground—he would sink like a stone with that on his back. Then the water was gleaming at his feet, and before he had time to think he had thrown himself in and was striking out desperately for the western bank.

No one was calling to him now. A crackling of shots from a pistol was followed by the louder, more ominous bark of a rifle. A slap sounded on the water to the left side of his head. He swam on steadily. He should be an almost invisible target, a black head against dark water. At this point the river was less than seventy meters wide. There was no problem in swimming across it—if he could avoid being shot on the way.

Thirty meters. Forty, and he was feeling the first surge of optimism. Then the whole river brightened around him. Every ripple and slip of waterweed became visible.

For a moment he thought it must be a Very light or flare. Then he heard the long, terrible whoosh of burning kerosene. A great tongue of red and smoking fire swept out above his head and across the river in front of him. After a moment the range shortened, and the licking tongue dipped to turn his hair to a ball of flame.

It seemed that the fiery jolt drove him straight underwater with no effort on his part. He was suddenly swimming a yard below the surface, eyes wide open. Above him, the river's surface was a sheet of flame. If he surfaced, it would be only to eat fire. Better to die underwater, from bursting lungs. He dived deeper, kicking himself along until his chest was exploding and his staring eyes could see nothing but black circles of stars. When his head finally broke the surface, he was at the brink of unconsciousness. He floated for many seconds beyond the pool of flaming oil and wondered why they did not shoot. Then he realized that the man who used the flamethrower had done his fellow marksmen a disservice. By creating a bright foreground, it had left them unable to see anything beyond. And at the same time the flames had made it impossible for anyone to follow him across the river.

Louis Villette dragged himself wearily onto the muddy western bank and lay there for a couple of minutes. If they shot him, that was bad luck, but he was too weak to move. After a few seconds he reached into his shirt and grasped the Cross. *Thank you, Lord Judas, for showing me the way.*

He was sodden and exhausted, and the surface burns on the back of his head were beginning to shoot pain down into his whole body. He was weaponless, friendless, and foodless, with the French lines still to cross—and he was wearing the jacket of a German soldier. None of that mattered. He was confident now, feeling strength growing within him. He could not have survived so much unless he were being saved for a great purpose, nothing less than the salvation of France. And the instrument to achieve that salvation was waiting for him back at Chateau Cirelle.

After a few moments of rest, Louis Villette began to claw his way up the steep bank of the River Meuse. His progress was slow. He dragged himself along with fingers so dirty, bloodied, and battered that they belonged more to the paws of a great ape than to the manicured hands of a great French aristocrat. He did not feel pain. He was on the way home.

CHAPTER THIRTY

Nothing on earth could offer a sensation like it: not sex, not food or music, not the sight of any natural or man-made wonder. Nothing. It was the thrill of the chase—the delicate scent of a trail that led back through time and space. This was how a tiger must feel when the first faint spoor of game came to its nostrils; or perhaps a kestrel, hovering high aloft and catching that trace of movement on the ground below.

Ellen Blake gently spread the books and bound scrolls across the width of the table and moved them so that the sunlight struck full upon them. The books came first—those she was willing to touch freely. They were bound in gray and brown leather. The gray volume was probably seventeenth century, the brown one more recent. They were in excellent condition, pages intact and bindings pliable. She put them to one side.

The scrolls were another matter. They had to be looked at more closely. She held a jeweler's loupe to her eye and peered at the edge of the rolled scripts. Two of them were parchment, thin and flawless lambskin vellum that had been scraped and whitened in lime baths and burnished to the finest quality. Ellen examined their cut and guessed that they were twelfth century. They had been well preserved and they could be touched—gently, to be sure, but safely.

The third scroll was a different proposition. It was papyrus, multiple thin strips of reed pith glued crosswise to form a rolled sheet that over the years had gradually grown more brittle and delicate. The inner surface was a pale blotched yellow, the color of moldering soft cheese. The document was obviously incomplete, cracked diagonally across the top and showing only a half line of writing. Ellen scrutinized the lettering. This scroll was far older than the other two. The style of cutting and gluing had gone out of use more than a millennium and a half ago, long before the Roman Empire had retreated from its holdings through the Middle East. Ellen placed the date at no later than third century A.D. and tagged it in her own mind as first century or earlier. An accurate dating could not be done without a long and careful analysis. That analysis, and a suitable delicate handling of the scroll, called for facilities available only in a major museum. She dared not open the roll further to look at the writing beyond the first few lines, in case the brittle material cracked or crumbled. What she could see was written in elegant and literate Greek in a faded shadow of ink that had once been brilliant violet—originally developed, she surmised, from indigo mixed with crushed lapis lazuli. The only words visible without opening the scroll—and she had to guess at some of them, the writing was so faint—translated as: ". . . said to them, go into the city. There you will meet a man carrying a pitcher of water. Follow him wherever he goes, and tell . . ."

Was this the Gospel of Judas? It was very similar to the Gospel According to St. Matthew, and it could well be an alternate translation of part of that Gospel. She was very aware of the danger of identifying a document to be what one wanted it to be—the "wishful thinking" school of archaeology had many practitioners.

Ellen automatically moved the delicate papyrus roll out of the destructive rays of the full afternoon sunlight and picked up the first of the vellum parchments. She unrolled it carefully, an inch at a time. It was written in black ink, with illuminated verse headings in scarlet. If that brilliant red were made from a variety of cochineal, and Ellen was inclined to believe it was, then she might have to advance her date of the document's production by a century or so. Had there been European reports of the use of the dried cochineal beetle for coloring inks as early as the time of Roger Bacon? She thought not, but she was not sure. The kermes insect was certainly in use then, and had been for many centuries, but it usually provided a purpler red. That detail could wait for verification.

She had deliberately postponed any inspection of the content of the scrolls until she had examined the parchment and the inks. Nothing she had seen so far in any of the materials had significantly changed her original perception. Now she turned her attention to the written content.

There seemed to be two separate documents on the first parchment. The first was written in a cool and exact Latin. The translation was easy.

1. This cannot be told except to the
Brotherhood, or to those who would be Brothers.
This is the nature of the three-fold way, the source
of power. The power lives with the Guardian. The
power is expressed through the Trinity of Gospel,
Cross, and Ritual. When the Guardian follows
these three, the power is given to him.

2. The Cross is the light of the World. The way
of the Cross is silver; the way of the Gospel is
stone; and the way of the Ritual is blood.

3. The way of the Cross is single, and comes
from the Cross alone; and the way of the Gospel
stands with the Gospel; but the way of the Ritual
stands with the Guardian, and must be found anew
within each man's lifetime.

4. The name of the Gospel is the Gospel
According to Judas; and the name of the Ritual is
the Ritual of Abraham; and the name of the Cross
is the Cross of Judas.

5. The Gospel was written by Judas Iscariot,
and the Cross was made by the hand of Judas.

6. The power of the Cross is invoked by
performance of the Ritual; only through the
sacrifice of the Ritual can power flow through the
Cross.

The second document on the parchment was more modern in style and showed the influence of a new writer. The Latin was less literate. There were odd lacunae, suggesting that the copy had been made from an incomplete document. It was also much fainter, and many words were questionable. By guessing liberally, and then adjusting those guesses to develop an overall sense of the document, Ellen slowly evolved a complete text. When it was concluded in her mind, she wrote out her own preferred translation. It read:

The account of events provided by the *Gospel According to Judas Iscariot* differs in both style and content from the "Synoptic Gospels" of the New Testament; most significantly, in the matter of the Betrayal and in the actions of Christ on the Cross.

The reasons for the differences should be self-evident. First, the New Testament Gospels were all written somewhere between 70 and 95 A.D.— forty to sixty years after the events that they describe. In consequence, all of them are *derived* documents. By contrast, the Judas Gospel was written by . . . (illegible line) . . . present at the events described and participated in them directly. This had two effects. First, there is an immediacy to the Judas Gospel lacking in any other gospel; and at the same time, there is a discursiveness to it, almost a randomness, reflecting the difficulty that a participant in events has in determining what will later prove to be significant. Matthew, Mark, Luke, and John had the benefit of hindsight. They also wrote as *evangelists*. Their desire to spread the Word of Christianity . . . (illegible line) . . . to provide logic where events seemed to offer none; to add supposition where the account was imperfect; and to omit detail that they judged irrelevant to their main message. To put the Judas Gospel into its proper perspective, it should be noted that although Judas himself may have written self-serving passages, Thaddaeus had no such motivation. Like Judas, Thaddaeus was contemporary with and a direct observer of Christ's last years on Earth; and, like Judas, he was one of the first twelve disciples.

In summary, although no human can write without bias, and that is as true of Judas Iscariot as it is of any other writer, the least biased, most

knowledgeable, and most sympathetic recorder of
the life and death of Judas Iscariot appears to be
Thaddaeus. He had been present at the time of
Judas's fall, and had nurtured the same ideas
concerning Christ's secular dominion. He edited
the words of Judas as a man of conscience; more
than that, he was one who, in the fullest sense,
could say, "There, but for the grace of God, go I."

As she wrote out the final words, Ellen was surprised to
see that the light in the room was fading. The sun was low
on the horizon and struck in to illuminate the far wall in gold-
red patches. She must have been working on the documents
for at least three hours.

She stood up and stretched, then took off her glasses and
rubbed at her eyes. She massaged the tense muscles in the
back of her shoulders, looking out of the window as she did
so. It would soon be too dark to work by natural light. She
crossed the room and poured a glass of water from the jug on
the dresser. What now?

The only other working surface in the room was the
writing desk, directly beneath the electric lamp. Ellen
turned the lamp on and was gratified by the amount of light
it threw onto the wooden surface. For the past twenty years
she had ruined her eyes struggling to decipher manuscripts
by candles and flickering oil lamps. The contribution of
modern technology to archaeology was by no means complete. Unlike some of her colleagues, Ellen welcomed the
newest tools. She carried the unexamined scroll to the writing desk and carefully untied the black waxed thread that
held it tightly rolled.

It was a longer document than any she had seen so far,
divided into six sections by multiple ruled cross lines of
sepia. Each section was written in Latin and headed by the
same decorative figure in vermilion, a stylized cross filled
with wavering crosshatched diagonals. The writing had
faded badly, more than on the previous scroll, and parts
were invisible even under the bright artificial light. Ellen
scanned the more readable parts, attempting to get an overall
feel for the document before she began the difficult job of full
translation.

> Go into the city. There you will meet a man
> carrying a pitcher of water. Follow him wherever
> he goes . . .

Her eye picked out that passage. She stood up, went across to the table, and brought the old and broken papyrus scroll over to the light. Her memory had served her well. The language was Latin now, rather than Greek, but the words she had read on the vellum parchment were the same as on the papyrus. She checked a little further, as far as she could see until the writing on the papyrus was hidden by the fragile curl of the scroll. The twelfth century parchment appeared to be a copy of the battered first or second century original.

Ellen turned her attention again to the vellum scroll. The translation was going to be a long and horrendous job. She was ready to plunge into it when she had another thought. What about the books? They were obviously much more recent. Could it be that they, too . . .

Within five minutes her new thought had been confirmed, and she was groaning at her own stupidity. Just as the vellum parchment contained a copy of the ancient papyrus translated from Greek to Latin, the older gray-covered book was itself a translation of the parchment—and this time it was in French and English! The summary commentary on the Gospel that she had so painstakingly converted from crude Latin was there, too, in French translation. It was different from her version only in small details.

Ellen shook her head at her lack of brains. Now she *had* to find out what this thrice-presented passage was all about. At some point she would want to make her own exact comparisons, Greek version versus Latin version versus English and French translations, but for the moment she was ready to cheat and go the easy way. She was too curious to wait. As the sun vanished from view, Ellen bent her head over the English version of the text.

FIRST FRAGMENT

Then Jesus said to the twelve disciples, "Go not to the cities of the Samaritans, nor seek out the Gentiles; but seek ye the lost sheep of the house of Israel.''

And Judas, named Iscariot, questioned Jesus, saying, ''Lord, thou hast given to us power against unclean spirits, and against all manner of sickness. How will we spread thy name abroad, that the Kingdom of the Lord may be established?''

Jesus stretched out his hand, and touched Judas, and looked on him, and said, ''Know this. The Kingdom will come, and thy deeds will be known.''

And it came to pass, when Jesus had commanded his twelve disciples, he departed thence to teach and to preach in the cities.

But they stayed, and spoke among themselves; and Judas said, ''We have powers. Should we not then serve our Lord's purpose? For it is written, The Kingdom of God is at hand.''

And Simon, called Peter, answered, ''Our powers come from him, and are nothing without him. We must follow his commands.''

And they went, each to his own way, to teach the Word. But Judas and Thaddaeus remained, and spoke again together, saying, ''What should we do, that the Kingdom be created? When will he manifest himself to the world?'' For Judas and Thaddaeus were impatient, and longed to see Christ's earthly kingdom.

SECOND FRAGMENT

Now Jesus was in Bethany, in the house of Simon the Leper. And the chief priests, and the scribes, and the elders of the people, assembled together. For they sought to take Jesus by subtlety, and kill him; for his word was heard in the city, and had weight with the people.

And Judas Iscariot heard of the meeting, and came to the palace of the high priest, Caiaphas, *in secret. And Judas said unto him, "What will ye give, if I deliver him unto your hands?"*

And Annas and Caiaphas, the priests, spoke together. Then said they to Judas, "Why would you betray him? Is he not your Lord?" For they were suspicious.

Judas said, "I am a poor man, with many debts." Which was true.

Then Caiaphas said, "So be it. Deliver him to those we will send, and you will be rewarded." And they covenanted with him for thirty pieces of silver.

THIRD FRAGMENT

And the first day of unleavened bread, the disciples said unto him, "Where wilt thou that we go and prepare that thou mayest eat the passover?"

And he sendeth forth two of his disciples, and saith unto them, "Go ye into the city. There shall ye meet a man carrying a pitcher of water. Follow him wheresoever he shall go, and say ye to the goodman of the house, The Master saith, where is the guestchamber?"

And his disciples went forth, and came into the city, and did as he had said unto them, and found a large upper room furnished and prepared.

They made ready the passover, and in the evening he cometh with the twelve.

And as they sat and did eat, Jesus said, "Verily I say unto you, one of you will betray me."

And they were sorrowful, and said unto him one by one, "Is it I?"

And he answered and said, "It is one of the twelve that dippeth his hand with me in the dish.

"The Son of Man indeed goeth, as it is written of him; but woe to the man by whom the Son of Man is betrayed! Good were it for that man if he had never been born."

And Judas stood forth and asked, "Master, is it

I?'' Then Jesus took a plate of burnished bronze, and gave it to Judas, and said, ''Hold it to thy face. What seest thou there?''

Judas looked, and saw Christ's dominion over the earth. And he rejoiced.

And Jesus said again, ''What sayest thou?'' And Judas spake, answering, ''Lord, I believe. When is the time of thy dominion?''

Jesus answered, ''That time is here already.''

And Jesus took bread, and blessed it, and brake it, and gave it to his disciples, and said, ''Take, eat; this is my body.'' And he took the cup of wine and said, ''Drink ye all of it; for this is my blood of the new testament. I say unto you, I will not drink henceforth of the fruit of this vine, until that day when I drink it new with you in my Father's kingdom.''

And Judas bowed his head, and rejoiced anew. For he heard in these words the promise of an earthly kingdom.

FOURTH FRAGMENT

And Jesus returned from prayer, and found his disciples asleep. And he saith to them, ''Sleep, take your rest. The hour is come, and the Son of Man is betrayed into the hands of sinners.''

While he yet spake, Judas came to him, and sat by him, and touched his hand. And soon there came a multitude with swords and staves.

And Judas saith, ''Master,'' and kissed Jesus. For he had given them a token, saying, ''Whomsoever I shall kiss, that same is he. Take him, and lead him away safely.''

And they laid hands on Jesus, and took him. And Jesus spake to them, saying, ''Are ye come out as against a thief, with swords and with staves to take me? I was daily with you in the temple, and ye took me not; but the scriptures must be fulfilled.''

And at Jesus' words the disciples forsook him,

*and fled, all save Judas. But he remained, for he
sought the revelation of Jesus' powers. And when
that came not, he was sore confused, crying
aloud, "What have I done?" And he followed
from a distance, watching all that happened
thenceforth.*

FIFTH FRAGMENT

*And in the morning the chief priests, scribes
and elders straightway held consultation, and
bound Jesus, and delivered him to Pontius Pilate.*

*And Judas stood in the shadow of a fig tree,
and watched from afar off.*

*Then Pilate asked, "Art thou the King of the
Jews?" And Jesus answered, "Thou sayest."*

*And Pilate said to the chief priests and the
people, "I find no fault in this man. I will chastise
him, but I will release him."*

*But they said, "He stirreth up the people
throughout all Jewry. Crucify him."*

*And Judas waited. But Jesus stayed silent; and
the robber Barabbas was released to the crowd,
for of necessity Pilate must release one unto them
at the feast. And Jesus was scourged, and
delivered to the will of the priests.*

*And the soldiers of the governor took Jesus,
and put on him a scarlet robe, and plaited a
crown of thorns for his head. And they bowed the
knee before him, and mocked him, saying, "Hail,
King of the Jews." And they spit upon him, and
took him away to crucify him.*

*And when they came to Golgotha, they parted
his garments, casting lots; that it might be fulfilled
which was spoken by the prophet, "They parted
my garments among them, and upon my vesture
did they cast lots."*

*Now when Judas saw this, his heart was
broken, and he could not follow. And he threw
down the thirty pieces of silver upon the ground,*

and departed, and hanged himself by the building of the weavers.

And about the third hour he was found, and cut down, and was placed within the house of Thomas the Weaver.

But at the sixth hour the body breathed, and Judas woke. And he took a knife, and stabbed his breast, so that the blood poured forth upon the ground. But he did not die, only lay a space within the building.

And he rose, and took himself to a high place, which is known as the Field of Stones. And he cast himself headlong down, and burst his body asunder on the rocks. But he did not die, nor was his flesh corruptible.

Then Judas rose, and walked through the city; and no one knew his face. And at last he went to the place of the crucifixion. And Jesus was on the Cross.

And Judas wept from afar off, and cried out, "Lord, forgive me, that I might be redeemed."

Then Christ lifted his bloodied head, and looked at him. And word came to Judas, "Go thou, and take the pieces of silver as they were paid to you, and make a cross from them. And ye shall be saved."

And Judas cried again, "Lord, what manner of cross shall be made, and in what wise shall it be made?" For his understanding was gone.

And the word came back to him, "As ye make the cross, so then shall be your redemption."

SIXTH FRAGMENT

Now no one knew Judas, and in his wandering he went to the house of Daniel, brother of him that had fed them at the time of passover. And he was provided meat there, as a beggar at the gate. But drink was not given to him, although his thirst was great.

And Judas left the house, and came at last to Golgotha, and found the thirty pieces of silver where he had thrown them down. For no man had seen them.

And he took the pieces, and went to a forge in the heat of the day, and there made a sand mold in the shape of a cross. And as he worked there came to the forge a streetwoman carrying a goatskin of sweet white wine, and a goatskin of cool water.

And Judas said, "Give me drink. For I am thirsty."

And the woman gave him water. But he said again, "Give me drink."

And she laughed, and said, "Here is drink enough. There is no wine without payment."

Then Judas took one piece of the silver, and gave it to the woman. And she was astonished at the amount, and gave him wine, and said to him, "What also do you now desire from me?"

And Judas did not answer. He took the silver, and in the forge made him a cross, the size of a man's thumb. And there were nine-and-twenty pieces of silver in the cross. And for three days and nights it stood hot from the forge, and cooled not. But on the morning of the fourth day, it cooled to a shining cross of silver.

And in that same moment the body of Judas dropped down, and his spirit departed from the world.

And no one knew the body of Judas. Three days and nights it stayed unseen by the potter's field, where lay the bodies of strangers.

And the body of Judas was not corrupted, until Thaddaeus found it, and took it, and prepared the body for burial; and in a moment the body withered, and was consumed from within, and showed a hundred wounds.

And Thaddaeus told the news of the death of Judas to the other disciples, and spoke it throughout the city.

When Ellen had finished reading, she sat for a long time without moving. The idea behind the early part of the document was not new to her; as early as 1857, Thomas de Quincey had suggested that Judas in his betrayal of Christ had been trying to force Jesus to display his Messianic powers and rise against the Romans. But the later fragments of the lost Gospel According to Judas—they were another matter.

They told a version of Judas's role after the betrayal that she had seen nowhere else. The Gospels and the Acts of the Apostles in the New Testament gave conflicting versions of the death of Judas Iscariot, but the Gospel here made those stories consistent with each other. And the description of the forging of the Cross seemed too specific and detailed to be an invention.

Ellen looked again at the ancient scroll. It glowed in her mind with its own light. This represented the single most important religious relic ever found. And a yet more precious item was still missing: the Cross of Judas itself. Its discovery would exceed any other, even the Grail from which Christ had drunk at the Last Supper. Louis Villette's cross-branded chest, combined with the presence of the Gospel and the ritual, convinced Ellen that the Cross must be close to hand.

She turned to the one remaining book. It was less promising. For one thing, it was more recent, and a first glance through the pages showed that it contained entries by many different hands. Some were neat, others totally illegible, and all seemed to be a hodgepodge of names and places, with what might be dates. They were apparently random, as though successive writers had chosen where they would make their entries without regard to what had been done before. Not even the languages were consistent; she found entries in English, French, German, Arabic, Spanish, Italian, Greek, and Latin. Before anything could be made of it, the information would have to be organized and laid out systematically.

Ellen went across to her bag, pulled out half a dozen sheets of blank paper, and set to work. She first made a list of everything that she could decipher. The entries that were illegible, or in a language she could not understand (there were two notes in Gaelic, and one in Basque), she ignored. For the moment she did not attempt to analyze each entry.

When that was done she started over, this time trying to

set everything into presumed chronological order. Alongside every date she wrote the location, if one was given, and the people's names. She found that she had dates ranging from 1092 A.D. to this year, 1916, and places scattered around the world—everywhere from India to East Africa to her present location in the Meuse Valley. With the list complete, she finally sat back and looked for any kind of pattern in the eighty-nine entries. At first there seemed to be none; then Ellen found that her attention was drawn again and again to certain items on the list.

    1208: Languedoc, France
    1231: Mainz, Germany
    1347: Venice, Italy
    1386: Isfahan, Persia
    1531: Lisbon, Portugal
    1685: Somerset, England
    1770: Paris, France
    1793: Paris, France
    1842: Kabul, Afghanistan
    1863: New York City, U.S.A.
    1885: Khartoum, Sudan

There was one inexplicable gap of almost a century and a half from 1386 to 1531 without a single entry, and another similar one from 1531 to 1685; but these dates and places struck chords of recollection.

Without any conscious intention on her part, Ellen's mind began to insert other information. The year 1208; that was when Pope Innocent III declared an outright holy war on the Albigensians in Languedoc, in the southwest part of France. Before the massacre was over, eight hundred thousand Albigensians had been killed and the whole sect exterminated. Twenty years after that, at Mainz, was the time when Conrad of Marburg had invoked the powers of the Inquisition with unique and terrible zeal. A century later, in 1350, Europe staggered under the full attack of the Black Death, the plague that would carry off almost half the people of the continent. The Black Death was often said to have been brought into Europe in Venice, in 1347.

Ellen could sense the whole picture now; every piece

made the next one easier to see. In 1386, Tamerlane had been in Persia. He had slaughtered more than seventy thousand people at Isfahan in a single day. Thirty thousand had died in the Lisbon earthquake, in 1531. At least twelve thousand had been murdered in the winter of 1842, during the British retreat from Kabul through Afghanistan's Khyber Pass. And every Englishman knew what had happened thirty years ago in 1885, when General Gordon's beleaguered garrison had been wiped out to the last man in Khartoum by the Mahdi's forces.

Ellen scanned the whole list. As far as she could tell, everything was consistent. This was a list of disasters, major and minor, natural and man-made, over the past seven hundred years. For instance, 1685 had been the year of the "Bloody Assizes" in the English West Country, when Judge George Jeffreys had put hundreds of people to death for their roles in the Monmouth Rebellion. The Reign of Terror of the French Revolution had begun in Paris in 1793. A generation earlier, in 1770, the same city had been the site of the great accident at the Dauphine's wedding, when a thousand people had been killed. That many had died in New York City in the Civil War conscription riots of 1863.

There was one problem with her interpretation. Many of the times and places were unfamiliar—and if they had been major disasters, she would surely have heard of them.

Very well. She leaned back. So this was a list of *events*, some of which were major misfortunes. A document of no more than minor interest. Unless—her mind threw the thought at her unbidden—*unless the Cross and Gospel had been present on every occasion*. Otherwise, why would these records be kept with the others?

It would explain those great gaps, too. The long disappearance of the Cross after the great earthquake, if it had been in Lisbon at the time, was not surprising. The miracle was rather that it had been found by some dedicated group of searchers— the Knights of the Twelfth Apostle—who would never rest until their most precious possession had been recovered.

The hour was well after midnight. Ellen took off her glasses, rubbed at her eyes, and listened to the chimes of the far-off clock in Chateau Cirelle's main hall. One-thirty. She ought to go to bed and look at the rest tomorrow. But it was impossible not to attempt the full picture and imagine her ornate vase re-created in its entirety.

A silver cross, made by Judas Iscariot in an attempt to atone for his role in the death of Christ. Together with a Gospel, written by an exact contemporary, recording the events. And a dedicated group, the Knights of the Twelfth Apostle, devoted to guarding Cross and Gospel with the ultimate aim of lifting from Judas Iscariot the name of betrayer. They also believed that the Cross, used with a certain ritual, could accomplish great things.

There was one major mystery: Who was the Guardian of the Cross of Judas in this generation? Everything that she had seen so far offered one simple answer: The current Guardian was Louis Villette, Marquis de Saint-Amè.

. . . and the way of the Ritual is blood. And later in the same document, *. . . only through the sacrifice of the Ritual can power flow through the Cross*.

Any barbarous rite, properly invoking the Cross by the Guardian, would have mystical significance. It would be a power for good.

And if the Cross were improperly invoked?

Ellen returned to the list of dates. Some might be acts of great good; but the easily identified ones were all times of great disaster.

She glanced again at the desktop. There was one more section of the book, and it was a short one. She would take a quick glance through it, then call it a day.

This one was much easier to read. It was in French, and messily but reasonably legible. There were three parts to it, two in ink that was already beginning to fade, the other freshly written.

The first part read like an extract from some other, longer work:

> The Rite of Abraham, when used correctly by a duly-appointed Guardian, can evoke the almost limitless powers of the Cross. Thus there is no question here of the *effectiveness* of the Cross, but only of the way in which a Guardian should seek to invoke its powers. . . .
>
> The clearest and most logical interpretation of

the Ritual of Abraham calls for the Guardian to make the same sacrifice as Abraham himself was asked to make: *the killing of his own child*.

To commentators and critics who find such an instruction unthinkable, or reject such an interpretation, these questions must be asked and answered:

• Was God's order somehow *easier* for Abraham to follow, than for any father today?

• Has something *changed* in the world, so that now we do not need to carry out God's command?

The answer to both questions is no. The scriptures must be followed. The duties of the Guardian must be discharged today, just as it was in the time of Abraham, or in the time of Jesus Christ.

Ellen read the passage twice. The assembly of evidence was complete and the fabric clear in her mind. The Guardians used a bloody ritual of child sacrifice to invoke the powers of the Cross for their own purposes. Regardless of the true properties of the Cross, there was no denying that the Guardians and the Knights *believed* in it and in the power of the Cross to amplify and realize the desires of the Guardian when his own child was sacrificed. Ellen might be skeptical, but the Guardian would not be.

She finally turned her attention to the second list. Again, it was a table of names and dates, these all from 1870, with the heading *Vessels for the Rite of Abraham*.

Lucille; served June 9th.
Louise; served June 29th.
Jacqueline; served July 12th.
Sophie; served August 14th.
Marguerite; served September 1st.

The list beneath it was much the same, but longer and more recently written. The dates were all for this year, 1916.

Rochelle Dufy; served January 28th.
Bernadette Lasalle; served February 13th.

Yvonne Mireau; served February 24th.
Helene Chalons; served March 4th.
Annette Seurat; served March 13th.
Therese Lisle; served March 22nd.
Isabelle Dozier; served April 15th.
Marie Givry; served May 12th.
Jenny Marshall;

The last entry brought Ellen sitting bolt upright. The words "Jenny Marshall"—with no date alongside it.

Cross, Gospel, Vessels; the very name "Ritual of Abraham" . . . *the clearest and most logical interpretation of the Ritual of Abraham calls for the Guardian to make the same sacrifice as Abraham himself was asked to make: the killing of his own child.*

Abraham had been told by the Lord to prepare his own son, Isaac, for sacrifice. But there was one inconsistency. Jenny was not the *child* of Louis Villette—from the look of it, she was his lover.

Ellen leaned back.

It made no sense—*unless Jenny was pregnant.* In that case . . .

Ellen jumped to her feet, pushed her glasses onto her forehead, and headed for the door. It was two-thirty in the morning, but that made no difference. She had to see Jenny at once.

With every light in the chateau switched off, the structure took on a different feeling. It was easy to make a wrong turn and get lost, even when you were going only through one turn and along half a corridor. Ellen Blake counted rooms carefully as she passed them, and knocked on what should be Jenny's door. No one answered. Not surprising, said Ellen to herself. At this time in the morning, all sensible people were asleep. She knocked again and opened the door, lifting the oil lamp to throw its light over the interior of the room.

Jenny was not there. Her bed had not been slept in.

What now?

The Marquis was away from the castle. So long as he stayed away, Jenny would be in no danger—unless she was with him already.

Or, a happier thought, Jenny might be with *Clive*.

Ellen went along to Clive Dunnay's room and eased the door open. It was also empty. As she was peering in, she heard a smothered giggle from far along the corridor, then an explosion of breath.

"Night-night, love," said a woman's voice. "See you tomorrow." Ellen heard a door being closed.

"Night-night, Penny-o," said a man's hoarse voice. There was a moment of total silence, then a sound of heavy breathing punctuated by out-of-tune whistling. It slowly approached Ellen along the corridor. She unshuttered her lamp and held it high. Walter Johnson was weaving his way toward her. When she had seen him that morning in William Marshall's room he had looked bleary-eyed and hungover. Now he looked drunk. He stopped, swayed, and stared at her.

"Dr. Blake. You know, I don't understand what I'm doing in this corridor at this hour, and I sure as shooting don't know what *you're* up to."

Ellen grabbed his sleeve. "Stand upright for another minute and listen. It's absolutely imperative that I see Jenny Marshall or Clive Dunnay. Do you know where they are?"

"Nope."

"Well, if you see either one of them, you tell them that it's a life and death thing and I must talk to them."

"Huh? Life or death thing." Walter was staring at her gravely, but it was hard to know if she was getting through to him.

"Yes. Jenny's life is in great danger. She's pregnant by the Marquis, and he is going to kill her so that he can sacrifice his own child, in embryo, to invoke the powers of the Cross of Judas. I don't know when he'll do it, but it could be anytime. He's already killed eight other women pregnant by him for the same reason. He's going to try to kill Jenny." She shook his arm fiercely. "Do you understand me?"

He was nodding, head bobbing like an amusement park doll. "Hmmph. Human sacrifice. Yep. The Marquis gets off on human sacrifice. Sacrifices his children. Yup."

Ellen shook him again. He canted away from the vertical, leaning against the corridor wall as he did so. He straightened with a great jerking effort, just before he overbalanced, and lurched away along the hall without another word.

Hopeless! Ellen glared after him in fury. She knew that Clive, Cecile, Walter, and Penny Wilson had gone off on some wild outing. Maybe Jenny had gone with them, and she and Clive had not come back. Or maybe they were in a bedroom somewhere in another wing of the chateau.

Ellen had run out of ideas. It was not practical to search the whole castle for Jenny and Clive. Everything had to wait for morning, when people would be sober and willing to listen.

Reluctantly, she headed back to her own room. She had to try to sleep, though what she had found out threatened to keep her awake for the rest of the night.

CHAPTER
THIRTY-ONE

Dawn came, and passed. Louis Villette slept on.

At seven-thirty, the guns began. He stirred uneasily, face-down on the rough grass. As the shells made their long arcs into French territory, the earth quaked. Explosions tore into virgin farmland. He heard and felt, but could not move.

It was smell that finally broke the barrier, the summer smell of burning hedgerows. That smoky tang called back boyhood, with the memory of children's laughter and endless evenings. Louis Villette drifted to wakefulness. A row of nearby bushes was ablaze from an incendiary shell, and the grass beyond was already black and shriveled.

He made a great effort, levered himself up on his arms, and looked around. Every gash in the land made its wound in his own body. Like France, Louis Villette lay trampled by German boots.

He rubbed his eyes with his knuckles. The morning was dour and overcast. There was no more time; this was *the* day. The swell of the German Army would pass through Saint-Amè, across the Voie Sacrée, and on until it descended on Paris. France would fall.

Unless he prevented it.

He felt for the Cross at his breast and shivered when his hands found nothing. He scrabbled at the grass in front of him until his cut and puffy finger-ends encountered the warm silver. The last thing that he remembered was sitting down, totally exhausted, and removing the Cross from his neck to look at it for strength and inspiration. For one second he had put it down on the grass. As his hand lost contact, every ounce of energy drained away. He had slept—and slept for far too long. He was miles from the chateau.

He looked at the Cross again, holding it at eye level and then touching it to his lips. *Everything, Lord Judas. Everything. I will give you all I have, surrender my life totally to your holy service. Only speed me to the chateau.*

He stood up and began to walk west. If he had to go on foot, he would do it. If it required crawling, he would crawl. Nothing must stop him. He held the Cross tight in his hand, feeling its power, and struggled on over untended fields and through rough woods. The world around him was tantalizingly calm and serene, full of the scents and sights of the vernal French countryside. Only the roar behind pointed out the existence of that other world, the world of war.

Finally he came to a farmhouse that was not deserted. An old man wearing a straw hat and holding a gun stood outside the barn, listening to the barrage. As soon as the Marquis was within earshot, he hailed the farmer. "Monsieur, if you love your country, lend me a horse."

The man stared at Louis Villette's wild appearance, but he showed no sign of fear. "Who are you?"

"I am Louis Villette, Marquis de Saint-Amè. I have just escaped from the Germans, and it is imperative that I get back to my home. The Germans are advancing."

"I guessed as much." The old man had a strange expression on his face. "More than guessed it, I knew. Yes, if you need one I have a horse. Return it when you can."

"What about you? How will you get away?"

"I have done all the surrendering to the Germans that I intend to do in this lifetime." The man pulled up his left sleeve to show a long, deep scar in his upper arm. "That was done at Sedan, nearly half a century ago, when our army surrendered. I laid down my arms with the rest, but I swore then that it would never happen again. I will stay and protect my farm. While I am alive, they shall not pass."

"Then stay, my friend and countryman." The Marquis hardly recognized his own voice. "Stay, and triumph. They will be stopped. I swear it to you. God will not permit such desecration of French soil."

"My Lord, if every Frenchman spoke as you speak, we would have the Germans back to Berlin in a month." The old Frenchman stood upright and saluted. "Bless you, sir, and Godspeed in your travel. Are you hungry?"

"I have not eaten for two days."

"Saddle the brown mare. I will find something."

In better times the farm would have half a dozen horses. Now there was only one, a placid brown mare, overweight and getting on in years; but she should be able to gallop the miles to Chateau Cirelle without dropping. An ancient, cracked saddle was nearby. The Marquis picked it up. As he was tightening the girths, the farmer hurried back holding a bottle of wine and a loaf of hard bread.

"The wine is good," he said. "And the bread is bad. But it is the best that I can do."

"You will not be forgotten. When this is over, come to the Chateau Cirelle. Anything that I have will be at your disposal."

"Thank you. I am sorry that I did not recognize you at once, my lord. I have seen you before, but never ragged and burned as you are now. You must have been through hell. I have spare clothes if you need them."

"Thank you, but I cannot spare the time." (The old man could not be more than five feet tall! Better to return home looking like a scarecrow than a circus clown.) "What is your name?"

"Merique Martine, my lord."

"I will not forget that name. We shall meet again in happier days."

"It is my prayer."

"Keep on praying." Louis flicked the reins and was off, riding the mare across the farmyard and into the open fields.

The old horse began slowly, but with the Marquis urging her on she warmed to the task. The guns behind were his own spur. That echoing roar drove him on, keeping him awake in spite of fatigue. One hand guided the mare along her path, the other clutched the Cross, drawing on its power to sustain his battered body. The bread and wine were gone within the first couple of miles (. . . *this bread is my body which is broken unto thee . . . this wine is the blood which is shed* . . .). He crouched low in the saddle, conserving his strength and musing over the events which had brought him here. Warmed by wine, he drifted into random thoughts.

The envoy, arriving in the bleak midwinter with his precious burden and his adjuration to duty. The Rite of Abraham. The arrival of Jenny, bringing an undreamed-of springtime to his heart. The German advance, the Cross, the duties of the Guardian. They were all interlocked by destiny, all moving into balance at one point of space and time. France would be saved. And Jenny . . .

The idea of her death moved him to sadness, and that sadness in turn filled him with alarm. He cared for her too much. It was a terrible mistake, to love beyond reason someone who was destined to be a Vessel. It was a weakness, one that must be fought with unshaken resolve.

And yet . . . Jenny . . .

The memory of her, her laughter and her love. If he were successful in this great undertaking, he would never again know happiness. He would be haunted forever by the knowledge of what he had lost, the sad thought of what might have been.

This was sacrifice, as great as any ever called for in the long history of the Ritual of Abraham. This was sorrow, like death itself. The question of the ritual's interpretation had been debated over the centuries by the scholars of the Knights of the Twelfth Apostle. They disagreed on many things, but on one point they were unanimous: the effectiveness of the Cross was proportional to the degree of suffering offered on its behalf. When he destroyed not only the unborn child but also the beloved, his heart's desire, that would be sacrifice indeed—supreme sacrifice, for a supremely great cause. . . .

He swayed in the saddle as he rode, and the branches of the trees along the road seemed to wave him on. Their leaves were trembling in the still air, already fearing the onslaught of the German advance.

As he drew closer to the castle, his feeling of urgency grew. He increased the mare's speed. Three times far-off peasants hailed him as he passed, but he did not slow or answer. He was late, late, *late*.

It was midmorning when he topped the final ridge and looked across the Aire River to Chateau Cirelle. He reined the mare and stared at the castle. It seemed incredible that it could be so peaceful, unaffected by the war or his own experiences of the past few days.

He had to take advantage of that quiet normalcy. His absence would have been noticed, and his return would cause a stir. Therefore he must complete the ceremony before that return was known.

He reached into his pocket to touch the Cross. *Be with me, Lord Judas. Guide my steps.*

He shook the reins. The weary mare stepped down the hill, forded the shallow river, and came to the stables of Chateau Cirelle.

CHAPTER
THIRTY-TWO

Jenny wakened at seven o'clock in Louis Villette's bed, shivering to consciousness from nightmares no different from reality.

She was heavy-headed and unrested, but it was useless to look further for sleep. Jenny rose and dressed, scribbled a note for the Marquis, and wandered out into the predawn silence.

After her father's death, yesterday had gone out of focus. Jenny remembered drinking tea in the lounge, elbows on the table, propping her aching head on her hands. She knew she had discussed funeral arrangements with Aunt Ellen and that everyone had spoken to her kindly and encouragingly; but of those conversations, little remained. Early in the evening Cecile had given her a glass of milk in which she had dissolved a packet of pale yellow crystals. "You need sleep," she had said. "That's the most important thing."

Jenny had obediently drunk the milk, then escaped at the first opportunity to Louis Villette's quarters. She needed him. But he had not returned to the castle. She lay down in his bed. Despondent and exhausted, she fell at once asleep.

And now, another day; one that was dawning cloudy and dark, with no breath of wind. From the east, sharp at seven-thirty, Jenny heard the man-made thunder of heavy artillery. A massive barrage was beginning. The roar of bursting howitzer shells was punctuated by the subsonic ground quiver of great field mortars. Jenny sat on the low wall by the southeast tower, a traveling cloak wrapped about her. She waited.

A little after seven-thirty, Harry Holloway drove his truck up to the tower door, hopped out, and disappeared inside. Ten minutes later he and Clive Dunnay emerged carrying a long canvas bag between them. In silence they carried it to the truck and lifted it onto the lowered tailboard. Both men stared at Jenny in surprise and dismay when she walked quietly up to them.

"Jenny! You shouldn't be here." Clive looked wretched, with the pasty gray face of a hungover man obliged to rise long before he was ready.

She said nothing, but walked across to the canvas bag. It looked so small, no bigger than a bundle of laundry. She put her hand on it. "What was it you used to quote to me, Clive? About being a man. Would you say it for me now?"

"What a piece of work is a man." Clive spoke gruffly. "How noble in reason, how infinite in faculty. In form and moving, how express and admirable. In action how like an angel, in apprehension how like a god. The beauty of the world . . ."

"Yes. That's it." Jenny stood silent by the truck, until Harry Holloway pulled at Clive's sleeve and said, "Come on, sir, 'round the corner and have a smoke for five minutes."

Clive gave him a nod of comprehension and the two men walked off side by side. Jenny stood with her hand touching the cold canvas. *Sleep peacefully. I'll miss you always, and I'll think of you every day of my life. I'll try to be a good daughter, and I'll love you forever. Good-bye, Daddy.*

She squeezed her tired eyes shut for a moment, then walked to where Harry and Clive were smoking rank French cigarettes and peering up at the strange cloud formations.

"Wondering if we're going to get rain, miss," said Harry.

"I shouldn't be surprised." Her voice was calm. "It's certainly very odd weather, isn't it?"

Both men visibly relaxed. "I'd better be on my way," said Harry. "Got a long drive ahead of me." He took Jenny's hand for a moment in his. "I'll drive very careful, miss."

Jenny nodded, turned abruptly, and headed for the door to the tower. Harry turned to Clive Dunnay. "Think she'll be all right, sir?"

"She's doing fine." Clive looked at the truck. "She loved

her dad more than anything in the world. I hope she's gone to get some more sleep."

"You should do the same, sir." Harry pinched out his half-smoked cigarette and put it back in his tobacco tin. "You look as though you could use it, if you don't mind my saying so."

Clive gave a grim smile. "I took my own advice to you and had a drink for the colonel last night. Then I think we had a drink for every other soldier we've lost in the war. We're going to need more liquor, Harry."

"Yes, sir. I'll collect some on the way back."

Clive watched as the truck started up, rolled off down the hill, and passed out of sight along the avenue of trees that skirted the fish pond. Full of his own memories of William Marshall, he went to Jenny's room and knocked on the door. There was no reply. He poked his head inside. The room was empty. She was probably in the dining room, looking for breakfast.

Clive considered joining her there; then his stomach rebelled at the thought of eggs or smoked fish. Even the smell would be too much. He and Jenny really needed to talk about their situation—she had said not a word, but she must have guessed about him and Cecile—but that could wait for a few more hours. Perhaps by then they would both be feeling better.

He went to his room, slipped off his shoes, and lay down on the bed. His head ached terribly. He closed his eyes. He had been an idiot last night, trying to drink every full glass that Walter Johnson had pressed on him. His stomach rolled uneasily.

God, but he felt bad! When he saw Walter, he would point out that not all the injuries of war were inflicted by the enemy.

His face was unshaven, the hair on the back of his head was burned off, and his ruined clothes showed the signs of two days of living rough. He could not go into the main body of the chateau without attracting just the sort of attention that he needed to avoid. He must lure Jenny to the cellars, and soon. But it must be done quietly and inconspicuously or all his efforts would be wasted.

Louis Villette hurried from the stables, across the grass

to the southwest tower. If only the door had been left unlocked . . .

It had. He sighed with relief. Within a minute he was in
his chambers, high in the tower. He closed the door and went
to the long mirror. A madman stared back at him, a torn and
dirty madman. Holding a hand mirror and turning around, he
was able to take a first look at the back of his head. The hair
had been seared to black stubble by the flamethrower, and
there were ugly burns. Yet he had been lucky. His instinctive
dive when the flame hit had saved him from fatal injury. He
had numerous cuts and scratches, but he ignored most of
them. It was his hands that concerned him. The cuts across
his palms made by the cell bars had not healed, and now they
were suppurating. His nails and fingertips had been ruined in
his scrabbling ascent of the gritty bank of the River Meuse.
They were seeping masses of pulpy flesh.

There was no hot water, but that was a luxury he could
manage without. He took a long drink from the china jug and
poured the rest of the water into the big earthenware basin.
He was about to plunge his hands in when he noticed the slip
of paper propped against the brandy glasses on the dresser.
If he had not been so preoccupied, he would have seen it
when he came in. He read it without touching it.

> My dearest Louis,
> I must talk to you. I'm pregnant. I'm sure of it.
> With Daddy dead, Aunt Ellen will want me to go
> back to England. I don't know what to do. Please
> see me the moment you get back. All my love,
> Jenny.

With Daddy dead—that was certainly news. Louis Villette
stood perfectly still. When had this note been written? Pray
God it was recent, something scribbled in the past few hours.
If she had already left the chateau . . .

He had to prepare for the ceremony, and he had to take
Jenny down to the cellars. *At once*, before any other complication could arise. She was with child—but if she left now, his
struggle through the German lines to Chateau Cirelle would
have been wasted.

The cellars first, then Jenny. But a note here, in case he

missed her and she came back to look for him. He went to his desk, picked up a pen in his ruined fingers, and scribbled a note on a sheet of white notepaper. The best place to leave it was where he had found her message—she would look there first.

Now to make himself presentable enough to pass through the castle without exciting comment.

He splashed water over his hands and face, wincing when it touched the seared skin. He dabbed himself tenderly with a towel and pulled a clean silk shirt over his head. There was not enough time for a shave, but he could make himself more presentable with a wide hat that partly covered his face.

He was rummaging in the cluttered wardrobe when the door to the bedroom opened without a knock. A woman stepped in and looked around. She was tall, with graying hair swept back from her face. Her eyes flashed with satisfaction when she spotted him.

"Louis Villette. Marquis de Saint-Amè!" She was a strong-looking, large-faced woman in her mid-forties. "You have returned. I have been looking for you since early this morning."

"Madam, you have the advantage of me." He put down the gray felt hat he was holding. Who the devil was this, wandering into his chambers? And how was he going to get rid of her? "You know who I am, but your identity is unknown to me. And I am not used to strangers barging unannounced into my bedroom."

"I am Ellen Blake. Jenny Marshall is my niece, and I am concerned for her safety. I went to her room last night, and again this morning, but she was not there." Her voice was cold and wary. "I feel sure you will agree that I have good reason to be worried."

His first reaction—*only a woman!*—was replaced by caution. He sensed her strength and her resolve. "Madam, I do not know what you are talking about, but I, too, am concerned for Jenny's safety. I returned less than an hour ago from captivity behind the German lines, with crucial information about a German advance. Jenny was here to greet me. She is saddened at her father's death, but she is perfectly well. With the Germans on the way, I have persuaded her that she should prepare to leave here. I suggest that you do the same, unless you are willing to be taken prisoner.''

The woman was shaking her head and looking calmly around his chambers. ''I don't believe you. Jenny would not consider leaving without talking to me. And you would never *allow* her to leave; she is too important to your plans. Where is she?''

The Marquis faced away from her, picking up and fiddling with the hat as he tried to hide his shock. The woman seemed to know everything. ''My plans? If I knew what you were talking about, maybe—''

''Don't bother, monsieur. I have read the Gospel, and the Ritual, and I have studied the list of places where the Cross has been in the past thousand years. I have even seen your own list of murdered women—your wretched 'Vessels.' You are a Knight of Judas Iscariot, and you are the present Guardian of the Cross. I am here to prevent my niece's murder. Where is she?''

''I am a Knight of the Twelfth Apostle, as are many other noblemen. The Gospel forms the foundation for our beliefs. But the rest, the idea that there might be an actual Cross, rather than merely a symbolic one, that is pure myth. The stuff of legends.'' His shirt was still unbuttoned, and he showed her his bared chest. ''You say I am the Guardian. Then where is the Cross? And as for my intending any harm to Jenny, I would not think of it. I am very fond of her. The things that you are suggesting—''

The woman opened her purse and calmly pulled out a revolver. It was one of the old Prussian ''elephant class'' with a lengthened barrel—by no means a woman's weapon. Louis Villette had seen one of those blow a hole in a man's chest big enough to show the whole heart.

She aimed it at him, and her hand was perfectly steady. ''I am sure you could go on talking all day. I thought it might come to this. You say Jenny is safe and well. Very good. I say again, where is she?''

She obviously knew how to use the gun. Louis Villette hesitated.

''Talk, sir!''

''Very well. The best way to end this nonsense is to let you see Jenny for yourself. We were intending to travel together as far as Bar-le-Duc. I told Jenny I would have a food hamper prepared, and she should select wine for the trip. She went to the wine cellar a few minutes ago, and I am sure that she will be there now. If we sit here and wait, she will certainly return."

"No. No delays. Lead the way, and take me to her."

"But at least give me time to change my clothes—these trousers, and these boots, they are the ones—"

Ellen Blake's eyes were hard and angry. "Take me to Jenny—*now*! I am not interested in talking until I have seen Jenny."

He shrugged. "Follow me."

He led the way out of the chambers and down the spiral staircase of the tower. At the foot of the stairs he turned, ready to lead Ellen Blake along the corridor. He paused. Halfway along, straightening a curtain, was Monge. The majordomo must not see Ellen Blake and the gun.

"Monge." He called along the corridor, and saw the other man straighten up and squint in his direction. "I have been away on urgent army business, and I must leave again this morning. I need a food hamper for two people. Have it ready in my chambers in half an hour."

"Very good, sir." Monge was peering along toward him, but from this distance he would see nothing out of order. "I will arrange it."

"Excellent." Louis Villette turned and went off along the corridor toward the northwest tower.

"I hope we are almost there," said Ellen Blake. "I have no interest today in guided tours of the castle."

"Two more minutes." Louis Villette spoke calmly. Within he was a volcano of emotions. *Two more minutes, and your damned interfering will be over forever*. He opened the narrow door to the cellar, squeezed through, and turned on the electric lights. "Very soon you will see for yourself that Jenny is all right. And you will owe me a massive apology. This way."

He started down the narrow wooden staircase.

Ellen Blake's misgivings increased with every step. When she went to bed she had been convinced that she understood the full situation. In the light of morning, she was less sure.

If she were right, would Louis Villette have gone anywhere without Jenny? She was his prize, his treasured sacrifice. He would have kept her at his side always.

And then there was the Marquis himself. He seemed so sincere and dignified, and he had obviously been through some terrible ordeal. Suppose that he had, as he said, just returned from behind the German lines? That seemed inconsistent with any ideas of Cross or ritual.

She had to see Jenny and find out her condition. Then all conjecture would end and she could plan the next step. She was sure of one thing. Her eyes had not lied. Jenny's name had been on the list of sacrificial victims; all that had been missing was a date.

The Marquis had halted at the bottom of the staircase, to look back at her over his shoulder. She waved the pistol. "Keep going. And don't make any wild moves. If you do, I'm going to shoot."

He nodded and moved forward. The cellars were old and moldering, with an underground chill that electric light could do nothing to dispel. Ellen wrinkled her nose. Something in the air did not smell quite right. It was not mildew or rotting timbers. It was deeper and older, wafting to her like a tainted breath.

They passed through a room filled with the trappings of medieval torture. Ellen noted that the instruments were thick with rust. "How much farther? Surely you're not telling me your wine cellar is next to a torture chamber?"

"We are very close. This was a shortcut only."

The next room was much more opulent, and at the same time more disquieting. It was a bedroom furnished with a broad, plush bed, carved teak cabinets, and gleaming overhead mirrors. And it had been used recently. Ellen noted the padded manacles and hanging harnesses, first with detached interest, then with alarm as she thought of Jenny. "And I suppose this is part of your shortcut, too."

The Marquis was not listening. He had gone over to one of the cabinets, opened it, and was staring inside. He turned back and faced Ellen, who brought the gun up to point squarely at the middle of his chest.

He shook his head. "I see how you know about the books. You have been here before."

"Never."

"My cabinets have been broken into, my manuscripts stolen, my personal property defiled. Where did you put them?" He took no notice of the pointing gun.

"Take me to Jenny. Then we can worry about your books. I assure you, I have no intention of stealing anything that belongs to you."

He stood with head bowed, as though in prayer, and finally nodded. "Through this door. We should find her among the white wines—Jenny will never drink red from choice. Close that cabinet as you come by, would you? The one by your right hand."

He was reaching for the door handle as he spoke. As Ellen's attention moved for a moment to the teak cabinet, he grabbed a metal statue on the table near the door, wheeled, and hurled it at her. She dodged, aimed, and pulled the trigger. The Marquis flung himself to the right, out of the line of the bullet. He rushed at her.

She was ready for him. She took two paces back, aimed again, and fired.

The first shot stopped his charge for a second. She saw the splash and spurt of blood on the lower right side of his chest. He staggered. Then he was coming on, anger flaring in his eyes. She fired again.

The third shot did it. This time he spun around, gave a guttural cry, and dropped to the floor. He writhed for a second, shuddered, and lay still. The room went oddly quiet.

Ellen stood, the crash of the shots in her ears and the smell of burned cordite in her nostrils. After a moment or two she looked down at the body, face upward in front of her. The bullet holes were welling with dark, venous blood, staining the white shirt. She could see the fiery red of burns along the back of the neck. She shivered.

"Jenny!" Her voice sounded hollow through the paneled room. "Jenny. Where are you?"

There was no reply. Could she be already too late? Or was it possible that he had Jenny somewhere down here, bound and gagged and ready for the terrible ceremony?

Ellen looked again at the Marquis. Now she was sorry that she had killed him. He was her only line to Jenny. She took a step closer and stared down. His eyes were closed, and she could see no sign of movement in his breast. He could be no further danger to Jenny—but if he had tied her up somewhere down here, he might even in his dying be the cause of her death.

She walked out of the room and looked along the corridor. No sign of any wine cellar. Farther along was a small locked door, of wooden planks with heavy crosspieces. She rattled at the lock with no result. She went back into the bedroom and knelt by the body of the Marquis. Might he have the key on him? It was a long shot, but she was reduced to long shots.

She felt for a pulse in his neck. Nothing, although the flesh was still warm.

She frisked along his sides until she came to the left-hand trousers pocket. Something was there, and it felt as though it might be a key. She reached her hand inside the pocket and touched metal, something attached to a long chain. A strange electric shock went through her fingers and up her arm.

Ellen pulled out her hand. She was holding a cross, a warm cross that glowed darkly silver in the electric light.

This was it. It had to be. She was holding the Cross of Judas, fashioned by the hand of Judas Iscariot and preserved through nineteen centuries. It had to be the ultimate moment, the summation of a whole life as an antiquarian. For a long, breathless moment she stared at it.

A hand reached up to close around hers.

She looked down and found herself staring into the bright blue eyes of Louis Villette. "Mine!" said that soft, deep voice. His other hand flashed up to knock the gun spinning across the room.

Before she could escape, those massive hands had lifted to circle her throat. It was a grip that she could not break.

He was squeezing, squeezing, squeezing.

From out of total darkness he had bobbed up, a cork in a tidal wave, thrust from the depths toward full consciousness by a power that he could not resist. Like a billowing reflection in a subterranean pool, he had seen her hovering dark above him, reaching out to steal from him the world's most precious possession. He had heard a voice saying, *"This must not be. This must not be."*

In the most powerful surge of energy he had ever known, he reached up to take her neck in his outstretched fingers. She had no time to recoil.

He squeezed.

The cry in her throat was choked off before it could be uttered. Ellen Blake's eyes bulged wide open. They were staring down at him, swelling from their sockets. The Cross fell from her hand onto his chest. As her face reddened above him and her legs began their drumbeat on the floor, he felt the Cross hot and secure against him. It cleaved to his skin. He did not notice the beating of her arms against his head and chest. He felt only the power. It was growing within him, building and building with the rushing urgency of an orgasm, surging up to find an outlet.

He shivered, looked at the tongue lolling from her open mouth, and hurled the unconscious body away. It landed in the middle of the floor, a contorted rag doll.

He lay back panting. By some miracle he was alive, and the Cross was with him. He gripped it tightly, lifting it from his chest to push it again into his pocket. Slowly and unsteadily, he rose to his feet. Blood was trickling from the bullet holes in his chest, but he felt only a memory of pain. There was loss of mobility in his left arm, more of a nuisance than a real hindrance to his movements.

He staggered across to sit on the bed.

How long had he just been unconscious, in that sleep like death after she had shot him? He had no idea. It might have been seconds or hours. He must attend to his wounds; then he must find Jenny and bring her here. Nothing had changed, except that those wounds made everything more urgent. He did not know how much time was left before his injuries took their toll.

Ellen Blake's shots had left dreadful, gaping injuries. Both bullets had penetrated deep and were still lodged in his flesh. Though there was little pain, the continued loss of blood was an immediate danger. A white sheet in the wardrobe was a good enough bandage. He tore it into strips and padded and bound both bullet holes as best he could.

And now for Jenny.

He was out of the bedroom and heading through the torture chamber when he realized that he was behaving like an idiot.

He couldn't bring Jenny down here and expect her to cooperate for even a fraction of a second with her aunt lying unconscious in front of her. He had to clean up.

Normally it would be easy enough. Ellen Blake would not be the first to disappear down the oubliette in the wall of the torture chamber. But would he be strong enough to carry her there, in his present condition?

Lord Judas, give me strength! For one more day, for one more hour. Thy will be done; and I will be your willing instrument.

He bent to seize Ellen Blake by both arms and began to drag her. A cold sweat poured from his forehead. It took a huge effort to get her to the chamber, a greater one to swing open the heavy stone panel of the oubliette. At last it was done, and he had her body on the very lip of the chute. He was pushing and turning it to begin its slide when he heard a new sound.

It was a woman's scream. It came from the door of the chamber.

CHAPTER
THIRTY-THREE

Jenny had walked to the dining room when she left her father's body, just as Clive had expected. But she did not stay there. She had no appetite for food. Instead she took a cup of coffee and again headed outside into the castle gardens.

She needed solitude, time to think. For an hour she sat alone among the spring flowers and the rumble and roar of distant guns. She was oblivious to both. If she were to honor her promise to her dead father, she had to resolve the situation with Clive, and with Louis Villette. And she needed to do it as soon as possible. She was not being fair to either man. But what was she going to say to Clive?

At last she headed back to Louis Villette's quarters. A knock on the heavy door produced no answer. Jenny entered. As she had feared, his rooms were still deserted.

Expecting to see her own note, Jenny walked into the bedroom and looked on top of the dresser. Her eyes widened. In place of her message was a new piece of white paper.

> Back at last—and what a journey! I was caught behind the German lines and had trouble getting home. But here I am. Jenny, my darling, I have urgent work in the cellar. It can't wait. If you can, join me there. I'll be in the bedroom, in Grandfather's chamber. Please hurry! Yours, Louis.

Jenny noticed that there was mud on the carpet and smears of mud and blood on the bottom of the note. Had he been injured? He would never mention it if he had. Louis made light of wounds. Just a scratch, he would say, of gashes that would send most men running for a doctor.

The quickest route to the cellar led down two flights of stairs and along a corridor. Jenny ran that way as fast as she could, her soft leather shoes making little noise. It was after nine, and the chateau was stirring to life, but most people were still thinking drowsily of breakfast. The stairs and corridors were deserted.

She found the little door that led down to the cellars, opened it, and slipped through. She didn't know where the light switch was located, but it didn't matter. She knew the direction to take her to the bedroom. Her feeling of relief at Louis's return was so strong that it lifted the black depression that had gripped her since her father's death. She wanted Louis to hold her, to say he loved her, to tell her that there was still something in the world worth living for.

The corridor was dark, but she could see lights ahead. Louis must be in the old torture chamber. She caught sight of his tall form bending over something. She wanted to run up behind him and embrace him before he even knew that she was there.

Jenny started forward. At the entrance to the long room she halted. Louis Villette had swung back the thick stone block that formed the opening of the oubliette. He was dragging something toward it, a bundle of green and gray rags.

She caught her breath. Those colors—that was Aunt Ellen's dress; she had been wearing it in Rembercourt. And the bundle itself. It was—it couldn't be—

Jenny gave a high-pitched scream. The Marquis dropped the unconscious body of Ellen Blake by the slippery chute of the oubliette. He spun around to face Jenny. She saw a crouched, filthy figure with bloodstained chest and scorched hair. He had stripped off his shirt and wore crude bandages around his ribs. The deep chest rose and fell in labored breathing. His battered hands looked huge, like animal paws. They slowly lifted from his sides.

"Jenny!" His voice was hoarse, and he stumbled across toward her.

She backed away.

"Jenny, don't run." He came closer. "I have to explain."

"Don't come near me. Don't touch me."

"Jenny, it's not the way it looks. Honestly." His eyes were bright and staring. He was only a couple of yards away from her, reaching out those awful hands. "You have to let me explain what's been happening—you're the only one who can help me."

She would like to believe him, but she could not take her eyes off those bloodstained hands. *Butcher's hands. Murderer's hands.* She shook her head. "No, no—stay away. I saw what you were doing. You were going to put her down the oubliette."

He was closer, only a step away. As he lunged forward, Jenny spun around. There was a tearing of cloth on the back of her blouse, then she was running desperately away from him. She could not face a flight through the unlit part of the cellars. Instead she ran the other way, down the long corridor. At the branch point she hesitated. The left-hand path was dark, too, but she had been along it before. It would take her beneath the grounds of the chateau, then up to the cloisters and the open air. If she could get outside, she stood a chance. There would be others to help her.

While she hesitated, Louis Villette was almost on her. He grabbed at her again, but this time caught only her necklace as she ducked under his arms and away. The thin chain broke, and she was running madly along the next corridor. This one was completely dark. She was forced to move with her hand held out to one side to locate the wall. She could hear the Marquis blundering along behind. The sound of his footsteps was getting fainter. He had been badly injured, and she could outrun him. But she could not run quietly. The great sobbing breaths that she was taking were more than loud enough for him to track her. The cloisters were not far ahead. She could see the light from the stairs.

Jenny turned to look behind her to see how far ahead she was. No more than ten steps. *Not enough.* She had to run faster. At that moment she ran smack into a waiting pair of outstretched arms. She was turned around, and was thrown back the way she had come. As she hit the ground, Jenny heard a staccato high-pitched voice cry out in an unfamiliar language. Then the Marquis had arrived and was crouching at her side.

Dolfi had been ready to shoot when he heard those running feet. There was no place for him to hide in the tunnel, no time to ascend to the cloisters. He had his gun out and ready when his eyes, adapted to the darkness, saw Jenny running toward him—with the Marquis close behind!

Dolfi filled with a huge satisfaction. Richter had forced him to skulk away here, hidden from everything—and now the Marquis and the Cross came falling into his lap like great ripe fruit. Ignoring the girl, he pointed his gun at the Marquis.

"No closer." Dolfi spoke loudly and clearly. According to Richter, Louis Villette was fluent in German. If not, so much the worse for the Marquis. "No closer, or I will shoot both of you."

Louis Villette halted at once, skidding to his knees next to Jenny. He glared up at Dolfi. "Who in the name of creation are you? And what are you doing in my castle?"

"Never mind who I am."

"You're German—how did you manage to follow me back here from the river?"

Dolfi took a closer look at the other man. Louis Villette was a mess. His bare chest wore a bloody bandage, his hair was burned off, his body and clothes were filthy. Was this shambling wreck the master of Chateau Cirelle, the man whom Charles Richter had described to Dolfi as "noble and dignified"?

"I followed you nowhere," said Dolfi. "As for my presence in this castle, it is now German territory. Its lands, buildings, and contents belong to the German government. I am occupying it in the name of Kaiser Wilhelm II and the German Empire."

"You are mad." The Marquis straightened and took a step toward Dolfi. Jenny remained crouched where she had fallen. She could not understand a word of what was being said, but whoever he was, the German-speaking newcomer was far less menacing than Louis Villette. The Marquis was only a couple of feet away from her, and his wounded body exuded rage and animal strength. In the pale light that filtered down through the cloisters she could see two bullet wounds, but he seemed to ignore them.

"You are quite insane," went on the Marquis. "Do you seriously believe that you can make threats to me *here*, on my own property?" He took another dragging step forward.

"Get back!" Dolfi lifted the pistol. He was ready to shoot to kill—until he realized he could not do so. Not now. The Cross was missing! A deep purple-blue patch of scar tissue was visible where it should have rested on the Marquis' deep chest. Instead of aiming for Louis Villette's heart, Dolfi sent a bullet to chip stone a few inches from the Marquis' feet.

"Back! I'm not joking. This is no longer your property. You can hear the bombardment for yourself. The German Army will occupy this chateau before sunset. The only reason that I have not shot both of you and gone on with preparations for the army's arrival is that you have something I need. And I have something you want—your life. I am willing to negotiate."

"What do you mean?" Louis Villette moved a grudging step backward.

"Your life, in return for the Cross of Judas Iscariot."

"I don't know what you're talking about." But the bloody hand went instinctively to the burn scar.

Dolfi made an impatient gesture with the pistol. "Don't waste my time and yours. You have the Cross. I want it. I am willing to throw in the woman, too, if you want—I'll spare her life, or if you prefer it I'll shoot her for you."

"I do not have the Cross." The Marquis touched his chest again. "I took it off to bandage my wounds. I was doing that when the woman discovered me. The Cross is still in the cellar."

"Then take me to it."

Louis Villette stepped back and stood looking silently at Dolfi. He was very aware of the Cross and chain, hot against his left hip. "But if I take you to the Cross," he said slowly, "and show you where it is, you will certainly shoot me. On the other hand, if you shoot me now you will never find it. I think we have a stalemate. If you shoot me, you will not get the Cross; if I give you the Cross, you will take my life. I would be a fool to show you where it is. Neither of us can do anything."

"I can do something." Dolfi placed another shot from his pistol an inch above the Marquis' right collarbone. If the man was reluctant to cooperate, it was time for invention. "Herr Villette, my orders were very precise. I intend to follow them to the letter. If you surrender the Cross to me, then I am on no account to kill you. My superiors know you, and they hope that you will cooperate with them in the occupation of this region. You will continue to control the area around Saint-Amè, just as you do now—perhaps with increased authority. However, this is conditional upon your surrender of the Cross to me. If you refuse to do so, my orders are explicit. I am to shoot you and continue my search for as long as it takes to find the Cross of Judas Iscariot. I am not a man to go against the orders of my superior officers. If you value your life, take me to the Cross."

Louis Villette hesitated, looking at Jenny and then back to Dolfi. Outside in the cloisters he could hear the artillery bombardment steadily growing fiercer. Dolfi's finger was tightening on the trigger.

"Very well. I will show you." Louis Villette turned. "Follow me."

"The woman first." Dolfi waved the gun at Jenny, urging her to her feet. "Tell her to lead the way. Then I want you at least two steps behind her. Tell her not to try to run away or to scream—I have plenty of bullets, and I will not hesitate to shoot a woman."

Louis shrugged and turned to Jenny. His voice was calm as he relayed Dolfi's instructions. She turned to go, then looked back, terrified at the idea of the Marquis right behind her. She was relieved to see that he kept his distance. He followed her slowly back along the corridor. She could hear his labored breathing, and the dragging of his feet on the stone floor.

At the entrance to the torture chamber Jenny halted. The oubliette was still open, but there was no sign of Aunt Ellen.

"Wait there for a moment." Louis Villette turned to Dolfi. "I heard what you said about orders. But still I do not trust you. I want the girl to come with me, and I want you at least five steps away from us. Then I will throw the Cross to you."

Dolfi scanned the walls and fixtures of the torture chamber. He had seen it before, with the grisly instruments and the long, altarlike table with its red cloth. But there was no guessing where the Cross might be. When he was not actually wearing it, the Marquis must have a good hiding place.

Dolfi nodded. "I will remain here. Do not go closer than four steps to the door to the bedroom, and do not make any sudden movements. Tell the woman the same thing. Then get the Cross. And hurry! This is taking too long."

Louis Villette spoke to Jenny and walked across to the red-clothed table. He reached down at the end of it to a carved wooden icon of a bearded man holding a chalice.

"Here." The Marquis scooped something from beneath the chalice's false bottom and tossed it toward Dolfi. There was a gleam of silver in the air and the twisting links of a chain. Dolfi instinctively reached up to catch it. As he did so, the Marquis called out urgently to Jenny and went ducking away through the door that led to the bedroom. Dolfi, distracted by the cross and chain that dangled from his grip, got off one shot before Louis Villette was through the doorway. It struck high on the back in the fleshy muscle between shoulder and neck, and then the Marquis was gone. The woman was crouched on the floor, her mouth an open O of fear and surprise. Dolfi lifted the gun again; but he hesitated. He looked at the cross, with its gleam of dull silver. He had it. The woman was irrelevant. Why waste another bullet?

He hurried out of the torture chamber. Since he did not want the Marquis pursuing him, he turned to close and lock the door. To his surprise, the woman was behind him, holding out her hands and crying in a frightened, beseeching voice. Dolfi shook his head and slammed the door shut. The Marquis de Saint-Amè apparently wanted the woman. Let him have her. Dolfi would settle for the cross.

He ran through the cellars as fast as he could. When he reached the cloisters he did not even look to see if he was being observed. The cross had to be hidden, safely hidden where Louis Villette could not hope to find it again; and the château must be made ready for the arrival of the Grand Advance.

His bandage fell off his head. Dolfi did not bother to replace it. He ran around the outside of the castle to the door nearest to Richter's rooms, then in and up the stairs. He did not care who saw him, and now in the perverse way of things he did not meet a soul. Without knocking he turned the door handle and pushed through into Richter's room.

"I got it! I have it!"

Richter had been shaving, with a basin of hot water, soap, and straight razor. He paused with his face half soaped and glared at Dolfi. "What the hell are you doing here? You're supposed to be in the cloisters."

"Damn the cloisters. I have it—I have the Cross of Judas!" Dolfi had been running with his pistol in one hand and the cross held tight in the other. Now he stretched out his hand and slowly opened it, palm upward. The cross lay there, its tarnished silver gleaming. "I tricked it out of the Marquis with a nonsense story about cooperation. Look at it! We have both the cross *and* the Grand Advance."

Richter was still standing with the razor in his hand. Now he put it down and walked forward. "We will have the Grand Advance. I cannot say about the cross."

"What the devil do you mean?" Dolfi was trembling with excitement. "Look, it is here. I got it from the Marquis himself."

Richter was shaking his head. "What you have there I cannot say. All I *can* say is that what you are holding is not the cross that I saw given to the Marquis. What you have is too big, the shape is wrong, and the cross I saw was dark and battered-looking. What you are holding is too shiny and smooth. You have been tricked."

Richter felt oddly pleased as Dolfi stared down at his hand. It would serve the bombastic corporal right! To be made such a fool of, and to have that fact clearly pointed out to him.

"You have blundered again," he went on. "Concentrate on the Grand Advance."

"We must have the Cross! It has to be in the cellars, down there with the Marquis. I'll go back—"

The man was insane! Richter shook his head firmly. "No! Absolutely not. You've proved it already, you don't know what you're doing when you're down there. You cannot even ask the way if you get lost! I will go, and I will look for the

Cross—don't argue, I know the cellars, I can move through the castle without being questioned, and I speak fluent French. You will do what you should have done in the first place: *stay in the damned cloisters*."

There was a long silence, during which Richter thought that Dolfi was going to refuse. Finally the corporal lifted his head to look at and through Richter. "Villette will regret this," he said quietly. "And so will all of France." What Richter saw in the other man's eyes made him feel sick.

As Dolfi slammed shut the door of the torture chamber, Jenny had pushed at it hopelessly for only a moment. Then she turned and ran toward the other end of the room. If only she could lock *that* door . . .

She was two steps away when the door began to swing open. Louis Villette stepped through and leaned heavily against the stone wall of the chamber. Blood trickled from the new wound in his back, and the bandages around his chest were stained with fresh red. He looked carefully around the whole room, hardly seeming to notice Jenny. Then he reached into his left-hand trousers pocket, pulled out a dark, battered Cross on a length of silver chain, and kissed it. He slipped the chain around his neck, so that the Cross lay against his bare chest.

He wandered into the middle of the room, looking thoughtfully at the long table. He made a tiny adjustment, straightening the crimson cloth. Jenny moved slowly back, never taking her eyes away from him. This was not the Louis Villette that she had known. The witty, intellectual host and the tender lover had gone. In their place was a dark, tormented animal, moving only to serve its own needs and instincts. She dreaded the thought of being touched by those filthy, blood-crusted hands. Surely those could not be the same fingers whose gentle movement over her breasts and thighs had given such delight.

His gaze, in its slow wandering around the room, moved to rest on her. "Jenny. My dear, dear Jenny." His voice was still the same, as soft and deep and warm as ever. "Lord Judas moves in a mysterious way. You flee, and I cannot run fast. Lord Judas sees that you might escape. He uses a German agent to bring you back to me, and then the False Cross of Apollonius of Naxos to get rid of the German. And now we are ready. We should delay no longer.''

He was advancing on her, not hurrying but making sure that she could not make any move that would get her away from him. She retreated behind the rack, behind the cage of the little ease, past the spiked open casket of the iron maiden. He came on steadily.

"Louis." Jenny was surprised to hear her own voice. "Louis, I am pregnant. Your baby, Louis. Don't do anything that would harm your baby."

He took no notice. He moved the torture implements as he came to them, effortlessly, making a wall that prevented her from running back along the room. "Come, Jenny." He was reaching out toward her, only a few feet away. "It is almost time. Didn't you hear the sounds for yourself? The German advance is ready to begin. If we are to stop it, you and I, there is no time to waste.''

She was shrinking back against the wall. There was no place left to go. His hand came down and closed like a steel manacle around her wrist. He lifted her until his face was close to hers. She was staring into those deep, bloodshot eyes.

"I love you, Jenny," he said, and it was the soft, thrilling voice of a lover. "I really do. In another time, or another place, it might have been different. But there is duty. Come, now, my lovely Jenny. We must do our sacred duty.'' He kissed her gently on the forehead, then lifted the Cross and touched it to her lips. The metal felt hot, too hot for simple body warmth, and there was a smell to it that made Jenny think of dusty villages and sun-baked rooftops. She recoiled, fighting to free herself from his grip. She screamed at the top of her voice.

He did not even notice. He touched the Cross to his own lips, murmuring, "*Lord, Lord,*" and lifting Jenny off her feet. Ignoring her struggles, he carried her along the room and placed her on the table in the middle, setting her down gently. Soon harnesses of dark silk, attached to each wrist and ankle, limited her movements to a few inches in any direction.

Louis Villette looked about him, then walked around the

table with dragging footsteps. He was still bleeding and the limp was getting worse, but he seemed as strong as ever. "I think that is everything," he said quietly. "Yes, everything. Very good. We can proceed."

He leaned over Jenny. Methodically, item by item, he began to remove her clothes.

CHAPTER
THIRTY-FOUR

When Walter Johnson was a child, a railway line had been built not far from his home in Dubuque. He would wake to the clang and clatter of rails and ties, and some mornings he would wander over to watch the workmen. His favorite part was when they were spiking the ties. One man would hold the long metal spike vertical, and the other would drive it home with booming strokes of a heavy sledgehammer.

That was what was happening now. He would hear a booming sound—sometimes the whole room shook—and then somebody drove a metal spike right into the top of his head.

It had been going on for hours. What were they *doing* to him? Walter groaned and opened his eyes.

He shut them again, hurriedly. He was looking at bright sunlight reflecting from something pale gold and shiny, too close to his face for him to be able to focus on it. He eased his head back on its cushion, wincing with the pain that the movement produced, and warily opened his eyes.

His head was resting on a soft thigh, and he was staring at a fleece of golden pubic hair that reflected the morning sunlight. He looked further, and recognized Penny Wilson's breasts. He couldn't see her face, because she had pulled a pillow across her eyes to keep out the sun. She grunted complainingly as Walter moved.

Walter grunted, too, as he tried to lift his head. *Not again!* Hadn't he learned his lesson last time? And hadn't Penny said she'd keep an eye on his drinking?

Apparently not. He looked down at his body, as naked as hers, and tried to remember what had happened. The four of them had gone off to Cecile's friend's house. He could get that far. And they had had a drink. And another. And after that? He had a vague memory of late-night lovemaking, but on the morning after there was no recollection of any pleasure—or even of where it had happened, or who it had been with. It could have been here, with Penny, or out on the roof with Monge's grandmother. And then he had left Penny—hadn't he? So why was he here?

He licked his lips. His mouth tasted like a gorilla's armpit. Dehydration, that was part of the problem. Better do something about it.

He eased his way over to the edge of the bed and reached out for the pitcher of water on the bedside table. He cautiously wet his lips, then took three small swallows. After a couple of loud belches, his stomach signaled that it was ready to accept more. Sip by sip, he drank half a pint of water and lay back on the bed, this time with his head next to Penny's.

He sighed.

A crazy country. Too much booze, too many good reasons to drink it. The war. It was all the fault of the damned war. It got blamed for everything else, might as well blame it for a hangover. Those boomings outside, they were shells—and big ones, by the sound of them. Every explosion drove another rail spike into his head.

His movements had been quiet, but they were enough to waken Penny. She rolled over toward him and lifted herself on her arms. Her hair hung loose to her shoulders, and her nipples brushed his chest as she leaned over to give him a light kiss on the cheek.

"Morning, sailor. Some voyage last night. How are you feeling?"

"Ooooooch!" he said. "Careful." There was no justice in the world. Just looking at her, he could tell that she felt fine and full of energy. "What am I doing here? I thought I left and went to my own room."

"You did—and you came back. For a nightcap, you said, and a little womanly sympathy for a wounded airman. And then I couldn't get rid of you. You don't remember those mad, passionate moments? I don't know why I bothered."

"I don't remember." He looked at her accusingly. "I thought you were going to stop me from drinking too much!"

"Are you kidding?" She sat up cross-legged on the bed, pushing blond hair back from her face. "It would have taken the Kaiser and fifty regiments. If it's any consolation, I'll bet Clive Dunnay's in worse shape than you are. He insisted on showing Cecile how he could drink a tot of rum standing on his head."

"Thank God I didn't try it. Or did I?" Walter held his head as another explosion, louder than usual, sounded from outside. "Jesus. What's going on out there? They sound as if they're right in the backyard."

"They're closer, that's for sure." Penny stood up and went naked to the window. "Nothing to see. Maybe we'd better go down to find out what's happening. I'd hate to find that while we were playing games here we'd lost the war. Can you get up?"

"Yeah." Walter swung his feet slowly to the floor. "Don't rush me, though. Tempt me with coffee and brandy, and I'll make it. Eventually."

Clive was sitting in the dining room when they got there. Once William Marshall's body had been taken away from the chateau in the early morning, Clive had gone to his room intending a ten-minute nap. He had felt queasy, and thrown up twice. Then he could face the food that had seemed so disgusting earlier; in fact, he was starving. And for the first time since it was broken, his leg didn't hurt or itch.

Before he headed for the dining room he had done a quick search of the first and second floors, looking for Jenny. He cursed when she was nowhere to be found. They had to have a serious talk with each other. She surely knew about Cecile, and he was almost certain about her and the Marquis. If their engagement was off—Clive hoped that it was not—then they ought to say so. Clive didn't want their talk put off any longer. But where was Jenny?

By the time Penny and Walter appeared in the dining room, Clive had eaten a pile of buttered scones and a plate of smoking-hot ham, and his feeling about Jenny's absence had changed from annoyance to worry. He nodded a greeting. Penny looked bright-eyed and sparkling, her hair carefully brushed and tied up on top of her head. Walter was unshaven and hollow-eyed, with a pale, fishy look to his face. He stared at Clive gloomily.

"Hear the guns?" he said. "What's happening?"

"There's a war on, lad. Actually, I don't know yet—but they're coming from Saint-Mihiel, and I'd guess we're seeing the beginning of a German advance." Clive pushed the coffeepot across to Walter, who was eyeing it longingly. "I say, do you know where Jenny is? I saw her first thing this morning, and now I can't find her anywhere."

Penny and Walter shook their heads. "Not since yesterday," said Penny. "You say you saw her this morning? Where?"

"Outside, when Harry was taking her father's body away." Clive grimaced. "Not very pleasant. I'd have felt even worse for her, if I hadn't been so hungover."

"You, too?" said Penny. "Well, boys will be boys. Did you try looking in her aunt's room?"

"Yes. I didn't find any trace of Ellen, either."

"Aunt Ellen," said Walter slowly. He was drinking coffee, and as the hot, sweet liquid went down his gullet he could feel an improvement in his condition, moment by moment. "Ellen Blake. My God."

"What's wrong?"

"I'm not sure. Either I saw her late last night and we talked together, or I was so drunk I imagined the whole thing. Jeez, was I drunk last night!"

"Yes, you *was* drunk last night." Penny snapped her fingers in front of his face. "Come on, don't stop there. Did you see Aunt Ellen, or didn't you?"

"I saw her. I think. I'm sure I did, out in the corridor before I came back to your place. And she talked my ear off." Walter closed his eyes and held them shut. "She was very upset. She was going on and on about Jenny being in danger. What she said was so wild, half of it went right past my head—I remember thinking, this is silly, she sounds in worse shape than I am." Walter opened his eyes. "I hardly listened to what she was saying."

"Walter!" Penny had seen the stricken look on Clive's face. "Come on, now, remember—you have to. Ellen Blake's a very bright woman. She doesn't get worried easily.

If she thinks Jenny is in trouble, we have to take it seriously. What did she say?"

"Well, she said she needed to talk to Jenny. Or to you, Clive. She said it was a life-or-death thing." Walter shook his head. "You know, I'm damned sure I must have dreamed this, because the way I remember it, she said that Jenny was in danger because the Marquis was going to turn her into a human sacrifice, so he could call on the powers of the Cross of Judas. Hell, I *must* have dreamed all this. A human sacrifice! And she said the Marquis had killed eight other women. And what's the Cross of Judas? It's all nonsense."

Clive and Penny looked at each other. "It sounds like nonsense," said Penny. "The Marquis isn't even here. He hasn't been at the chateau for days."

"There was one other thing." Walter looked awkwardly at Clive. "If I'm telling you what I think I remember, I ought to tell you everything. Ellen Blake said that Jenny is pregnant—but it's all nonsense, we know that."

There was a long silence.

"All right, so it's nonsense," said Clive at last. His face was pale, and his backbone felt like a column of ice. *Pregnant?* Walter didn't know it, nor Penny, but if Jenny was pregnant it certainly was not by Clive. If she was pregnant, then it had to by the Marquis. And that turned the abstract possibility he had thought of earlier into something real and sickening. "If there's nothing to any of this," he said at last, "then where is Jenny, and where is Ellen Blake?"

"I bet I can find Jenny," said Penny abruptly. "I'll bet there's some simple and normal explanation for all this, nothing to do with crosses and human sacrifices and murders. You're getting upset about the Marquis, and he's not even at the chateau. Clive, did you look in the stables?"

"No. Do you think that—"

"You know Jenny. She loves horses, and she must be feeling terrible about her dad. I'll bet she went off for a ride by herself, or maybe talked her Aunt Ellen into going with her. You two stay here and have more coffee. I don't want any, and I'm in a lot better shape than either of you. I'll see if Jenny has been at the stables, and I'll check to find out if there's a horse or two missing."

"Do you think she'd go for a ride with the weather like

this?'' Walter jerked his thumb toward the window. "I can't tell if it's going to rain, or blow, or what. It's gray and horrible-looking.''

"And so's her mood, I'll bet.'' Penny was on her feet. "Sit tight, Walter. I'll be back.''

"Good old Penny,'' said Walter after she had left. "My dream girl—but don't tell her I said so. Come on, Clive, cheer up. I'll bet she's right, dollars to donuts she finds both of 'em in the stables or out riding.''

"I hope so. But I have this bad feeling, Walter. Something's wrong, and I can't put my finger on it.''

"Damn right something's wrong. It's called the war. It drives everybody crazy. Relax, man, and see what Penny turns up.''

As he was speaking, Monge had quietly sidled into the dining room. He looked at both men, but he addressed himself only to Clive, in French. "Luncheon will not be served for another three hours, sir.''

"What's he want?'' asked Walter as Monge stood waiting.

"I think what he really wants is to kick us out,'' said Clive grimly. "But what he *says* is that we won't get lunch for another three hours. Want more coffee?''

"Yeah, why not?'' Walter looked up at Monge and addressed him in dismally bad French. "Monsieur Monge''— he pronounced it to rhyme with "sponge''—"have you any idea when Monsieur le Marquis will come back?''

Monge gave him a look of funereal satisfaction. "Monsieur, the Marquis has already returned. He is here at the chateau.''

"He is?'' Clive cut in. "When did he get back? And where is he now?''

"I am not sure when he returned, but I saw him less than an hour ago. He was going along one of the corridors that lead from the northwest tower.''

"Alone?''

"No. With a woman.''

Clive groaned, but Walter, who had understood most of the exchange, asked, "Who was she? Mademoiselle Marshall?''

"No, sir. I was not close enough to be sure, but from the colors of the clothing I feel fairly sure that it was Madame Blake.''

"What's he say? What's he say?" Monge's reply had been too quick for Walter.

Clive had taken a deep breath of relief. "It's all right. It was Ellen Blake, not Jenny."

"Boy." Walter shook his head. "Thank God for that. I still don't believe a word of it, but I was getting worried there for a minute. Ask him where they were going."

"I'm not sure, sir," said Monge in reply to the question. He was showing increasing signs of impatience. "There are no rooms in that direction. It is most likely that they were going to the cellars. And now, sir, if you will excuse me . . ."

"The *cellars*." Walter was baffled at Clive's translation. "Why the devil would they go there?"

Clive was looking relieved. "Because Ellen's an antiquarian—an archaeologist. The cellars are the oldest part of the castle; she'd be most interested in them. He's probably showing her 'round them. Now, if we just knew where Jenny had got to, I'd be happy."

"Maybe she's with 'em. Do you think we could get Monge to show us how to get to the cellars?" The stooped figure was already edging out of the dining room.

"He certainly doesn't want to. Let him go." Clive stood up. "I've got a better idea. I know someone who can find her way around the castle a lot better than he can: Cecile."

"Have you seen her today?"

"Not since three o'clock this morning. If I know her, she's still asleep."

"You're going to tell her all that human sacrifice stuff?"

" 'Course not." Clive was heading for the door. "But she knows the castle, and she'll take us to the cellars. It's time she woke up anyway. Let's settle all this and get back to the normal messed-up routine."

CHAPTER
THIRTY-FIVE

They stood outside her door for a moment before knocking.

"What are we going to *tell* her?" said Walter in a whisper. "You can't start on that stuff about her father and Jenny—it's going to turn out to be all rubbish, and you'll never be able to look her in the eye again."

"Don't worry, I won't scare her. You wait here for a minute while I see if she's up and about. And let me do the talking." Clive tapped on the door and went in.

Cecile was not asleep, far from it. And she was, to Clive's relief, considerably more clothed than when he had last seen her. She was sitting at the long dressing table, barefoot but wearing a morning dress of yellow and blue bright enough to hurt hungover eyes. The sunny smile she gave him suggested that after a refreshing sleep she was ready for another day of partying.

"Well, good morning," she said. "I *wondered* if you'd come and see me this morning. I know the Englishman's style, love them and leave them." She stood up and came light-footed over to Clive, reaching out her arms. She paused when she saw Walter at the door. "Hey, what's—"

"That's not why we're here," said Clive. He reached out and took her hands in his. "Cecile, did you know that your father is back?"

"Why, no, I didn't. But that's wonderful, I was beginning to get very worried. He's been away before, but never for so long."

"Cecile, we have to see him. At once." Clive's face and voice were grim. "It's important, and it concerns the war."

"Well, do it, then. See him." Cecile sounded hurt at Clive's coldness, after the night's warm intimacy. She took her hands away from his. "You know where his chambers are. I'm sure he'll talk to you whenever you want."

"He's not there. I haven't seen him since he got back, but Monge says he went down to the cellars."

"Probably. He works down there a lot. I don't blame him, it's been so noisy this morning with all the shelling. He comes up at mealtimes, though. If he's in the chateau he'll be there at lunch, and you can talk to him then."

She started to move toward the long dressing table, but Clive took her hand again in his. "Cecile, it's important that we see him now. And we don't know our way in the cellars. Would you take us down there, as a big favor? So we can talk to your father?"

She stared at his serious face and sighed. "You men! It's always the same, everything in the world is serious, everything is a crisis. All right, I'll take you. Give me a minute to put on a pair of shoes."

She went to the wardrobe, while Walter Johnson stared around him in fascination at the mementos of Africa scattered around the room. He wandered across to the dressing table and randomly picked up and stared at a couple of the bottles and jars scattered over its surface.

"Don't mix those up!" said Cecile, bent over and rummaging in the wardrobe.

"I won't." Walter cleared his throat self-consciously and looked at Clive before he spoke. "Cecile, did you ever hear anyone at the chateau talk about something called the Cross of Judas?"

There was a laugh from within the wardrobe, and Cecile's dark head poked out to stare at him. "Not you, too! It was bad enough with Charles quizzing me—"

"Charles?"

"Charles Richter. He says he saw somebody at the chateau back in March, trying to give Papa an old cross that he called the Cross of Judas. Charles asked me about it, but I didn't know a thing. You ought to find him and ask him."

Clive and Walter Johnson exchanged looks. They had

talked several times about Charles Richter's function in the war and at Chateau Cirelle, without ever reaching a satisfactory conclusion; his night trip down to the Aire River was still unexplained, though Clive was convinced from his furtive manner that he had been up to something illegal.

Cecile slipped on a pair of low-heeled shoes of soft leather and led the way out of the room and along the corridor. "Just around the turn," she said. "We'll find a door that will take us to the cellars. Then you can—well, speak of the devil!"

As they rounded the corner, they saw that the little door was already open. Standing in front of it was Charles Richter. He stared at them in surprise, his hand on the latch.

"Richter!" shouted Walter, hurrying forward. "Are you looking for the Marquis, too?"

Charles Richter had had no time to decide on his story if anyone asked what he was doing. He walked over to Cecile and kissed her on the cheek—it gave him one more second's thinking time.

The first rule of lying: *Keep as close to the truth as possible*.

"I am looking for the Marquis, as a matter of fact." Richter gave Cecile a worried look. "I'm glad you're here. Maybe you can help with him."

"With Papa?" Cecile's eyes widened. "What's wrong? Is he hurt?"

"I don't know. I haven't seen him, myself. But one of the wounded French soldiers who came to the chateau yesterday saw the Marquis, and he says Louis looked quite a mess. Evidently he's been behind the German lines, and through quite an ordeal. And it seems to be affecting his behavior. The soldier said that your father was heading for the cellars."

Cecile looked devastated. "Poor Papa," she said slowly. "If he was captured, and hurt—"

"Cecile, I don't think you should go to the cellars." Richter put his arm around her shoulders. "In fact, I think I ought to go alone. If Louis is hurt, or if he's mentally unbalanced because of what he's been through, the fewer people he sees, the better. I know him well, I'm an old friend—"

"Did the sick soldier say anything about a woman with the Marquis?" asked Clive.

Richter stared at him. How much did the others know? If

they knew that the Marquis had Jenny, it would do no good
to lie to them.

"Yes, there was a woman with him."

"Ellen Blake?"

"No." *Ellen Blake?* Now Richter was baffled. What did
Ellen Blake have to do with anything? "No, the woman was
Jenny Marshall."

If he wanted to get to the cellars without the others, it was
the wrong answer. Clive was pushing him aside and hobbling
through the door before the words were out of his mouth.
Walter Johnson followed. As he went through the door, he
turned to Richter. "I don't know where you fit into all this,
and I don't know why you were on your way to the cellars.
But if you want to help, come on."

"Yes, yes, of course. I'll do what I can." Richter paused
and looked at Cecile. "But if there's anything going on, dear,
I don't think you should come with us. I know the cellars
well enough. You stay here."

"When my own *father* may be in trouble?" Cecile was
pushing past him. "Don't talk nonsense. I know the cellars
far better than you—better than anyone except Papa himself.
Come on. Down these stairs."

They were soon in the first of the gloomy passageways. It
was dimly lit by naked bulbs suspended from wires snaking
along the low ceiling. Clive could hear the distant echo of
dripping water, and the cement and naked rock around him
glistened with moisture.

"Old as the hills," Walter was saying. "Jesus, what a
place. Did people once *live* down here?"

"Only during siege," said Cecile. Her dress was too light
for the chill of the cellars, and she was shivering bare-armed
as she walked. "The new chateau was built on the original
foundations a couple of hundred years ago. The old castle
was fortified against assault, and when anyone tried to capture
it, the garrison and all their families came down here. In one
siege, they lived underground for over a year."

"What happened then?"

"That siege had a happy ending. They were relieved
by—"

She stopped with a grunt of surprise. Coming slowly toward them, supporting herself against the cold stone walls,

was Ellen Blake. Her face was pale and sweaty, and her bruised neck was swollen as wide as her head.

Cecile took her arm. "What happened?"

Ellen gave a pained, husky croak. She turned to point along the corridor. She waved them onward, pushing at Cecile's arm. "Hurry." The whisper was hardly intelligible.

Walter Johnson hurried past her, leading the way. They had left the bare stone walls of the tunnel and were arriving at a point where the cellars changed character. In front of them was a heavy door, and beyond it a well-lit chamber with paneled walls, carpeted floor, and elegant furniture. Carved cabinets sat along the walls, and in the center of the room stood a wide bed with red satin covers.

They paused in the doorway. "Now, I could stand being besieged in here," said Walter.

"My great-grandfather's room." Cecile took a step forward. "This work was done less than fifty years ago."

"What a place!" Walter was staring at the padded straps on the bed and the loops and harnesses hanging from the mirrored ceiling. "What are all these things for?"

"Maybe I'll show you some other time." A little of Cecile's old spirit had crept back into her voice.

Beyond the elaborate bed, a broad oak door led through to another room. At the moment that door was barely ajar, just enough to see that the next room was well lit by powerful electric lights. Walter had taken one step toward it when a dreadful, despairing scream rang through the cellars.

"What the hell is that?" said Walter, at the same moment as Clive shouted, "Jenny!"

"Where did it come from?" Walter looked around in confusion. The acoustics of the room made the echoing scream ring out from all directions.

"That way!" Cecile pointed. "In the torture chamber."

Richter was already running toward it, making good speed in spite of his crippled leg. Clive followed him, sick at heart. For the love of God, a *torture chamber*? What was this place?

Richter was at the door. He pushed it open and stood aghast. "Louis! What are you doing?"

A long, narrow altar spread with a scarlet cloth rose up in the center of the stone-walled room. Around it stood implements of torture, black-stained and ominous. On the walls, powerful electric lamps in metal brackets illuminated every detail of the interior. At the center of the room, bending over the altar, was a tall man. Disheveled and burned, he was wearing nothing but tattered trousers and crude wrappings of bloodied sheet. Even when the figure turned in response to Richter's shout, so that Clive could look directly at the face, it was hard to recognize the distorted features and sunken eyes as those of Louis Villette. But the rage and resolve stamped on that face could not be mistaken.

In his right hand the Marquis held a long knife. Its edges reflected the electric glare like slivers of ice.

There was another heart-stopping scream. It came from the figure lying on the altar. She was naked, bound hand and foot by cords of dark silk. Her pale body was unable to move more than an inch or two, despite its desperate writhing.

"Jenny! Jenny!" Clive was screaming at the top of his voice, trying to push past Richter into the room.

The other man held him back. "Don't be a fool—you're injured, and he's crazy. I'll handle this." He was fumbling at his waist, trying to free his pistol, when the Marquis stood up straight. His eyes glowed, sparks of bright blue at the end of dark tunnels. They were the eyes of a rabid dog. Louis Villette gave a great, wordless roar, dropped the knife, and rushed at the door.

Richter instinctively flinched back. Clive stood his ground, and the Marquis was upon him in a second. Clive punched as hard as he could, aiming at Louis Villette's jaw. His arm was batted to one side. The massive hands reached out to seize him by the front of the shirt and hurl him backward, straight into Walter Johnson. Both men fell to the ground. Clive saw the gun plucked from Charles Richter's grasp. A great fist smashed against the side of his head and threw him on top of Clive and Walter. As the three men lay in a struggling heap, Clive heard a snarl of triumph. The door to the chamber crashed shut again.

"Jenny!" Clive struggled to his feet and flung himself against the solid wood of the door. It did not give a fraction of an inch. "Jenny!"

He was hammering uselessly on the panels when Cecile ran

to stand next to him, her face bewildered. "What happened? I couldn't see, you were all standing in the way. Was that—is that—"

"It's the Marquis." Clive struggled for self-control. "Your father has gone crazy. He's got Jenny in there, and he's going to—to—" To slash her open with that carving knife, like a butchered animal. He couldn't say it. He didn't want to think it. "We have to get in and help her. Cecile, is there another way? Some way around, to get into the torture chamber?"

All three men were on their feet, clustered about her. Cecile stood, her fist at her mouth. "There's a door at the other end—but it may be locked."

"We have to take that chance."

"No, wait." Cecile was clutching his arm. "There's a better way. The spectators' gallery! We can go that way, and it can't be locked."

"Do you know it?"

"Yes." Already she was running back through the room. "This way. Follow me, all of you."

She had screamed, cursed, wept, stormed, and begged for mercy. Jenny wondered if he could even hear her. Had his experiences away from the chateau somehow destroyed his hearing, as well as his reason? Yet he had heard well enough when he was talking to the German soldier. . . .

Jenny strained against her bonds for the fiftieth time—uselessly. Louis Villette was moving around the table she was lying on, setting in place two tall red candles. They were quite unnecessary. The electric lights threw a harsh white glare over everything. Jenny stared at the torture implements. Please God, they were only old and useless relics.

"Louis." Her voice was hoarse with screaming, and she kept it low and pleading. "Louis, I know you've been through a terrible time. Why don't you let me go now, and we'll find a doctor for you? You need help, Louis, you're badly wounded."

No reaction. What in God's name was he going to do next? If he intended to kill her, he had had ample opportunity.

He moved to the end of the table, lit the candles, and sank to his knees. She heard his voice, soft and deep, and she struggled to understand what he was saying. He was speaking slowly and formally.

"For this greatest of causes, I call upon the greatest of powers. Through the offering of life's blood, the chained spirit will move to this altar from the place beyond, from the place we feel but never see."

Jenny twisted against the silken cords. *The offering of life's blood.* Oh, God, he's talking about killing Aunt Ellen. Or worse . . .

The Marquis continued. "Lord Judas, who lives still in this Cross, teach the way of atonement, as the Cross was shaped for your atonement. Lord, who alone of the Apostles learned what lies beyond good and evil, teach me. Teach me self-sacrifice, as you made sacrifice. Give me resolve, as you were resolute. Lord Judas, accept this offering, flesh of my flesh."

Jenny raised her head as Louis Villette stood up. He was holding a long, straight knife, with a gleaming silver blade. He took a box full of dark, crumbling material like dry earth and began to rub it along the knife blade. As he did so, he began to speak again. This time she could understand nothing. He was speaking what sounded like Latin, pacing around the table where she lay. She could see his hand trembling on the knife, not with weakness but with a suppressed power.

He was looking down at her tenderly. The cold point of the knife touched her bare body. She felt its chill on the tip of each breast, on her neck, her shoulders, her navel, on the tender inside of her spraddled thighs. There was no sensuality in his movements. He was gazing into her eyes, thoughtfully, caringly, unaware of the terror in her face.

"You are very lovely, Jenny," he said, and his voice was as soft, warm, and tender as it had ever been. "How I shall miss you, how very much. My sweet, sweet Jenny."

"Louis, please let me go." Jenny could hardly hear her own voice, it was so weak and unsteady. "Please. *Please.*" Staring at that terrible knife blade, Jenny realized a truth that she would have denied twenty-four hours ago. When her father died, the world had seemed to end. There was nothing left to live for. Now she knew how false that was. She wanted to live, wanted it desperately. She wanted to survive the war, marry Clive—poor Clive, who had been so badly injured, whom she had hurt worse. She wanted to have his children, see them grow to their own maturity, become a watching and worshiping parent . . .

But that knife, dazzling as a Christmas tree ornament in the harsh lights, was going to end it all; all her hopes, all her dreams. Now the real tears came—not tears of rage, but tears of despair. Her cry was a wail of sorrow and futile anger.

In that darkest moment, when she had given up all hope, she heard the shout from the door of the chamber. Charles Richter stood there—and then Clive, by his side, their faces distorted by shock and horror.

"Clive! Help me."

He did not hear her cry, she was sure of it. Louis Villette dropped the knife, bellowed his defiance, and rushed to the open door. While she struggled with new energy against her bonds, he seized the men and threw them back with terrible strength into the other room. In spite of his wounds, the Marquis was filled with an impossible energy. He smashed the door shut and secured it while they were still struggling on the floor.

For a moment he looked spent. She saw him lift his hand to his chest, and his shoulders sagged. He turned to her. "Intruders! Enemies! Unbelievers! To defile this sacred place . . ." He spoke those words to Jenny in English, then lapsed into mumbling French that she could not follow. The physical effort had opened all his wounds again, and blood was flowing freely down his bare back and chest. With painful slowness, he stooped and picked up the knife. She heard a great groan as he placed his hand low on his left side.

She thought he was coming across to the table, but again he paused, frowning and listening. There was a sound of running feet from the other room. Louis Villette shook his head, laid the knife on the table, and limped across to the wall of the torture chamber. A great spoked wheel protruded from the stone. He began to turn it, grunting with effort. At last it would turn no further. He dropped to his knees, as though about to fall unconscious, but rallied after a few seconds. Jenny heard a muttered incantation. He.levered himself up and stood swaying like a drunkard.

He staggered back to the table, where Jenny had been

making desperate efforts to get her right hand far enough over to grab the blade. He shook his head as though to a child. "No, Jenny. You must not do that. Everything is finally ready. And this time I have armed the safeguard to this chamber. We will not be disturbed."

He stood upright again, knife in hand, alongside the table. The point was facing down, directly over Jenny's bare abdomen. She was too frightened to scream. Her naked skin, chilled by the damp air, already held the coldness of death. She could hear his harsh, uneven breathing. His bloodied right hand was perfectly steady.

"*Lord Judas.*" He had taken the Cross on its long chain from his chest and was holding it tight in his left hand. "Lord Judas, heed my prayer. You have protected me, you have delivered me from my enemies for this great purpose. My life and soul are yours. Like Father Abraham before me, I offer this second life, my child, the product of my love. Take this blood, flesh of my flesh, and grant this in return: the end of the earthly power that seeks to tear through this Holy Land of France. *Ut bellum desineat, nunc potestam crucis sanctae invocamo . . .* that the war may cease, I now call upon the power of the Holy Cross. . . ."

His hand lifted high and began to descend. Jenny watched it with a sick and disbelieving horror. It was impossible; it couldn't happen. That knife would slit through her unprotected belly, slash delicate skin and soft muscle. The glittering point, already ruby-red with anticipation of her blood, would plunge deep within her. . . .

The air in the chamber seemed to freeze, to crystallize around the knife like an ice cloud.

"Take this offering, Lord Judas"—the knife was touching her belly—"and with this stroke I yield my very soul."

Jenny opened her mouth and gave a final, despairing scream. As she did so, her voice was echoed by another cry from somewhere above and to one side of her. She could not take her eyes off the knife, could not look at anything else in the world. But the Marquis had paused, his knife touching her skin. He was staring at the Cross in his left hand, his mouth open. The Cross was glowing, incandescent, far brighter than all the lights of the room. Brighter, impossibly bright, the heart of the sun itself.

Louis Villette was staring, incredulous. "*Before* the sacrifice, and the Cross is aglow? That cannot be." His voice was shaking and uncertain.

There was a titanic crash of thunder, louder than any thunderstorm since the beginning of the world. The room shook. Jenny felt the table buck and tremble beneath her, while Louis Villette fell to his knees and dropped the knife.

The Cross blazed on, brighter than ever.

Louis Villette, on his knees by the table altar, looked again at Jenny. A strange expression crossed his face. He threw back his head and howled, with a voice louder than the thunder itself.

CHAPTER
THIRTY-SIX

They ran back across the bedroom: Clive at the edge of panic, Richter grim, Cecile puzzled, and Walter Johnson filled with the rush of adrenaline that he felt in an aerial dogfight. "Another way," he said urgently to Cecile. "You say there's another way in?"

She was leading, with Walter just behind her, but she did not seem to hear. "He must be sick," she said. "*Really* sick. Something's terribly wrong with him. We have to help him."

No kidding, thought Walter. *Something's wrong, right enough. The guy's a loon.*

Cecile paused in the corner of the bedroom and pulled back a heavy wall tapestry of a hunting scene. Behind it stood a narrow doorway perched above a stone step. She turned the brass doorknob and it clicked in her hand. "No lights," she said. "Can't be helped. Come on, hurry!"

Walter heard her footsteps clatter on the stairs. He followed her up steep, winding steps of old wood that creaked beneath his weight. He had been right on Cecile's heels, but when he felt the sway and give of the steps, he paused and turned back to Clive.

"One at a time! The stairs won't hold the lot of us."

Cecile had been moving nimbly and very fast. She was already at the top when Walter was halfway there. He hurried after her, annoyed at falling behind. His head was just above floor level in the spectators' gallery when Cecile ran to the balcony that looked out on the torture chamber.

He saw her shin come into contact with something close to ground level—a tight gray cord that gave under the pressure of her leg.

A melodious thrumming sound rang out through the spectators' gallery, like the plucking of a giant's harp. Walter heard a whirring like pheasants' wings and something bright flashed past his eyes, too quick to track.

There was a single, terrible scream from Cecile. Walter felt a splash of hot liquid on his face. He looked up, just as Cecile's body came tumbling to the floor of the gallery. She rolled toward him, her torso run through by multiple rusted iron skewers. He could see wicked barbed darts buried deep in her neck, two in her chest, two in her belly. Bright arterial blood was gushing from her throat. Walter looked across to the wall of the gallery and saw another dozen crossbow quarrels there, driven deep into the hard wood. One of them must have missed Walter's head by only a couple of inches.

As Cecile's body rolled over and lay limp, a monstrous crash of thunder shook the whole castle. Walter had to cling helplessly to the sides of the staircase, waiting for the shivering of the structure to die down.

"Get a move on!" Clive's voice came urgently from the bottom of the stairs as the roar of thunder died away. "We can't come up with you hanging around on the steps. What's your problem?"

"The Marquis. He set a trap." There was no point in trying for a longer explanation—the others would see for themselves as soon as they got to the top of the stairs. Walter wiped blood from his eyes, went the rest of the way up the staircase, and advanced cautiously to the waist-high railing that crossed the edge of the spectators' gallery. With one trap sprung, there might be others. He heard Clive's steps on the stairs, and the horrified exclamation when he saw Cecile's body.

"A trap!" Clive could hardly speak. "He set a booby trap!" He hobbled forward to the balcony, his leg aching from the effort of climbing the stairs.

"Let's hope there aren't any more." Walter was staring down into the chamber. The two men were vaguely aware of Charles Richter's ascent of the stairs, and of his groan of horror and disbelief when he saw Cecile. Clive alone caugh' Richter's distraught and unthinking words as he knelt by th body. *"Cecile! Ah, mein Liebchen, mein Schatz. Ah, nein, nein."*

Clive registered the German words, but he paid little attention to them. Like Walter, he was stunned by the scene below.

The room was as bright as a hospital operating room. Jenny lay naked and spread-eagled on the red-clothed altar table, her wrists and ankles chafed and reddened from useless tugging at the silk cords that held her limbs. Clive saw her eyes, round with horror, and her cheeks so pale that they seemed already lifeless. She was whimpering, high in her throat, and staring off to the side of the table.

The Marquis was there, kneeling. One scarred and bloody paw held a long-bladed knife, the other gripped a glowing cross secured around his neck by a long, silver chain. His chest was bare except for two strips of ragged bandage, and three bullet wounds on chest and shoulder were seeping blood. He was gazing at the Cross and silently weeping. Clive could see tears running down the haggard cheeks and stubbled chin. The eyes of the Marquis were closed.

"Cecile!" Louis Villette rocked backward and forward on his knees. "Oh, my little Cecile. I swore it would not happen, that this child would never be sacrificed. I failed you. Cecile, forgive me."

His eyes blinked. He glared around the brightly lit torture chamber, then staggered unsteadily to his feet. "I understand, Lord. Even this. Total sacrifice—my daughter, my child, my love—all. The sacrifice must be *total*, or end in failure. Lord, I understand." He allowed the Cross to fall to his chest, and groaned as though it seared his skin. Lifting the knife, he turned toward Jenny.

Walter gave a wild yell, swung up onto the railing of the gallery, and dropped eight feet to the floor of the chamber. He landed cleanly and ran straight at the Marquis.

The impact of his body drove the Marquis backward just as the knife was swinging down to Jenny's bare belly. Walter grabbed at Louis Villette's wrist, cursing his wounded arm as he did so. He was trying to fight someone of incredible strength, and he was doing it one-handed.

The two men were eye to eye. There was no flicker of recognition on the Marquis' face. He hardly seemed to see Walter as the knife slowly turned again toward Jenny. Walter could not stop him, he knew it. The crazed Marquis was just too strong.

Walter let go his grip, stepped back a pace, and kicked Louis Villette as hard as he could in the testicles.

There was a grunting wheeze of pain, and the knife wavered. But in a second or two it was lifting into position again, with the downward-facing point aiming a couple of inches below Jenny's navel.

Clive had watched Walter's plunge to the floor of the torture chamber, but he knew that such a leap was impossible for him. There was no way for him to take all the weight on his one good leg, and the impact might refracture his broken shin. The urge to watch what came next was almost irresistible, but Clive turned his back on the scene at the altar and swung himself over the balcony of the spectators' gallery. He lowered himself steadily until he was hanging by his hands from the edge, then dropped the remaining couple of feet. He landed evenly, giving his hurt leg no more than a painful jar. He turned at Jenny's despairing scream to find the glittering knife blade coming down once more. Ignoring the jag of pain from his leg, Clive hurled himself at the Marquis.

He hit him in the back, squarely though without much force. At the same moment Walter Johnson kicked violently at Louis Villette's knee. The knife slipped sideways in its descent. It drove into the tabletop an inch from Jenny's side.

Before Clive could recover his balance, the Marquis had jerked the blade free and was aiming another blow at Jenny. Clive was impotent to stop him. Walter, his injured arm toward the Marquis, could not prevent the downward plunge. Instead, he dived forward to shield Jenny, covering her body with his own. The knife went into the back of his left shoulder, piercing under the collarbone and thrusting deep into Walter's chest roughly midway between shoulder and breastbone.

Walter gasped with pain and rolled off Jenny's body. The knife was suddenly slippery with blood, and Walter's turn wrenched it from the hand of the Marquis. Walter fell to the floor close to the table. He lay there faint and nauseated, the knife still in him.

Louis Villette stood silent. He seemed dazed, but after a moment or two he began to look around him. He was seeking the knife.

"Louis! Louis Villette!" The shout sounded loud through the chamber, echoing from the bare stone walls. It was Charles Richter, crying down from the balcony in an angry and tormented voice. "Look what you have done, Louis. She is dead. Your trap killed your own daughter."

He was standing at the edge of the balcony, tears flowing down his cheeks. In his arms he held the torn body of Cecile. He called again. "See her, Louis. See what you have done."

If Richter was hoping to distract the Marquis, it was useless. Louis Villette shook his head, cried, "Cecile, Cecile," in a great, heartbroken voice, and touched the Cross around his neck. His maddened eyes caught sight of the knife handle sticking out of Walter Johnson's shoulder as Walter tried to crawl away under the table. He reached down and grabbed it, pulling it out with one quick jerk.

Walter screamed in agony and fell forward.

"No, damn you. You won't." Clive grabbed a long pair of metal pincers from the top of an iron brazier. He hobbled forward again toward the Marquis, at the same time as Charles Richter came scrambling over the edge of the balcony and dropped to the chamber floor.

Clive smashed Louis Villette across the shoulders with the pincers, a blow that should have been hard enough to cripple him. The Marquis merely shook his head, like a dog throwing off water, and said in a guttural voice, "For France, Lord, for France. Hear me, help me."

A second blow with the pincers, aimed at Louis Villette's seared scalp, missed when the Marquis suddenly turned back to Jenny. But now Charles Richter had arrived. Weaponless, he jumped squarely onto the Marquis' back. His weight drove the Marquis down to the stone floor, but he did not release his hold on the knife. He was reaching up and back with it, and Richter was forced to release his own hold or be slashed across the neck. Richter dropped to the floor and rolled quickly away from the knife's reach.

Charles Richter and Clive Dunnay were now between the Marquis and Jenny. The Marquis did not seem to notice them. With his eyes intent on Jenny, he blundered right at them, knife raised. He smacked squarely into the two men, elbowed them aside, and continued, pushing through to Jenny's side.

A desperate push from Clive at Louis Villette's descending

right arm diverted another vicious knife thrust. The knife quivered deep in the table.

Before the Marquis could pull it out, Clive and Richter had moved to brace themselves against the altar table. Instinctively working together, they used the weight of the table to give themselves good leverage and thrust the Marquis backward. He staggered a few steps, arms waving for balance, then came to a halt at the other side of the chamber. He stood, chest heaving, against the open spiked lid of the iron maiden. He was off balance, unsteady and weaving on his feet.

Clive looked past Louis Villette at the field of rusty iron spikes that stood behind the Marquis.

He realized at once what they had to do. "Richter. Come on!"

He ran at the Marquis and hit him square on the left side of the chest as hard as he could. Charles Richter was just behind him and smashed into the right side of Louis Villette's chest a fraction of a second later.

The Marquis was slammed backward into the open array of long spikes. His mouth opened wide in a silent scream of agony. Eyes popping open, he made a desperate effort to jerk himself forward from the lethal spears of the iron maiden.

He was close to succeeding when Walter Johnson, legs weak and wobbling from shock and loss of blood, staggered forward to add his weight to Clive's and Richter's.

"Push!" cried Clive. "All together."

There was one last growl of defiance and hatred from the Marquis, one last blood-dimmed surge of effort from the other three. Louis Villette was driven back, all the way, back until the rusted ends of ten-inch spikes burst from his throat, chest, and belly. The Marquis gave one high-pitched scream of pain.

The cross on his chest was glowing again, with a brighter and fiercer light than ever.

As the chamber shook with the vibration of another great thunderbolt, Louis Villette slumped forward. He shivered once, then hung limp in the awful and gaping embrace of the iron maiden.

The first lightning strike had been confusing as well as frightening—it might have been anything: earthquake, lightning, or a monstrous shell falling on Chateau Cirelle. The second one left no doubt as to its nature. As the explosion sounded through the cellar, a vast blue spark leaped from the ceiling and crackled its way along the metal frame of the rack to the floor.

Jenny, tied tight to the sacrificial altar, felt a tingle through her whole body. The table she was lying on was filled with electrical charge. She turned her head. Her hair was surrounded by a golden nimbus, each strand standing away from its neighbor. At the other side of the room the impaled figure of the Marquis jerked and smoked on the iron maiden, while powerful surges of current ran through the coffin's frame to the ground.

She saw Clive stretch out his hand to grab the Judas Cross from Louis Villette's breast. In a half faint she called, "Clive, Clive—no!" She wanted to reach out to him, wanted to warn him, but her bonds bit deep into her flesh. She could not move, and her voice was weak and trembling.

Just before Clive's fingers made contact with the Cross, Richter grabbed his arm and pulled it back. "Don't be crazy, man. You'll be electrocuted—look at him!"

The Cross was aglow, sizzling and spitting its way deep into the flesh of Louis Villette's mangled chest. Every part of the Marquis shimmered with a halo of charge, ballooning his clothes away from his suspended body. While Clive stared, Louis Villette spasmed and writhed like a mechanical man. New discharges flashed through him. His skin was smoking, blackening, fat bubbling from melting blisters. The current was cooking him, igniting chest hair and burning off eyebrows and ears.

While they watched in horror, the lights in the cellar flickered for a moment, blinked out, and came back to full strength.

Clive stepped backward. "Let's get out of here! If we lose the lights while we're down in the cellars, we're in more trouble."

He turned away from the body of the Marquis and headed toward Jenny.

Ten minutes ago she had never expected to be free of her bonds alive, never expected to see Clive again—but now he was coming to free her! The hope that swelled inside her was almost unbearable. It filled her whole existence . . . to be untied, to be free, to be able to move again. . . .

But he would have to be quick. The smell of burning wood was strong, even this far below ground. There must be a fire in the chateau—and a big one. Jenny watched as Clive came to her side, his eyes intent and concerned. He cut the silk cords holding her with the same knife that Louis Villette had intended for the sacrifice. She could see his hands shivering as he did so. One by one the cords were severed. When she was finally free and sagged against him, not far from collapse, he swept up the altar cloth and wrapped it around her naked body. She clung to him, to his solidness and stability.

"Can you walk?" He was cradling her against his chest.

She nodded faintly. She felt almost warm again, safe again—she had been so cold, so vulnerable, stretched naked on the altar.

"Let's go." Clive turned. "Richter, give Walter Johnson a hand."

Richter had been standing motionless, staring at the Marquis with a mixture of pity, horror, and disgust. After one last look at the cross, he went to help Walter Johnson to his feet. The American was bleeding profusely, but with Richter's help he was able to walk.

Clive was half carrying Jenny as they left the chamber. She clung to him, fighting off the trembling that threatened to take over her whole body. She closed her eyes and let him guide her steps. *Be strong.* There was no reason for trembling now. She trusted Clive more than anyone in the world. He would take her to safety.

They were just outside the torture chamber and into the main corridor when the lights flickered off, brightened dramatically for a few moments, and failed totally. In the last moment of brightness, Clive stared at the path ahead. He held tight to Jenny and waited until Charles Richter and Walter Johnson came up on his heels.

"Hold the back of my shirt and stick close." Clive felt a hand grasp him at the waist. "Good. I think I can line us up with the staircase. Walter, can you manage stairs?"

"Don't know." Walter's voice was very low.

"I've got him," said Richter. "Go on, man, let's do it. I don't like those sounds."

The smell of burning was worse, acrid in their nostrils. They could hear a crackling roar from above. Clive held Jenny tightly in one arm and reached for the stone wall with the other. She felt the floor icy on her bare feet, but it was nothing. The urgency to get away from this awful place filled her.

They went slowly upward, expecting to emerge into the interior corridor where they had entered. Instead they found themselves in the open air. Torrential rain deluged them, and they were buffeted by a gale-force wind. Within seconds, Jenny was shivering again.

She looked at the unfamiliar scene around them. The lightning had struck this corner of the Chateau Cirelle with explosive force. The sturdy superstructure had been demolished; nothing but rubble remained of this wing's first or second floors, and the rest of the building was ablaze.

They waited for Richter and the wounded Walter Johnson to struggle the rest of the way up the stairs. Richter nodded to show that they could go on. Clive hugged Jenny to him, put his head down, and butted on through the storm. All the chateau was smoking and steaming, and the only safe place seemed to be the stables.

The downpour was like a waterfall. Within a few yards they were soaked to the skin. It was scarcely possible to breathe without taking in water. Jenny felt spongy mud squirting up thick between her toes. When they had ten yards to go she heard a cry of horror from ahead of them. She squinted through the driving rain and saw Penny Wilson running from the stables to meet them. Her blond hair hung in dirty streaks down her face, and her dress was a shapeless rag. Behind her, face pale and swollen neck wrapped in a long woolen scarf, walked Aunt Ellen.

"Walter." Penny ran right past Clive and Jenny. "Walter—my God, your shoulder—the blood!"

"It's all right." Walter put his arm around her waist. "Look after Jenny. She needs help more than me."

But as he said it, Walter was sagging forward into Penny's arms. With help from Ellen Blake, she half carried, half dragged him to the shelter of the stables.

Jenny had recovered enough to stand upright when Clive took his arm from around her waist. She steadied herself against him and pulled the red cloth tight about her. The two of them stood silently in the howling storm, staring back at the chateau. Jenny shook her head, and clusters of water droplets sprang from her hair, the color of dark honey from its sudden soaking.

The castle stood before them, half destroyed, but still massive and solid. Jenny knew she would never forget the chateau—or its master. They had taken away the life of her father, and almost claimed her own life and Ellen Blake's. She and the others had escaped by a miracle.

Jenny leaned close to Clive and put her cheek on his chest. "Clive, I can't believe that I'm alive. When he slammed the door in your face and locked you out of the chamber . . . he was ready to stab that knife right through me, he had it touching me . . ." She put her hand to her lower belly. "And then Cecile screamed, and the Cross glowed, and he stopped. And then he started howling like an animal. . . ."

She could say nothing more, though she wanted to huddle close against him and talk to him forever. There was another fearsome lightning bolt and a roar of nearby thunder.

"Inside!" Clive was leaning to shout in her ear. "We can talk later, when you're dressed and dry."

Jenny turned to him, her eyes wide open and staring at him. He wondered, was she all right? She had been through so much.

Instead of speaking, Jenny reached up one arm, pulled his face down to hers, and gave him a fierce wet kiss on the lips.

He stood there like an idiot, stunned by the intensity of her embrace. Before he could respond, she walked forward into the stable, leaving Clive and Charles Richter standing outside together.

The Frenchman did not bother to shelter under the eaves of the stable. He stood motionless, head hanging down, and stared back at the burning castle. *So this is where your damned Cross leads, Dolfi. To more death and destruction.*

Clive stepped to his side. Jenny's kiss had made him feel warm all over. But was Richter all right? He seemed totally dazed. Clive tugged the other man's sleeve. "I don't understand what happened back there. Why did Louis Villette stop, when he was all ready to kill her?"

Richter was staring at him, stony-faced. "Still you do no

understand? I understand only too well. Louis Villette set that trap, expecting to catch me or you. He did not even know Cecile was in the cellar. When the trap killed her—his own daughter—the conditions for the sacrifice had been fulfilled. And when the Cross glowed, *Louis knew what he had done.* You heard him roar with grief. It stopped him for just a few moments—he was still ready to sacrifice Jenny, too—but Cecile's death gave enough time for us to reach him and save Jenny. But Cecile, my poor, innocent Cecile . . .''

He bowed his head. Grief was still growing within him.

"If I had tried to grab the Cross down there from the Marquis . . .'' Clive paused. "You know, you saved my life. I would have been electrocuted.''

Richter shook his head. He felt nothing. The deaths, first of Cecile, and then of his friend the Marquis, had left him empty, incapable of any feeling except misery and revulsion at his own role in all this. What did it matter, any of it?

Clive Dunnay was staring at him thoughtfully.

"You saved my life. I think maybe I'm about to save yours.'' Clive looked around him. His words would be carried away by the gusting wind. No one but Richter could possibly hear. "I think I know what you are, and what you've been doing here—and if I dig a little bit, I feel sure we can prove it. But you helped to save Jenny, and you saved me. So I'm giving you a chance. Start now, and get back to your own side—today. That's all the time you've got. If you are ever caught on French soil again, you know what the punishment will be.''

Clive had expected an indignant denial, perhaps an argument. Richter instead stared at him dull-eyed and waved his hand out to the north and east, across the sodden fields.

"Does it matter, Captain Dunnay? Does another death matter? One more German, one more Frenchman, one more Englishman—does it count, when our generals are playing their game in millions? The world is mad, Dunnay, madder even than I realized. What we have just seen is nothing. Worse things happen on the front every single day. Hopeless. It is all hopeless.''

He turned and walked away.

Hopeless? thought Clive. Is it truly hopeless?

He watched Richter heading dejectedly south, his way lit

by lightning flashes, toward the road that led to Saint-Mihiel. As Richter reached the avenue of trees on the chateau approach road, he turned. Facing back toward Clive, the spy gave a formal salute.

Clive returned it, watching until the other man was out of sight. The vapor of his own breath was the only touch of life and warmth in the cold rain.

At last he sighed and moved to face the castle. The scene that met his eyes was like a strange dream. The wounded soldiers from the French bivouac had been roused by the storm and the lightning blast that followed. All who were capable of walking had emerged from the tents. Now, lit by the flames of the burning chateau, they moved toward the stables, a rain-soaked group of the walking dead. Armless, legless, eyeless, in sodden bandages and drenched nightclothes, they struggled on. Helping, guiding, encouraging each other.

Hopeless? Only if men and women gave up hope.

The soldiers had not. Clive could not. Jenny was alive, and life carried its own hope, its own promise of renewal.

Clive stood for one more minute bareheaded in the downpour. Then he, too, turned and headed for the shelter of the stables.

CHAPTER
THIRTY-SEVEN

The lightning had come out of a still, overcast sky. From his vantage point in the cloisters, fifty yards from the main building, Dolfi saw lines of white fire run from the southwest tower and plunge in sizzling lines of steam down to the ground. There was a gigantic, ear-shattering roar, too loud and too immediate to suggest thunder.

Dolfi cowered under the covered cloisters and stared up at the sky. Two seconds ago it had been a dark, dull morning, with an uncertain prospect of rain. Now black storm clouds were streaking from the west, and a great wind swept over the castle.

And the castle was on fire!

He could see smoke pouring out of it in four different places, thick columns of black with licking orange-red tongues at their bases. He glared at them in fury. Charles Richter was somewhere in that burning building. The chance that the other man would have the nerve to pursue the Cross when the chateau was ablaze was close to zero.

Dolfi swore. He ran down the stairs that led from the cloisters to the cellars. Even now, with Chateau Cirelle falling about his ears, he was not ready to give up. He would risk a final sortie for the Cross.

As he reached the corridor leading to the main part of the castle, the electric lights flickered twice, then failed completely. He cursed again. The lightning bolt—it had destroyed the generators. But he had—*Gott sei Dank!*—not emptied his pockets of the candles and matches stuffed into them the previous morning. It took twenty precious seconds to strike a light in complete darkness; then he was ready to go forward again. Shielding the flickering flame with one hand, he moved down the corridor.

The candle provided him with a faint circle of vision, up to maybe five meters in front of him. He could smell burning wood and hear the groan of collapsing timbers. The cellars seemed deserted. He went on until he heard a faint slamming of doors ahead.

Where was he now, and where had the sound come from?

The torture chamber. Dolfi gripped his revolver and walked slowly forward. There was no way to hide his arrival, since the circle of light moved with him. He was a perfect target.

When he came to the door of the torture chamber that he himself had slammed shut in the woman's face, he hesitated for a long time with his hand on the door ring. If he went through, he would probably have to face the Marquis again— and this time Louis Villette might be armed. Dolfi knew that his earlier shot had been too high; it would have inflicted no more than a flesh wound. But what other options did he have?

He slipped the lock and turned the ring. This was a case where risk could not be avoided. The Marquis had fooled him once over the Cross, but it would take a lot to fool him again.

The door swung open slowly and noiselessly. He stepped through and held the candle high.

For a few moments Dolfi thought that the room was deserted. There was plenty of evidence of recent activity, with weapons and torture instruments scattered around and three separate stains of blood on the floor. But the people who had fought each other so hard had all disappeared.

The tension in Dolfi was replaced by swelling disappointment. He had been so near to the Cross, so close to winning it. It was maddening! In his anger and frustration he lifted his revolver and fired a shot along the room, hearing the bullet whine in ricochet off the cage of the little ease and onto the metal hooks of the *ungulae*. As the echoes of the explosion and the bullet's impact faded away, Dolfi heard a long, faint rustle, as of charred paper moving in a breeze. It came from nearby—from something only a few feet away.

He jerked back in surprise. The candle flame wavered and

almost went out. He recovered, held still, and looked over to the right.

He had been wrong. The room was not empty. Louis Villette was here, almost unrecognizable. He had been impaled face-outward on the rusted spikes of the iron maiden. Two long blades ran through his body at kidney level and their ends stuck out of his belly. Another had caught him high in the back, near the nape of the neck, and bright arterial blood was dripping from its exposed point. A fourth spike speared his lower back above the buttocks and emerged near his groin. The skin of his spitted body had been baked and seared to a black crust that seeped blood and lymph fluid. He lacked body hair, and his ears and nose were burned to misshapen stubs.

The Marquis hung from the iron maiden in a contorted death agony. He had suffered his own form of crucifixion.

Dolfi stepped forward, and as he did so the blackened hands of the Marquis lifted. He was not dead! He was reaching for the sides of the iron maiden, pushing down, painfully levering his body away from the terrible spikes. When the candlelight fell on his face, the Marquis lifted his head. Blood dripped from the corners of his mouth, and his seared eyes were sunk deep in their sockets. Yet he went on: slowly, single-mindedly, inching himself off the iron maiden. He seemed unaware of Dolfi's presence as the other man approached and brought the candle close to the Marquis' chest.

The Cross! There it was, against the ravaged chest, dangling from a silver chain around Louis Villette's neck. And this time there was no doubt. The candlelight fell on the true Cross of Judas, tarnished and battered, dark against the mangled flesh.

Dolfi hissed between his teeth and reached out his hand. As he did so, the head of the Marquis lifted to look him in the eyes.

"No!" The voice was a gurgling, blood-filled rumble from deep in the throat. The Marquis turned his head down to gaze at the Cross. "*Do not permit this. I gave everything—my life, my soul. No!*"

"Yes!" Dolfi took the Cross in his hand—hot against the charred chest, hot to his touch—and jerked it to rive open the links of the chain. There was a moment of resistance while the Cross stuck firm to the seared chest; and then Dolfi had it. The chain snapped. The Cross slapped into his hand so firmly and cleanly that he did not need to close his fist. He jumped backward, almost falling, and the Cross stuck hard to his palm.

At that moment the Marquis gave a shuddering groan. *"No, Lord, no."* His back arched, driving the spikes deeper. Blood poured anew from all his wounds. The burn fissures cracked open, and the body went limp. Louis Villette, Marquis de Saint-Amè, Knight of the Twelfth Apostle, Forty-fourth Guardian of the Cross of Judas, was dead.

Dolfi did not give the Marquis another look. He turned and headed back the way he had come. In less than a minute he had ascended the stairs and was in the cloisters. While he had been gone, the thunder and lightning had led to a fantastic rainstorm. Dolfi had never seen such rain. It sheeted down from a black sky, swamping everything, rebounding feet high from the hard soil in spurts of spray. Clouds of white steam were rising from the ruined chateau as the falling water met the flames.

He turned and looked east. If anything, the sky was blacker there. Forked lightning flickered incessantly in the dark sky. There was still an ominous rumble and roar from over toward Saint-Mihiel, but now it was thunder, not gunfire. Dolfi could imagine the scene. The Grand Advance would be grinding to a halt as the great gun carriers and armed vehicles sank to their axles in thick mud. A storm of this intensity made armored attack impossible. The Grand Advance, Germany's thrust to bring a rapid end to the war, must be postponed. Who knew when the chance would come again?

Dolfi stared at the Cross, dark in his hand. He left the shelter of the cloisters and began to walk east. He forded the Aire River and went steadily on. Less than ten miles away lay the German lines.

The rain sluiced down, soaking him and battering at his unprotected head. He laughed, blinking away the rivulets that ran down his dark hair and trickled into his eyes. The Grand Advance might be thwarted, but he was not downhearted. This was not Götterdämmerung, the twilight of German great-ness; it was merely a temporary setback. He had wanted the advance to succeed, desperately, but at the same time he knew that it was not a great plan. It was a piece of warfare from the last century, the brainchild of a general who was stuck firmly in the past. The future of war lay elsewhere, in modern ideas, new armaments, twentieth century technology, daring thinking.

Dolfi walked on across the drowned fields. The eye of the storm seemed to hover above him. Although the distant woods shook and swayed with the power of the winds, where he walked all was peaceful. The rain here had stopped. When he looked straight up, it was into a circle of clear blue sky.

He stared again at the Cross in his hand. For all its history, and his struggle to possess it, it was not impressive in its appearance. He was holding an X of dark silver, crudely—almost carelessly—made. The four arms were not quite the same size, and their L-shaped endings all bent at slightly different angles. The grooves along the arms were filled with old grease and dirt. The Cross had a battered look, a *used* look.

He clutched it tight in his right hand. Its appearance was irrelevant. He knew its powers. He knew he would reach the French lines, knew he would pass safely through them to rejoin the German Army. The Cross would carry him. Already he could feel its power, lifting him, bearing him up, strengthening him. He could see beyond today, beyond tomorrow, across the years. With the Cross in his hand, a perfect future stretched before him, as bright in prospect as that circle of blue far above his head.

He lifted his face. All around was rolling thunder and driving rain, but where he walked the downpour ceased. He was at the center now, at the axis of the world. He would remain there.

Dolfi strode on through the storm at the head of an invisible triumphal procession.

ABOUT THE AUTHORS

CHARLES SHEFFIELD's novels include *One Man's Universe, The Mind Pool, Godspeed, Cold as Ice,* and the Heritage Universe and Proteus series. His novel *Brother to Dragons* won the John W. Campbell Memorial Award for best science fiction novel of 1992. *The McAndrew Chronicles* won the Japanese Sei-un Award for 1991. "Georgia on My Mind" won the Nebula Award for Best Novelette in 1993. His nonfiction works include the bestselling texts *Earthwatch* and *Man on Earth.* A mathematician and physicist by training, he is past president of the Science Fiction Writers of America and a Fellow and past president of the American Astronautical Society.

DAVID BISCHOFF worked in television during the 1970s and since then has been a full-time writer, with books published by most of the New York paperback houses and several hardcover houses as well. His writing has been translated into a dozen languages. One of his recent novels, *Grounded,* appeared on the *New York Times* bestseller list. His shorter fiction has appeared in such magazines as *Omni* and *Analog,* as well as in numerous original anthologies. His previous collaboration with Charles Sheffield, *The Selkie,* was a *Los Angeles Times* bestseller. Bischoff presently lives in Eugene, Oregon.